RUIN'S
WAKE

RUIN'S WAKE

PATRICK EDWARDS

TITAN BOOKS

Ruin's Wake
Print edition ISBN: 9781785658792
E-book edition ISBN: 9781785658808

Published by Titan Books
A division of Titan Publishing Group Ltd
144 Southwark Street, London SE1 0UP
www.titanbooks.com

First edition: March 2019
10 9 8 7 6 5 4 3 2 1

A CIP catalogue record for this title is available from the British Library.

Printed and bound by CPI Group (UK) Ltd, Croydon, CR0 4YY

For Al,
who made it all happen

Bask 2 – 498

I had to rid myself of Melthum. The man was insufferable, and worse, unreliable. His bumbling efforts to manage my appointments and correspondence reflected poorly on me, and that I will not tolerate.

So much of position is dependent on keeping face here at the vaunted Karume Elucidon – I am measured not merely on the papers I write, but how well my department is organised, though I – like all of my faculty colleagues – couldn't care less about the right forms going in the right bins, student assessment, inter-departmental statistics. The face of it – the conceit – is that efficiency is as vital as discovery, though in truth the former trumps the latter in this glorious Hegemony of the Seeker.

Melthum had been my assistant and occasional bed-warmer for so long I barely noticed him, no more than I would the pen I use to sign or the chair I pull up to my desk. I certainly noticed him when he tried to plead his case, bleating in that dreadful provincial accent of his. When he persisted, I slammed the door in his face and advised him to try the fucking military (which he never shut up about anyway). Maybe getting shot at in some border action would give him some vim – though I doubt, for all of his admiration and exaltation of the soldiery, he really has any intention of putting himself in harm's way. Doubtless he'll scratch at someone else's door for his grant money, and there is enough vanity among the faculty that he'll likely get it. Just not in my department.

Department – it sounds so grand. The name conjures images of shuffled papers and sage nodding in all-night pushes; rooms full of desks, the ceilings chattering with rapid keystrokes as serious boys and girls process important data and compile heavy archival volumes for posterity.

As it is, the Department of pre-Ruin Cryptoarchaeology comprises only myself, Professor Sulara Song, and two underachieving postgrads who couldn't do any better (academically, as well as with each other) and, until recently, the assistant and administrator Melthum. Now my truncated 'team' of two is, I'm sure, as much looking forward to taking their directives from me as I am to addressing them directly.

On to the paperwork, in which the idiot barely made a dent despite ours being the smallest department in the Elucidon. I've requested a replacement, although, given how most of my formal requests die alone in a darkened corner of the Dean's office, I'll square my shoulders against a long haul of tedium.

Despite the drudgery, I can at least look forward to not seeing that rodent-like face peering around the door and the awkward silences when he assumed a few throwaway rolls in bed permitted him to see me as anything other than his superior.

Bask 9 – 498
I am packing up the department for the move to the Makuo glacier. Paperwork, endless reams of the stuff, dogs me at

2

every turn. I would draft in the other two to help if I didn't think their heads would implode from the need to consider more than one thing at a time.

So much to do, so much equipment to be requisitioned, so many permits to be filed. Moving house is hard enough in this city, let alone shifting a team of people three hundred klicks into the frozen north.

...but of course, I forget. With all that has gone on I neglected to keep this log updated. To wit:

The oaf Fermin marched into my office three days ago and stood in front of my desk looking mightily pleased with himself. Someone – presumably heralding imminent senility – decided the greasy shit was fit for an assistant professorship and now he struts about as if he owns the place. Come to think of it, he's looked that way ever since the Elucidon overruled me in giving him a fail for his undergraduate Heritage module. In his eyes, that was quite the victory, I'm sure.

Anyway, I made sure Assistant Professor Fermin had a good wait before I raised my eyes to acknowledge him, and when I did so I just stared at him in silence. This had always made his upper lip sweat when he was a student, and it seemed nothing had changed. He fussed with his nails, shuffling from foot to foot, then blurted out what had obviously been meant as a triumphant, pre-prepared speech.

The survey I'd commissioned with his (ha!) department – Geology – had turned up some results. Again, I waited in silence. In fact, I began to drum my fingernails on the desk because I know how wickedly unnerving he finds it. The oaf spat it out – in the north, they'd found something that

3

might be pre-Ruin. After a pause, I gave him some cold formal words of thanks and indicated he should leave the sheaf of papers on my desk. He dropped them and made for the door, and only at the last minute did he seem to regain some of his forced humour. His face took on a look halfway between elation and satisfaction – triumphant, you might call it. Despite myself I snapped at him, asking what was so wonderful that he felt the need to take up more of my time.

Maddeningly, he nodded at the papers on my desk.

'You'll see,' he lisped.

Skies, I loathe him.

Ice, you see. Almost 1.5 kilometres of ice between the surface of the glacier and the bedrock, and in between all manner of fissures, faults, melt-lines and geological waste dumps. That was what the idiot was so happy about, because he knows I am obliged to go. It has been years since any undergraduate applied to major in Cryptarchaeology, which has whittled away at our share of the budget, our designation reduced to 'research-only' – just one step up from 'shuttered'. We have scoured the old dig sites over and over, sucking every drop of evidence from them (which would fill a medium-sized beaker, at best). The Elucidon, taking its lead from the wider Hegemony, is touchy about anything to do with the pre-Ruin that is not an out-and-out condemnation; they would need little encouragement to allow the already obscure department to dry up and disappear – without me, I'm sure this would already have happened.

So, Fermin was right in his assumption – I have to go, and it will be hard going on me, a woman of middle age (the mirror tells me, unfailingly), and though I try to keep myself fit and healthy (erstwhile rolling with assistants, for example) I am hardly prepared for an expedition into the harsh ice fields.

But they have made a miscalculation, a misstep guided by male arrogance, pride and a lack of attention to detail that is particularly heinous, for all that they claim to be scientists. They assume I'm past it, ground down by the years and lacking the vitality necessary to make anything come of this; in truth, I cannot gather my things fast enough. The years are rolling off me as I prepare to *do* something, finally, after an aeon of mouldering in these rooms with the dregs of the student body to assist me. I'm an undergraduate again on my first field expedition, too full of excitement to know which warm liners to pack or which boots to wear.

There might be nothing up there more than a cavern or an intrusion of granite that has confounded poorly calibrated sensors; on the other hand, I might reach out and lay my fingers on something from before the world I know was made, and feel its legacy on my skin.

Bask 10 – 498

The Dean accepted my research proposal with alarming speed. I'm sure the rest of them are having a jolly good laugh about sending me off to freeze. He won't be smiling when he sees the size of my equipment requirements. And they'd better give me an able assistant, or I'll come back and haunt the bastards for ever.

Groan

Death had receded, and the flat expanse of the steppe welcomed the return of the pale, waking light. The ground was frozen below the surface but the cap ice had begun the slow melt, releasing its grip on the broken walls and streets of the old mining town. Ras's burning arc was shallow and cast long shadows over the broken water tower, the old dormitories, the ore processors with their silent conveyors. The strip mine's pit gaped, the great conical hole in the permafrost presenting its open maw to the milky sky. No one remembered the place's real name. It was just the Groan. Nobody else came here any more.

Cale contemplated the white stone block in front of him while he got his breath back. It was taller than him, its rough-hewn sides criss-crossed with straps. The lifter-field unit he'd used to haul it out of the pit had barely held together and the block, even in the anti-grav bubble, had been cumbersome. It stood now, stark against the sky on the gravel apron that brimmed the lip of the pit as he ran a callused hand over it, feeling the roughness on his palm. This one would become his tenth Face, and he knew it would be his best. The pale granite stared back at him, flat, unyielding, devoid of the features that would emerge: jawline, brow, eyes, lips. There was still so much to do, so much preparation, before he could so much as pick up a chisel.

The Death had been especially long this year and the ice had draped itself over everything, layer on layer, during the cold months. A particularly large build-up had caused a section of the mine's spiral access track to shear away, leaving the rock beneath exposed and saving him many days of surveying and excavating. The next stage, the cutting and hauling of the block, had been more dangerous due to the sheer rock face; even now, powered down, the lifter unit gave off a smell like burned hair that showed how close it had come to failing on him. The motor housing ticked and creaked as it cooled in the sharp air. Then the wind gusted from the west and the giant pit behind him emitted the deep bass note that gave it its name.

The Groan's call filled the tundra and drowned out everything for a few heartbeats, so he didn't hear the skimmer at first. When the uneven pulsing chug of its engines finally made itself known, the heavy utility vehicle was almost upon him. He could see where it had kicked up a trail on the thawing track which wound its way from the hills to the east. The narrow road took in a half-circuit of the circular rim of the pit before ending near where Cale had set up his tools. The rust-red skimmer was bulky, old and jury-rigged, listing under the weight of its cargo, a haze of compressed air distorting the underside.

7

Cale dropped his heavy gauntlets on the workbench and shrugged out of his booster harness. He shifted and stretched in his protective suit. The sweat from the work was still lukewarm between his shoulder blades, though his ears and cheeks were raw from the cold and his breath misted the air. There was a moment of dislocation, until he caught up with himself, remembering that the landslip had saved him those two weeks – normally the first supply run of the year would find him deep in piles of excavated mud. A reminder of last year's dig lay nearby next to the broken security fence: the engine he'd cobbled together from scavenged parts, when the permafrost had been so hard he'd had to jet-blast it just to be able to break the surface.

The skimmer – grav-trailer bobbing along behind like a leashed larg – pulled up at the edge of the apron. There was a mechanical sigh, followed by the grateful ticking of cooling metal as the skimmer powered down and the cab door popped open. The old man from the village jumped down, the vehicle barely shifting on its air cushion. He wriggled his shoulders inside the big oilskin jacket. He wore a thick cap with flaps that hung down over his stubbled, hollow cheeks. He caught Cale's eye, a mitten rising in greeting. Cale returned the gesture and went to meet him.

They rode the short distance back to the hangars in the skimmer. Once there, Aulk was all business. Cale could see the Groan's shadow in the fisherman's hesitant step and furtive glances over his shoulder. The place had a reputation amongst the locals, and because of it he had to pay well over the odds for these supply drops; only cash and the occasional bottle of rakk kept the old man to his word, making the seasonal journey from the village over the hills. Aulk was not unfriendly but always eager to be gone from this eerie place and him, the strange foreigner who lived with the ghosts.

Cale had been alone for so long he found he'd lost the knack for conversation, so the talk was minimal as they worked.

'Lift that, on three.'

'Pass that down.'

'Careful there.'

For the first time in a while he was conscious of how he must look: his hair and beard unkempt and matted after the months of dark isolation, and now mussed with sweat. The mad hermit and his rocks. Just another reason to stay away.

The unloading took longer than usual and he could see Aulk checking Ras's position in the sky every so often. The first drop after the dark months was always the biggest – power cells had run low; fish, meat and vegetables were distant memories. For the last month he'd been on reclaimed military field rations that all tasted identical – fine as long as you didn't look too closely. He was heartily sick of them.

Another, second lifter-field unit, the twin of the one he'd used that morning, helped shift the heaviest crates into the open hangar, then Aulk let him haul the rest. Cale towered over the village man and his thick arms could carry twice the load. He noticed Aulk's limp had got worse during the Death, and he was even less help than usual. The old man shuffled about, offering the odd grunt of encouragement, occasionally holding out a steadying hand. Cale found himself sweating again and a tired old voice at the back of his mind told him he should start exercising. As usual, he ignored it.

By the tail end of the afternoon all the crates were piled up in the hangar he used for storage. The unladen skimmer floated a half-metre higher off the ground; Aulk had powered down the trailer and stowed it away. Cale leaned on some crates to catch his breath, feeling the wetness that had spread from his lower back. Neither man spoke for several minutes. Aulk cleared his throat as if to start talking but hesitated; Cale saw him looking over at the Faces, all nine of them lined up on the empty concrete square, their frozen expressions facing north.

He wondered if there was some significance to it, some unthinking reason why he'd arranged them that way. The carved blocks of granite charted his time here, one for every year. With each one he'd got better as he'd learned: how to visualise the shape inside the block, how to chip and wedge and scrub and polish until it emerged. Always the same subject, a woman's rounded face with shoulder-length hair and a half-smile playing over her lips. Every year, he got a little closer to her.

Aulk shuffled and Cale knew he was about to ask about the Faces, but a gust of wind came barrelling over the plain, passing over the open mouth of the Groan and making it sing like the top of an enormous bottle. The low, mournful note vibrated through the ground and the air all at once, pounding eardrums and shaking bones. Aulk's eyes widened, his jaw slack. He took a step towards the skimmer as though something invisible had pushed him, gripped the cab's handle, but did not open it, standing stock-still as the noise died away.

Cale stood up straight and stretched as if he'd not seen anything. He gestured at the entrance to his home. 'Come on. Let's go have a drink.'

The two men sat at Cale's only table nursing earthenware cups of hot rakk. Aulk looked a little calmer indoors. Cale watched him take regular, rapid slurps, the weathered old face twisting into a grimace of pleasure with each. He brushed the base of his own cup back and forth over the pitted wood, painting it with a tiny spill of liquor, waiting for the right time to break the silence.

Aulk smacked his lips and caught Cale's eye. A minute nod of the head, acknowledging the quality of the drink.

'Good?' Cale asked.

The fisherman nodded. 'Good.' He clasped the cup between his palms to soak up the heat. 'Now I know how you can stand living in this Sky-forsaken place.'

'I like the quiet,' said Cale. He put his drink on the table between them and sat back in his chair. 'The stone is good.'

Aulk made a sucking noise between his teeth. 'Stone don't keep a man warm. Can't eat or drink stone. I wouldn't live out here for all the money in the world.'

'I have what I need.'

Aulk's brow remained furrowed. 'Bad place. Can't be good for a man to be out here this long.' He looked Cale over with a critical eye, like he was searching for some outward sign of something wrong.

Cale shook his head. 'It's an old mine. Nothing more.'

'You've heard the stories.' Aulk took another battery of sips.

Cale had, many times over the years, and never the same tale twice. It had been a war, some said, that chased the miners away; others said a plague. A couple of years before, Aulk had stayed for one more cup than usual and had spun a yarn of his own about the miners being driven mad. It was the Lattice, he'd said: out here, alone in the barren tundra, they couldn't bear those dark claws blocking out the lights in the night sky and dragging great shadows over the land during the day. With nothing but flat, iron earth beyond the town limits stretching to the end of the world, the horror of the thing was too much to bear. One night, as one, they'd all risen and walked to the lip of the Groan, tossing themselves in without so much as a scream. They were still there, he'd slurred, glassy eyes staring up through the dark waters, waiting.

Waiting for what, Cale had asked, but the old man shook his head and refused to go on.

That time was vivid in his mind as he watched the fisherman finish his rakk. It always came back to the Lattice, in the end, wherever you went. Raised in the Home Peninsula and a product of the best academies his father's rank could afford, Cale could count himself as an educated man, but even he felt an ominous stirring whenever he looked up, day or night, to see that huge, complex intertwining shape hanging there. It was the sheer scale of the thing that brought on a kind of vertigo, giving form to the immense distance between the ground and the outer shell of the world, the roof of all existence.

Aime had been the only one who'd been willing to talk about it. Her guess was that it was a leftover from the ones who'd come before, something even the Ruin couldn't obliterate. It was a monument of a forgotten people, she'd said, meant to inspire wonder, not fear.

For an instant the smell of her hair against his face was everything.

Rising, he gathered the mugs and went to refill them from the kettle. 'I've heard some of the stories,' he said. 'Do you ever wonder what it was for?'

'The pit? Why would I?' Aulk accepted the full mug. 'Thanks.'

'Not much in the way of minerals around here. Certainly nothing worth something so large. The mine, this whole town. I wonder what they were digging for.' Cale had pondered this many times, in the quiet months when the cold kept activity to a minimum. Why scoop a cone two kilometres across and one deep into the barren steppe?

It wasn't just Aulk who was reluctant to discuss the Groan – he'd never heard a straight answer from anyone and now he rarely brought it up. It was difficult enough getting people to talk to him, like he'd been tarnished by the place.

'I catch fish,' said Aulk. 'I try not to think about it. Place gives me the shivers.' He shrugged. 'Who the hell knows?'

Leave it alone, is what you want to say, Cale thought. It was difficult to look past the stories your grandam told you.

The fisherman launched into his freshened mug of the fiery amber spirit. Cale filled his own and returned to the table. There was something in it, he had to admit. Sometimes, when Ras began to lower in the sky, he'd find himself hurrying to get indoors to light and warmth and shut out the wind howling over the broken old buildings. That

13

sound: nothing more than a meeting of wind and geography, the rational part of him said, though even after all these years it could still shake him awake with hackles raised.

At least I have peace, he thought.

He looked up at the ribbed ceiling of his home. The long, arched metal structure looked like it had once housed mining trucks or even light aircraft: there was a hint of grease that time had never fully scrubbed away. Its shape had been proof against the weight of built-up ice, though thawing the coffin of frozen water around it had taken many days when he'd first arrived. It was comfortable now with the windows sealed and the concrete floors sheathed in thick carpet. The wooden partitions that made up rooms cut down the echoes and he'd filled every bit of empty wall with old books and older landscape pictures – the only reminders of the world he'd left behind – and added lights to all the rooms, staving off some of the oppression of the dark months.

Cale let the silence stretch, content to listen to the ticking of the old chrono in the corner. It, and the dark wood chairs they sat in, had come from the ruins of an administration office in the town – he was careful never to mention this. There were book piles dotted around on tables and chairs, empty bottles, unwashed plates in the sink, making him wish he'd thought to tidy some of it away.

The place must reek of me, he thought.

He hated the Death that kept him shut indoors and away from working on the Faces, his sole vocation robbed by swirling winds that cut to the bone. Nothing to do but drink, read and try over and over to get a tune out of the old bandothal on the wall. There were faded patches on the fretboard where Bowden's hands had marked the wood and he could still hear how it had sung under his deft, young fingers. He wondered for the thousandth time why the one thing he'd brought to remind him of his son was something he could not hope to master – the stubborn strings only whined in his thick hands. Every time he tried to play only reminded him of that last time, when words had cut the air with the heft of resentment. The memory of their parting always came on fast and had him abandoning the instrument for a bottle of something strong and dark as remorse threatened to swallow him down. After the second bottle, he'd shout his questions to the empty room, but the stubborn bandothal gave him no answers. The pale light of the Wake was always a blessed relief.

There was little reason to worry about how the place smelled, he realised, coming back to himself: Aulk's own powerful odour of fish and engine grease pervaded the air. The warmth of the room and the drink had relaxed the fisherman, now resting his feet on the open rakk crate as he contemplated the ribs of the vault above him between longer pulls on his steaming mug. Cale leaned back into his own chair and savoured the feel of the rakk's sweet-burning vapours jumping up his nose and down his throat before spreading heat to his fingertips and toes.

'How are things in Endeldam?' he asked.

'Oh, same, same you know.' Aulk took a gulp, his brow creasing. 'Long Death this year. Ice was thick. Fish were slow to come back.'

'And now?'

'Buggers turned up, so no bother. But, ah… there's this

new Factor in town, and a new official means more...' he rubbed a finger and thumb together. 'Always more tax.'

Cale nodded. 'And... your new wife?'

Aulk brightened, easing his shoulders back and giving a contented sigh. 'Fat and warm. Soft-like, eh?' He winked. 'She's, ah...' Aulk held cupped hands out in front of his belly.

'Already?'

'Of course she is!' A twinkle in the old eyes. 'For fishers the Death is mighty dull, unless you like drilling holes in the ice. So, instead, we get drunk and... drill holes.' He hooted and slapped his knee, then doubled over with a rattling fit of coughs. 'Bad Death, though. Too long,' he said, cuffing moisture from his eyes.

There was silence for a while as Cale made another trip to the steaming kettle to refill their mugs.

'Ah.' Aulk straightened like he'd just remembered something important. 'Got... got s'mink for...' He rummaged through his numerous pockets, then his small backpack, finally finding what he was looking for with a satisfied grunt. 'Came just last week, first ship to break through.' He handed the object over, a light brown paper package that had paled and stiffened at the edges. It was still sealed.

Cale turned it over in his hands, examining it. His name was written on it in thick handwriting he recognised. He gave it an experimental squeeze. The thick paper crunched under his big fingers – there seemed to be something rigid inside.

'Would've brought it sooner but, well...' Aulk let the words hang.

Cale ripped open one end of the package and carefully tipped out the contents – a metal cylinder rattled on the table and came to rest. He picked it up – heavy, dull gunmetal, flat-ended and as long as his forearm. At each end was a stud, one blue, the other black. He held it level in front of his face.

'What is it?' The fisherman's eyes were locked on the cylinder.

'A message capsule,' he replied. 'My… friend in Keln uses them. Old tech. An affectation of his.' Cale pressed the blue stud and there was a click, followed by an electronic chirp. A flat, glowing rectangle sprung into existence, then flickered out again. He slapped the end of the cylinder against his palm and the screen popped back to life, filled with lines of blue code. Through the translucent display, Aulk's eyebrows disappeared under his hat.

'Old, you say? Makes radio relay look like carving on wood.'

'Not many of them left now.'

Then the screen flickered again. A man's face appeared, staring directly at the camera. It was fleshy, round and completely bald.

Aulk snorted. 'Soft city man, I see that.'

'Brabant is his name. And you'd be surprised.'

'Looks well fed.'

'He arranges the payments for my supplies.'

The fisherman went quiet.

Cale waited for Brabant to begin. His friend's heavy jowls always made him look sombre, but there seemed to be something else this time – perhaps a tightness around his eyes or a rigid jut to his jaw.

'Cale,' fuzzed the voice, coming at them as if from the

17

other end of a long room. 'Brabant here. Well… you know that.' He looked down, seemed to be toying with something.

Disquiet seeded Cale's belly.

'Look, I'll come straight out with it, it's bad news. Bowden's hurt. I mean, he's been hurt. I got a… I got contacted by the Army. I know you parted on bad terms but… well.' Brabant passed a hand over his face and rubbed an eye. 'Skies, I wish you were near a relay station, Cale. I don't even know if this is going to reach you…' He took a deep breath. 'Details are sketchy – you remember what the military's like. Some police action down south. Something happened; he did something bad before he was injured. And now he's in a lot of trouble.'

The world beyond the screen dropped away until there was nothing in the universe but that glowing square and sad eyes in a tired face. There was a dark hole above Cale's breastbone that felt like it might suck everything into itself. He forced a halting breath.

'He's been sent to Sessarmin, the sanatorium,' continued the recording. Brabant's eyes stared straight at the camera. 'You know what that means. How bad it had to have been to get him sent to… that place.' He looked away. 'They say he's critical, but stable. But he's not waking up, Cale.'

The hole grew, swallowing him whole until only the pounding in his ears reminded him that he was alive, sitting with shoulders hunched, eyes unblinking and starting to water.

'That's it. I'm really sorry to have to tell you this. I don't know if this message will reach you in time, but… well, there you have it. Go well, old friend. Get in touch.' The screen flicked back to code.

18

Without pausing Cale hit the blue stud and listened to the message again. On the other side of the world, Aulk shifted in his chair and cleared his throat.

It was a mistake – another plea from Brabant to come back to the world, that was all.

The words came again, each one a bullet impact. Cale's disbelief died a little more with every shot, replaced by a creeping, hollow horror.

He's not waking up. The words were an ice burn.

He hit the black stud and the screen flicked off. With slow, deliberate care, like it might shatter, he placed the cylinder on the table. He leaned back, closed his eyes and let his head droop with a long, rasping breath.

Oh, what the hell, he thought. *What the hell.*

A lifetime ran past, a flurry of memory, scenes jumping out of the flow but disappearing before he could focus.

A small, soft hand holding his weathered fingers.

Aime walking away, smiling over her shoulder.

His son's face twisted in anger, looking too much like his own.

His hand whipped the table with a gunshot slap; rakk spilled; the cylinder rolled off and thunked on the carpet. Aulk jerked back, his eyes wide.

Cale inhaled through his nose, then stuttered the breath out past his teeth. He was standing, he realised. Looking at Aulk's huddled form, he realised just how much smaller and skinnier the other man was – in that moment he looked almost childlike.

Slowly, he held up his hands. 'I'm sorry. Bad news. Very bad news.'

The fisherman knocked the table with his knee as he stood. He downed the dregs of his rakk. 'Look,' he said, 'I'll go. You need time to yourself. Terrible news.' He nodded, agreeing with himself. 'I'll be back in a couple of months, but if there's—'

'Wait,' said Cale. The sucking hole was still there but he held himself from its edge by force of will. His hands had stopped shaking, and he knew what needed to be done.

'Give me a few minutes,' he said. 'I'm going to need a ride.'

i. Karume

The Major was still asleep when she got up to make breakfast. Kelbee moved slowly, carefully, as she did every morning, not wanting to wake him. The rough tiles were cold underfoot as she drew a thin robe about her shoulders. She shivered as she searched for her slippers at the foot of the bed, but they were not where they should have been. Maybe he'd knocked them into a corner of the room. He'd come home late and she'd had to help him stagger to the bedroom, had to pull off his high boots after he collapsed onto the bed.

Kelbee gave up on her slippers, padding barefoot along the short hallway that joined their bedroom to the kitchen and lounge of the apartment. She paused to greet the Seeker, bowing deep to the portrait set on the otherwise plain wall reserved for it. As she straightened she spotted a fine layer of dust on the frame and felt a twinge of worry that someone might see it. She flicked a furtive finger across the polished wood, thankful that he'd been too drunk to notice last night.

The lined flooring in the kitchen felt clammy, like the skin of a fowl. The district's power was still off at this early hour but the seals on the cold cabinet were in good repair and there was no smell of rot as she reached in. Kelbee took out a silver tarn, three fingers wide and as long as her hand, feeling a few delicate scales flake off on to the floor as she moved it to the counter.

With a small, sharp knife she cut the barbed fins away, and with quick, practised strokes scaled the fish into the sink. The dawn was coming, the faint light peering through the window in front of her as she worked, glinting off the scales in the basin.

Kelbee turned the tap to rinse the smooth fish and the pipes gave out a chopping groan. Startled, she shut off the water and listened for any sound of him stirring. She waited, tensed like a bird on a branch, but there was nothing; the apartment was still, save for the trickle of water down the drain.

Exhaling, she continued, drawing her knife along the tarn's belly line from throat to tail. She used her thumbs to ease its silky guts into a bowl, then covered the quivering red mass with paper and set it aside for the end of the week when she'd make fish sauce. The Major liked her fish sauce, as long as the smell from the rendering was gone by the time he got home. She knew he liked it because he grunted when he ate it – a single grunt was high praise. The commonplace merited only silence. He only spoke aloud when the food was not to his liking and she remembered both times that had happened.

Two more cuts of the knife, running along both sides

of the backbone, then she peeled the fillets away from the ribs, leaving the spine gaping on the board like a trap. She scooped the tender cheeks from the head before dropping the carcass into the waste bin under the counter, which let out a burst of cloying stink as the lid was lifted. The glue-makers only called every two weeks and she knew she'd have to burn more of her precious stock of incense to cover the smell until they came.

Kelbee took a pair of tweezers and set to plucking out a few stubborn, bristle-like bones from the fillets. Ras was up over the horizon now, hidden behind tendrils of low mist so she could look directly at it without having to squint or turn away. As she worked, it rose further until it broke free of the mist and passed behind the enormous edifice of the Tower, just two klicks from their small apartment, casting its shadow over her. She set the fillets down in the sink, rested her palms on the smooth ceramic lip and watched Ras's bright corona haze the edges of the giant pyramid.

This was her time, a moment for herself every morning. When Ras emerged, she would continue with her day, but for these few minutes she could just stop and stare at the quiet city. It was so still she could pretend it was a model, perfect and serene under a glass case, like the one in the Unity Museum. Over there were the tall trees that bordered a municipal park, where citizens could take the air and which she crossed every morning on the way to work. Apartment buildings just like this one stood in neat, numbered rows, marching out from the centre of the city like the spokes of a giant wheel with the Tower at its hub. If she were to just crane her neck to the right she would make out the square charcoal bulk of the building where she worked; she didn't, leaving the smell of bodies working close and the heavy chatter of sewing engines for later, when she could no longer avoid it. This time, now, was for her.

Every day, for these quiet turns of the dial, she could stop and remember how it felt that first day in Karume. The first time she'd seen a skimmer humming along the street on a cushion of hazy air, she'd stared at it open-mouthed, a dumbstruck country girl. Then the terrifying bulk of the Tower, taller than anything she'd ever imagined; a pyramid that seemed to join heaven and earth. Even after years of living in its shadow, she still marvelled at the madness of its scale. Reaching out, she ran a finger down the pane of glass, as if she might feel the hundreds of floors and balconies of the monolith as rough bumps under her fingertip like the scales of the silver tarn.

Ras emerged from behind the Tower – the moment was over. The light was piercing in the clear morning air, so she lowered the blind partway, and, as she did, felt the dull ache of her collarbone. She rubbed at the bruise, remembering. The Major's breath had been rank with drink and he'd been asleep in minutes. Later, he'd woken, fingers grasping and insistent.

She patted the fillets dry with a cloth so the oil in the pan wouldn't spit and wake him. She noticed a red light blinking on the rice steamer and knew the power had come on. This was a good thing: with fewer pans to wash she wouldn't have to rush to work.

And, said a small voice at the back of her head, you might have a few more moments with him.

24

Her heart hammered in her breast and she wrestled the thought away – too dangerous even to think about it here, she couldn't risk so much as the hint of a smile or a blush, so she distracted herself by adding rice and water to the grey cylinder and set it to steam, then rubbed salt into the fish, spreading it with her fingers. When it was time, she opened the top of the steamer and laid the fillets over the top, setting the timer, then busied herself with scrubbing down the countertop and hunting the floor for the last few rogue scales. Her breathing slowed and the panic flowed away.

Just thoughts, she told herself. No one could know. She noticed the chipboard door of one of the cupboards had started to warp with age and moisture, then the steamer drew her attention with its soft buzz. Under the hood the fish had lost its translucency and become firm. She tipped the whole lot, rice and fish, into a large, glazed serving bowl and mixed it together, the fish flaking just as she'd hoped it would.

She heard him move as he rose and though she'd heard the same sound every day for six years it made her breath catch in her throat. She forced herself not to pause, adding a pinch of smoked spice, some salt and a few drops of dark sauce to the mixture. He was in the shower now; she could hear the water splashing and the rasp of him clearing his nostrils into the drain.

She filled two bowls with rice and fish and touched the panel to turn on the strip lights in the living area, glad she'd had the presence of mind to set the table last night. She set both steaming bowls out and took one of the chairs to wait for him, her gaze lowered.

The Major came striding into the room and she pulled her robe tighter. He was clean-shaven and dressed in his uniform, save for his boots and hat, which she'd already placed by the door. He joined her at the table and set about his food without a word. He didn't bother to look at her, shovelling rice into his mouth, smacking as he chewed. A snort, then he went quiet. Kelbee's shoulders froze. Looking up, she saw him chewing slowly, his brow creased. He spat the mouthful out onto the floor.

'This is terrible.' He went to put the bowl down but missed, catching the edge of the table. Kelbee watched it as if in slow motion, tipping, spinning, finally hitting the floor with a crash that spilled the white-grey mixture over the tiles.

He rose. She inhaled.

He walked past her and began pulling on his boots. While his back was turned she took a spoonful from her own bowl and sampled it with care. There it was – a few bullet-like grains that clustered around the chunks of soft fish – the steamer must have another leak. She'd have to find it and repair it before she left and clean up the mess. There would be no early walk today.

She heard him straighten behind her and rose to face him. He'd put on his peaked officer's hat.

'No more damn fish,' he grunted. 'Get some meat in.'

'Yes, sir.' Kelbee bowed her head.

For the first time that morning, for only an instant, their eyes met. He was not much older than her, still in his thirties. His face was young, severe but unmarked except for dark shadows under his eyes. His body was trim in the uniform, fit and lean. His hands were slim and strong. His eyes were bleary today, but ordinarily were piercing, as if seeking out threats; he looked like a tree branch held back by brambles, ready to snap forwards with terrifying swiftness.

He would have been handsome, she thought, if it weren't for the wide mouth, too big for his face. She'd fallen in love when she'd been given to him: the tall soldier in his crisp uniform whose name she'd heard once when the Teller read it out and vows were exchanged, then never again. It had been so long that she could no longer recall it; he was the Major, always, and she'd not had the strength or the will to climb over that wall.

He broke the contact, looking away.

'I'll be home late again,' he said, adjusting his cap. He looked at the mess on the floor, then back at her. He looked for a moment like he might apologise, but it passed. 'Work hard,' he mumbled. He keyed the door and it slid open with the squeak of rubber on rubber, then he was gone.

A strand of her blue-black hair came loose over her eyes and she brushed it back behind her ear. She noticed four small red crescents in the meat of her palm where her nails had dug into the flesh.

Gloves today, she decided, and maybe a scarf.

Her morning commute took her through a tight warren of alleys at the base of the apartment block and out onto a thoroughfare. A few other women were making their way to work; at this time of the morning, with their eyes downcast and with purposeful strides, they could be going nowhere else. She must look the same to them, with her hat pulled low over her eyes and her collar turned up against the wind that blew down the long street, ruffling the gaudy red and blue Quincentennial banners. In this middle-ranked district there was little street traffic at this time of day, apart from the occasional skimmer making a delivery. One was backing out of an alley, beeping as it reversed, a shopkeeper waving the driver out as a boy in trousers too short for him stacked the boxes that had been delivered. One split in his hands, sending dark berries scurrying over the pavement. Kelbee crossed to the other side to avoid the mess as voices rose.

The words of the Seeker droned from the screens mounted on high posts spaced evenly along the street, as they did every day. The muffled utterances echoed off the shop fronts and windows, following her steps. The city was stretching, coming to life as she passed. At the end of the street she came to a checkpoint where her pass was scanned. She felt the usual jab of fear in her heart as the policeman looked her over, then kept her relief hidden as he waved her through, turning to the next person in line.

Beyond the barrier lay the park. Kelbee followed the white gravel path that cut through the grass, heading towards a row of skeletal trees on the far side. In the centre of the park was a wide gravel circle. She joined others who milled about the feet of a Teller, the morning ritual already begun. The platform on which he stood, red-robed and straight-backed, was at head-height to the assembled crowd and set before the gleaming statue of the Seeker, gazing with beatific eyes over the sweep of the park and the city blocks that fenced it. The Teller was mid-flow when she edged in.

'...cast down the ignominy of the old world, the corrupt, the decadent, the vile. He built the Walls that keep us, wrote the Principles that bind us and set us on the path to the exalted Inner Victory. For who was saved when the waves came? Who emerged from the broken world, ready to sow anew? For this, we give everlasting thanks to Him, our Eternal Leader.'

A speckling of mutters replied, tired voices repeating their daily catechism. The Teller's eyes flashed, and the words of thanks were repeated, this time with greater gusto. By his side a Factor stood mute, eyes attentive, one hand on the pistol at his hip.

'Bow, for Temperance,' the Teller intoned. 'For Vigilance, Modesty, Abstinence, Fortitude, Restraint, Obeisance, Fear and Love. They shape the lives we lead in His name.'

For each Principle of Inner Victory, they bowed to the likeness of the Seeker, the group rippling like grass, the timing ingrained. Kelbee, though a country child, knew the rituals well enough after six years in the capital. She also knew every bow was watched for appropriate veneration.

She waited her turn, then stepped forward to press her fingertips against the golden foot, the metal polished by thousands of daily caresses. The great eyes, high above, ignored them all.

Respects paid, she continued on her way. She was behind, and work was to start soon, so she picked up the pace though her bag rubbed against the bruise on her collarbone, restricting her. She passed through the border of trees, noticing that a few were beginning to bud even though the air still bit at her cheeks. As the Death faded into the

Wake the mornings were brightening, the skies clearing; she hoped the birds would return soon to rustle at the branches, filling the grey air with their songs. No branch had been spared decoration for the upcoming celebrations, blue and red garlands strung between them like the web of a great colourful raknud. The time away from work she was looking forward to, but the parades... The parades were exhausting, mandatory affairs for a military wife.

Fortitude, she thought to herself. *It's your duty.*

The wind cut across her face as she emerged onto the park-girdling street, making her hunch her shoulders against the chill. When she reached the charcoal-grey lump where she worked, her heart sank: the queue stretched almost to the far corner of the building. Several floors above, the klaxon would be about to sound the start of the working day and if she was seen to be missing there would be consequences.

She made her way past blank morning faces until she reached the tail, and there he was, waiting. He saw her and a brief smile flashed over his lips – a mere flicker of clouds parting to anyone but her. She didn't dare return it as she joined the queue behind him and a little to his left, so she could see the nape of his neck where it dipped beneath his collar.

Nebn's head turned a fraction. 'Morning,' he murmured. A simple greeting between acquaintances. A pounding of drums.

'Yes,' she replied, her ears thick with hot air. She turned her head, embarrassed she couldn't think of anything better. When she looked back he'd turned away again.

The minutes dragged on, and for all the closeness to him

stole her thoughts away there was a nagging in the back of her skull that every person in the queue in front of her was making her tardier. After what felt like an age, they shuffled into the foyer and waited to pile into one of the big elevators. When the car came, they managed to stand side by side as it rose through the building, watching the glowing floor numbers count up. Her fingers were a breath away from his, the air between them. Behind them, a man snorted. A woman was chatting to a friend about the upcoming parades and the feast days. Kelbee felt, more than saw, Nebn's face turn towards her a fraction.

'How was the park this morning?' he asked. 'Pretty, eh?'

She nodded back and smiled. He smelled of woodsmoke and soap. He was tall, the tallest in the elevator, though he stooped. She allowed herself a glance: liquid-bright eyes, a sharp chin and cheekbones softened by crow's feet and crescent dimples around his mouth that formed deep pits when he smiled, which was often. His lips were thin and firm – just that darting look brought a flash of memory, of softness and the taste of mint on her tongue. His hands, held by his side, were strong and soft. Before she could allow herself to remember how they'd felt on her skin she forced herself to look away, anywhere else.

He'd been working on a faulty heating unit on the day she'd first seen him. The elements often broke and turned the chilly factory floor unbearable – the number of accidents from fumbled shears were always worse during the Death. Contracted workmen were transient visitors and didn't talk to the women in the factory unless it was to order them out of the way.

Kelbee had been carrying a heavy bobbin from the storeroom down a narrow side corridor when it spilled from her numbed hands and hit the floor with a metal clunk, spinning into an overalled, helmeted workman, unspooling as it went. She'd expected at the very least jeering, or even a call to the monitors to reprimand her for her clumsiness. Instead, *he*'d been there with his kind face and gentle words. He'd not said much but had helped her gather up the thread before giving her a parting smile and returning to his task. It was only later that she realised they were the first words she'd had from a man in years that hadn't been an order or a grunt of disapproval.

She'd spied him coming from another side of the park the following day, converging on the Seeker's idol for morning worship just as she was. As she'd mouthed along with the Teller, she'd shocked herself by imagining what it would be like to walk alongside him, running the conversation over and over in her head, playing both parts. After, she'd even sped up to catch him, but when she was almost in earshot her nerve went and she ended up hanging back.

The next day, he'd waited for her at the edge of the park and greeted her with deference, even reserve, but behind the words were smiles that licked her like a shock of lightning. Then, later, in a place hidden away from prying eyes, the outlines of his body had melded with hers as they broke every rule she'd ever known.

The elevator continued up, dropping off people until it was empty but for the two of them and an older man leaning against the back wall, looking for all the world like he was still asleep. Kelbee felt the silence like a thick blanket.

'I love the Wake. It's like everything's... swept clean,' she murmured, wishing she had a better way of saying it.

Nebn nodded back with a small smile, and she cursed her awkwardness. Then it was his floor and he said goodbye before stepping out. The older man started awake and rushed past the closing doors, bumping into Nebn as he turned back. He mouthed the word, 'Goodbye,' at her; their eyes met and she felt a flutter just above her stomach.

When the doors closed she realised her cheeks were burning and her smile reached the corners of her face.

The factory floor was already filled with clicking and whirring as the garment-makers began their day. A few were still drifting back from the commons area and heading for their workstations. A glance at the chrono told Kelbee she'd missed the pre-work salutation and exercises, but there were no monitors nearby so she slipped in behind a shuffling group of women and did her best to blend in. At her station, keeping her face down to hide her rapid breathing, she shrugged off her coat but left her scarf on – she didn't much feel like being the subject of gossip this morning.

Like the other workers she wore a light blue shirt and trousers, and she'd pulled her hair back into a tight bun that slipped easily under the hairnet. She pulled on a white cloth facemask and climbed onto the high chair bolted to the floor behind a clunky, rust-stained sewing engine. Strands of black and brown cotton hung from the ceiling, joining the machine to a narrow metal frame suspended overhead. This ran along to a cluster of bobbins dangling in the centre of the six sewing stations, supplying them all with thread like puppets in an oversized koktu show. There were four sewing clusters like this one on the floor, and the air was alive with the dull rattle of chattering industry.

From a stacked trolley by her side Kelbee pulled the topmost garment, a pair of rough-stitched trousers. Setting her head down and her feet on the pedals, she began to hem with smooth, practised passes. The needle before her whirred up and down, leaving a neat line of stitching across the rough brown fabric.

The other five women in her cluster were doing the same, heads bent and eyes intent on their work. As Kelbee worked, the pile on her right shrank and the one on her left grew. When it became ungainly, she stopped and hefted it over to a wheeled cage at the edge of the circle of machines; when that was full, a porter in red overalls appeared to push it to the next stage in the production line. There was no talking, only the chatter of the machines, the rumble of the bobbins and, faint under everything else, the tinny echo of State music. It was there to inspire them, they'd been told.

On most days Kelbee could go into a trance-like state where her hands and eyes and feet all worked in unison without the need for much guidance, but not today. Little things kept distracting her, like a fly darting past her eyeline, or a particular note in the music that grated on her. Her collarbone rubbed raw against the rough material of her shirt and she could not get comfortable on the stool.

The memory of that morning in the elevator kept repeating like a broken film in her mind, flashing over and over as she imagined all the ways the conversation could have gone, but hadn't. She saw where his eyebrows met at the bridge of his nose and drew further down, passing over the tip and to where his lips lay, slightly parted and flecked with moisture, white teeth peeking out from behind. She tried to shake it away, but still the memory of that mouth came back to her again and again. She'd seen more than smiles from it, greetings of a different kind as it had played over the rise and fall of her body; the recollection was a tingle that excruciated, making the room seem hot and close around her. Sweat ran down the curve of her neck. She tried to keep her mind on her work, desperate not to move her mind's eye any lower on his body, to those other places of him, but it was no good. Even thinking about his eyes fogged her head, remembering herself looking at him looking at her in the afterglow of that dangerous, beautiful thing they'd done, feeling like he could see past her skin – what she was thinking, feeling. It terrified her; she craved more and more. No one else had ever looked at her, touched her like that. Certainly not the Major.

The thought of her husband was an icy slap of reality. His face, fleshy and flushed, caught in the half-light from a crack in the blinds. It was her duty, she knew, to submit to him, but his fingers had been cold and his grip painful. She'd known better than to cry out – he was drunk and didn't know he was hurting her. Then, after, she'd been discarded, her function fulfilled. Despite herself, she shuddered.

Someone was there. Glancing up, she saw a floor monitor standing on the other side of the desk, his head poking over the top of her machine. Ganada, who liked to watch her. His tiny eyes were even narrower than usual.

35

'You were late,' he said, his voice nasal.

Kelbee tried to look blank. 'Mr Ganada?'

He walked around to her side of the desk. He was small and portly, made even shorter by his hunched shoulders. Speckled hair receded back from a sharp point in the centre of his forehead and he had the habit of rubbing his knuckles as he talked. He smiled an oily smile as he drew a baton from his belt and rested its tip on the desk. 'I saw you. You missed the callisthenics.'

There was no let-up in the sound of the women around her but Kelbee knew they were listening. 'I'm sorry, sir,' she said. 'I was delayed at home.'

'That's no reason. If chores keep you, rise a little earlier, no?' He lifted her chin so she was looking into his murky brown eyes. 'Is that so hard?'

'No, Mr Ganada.'

'No, Mr Ganada,' he repeated, sing-song. 'It's very simple. If you miss the morning exercises you will become unfit, which means you will be less efficient, which means I will have to move you back down the line. That's how it works.' His tongue darted over pale lips. 'You don't want me to do that, do you?'

'No, sir.'

'I've had my eye on you; you're one of the good ones. But rules are rules, girl, so I have to give you a stamp.'

'Sir, please—'

There was a crack like a pistol shot as he smacked the metal desk with his baton. Kelbee heard another woman gasp, which drew an annoyed look from the monitor. Then he held out his hand.

'Your book. Now.' The smile was gone.

Kelbee felt inside her bag with trembling fingers for the slim black notebook. The pages were blank and unmarked.

'Hmm, your first one,' he said, the sickly grin back. 'What a good girl you are.' He drew a heavy metal stamp and an ink sponge from a pouch and pressed them together.

Kelbee's heart was beating fast. She would have to get the Major to sign the stamp and present it back tomorrow. He would be angry. He would hit her, she was sure of it. It might be bad. She'd never been cautioned herself, but she'd seen other women who had come in with bruising on their faces. Once, a girl she'd shared lunch with had been given a stamp for dropping a pail of black dye on fresh cloth and hadn't returned for days; she still refused to speak to anyone, save for the monitors, and when she did her words were muffled.

Just as the monitor was about to stamp the page there was a loud crash from a few rows over and a high-pitched scream. Kelbee craned her neck and saw a crowd was gathering over by the cutting tables. Ganada, the stamp held in ink-stained fingers, took a step away from her desk and called out to a colleague.

A thin wail carried over the factory floor.

The monitor swore. He dropped both stamp and sponge into his pouch and rushed over towards the growing crowd. 'Get back to work!' he shouted as he pushed his way through. A few minutes later he reappeared with another monitor, carrying a young girl towards the double doors at the far end of the room. Her head was lolling and her arm was clutched to her chest. The light blue shirt was stained dark.

37

The cutting tables, where everyone started when they joined the garment factory. Accidents with the heavy automated shears were common; Kelbee had seen women with missing fingers, or in some cases whole hands. She'd come away unscathed herself, but it looked like this one had not been so lucky. Poor girl, she would go no further with an injury like that. She'd likely be looking at the shears that cut her for the rest of her life.

There was a piercing screech from the speakers and a voice barked, telling them to get back to their tasks. Within seconds the busy hubbub resumed as if the incident had never happened. Kelbee saw her book, still perched on the edge of the desk, the pages unmarked; she snatched it and dropped it into her bag before returning to her sewing.

Keep working, she told herself, *don't draw attention. You might get away with it.*

At the end of the day Kelbee's eyes felt as dried out as the clothes she'd been working on. It was late and she was alone in the elevator, thinking about what to make for dinner when there was a chime, and she realised it had stopped on Nebn's floor. It was too late for him to still be at work but hope flared in her chest, hope that he would walk in and give her that smile that made everything seem better. Instead, two middle-aged women entered, deep in conversation, and the doors began to close.

She heard a shout, then a hand wedged itself into the gap and pushed the doors back open. Nebn stumbled into the elevator as if pushed. His hair was damp at the neck and he looked like he'd run for it. He saw her there and grinned.

They walked together for the first time that evening. As they reached the park, he paused at a garland of blooms that had been set out for the parade. He looked both ways, then plucked out three blue flowers, but waited until they were well under the trees before he stepped close and gave them to her.

A whispered invitation.

She nodded.

Endeldam

Cale and Aulk made their way into the range of bald hills that split the wide steppe from the coast, following an ancient road. The occasional pothole jostled the cab of the bulky skimmer truck. Cale didn't speak much. His breathing had settled after the first hour, but every so often the words of the message – pressed against his heart inside his jacket – rang in his head and panic would creep up, making the blood boom in his ears.

The cab was cluttered and close, made closer by their thick layers of clothing. Despite a trickle of warm air struggling through the vents, the cold from the mountains had seeped in. As Ras's light began to fade, Aulk fished blankets from behind the seats and offered one to Cale, who nodded in gratitude before wrapping it about his legs and body, leaving only his head exposed; like everything in the cab, it reeked of engine oil. The fisherman fiddled with the ancient radio unit, finding only static.

'How long to your village?' Cale asked.

'Some hours yet. Still going up, need to start going down.' Aulk prodded the radio one more time as an afterthought. 'Got to get this bastard thing fixed,' he muttered.

'Shouldn't you watch the road?'

'Nah, pretty much drives herself. She's a good old beast, though she don't look it.' He patted the cratered grey dashboard.

Cale gazed out of the side window as they wound higher and higher above deep, shadowed valleys. Evening had set and was leading the night in. The peaks began to feel like walls pressing in on him.

He's not waking up, Cale. No matter what he did, he couldn't get those words out of his head.

Aulk cleared his throat. 'Here,' he said, blowing on his fingers. 'Did I tell you about this fish I caught with two heads? I was out, before the cold set in, with my brother's boy. Feckless prick he is, but good in a storm. Anyway, we was out past the point...'

Cale settled, allowing the chatter to wash over him. His lids felt stone heavy and his gaze kept wandering back to the crags and peaks outside. On his side of the road the edge dropped away, just a jagged line between earth and empty air. The light was faltering now and the headlamps flicked on, carving twin cones into the gloom.

'...he says to me, where's the bait? Where's the bait? And I says, you was meant to pick up the fuckin' bait! And then *he* says...'

The gloom deepened until Cale could no longer see the bottom of the ravine. His head felt so heavy on his neck. Aulk's voice was a steady drone at the edge of the world.

'...Endeldam. Lived there since I was born. My da and his da too, going way back. He said since before the Ruin, but never believed that. Got a load of cages for catching redcrumn out past the point. Sometimes follow the breeze further out and net a charce or three, and if luck really opens her ankles maybe even a naru. Got three boats now, from the one I got from Da...'

Another voice slid in, smooth as a razor; a whisper at the edge of hearing, muffled as if by a great distance. It slipped into the cracks of the fisherman's chatter, blending with his rough tones and singing its own sibilant song.

What about you? it said. *What have you ever made that lasted, old man?*

'...you can stay as long as you like. Nowhere else to go, anyways. Little chance of finding a berth these days...'

Nowhere to go, not for you. Not any more.

'...cargoers barely come these days, once or twice a season maybe, for scraps. It's that bloody fishery, ain't it? On the other side of the bay. They say to me, why bother with your bony catches? Your measly snappers? The shits...'

Though his lids were closed, Cale could see the cab of the skimmer, darkness leech-like against the dirty glass. As he watched, it began to seep in, an inky mist pouring into the cab; pooling in the foot wells, rising higher, higher. The headlamps cut through the murk ahead, which was now thick as earth, and they tunnelled ever onwards, delving deeper even as it engulfed them. He opened his mouth to shout, scream at the fisherman to stop his mindless chatter, to pull them away from the mire that was swallowing them, but no sound came out.

'...livelihood's going down the crapper, but it's supply and demand, they say. Just pay your tithe on time like a good boy...'

Stick to the rules and no one gets hurt, wasn't that it? Wasn't it, sir?

'...you'd want to live next to an old ruin, anyway? You ain't a murderer as I can measure it, and no dissident. Still, two wives and a brood of kiddies ain't cheap...'

Even the beams of the headlights were fading behind the swirling, liquid dark. It was as cold as death. The mist rose up to his mouth and he tried again to scream but couldn't.

'...new Factor threw a whole family out on the street for not paying the tithe. Scratching a living from some cave, moss and berries. What a waste...'

All a waste. A cold-eyed waste, said the other voice. It was louder now, drowning out the fisherman. It was angry.

Where were you when that jackbooted son of a bitch took them? They looked up to you.

Let me go, old man.

'No!' Cale awoke with a start. There was no mist. His heart pounded a tattoo.

Aulk was staring. 'Bad dream?'

'Mmm.' Cale shifted his shoulders; the blanket had slipped down and he was frozen. The anger from the other voice lingered, resonating as if it had been real – anger like a hot ball in the centre of his chest.

'You were talking in your sleep,' said Aulk. 'A woman's name, maybe. Dunno.' The old fisherman shrugged. He offered over the rice pocket he was munching; Cale thanked him but waved it away.

Outside the window, Marna was cut in three by the limbs of the Lattice and threw jagged silver shards across the mountains, lighting the highest peaks like beacons. Cale found a spot on the dashboard, a divot burned black long ago by dropped ash, and stared at it until he felt calm return.

Aulk finished his rice and tossed the wrapper down by his feet. 'Know what?' he said, turning to face Cale. 'Caught a ray with three tails once. Ever seen one of those?'

By the time Marna's pale light had cleared the Lattice their skimmer truck had begun its descent towards the sea. Aulk's constant babble helped keep the night at bay but Cale didn't sleep again. His eyes felt gritty and his neck was stiff against the headrest.

Finally, their headlamps rounded the last bend and led them into Endeldam. The village was mostly dark, with only a smattering of lights. Cale found it hard to picture the shadowed streets from the hazy memories of a handful of visits. Was that a house he recognised? Had he walked that path? In the night, everything seemed foreign and new. A few windows were still lit – some by electrical light, some by the flicker of candles. Only the bar on the central square showed any real life under its loud, neon sign. He heard the pumping of music as they passed; a man was pissing up against a wall, swaying on the spot, steadying himself with one hand. They carried on down the hill.

Aulk's house was set back some way from the road, with a gravel driveway flanked by tilled patches of dirt. Cale could make out rows of sticks set out to carry the Wake's new creeper-beans. A chain-link fence marked out the plot, with the neighbours' houses some distance away in the darkness. The building itself was two floors of wood plank, the reddish bolma interspersed here and there with driftwood, Ras-bleached and wave-polished. A raised porch of decking fronted the place, lit by the soft glow of storm lamps, the walls hung with trophies from the sea: gaping shark jaws and stinger-tails. The windows were shuttered, the light from inside peeking out through gaps in the wood. Everything was deserted except for a single figure, sitting in an old rocking chair, its face in shadow.

'Very quiet,' said Aulk. 'Where are they all?'

Cale saw more lines than usual across the fisherman's brow.

They stepped down from the skimmer and stretched, welcoming the freedom of the chill air. Cale caught salt on the breeze and, almost too faint to make out, the crash of waves. He reached into the cab and grabbed his holdall, dropping it at his feet while Aulk took a few steps towards his home, craning to make out the shadowed figure.

It stood, the muted light revealing its features.

The face looked boyish in its roundness, out of place between the peaked hat and stiff uniform collar. A young man, with hair clipped short, precise, like the starched uniform he wore. Polished buttons glinted, black boots hugged slender calves and swallowed the light. He looked like a boy playing dress-up. A serious, dangerous boy.

'Citizen,' he said. 'You're out late.'

'Evenin', sir,' Aulk mumbled. 'I, um, I didn't know there was a curfew.'

'There isn't. Yet.' The slight figure stepped down from the porch into the gravel of the driveway. 'I was in the area and thought I'd pop in. A social call, you know?' The eyes turned to Cale and they locked gazes. 'Who's your friend?'

Cale answered. 'Local craftsman.'

'Is that right? Local craftsman? I didn't know we had any, local or otherwise. No, no.' He made a show of looking Cale up and down. 'I don't know you. You're not on my lists.' He took a step forwards; he was a whole head shorter and had to tilt his chin upwards to maintain eye contact.

'I doubt I am,' said Cale. He heard the fisherman draw in a sharp breath. *Don't make trouble*, he reminded himself. 'I live out on the steppe. At the old mine. Aulk is a friend.'

'Really? I don't recall him mentioning you before, friend.' The silence stretched. A sudden smile cracked the boyish face, though it didn't reach his eyes. 'Where are my manners? I'm the Factor of this armpit of a town.' He pointed a gloved finger at his epaulette and the gold bars that showed his rank.

'Pleased to meet you,' said Cale.

'Likewise, I'm sure. Your name?'

'Cale.'

'And you have your papers?' The Factor held out his hand, smile fixed like wax. 'I'd like to see them.'

'I'm not sure where I put them. It's dark.'

The Factor's gaze didn't waver. He cleared his throat and began to quote. '"Citizens are required to have their papers on hand at all times. They must present these to any official or representative on request and without delay." That's the law. As you can see, I'm the representative or official.' He pointed again at his rank bars. 'So, again. Your papers.' The smile had vanished.

Aulk, fidgeting, cut in. 'Hey look, Factor, we just had a long journey. My friend has all the right papers and I'll vouch for him. Besides, he's right, it's dark like a fucking cave out here. And cold, eh? Maybe we can have a drink, sit down and... well, have a talk like reasonable men. What do you say?'

The official's eyebrows lowered.

'I think I have them here,' said Cale. He crouched and rooted around inside his bag, drawing out a plastic wallet. After a slight hesitation, the Factor took it and began to leaf through the card sheets within.

Cale caught Aulk's eye, who nodded in mute gratitude.

The Factor scowled in the half-light. 'That's... hmm. What *is* that? I can't see a damned...' He breathed a long sigh. 'Oh, it's too dark out here. How do you expect me to read this without adequate light, eh?' He put the cards back in the wallet and tossed it at Cale's feet. 'I am not satisfied, citizen. Even in this piss-awful light I counted only four documents in there – the standard now is seven, eight for migrant workers.'

'I've been away from things for a while.'

'I can see that. Anyhow, you'll present yourself to my offices tomorrow morning and my staff will run the necessary checks. There will be an administration fee. But at least we've been introduced, eh?' The thin smile reappeared. 'I know your face now.' With that, he straightened his tunic before brushing past Cale, heading for the main road.

Cale kept his eyes on the middle distance.

Halfway to the gate, the Factor paused. 'Aulk,' he called over his shoulder. 'I'll expect you in the next couple of days. There's still the matter of your outstanding tithe.' A crunch of gravel. 'A pleasant evening, citizens!'

Aulk called out a hurried, 'Night, sir!' but was answered only by faint whistling, moving off into the distance.

As they crossed the threshold Aulk's household erupted into homely chaos. Children appeared from every side, jabbering questions at their father while his two wives fussed with coats and hats. Cale's overcoat, stiff with the cold, was taken with a disapproving cluck. The older children stood apart, eying the newcomer with suspicion. The front room doubled as the kitchen and was lit and heated by a large metal stove in the centre, its black pipe disappearing up into the eaves.

One of the younger boys stood in front of Cale and stared up with a defiant gleam in his eye. 'I'm Jeb, and I'm six. Who're you? Why's your beard so big? Are you a demon?'

Aulk shooed the boy away and tugged at Cale's sleeve, guiding him over to a wooden table. They both sank onto benches polished smooth from use. Thick broth with chunks of fish was ladled into bowls by the younger of the wives while the other corralled the offspring into another room. The two men ate in silence as the household settled down for bed. After the first spoonful of spiced stew Cale found he was ravenous. Aulk poured two large cups of rakk and they both drank deeply without toasting.

After the stew, both men found easy chairs by the fire that had burned low in the stone hearth. Aulk added a thick chunk of wood and poked at the embers until little flames licked at its sides. The log sizzled, spat, then settled down to a slow burn, its cracked underside glowing cherry red.

'I need to get back to Keln,' said Cale.

'Roads through those hills are still bad,' replied the fisherman. 'No buses. Trade runs won't start for a few weeks when the landslips are cleared.'

'A ship, then.'

'No boats going any further than a few klicks. It's not what it was, this place. Big berths have all rotted. Ships go across the bay.'

'I have to find a way.' Cale was about to go on, but the thought of Bowden cut him short. He lowered his head, finding distraction in the calluses on his palm.

Simple tools for a simple job. Then, *What if I'm not there in time?*

Aulk watched the fire for a few moments, silent. 'Tomorrow,' he said. 'There's a market. We might find a man, and he might take you.' He yawned and stood, fishing out a heavy blanket and tossing it over. 'You'll be warm by the fire.' He grunted, then nodded his farewell. Cale thanked him and watched the old fisherman disappear behind the curtain to his bedroom.

Sleep crept up on him sooner than he thought it would but his night was full of endless climbs up steep hills as the rain made the mud worse, both sticky and slippery, and every inch was a battle, and then he was at the top and Aime and Bowden were there together, waiting for him, smiling at each other though they'd never met, and no matter how hard he tried to run to them the mud held him in place.

•

The market crowd murmured as breath misted the morning air. There was anticipation, a gentle susurration of waxed coats brushing together and low conversation. A few dozen men had gathered in a corner of the marketplace; fishermen mostly, a scattering of fishmongers and other traders. They milled, swapping greetings and gossip, complaints about the weather and the size of the last catch. Feet shuffled and stamped and hands were thrust deep into warm oilskin pockets; ruddy cheeks puffed out and blew into cold, laced fingers.

The marketplace was roofed but open-sided and stood at the intersection of the town square and the main road. The square had been used for a festival recently, judging by the withered, flapping remnants of bunting, but now it was being used as parking, the flat gravel pan half-filled with utility skimmers and old, wheeled trailers.

Cale and Aulk stood at the back, waiting for the auction to begin. In front of the crowd, lying in neat rows, was the morning's catch. Each grey torpedo had been de-tailed, beheaded and gutted. Smaller fish rested in crates of ice but the still-frozen naru – some as long as a man lying down – rested on the wet concrete floor. A powerful brine tang came from the carcasses, though there was no rot. The catch, Aulk had told him, would have been pulled from the ice-holds only an hour before.

Last night the fisherman had told him this was the best place to find sea captains that would take cash and turn a blind eye, though there seemed to be few men here from outside the community. What had once been a thriving fishing town had visibly withered – the marketplace could have held four times this many people.

An elderly man with a wrinkled neck dragged a footstool out in front of the crowd and mounted it as conversation died away. He closed his eyes, and after a moment of silence began to call out in a low, rolling chant.

'Allzooooo! Naru-meskan. Allzoooo! Kandak merek...'

Cale didn't know the words, but it was clear the auction had begun. The chant waxed and waned; in the pauses others from the crowd replied in the same lilting dialect. It seemed rehearsed, like a ritual, a chanted prayer led by the old man perched on the stool as the high priest. Amid the noise fingers pointed and stock moved – somehow, deals were being struck. A number of the men began to walk up and down the rows, stopping to dig a fingernail into this head or that tail stump, bringing the flakes of frozen fish to their mouths or rubbing it between their fingers.

'Checking for quality,' said Aulk, answering the unspoken question.

The monotone rolled on, regular, punctuated by the shouts from the crowd. The noise broadened until Cale wondered how anyone could single out an individual voice. Through it all the old man on the stool's face was serene; occasionally he would glance at one of his helpers and they would go to speak with individual buyers, but his chant never faltered.

'How does anyone understand what's going on?'

'Old language,' answered Aulk.

'The Factor knows about this?'

'We don't speak it when he's around.'

Cale acknowledged this with a nod. *We, not they*, he thought to himself. Old ways still clung on this far from Karume.

He began to spot patterns amid the chaos now – they were there if you took the time to watch, like whorls of rainbow oil over water. Each time a deal was struck an assistant pinned a yellow strip of paper into the flank of the fish, then the buyer would hook it at the gills and drag it away; the big frozen naru skidded and clattered after their new owners on the wet concrete. Other men walked off carrying crates of the smaller fish, heading for their trailers.

Just then Cale noticed the outsider. He was dressed differently, in clothes that looked newer, his bright yellow coat standing out from the leather and sackcloth. Under his jacket he wore a crimson shirt and grey trousers tucked into black rubber boots. He looked unsteady on his feet and his face was flushed under thick stubble; he stood with his arms crossed, watching the sale, seeming to take no part in it. After some minutes, Cale saw him scratch his cheek and beckon one of the assistants over.

The man in yellow indicated around a dozen big naru with a sweep of his arm. The assistant's eyes went wide and he mirrored the gesture as if to confirm what he'd heard. This earned an impatient nod, then a large bag changed hands. Whatever was inside it quickly wiped the uncertainty from the assistant's face and he turned to gesticulate at the auctioneer. The bag was spirited off as more men in bright jackets arrived to take the naru haul away. Cale watched them take the frozen carcasses over to a large skimmer parked right at the edge of the market.

'Him,' said Aulk, leaning in. 'Over there. That's the captain you want.'

'I see him.'

Yellow Jacket waited for his men to remove the last of the naru before following them out. Cale watched him, now only distantly aware of the buzz of the auction around him.

Aulk tapped him on the shoulder. 'I'll talk. Easier. Met him before.' He indicated that Cale should stay where he was and headed for the heavily laden skimmer.

As Aulk weaved his way through the crowd, one of the big carcasses slipped off the trailer and hit the road with a loud crack. The youngest of the crew, a red-haired boy standing on top of the truck, had let the big fish slip out of his grip; the boy's face flushed with embarrassment. The captain bellowed, brandishing his fist, then flinched as Aulk tapped him on the shoulder; the curtness of the captain's reply was apparent from the way the old fisherman's head jerked back. There was a brief verbal altercation, then the situation appeared to be diffused.

They spoke for several minutes and, once, the captain shot a glance in his direction. The conversation ended with both men shaking hands.

Aulk pushed his way back to Cale's side. 'He will take you to Keln, but he wants a lot of money.'

'He can have it.' With Brabant taking care of the bills for supplies, Cale had barely spent any of the money he'd brought with him ten years ago. It would be enough, and if not then there would be more when he got to Keln where old accounts lay dormant, the relics of a more complicated life.

He can have the whole damn lot, he thought, *if he just gets me there.*

'I told him that already. He's moored at the fishery up the coast, taking on bulk stock. This is all special order. Sells for more, apparently.' He indicated the auction still going on behind them. 'He said he'd pass near tonight on his way to Keln. I can take you out, but we have to be quiet.'

The captain's men had finished retrieving the naru from the road. Some stray largs had gathered and were eying up the loaded truck, sniffing the air with wet noses. One of the crew yelled; a lobbed stone scattered the pack, sending them yipping away into the nearby alleys. The captain went over to the youth who'd dropped the fish, clipped him behind the ear, then climbed into the cab of the skimmer.

'He'll do,' said Cale.

Aulk shifted, his discomfort writ large. 'Listen, last night. The Factor. When you go, there'll be questions. It could be difficult.'

Cale saw the worry in the old man's eyes. He was asking a lot of this man who owed him nothing. 'If it was your son, what would you do?' he asked.

Aulk nodded at the ground. 'I would go.'

'I will make things right. I'll see him now. Your family will have nothing to worry about.'

Aulk didn't meet his eye, grunted.

Cale put a hand on the fisherman's shoulder. 'I'll deal with him.'

That made the fisherman look up. 'I don't like your voice when you say that.'

The Factoriat was a short walk from the marketplace. The buildings in this part of town were stark concrete and barred windows, a world away from the driftwood huts by the sea.

The office building itself was squat and angular; from the approach it looked more like a fortification, the dark, narrow windows flanking the main doors like gun ports. Cale fought down the nagging urge to find cover as he walked up.

Inside, a functionary with bored eyes pointed him to an empty row of seats along the wall. Cale sat and waited, his eyes playing over the low-lit room that even in daylight conspired to be gloomy and oppressive. The walls were thick with deep crimson tapestries bearing the gold-stitched profile of the Seeker. The hangings muted every sound and the place smelled stale. He wanted to push the doors open and let the air in, but forced himself to sit still and wait for his turn.

This is how they did it. It was all part of how they kept you in line.

The Seeker's portrait hung in pride of place above the reception desk, red and blue garlands adorning it. Cale thought of all the festivals he'd missed. Was this the year of the Quincentennial? Or had that been the year before? He couldn't be sure.

A little further away, on the same wall, hung another painting. A tall, bald woman with sharp green eyes stared from a gilt frame. Her mouth was set in a proud, narrow smile. Fulvia arc Borunmer, Venerable Guide, Chief Marshal of the Seeker's Military and Holder of Keys. She'd acceded to her office the same year he went into exile; this new Factor and this new, oppressive building had all the hallmarks of ambition and spreading influence. She'd not been idle.

After what felt like an age he was summoned through

another set of doors and down a corridor to a large office. The room was rounded, the walls lined with wood panelling and polished to a high sheen. The floor had been lowered to allow for a higher ceiling, so he had to take three steps down before his feet met thick carpet. Unlike the rest of the place there were tall windows here bringing in daylight. In the centre of it all, behind a large wooden desk, sat the young Factor, writing with his head down. He didn't look up as Cale approached but dismissed the functionary with a flick of his wrist.

Cale remained stone still while the Factor's pen darted over the page, waiting him out. It was an old trick, meant to put him at a disadvantage, one he'd used himself in another life.

Be patient. Look at the wall. Don't allow the itch to set in.

After several minutes, where the only sound was the scratching of pen on paper, the Factor raised his head. His voice was tinged with annoyance. 'Ah. You.'

Cale didn't speak, drawing out the game.

In the light of day, the Factor looked even younger. His uniform seemed oversized, as if he'd had to borrow it. 'What can I do for you, citizen?' he snapped.

Cale placed his papers on the desk. 'You wanted to review these. So, I've brought them.'

The Factor pulled the papers over but left them in their wallet. 'What's your business in Endeldam?'

'I'm passing through.'

'Most come here for three things: drinking, fishing and fighting. You don't seem like you want any of those, so what is it really?'

Cale kept his tone neutral. 'It's as I said.'

The Factor tutted, exasperated. 'This isn't a port. This is a shithole broken fishing town. How are you planning to get anywhere? No vessels here are sanctioned to go beyond the bay, by my order.'

'Perhaps I'll go by land.'

The Factor gave him a long look. 'We'll see about that.'

Cale cleared his throat and summoned all the humility he could muster. 'I have something important I have to do and I have to leave tonight. I am asking you, with all respect, to allow me to pass through your district. Sir.'

The Factor sat back, steepling his fingers under his small chin. 'I'm sorry, citizen, but that won't be possible.'

'Factor, you must understand—'

'No, *you* must understand. This is my district and I say who comes and goes. I like order. Now some fat old man turns up and says he's lived unmonitored for years and I want to know how this happened. It is unacceptable—'

'Your predecessor, perhaps—'

'Don't interrupt me! I won't have it.' His face flushed, red splotches spreading out from his nose like wings. There was a moment when Cale thought he would go on shouting, but he took a breath and gave him a thin smile.

'There is nothing about you on file,' he continued. 'I checked already. You are a surprise to me, and I'm not accustomed to surprises. They reek of inattention. So, here's what's going to happen, *citizen*.' He slid the papers back over the desk but kept his slender hand on top. 'I want to know everything there is to know about you, like I know everyone else in this place. This may be a lowly posting but I will not allow that fact to erode standards, as my predecessor did.

57

You and I are going to have a chat.' His eyes flashed in the pale light from the windows. 'I'm afraid that will take quite some time. Whatever you had planned will have to wait.'

Cale looked down at that smile. He thought of Bowden lying in a bed, in pain. The Factor's hand was pale, almost blue at the knuckles, the skin soft and unmarked by hardship.

Somewhere else, Bowden bled.

His heart beat in his chest, blood charging his ears, pounding. He knew what was coming; this time he made no effort to stop it.

The Factor was halfway over his desk before he knew what was happening, Cale's grip fast on his wrist. The official gave a startled yelp, immediately silenced as Cale took him by the throat and slammed him against the heavy wooden foot of the bureau, pinning him. The blotched face twisted, eyes bulging with terror. He struggled to shout for help but Cale pressed harder against his windpipe so only a gurgle came out. He leaned in close, so their noses were almost touching.

'Listen to me. I am not here for trouble. You will let me pass on.' The Factor's face was going a shade of purple, so Cale slackened his grip just a fraction, allowing him to suck in a breath.

'You'll die for this,' he rasped, fear vying with murderous rage. 'I'll see you burn.'

Cale placed his other hand on the Factor's cheek, cupping it like a lover. He settled his finger in the small hollow behind the ear. 'No,' he said in a grating whisper. 'You won't.' With a sharp motion he jammed his finger upwards between ear and skull.

The Factor's mouth flapped and his eyes rolled back. He

whimpered, his feet scrabbling on the floor as he tried to push himself away from the source of the pain, but he was held fast.

Cale kept his finger on the pressure point for a few seconds then pulled away. The Factor gasped, and this time the fear was naked on his face.

'I used to be good at hurting people,' said Cale. 'So you are going to listen. I'm leaving and you're going to let me. I'll make no more trouble for you and leave town tonight. You can pretend I was never here. Understand?'

The Factor's eyes were red. Cale could see he was a stranger to pain or threat. Just a little boy in a cheap uniform.

'Yes,' he said. 'Please, stop.'

Cale continued. 'I was never here, so no one else saw me. If I find out anyone had trouble from you on my account, I'll come back in here.' He applied a tiny amount of pressure with his finger and felt the Factor squirm.

'I won't!'

'No questions?'

'No questions!'

Cale waited, just a breath, then released his grip. The Factor curled into a ball on the floor, sucking in gasping breaths. He looked more like a child than ever, and for an instant Cale felt a pang of remorse. Before it could take hold he turned and left, closing the door behind him with a soft click.

As he made his way back down the hill to Aulk's house, the impact of what he'd done hit him. He'd felt a spectre of old pride surface in that office, satisfaction at watching the jumped-up little man squirm. It was the kind of conceit that had brought him here, to this isolation, and now even the scent of it sickened him.

59

This is taking care of it? Old fool. You think he'll keep quiet when you've gone?

There was a good chance the young Factor would retaliate out of pride, no matter how scared he'd been. Aulk and his family might still suffer because of him.

He should stay, straighten things out. Aulk had opened his home to him, helped him.

But Bowden was over the sea, dying.

Bask 28 – 498

The seals on the laboratory failed yesterday, meaning we had to evacuate to the canteen section of the habitat until they were repaired. The damned things weren't properly fitted and the outer layer was letting in enough wind to cause contraction on the inner, or that's what they tell me. I told them to conduct repairs as fast as possible but I know they took their sweet time getting about it. Maddening, that crew of muck-rakers. 'We're excavators, not maintenance!' they bleat, as if there's some sort of idiot hierarchy I should be referring to.

This – that is, the Alaimansk research outpost, named after the place closest to it on the map – is a deadened wasteland perched on the Makuo glacier. It is a nowhere place. I look out of any window, and all I see is vast, unending white without so much as a boulder to break it. I know there are mountains to the south-west, but on even the mildest days the wind kicks up the powder and renders the sky a few hundred feet away as monotone as the ground. The Bask does not touch this part of the world. In my first few days here, before the tedium set in, I found the sparseness refreshing. A kind of savage beauty, wind-scoured and ever-changing. It was like the world was a fresh, untouched whiteboard, uncluttered with words or numbers – a quintessence of potential. You see how it was? How close I came to turning sentimental?

Never fear, though. Weeks of the stuff sapped me until I saw the landscape for what it is: barren and lifeless. It gnaws at the soul, this lack of colour.

ADDENDUM

We processed the results of the mag-return this evening, and I can't help but be carried by my enthusiasm. There really is a large foreign body of some sort there. I will rerun the scan just to make sure my two imbeciles didn't screw it up somehow, but I dare to hope. Hope that there is something worth the effort under all that ice, hope that we didn't come all the way out here for nothing.

The scan that has me so unusually keen shows a void some 20 metres beneath the rock surface which is itself 1,200 metres (give or take a metre) under ice. It is dome-like in shape, 10 metres in diameter and 4 metres high at the apex. There are indications of low-density occlusions beneath a dense outer shell, most likely ice and sediment, so the void may be much larger when cleared.

It could be nothing more than a volcanic intrusion or some unusual product of glaciation. Even if it is pre-Ruin, it may be nothing more than a ball of garbage, a waste-dump. But something about the regularity of the void's inner curve – it is almost too precise.

It's late, and I have a cold bed to go to. Tunnelling starts tomorrow, and I need to be fresh.

•

Bask 45 – 498

I have spent the last two hours arguing with those fools. Shivering in that tiny site office, breathing in their body odour and the rank steam issuing from their mouths.

They likely talk down to me because I am a woman. They have the nerve to tell me they are overstretched, as if how they manage their shift patterns is any of my concern. I maintained my position – the current schedule is quite achievable, in fact desirable. I'd rather have it done before Death arrives. But they puff their cheeks, complain about *contracts* and *adverse conditions*. Will no one save me from this tedium!

After an hour of watching the four of them carry on like this, I'd had enough. I threatened them, in matter of fact, with replacement and blacklisting and they knew I meant it. I made it clear I'd bear the delay of acquiring new staff if pushed (though it would present me with even more damned paperwork).

It was worth it, to see their asinine faces drop like they'd been kicked in the nethers. They backed down after that. This might be the back end of a frozen nowhere but the pay is good – far too good for the likes of them, in my opinion.

Imagine: being able to get on with the work I already have without being dragged into trivialities. And to have people who respect the framework of responsibility! Workers work, why should it be any other way? How would they like it if I barged in on them with questions about this or that pre-Ruin artefact? They have already cut down through almost a kilometre of ice – all I need is for them to finish what they agreed to do in the first place.

Where the hell is my new assistant?

Sleep 15 – 498

Finally, I can begin in earnest. The void has been breached.
I have been going to bed later and rising earlier just to fit as
much in as possible, and it is still not enough.

The problem, the diggers told me (they are suitably
deferential now), was the shell. Delving through the ice was,
if energy-hungry, little more than rapid, precise melting. The
drills had chewed into the bedrock with barely a pause, but
then they'd hit the intrusion itself and had blunted in just
seconds, though the diggers assured me they were of the
best tungsten carbide. We barely scratched the surface.

We had to sit on our hands for weeks while we waited
for corundum bits to arrive, but those made no impression
either. The noise from the shaft was appalling, like the
scream of a wounded animal. There was an explosion. One
of the diggers was killed.

After some wrangling, I sourced an old plasma lance
from a contact in Keln; where it came from, who knows?
Stolen from the military or most likely shipped from
Aspedair. The cost was horrific, but it was the right choice.
After a few hours we broke through to the chamber inside.
I went down immediately, before the smoke had cleared,
despite the fretting and fussing of my researchers (they've
had some sort of lover's quarrel and have become sullen,
trying to outdo each other in fawning on me and firing
waspish barbs at each other). I ignored them; I wouldn't
wait a second more to see this thing.

The void is, as I surmised, not a natural formation. The dome appears perfect; some manner of super-hard, non-conductive alloy. The floor is packed dirt and ice, built up over centuries. I estimated on the fly that if the chamber were in fact a sphere, I would be standing around three-quarters of the way up on a plug of dirty ice.

I must be cautious because my mind wants to run away with me. It still stings, the mockery the Elucidon poured on me when I delivered my paper on Master Computers. The evidence was all there, built up over many years of painstaking work; hard digs and long dark hours poring over barely legible glyphs on ancient storage devices. The pre-Ruin was a *connected* world in a way that we can barely fathom; everything from homes to vehicles to factories, to the very Lattice itself – it all communicated. There are dark gaps in all of it – something else that only reveals its shape by its effect on the rest of the system. I gave them the name Master Computers not because I believed them to be anything so unsophisticated, but because it was the only way to explain to the rest of those dullards what these things might be. Something had to *run* the system!

My younger self was more prone to injury. No evidence, they said, no proof. Even as their flat dismissal of a mountain of corroborating sources stabbed at me I could see the cowardice behind their eyes – the mere suggestion that the pre-Ruin was anything other than an anarchy making them sweat – and this coming from an upstart woman! As it often does, fear of the unknown rests easily on the couch of ridicule.

The diggers are melting the stuff away as I write – we will begin mapping and sampling. I try to keep my hands from shaking, to tell myself to be measured, but this thing is so large and so artificial, so unlike anything we've found before. *What if*, says the little voice. *What if this is* it?

I must confess, I have not felt this excited in years.

Alec IV

The pitch of the ship had Cale lunging for the side again. With nothing left to come up he dry-heaved over the rail, his jaw locked wide. The wake was a white trough carving through the waves and in the low grey sky some aryx coasted on the breeze with occasional, languid flaps of their scooped wings as they tracked the giant cargo ship. Their screeches mocked him as he felt another lurch in his gut. Though the cargo of frozen naru carcasses was packed in ice far below everywhere reeked of dead fish. It was as if the sweet-sick stench, the birds and the listing of the deck conspired to torture him.

He'd always hated the sea.

Cale's lips were cracked and dry, but out of habit he wiped the back of his hand across them. His tongue felt like sand, though as bad as he felt he had to admit that, after three days at sea, it was getting better. An open deck was better than his coffin of a cabin and if he stood with his face full to the wind the smell almost went away; this morning he'd nearly made an entire lap of the deck without vomiting. Small victories. Out beyond the rail the sea stretched unbroken.

It had been three nights since Aulk had taken him out in the dead of night, his puttering launch holding station beyond the headland, waiting for the cargo ship to pass. They'd matched speed with the hulk and he'd clasped the old fisherman's hand in brief thanks before clambering up the side on a thin rope ladder. At the top, he was pulled over the gunwale without ceremony; he didn't see the launch drift away behind them, though even now, he could imagine the weathered face with its worried old eyes as it watched the big ship disappear into the night.

I'm sorry, he thought, wishing he could send the words back to Endeldam on the wind. *I brought you only trouble.*

The aryx were calling to each other overhead as he caught the sound of a snigger down the deck. The crew were enjoying his discomfort. Especially the big one, the hulking bosun who ran the crew hard, his heavy hands and ready snarl keeping order. Cale hadn't seen the captain since the market and it was clear that true authority rested on the senior crewman's wide shoulders. He could be heard now, at the other end of the deck, his deep voice booming at some unfortunate hand.

The crew were terrified of the bosun – it was written on every word and gesture. He was the biggest man on the ship, even taller than Cale, with a wide-legged swagger and knuckles that were as calloused and flat as any prize fighter's. Small eyes under heavy brows swept the air as if offended by everything. The first time they'd crossed paths there had been naked challenge on the man's face – a dominant larg guarding his patch. Cale had averted his eyes but knew it hadn't been enough. As an unknown quantity, he was a threat until proven otherwise. The crew felt the tension and avoided him, though some made fun of his landsman's stomach, loudly, probably hoping the bosun would notice.

He heard someone approach from behind and stand next to him at the rail. The red-haired boy, who'd dropped the naru carcass back at the fish market, flashed a nervous smile and offered a battered metal mug.

'Here,' he said. 'Drink this.'

Cale took it and eyed the contents. Grog, still steaming from the galley kettle, a dark and pungent mixture. He took a sip and coughed as the fumes jumped up his nose. 'Will this help?'

'Not really, not with the throwing up.' The boy's face was very pale, wind-bitten cheeks almost as red as his bright mop of hair. Like the other hands he wore a yellow jacket against the spray. 'Only time at the rail gets rid of that.' The smile was earnest, at the fringes of desperation.

'Encouraging,' said Cale, taking another sip.

'I'm Derrin, but everyone calls me New Boy.'

'New Boy?'

He nodded. 'Even after a whole year. Not a lot of imagination, this bunch.' He glanced around in case anyone had heard. 'Don't tell them I said that.'

'They don't seem to want to talk.'

'The bosun doesn't like you. He doesn't like anyone, especially new people. They're just trying to get on his good side. Or stay off his bad one.'

'Suits me.' Cale watched the aryx swoop overhead. The boy was waiting for him to go on. 'I'm Cale,' he said.

'It was me that pulled you aboard the other night.' Derrin drank, grimacing. 'Odd for us to take passengers.'

'Odd for me to be one.'

They watched the waves for a while. A large one formed a little way off, racing over the top of its fellows, cutting a line against the pattern until it beat itself to nothingness against the iron of the hull, throwing spume back across the surface and spray high into the air.

'Look at the horizon,' said Derrin, pointing with his free hand.

'What?'

'Keep looking at the horizon when you feel the retch coming on. It helps.'

Cale did so, trying to find the hazed line between sky and sea. After a few minutes, he did start to feel a little better. 'Thanks for that. And the drink.'

Derrin looked delighted. 'No problem. A week, and you won't have to think about it.' He tilted his head to indicate some nearby crewmen, hauling crates. 'I'll bet they all had it the same. I did. Only the bosun was born with sea legs.' Worry darkened his face. 'Doesn't even go on land when we're in port. Makes us bring his fun aboard for him.' He looked down at his feet. 'I keep out of his way. You should too.'

'I was planning to.'

A deep bass shout carried over the deck. 'New Boy, you puke! Get on with it, or you're going over that rail!'

Derrin shot up straight, fumbling his mug. It fell, spilling

70

its contents as it bounced from the rail before tumbling into the foaming wake. He called out a stuttered apology and gave Cale a rueful look before shuffling off down the deck, shoulders hunched, head lowered. He took a mop from a bucket and set about cleaning the deck.

Cale saw the bosun was staring from the other side of the deck. He held the gaze, taking another sip of grog. He raised his cup. The bosun kept staring. The moment stretched and Cale felt his hackles rise. The bosun turned his head so one eye was pointing at him, then slowly tapped his skull with a thick finger. *I'm watching you*, it said. He bared his teeth, then turned and went below. Cale watched him go, his jaw aching.

The days on the *Alec* went by without much to tell them apart. The cabin Cale shared with a sullen crewman was tiny and stank of unwashed bodies. His bunkmate had had the place to himself until now and resented the invasion; the first two days of Cale vomiting into a bucket had done nothing to build bridges. Since then an unspoken agreement grew, where both men would avoid each other if at all possible. After finding his way to the main deck, Cale spent most of his time there anyway.

At first, he took his meals in the galley. The food was ship's biscuit and fish most days. The water had the mineral-metallic hint of the recycler about it and the cook kept a kettle of grog on the burners for the crew. Cale suspected he would be turned away if he asked for some of the dark brew so he stuck with water, using the cup Derrin had given him.

One day, as he was leaving the galley, the bosun stopped

in the hatchway, blocking it. The big sailor glowered at him, daring him to make a move. Cale held the gaze for a heartbeat before moving aside. The bosun snorted and swaggered past, tailed by two sniggering cronies. After that, Cale ate in his cabin.

He made daily laps around the deck, ignoring the sideways glances and mutters of the crew. Even those who weren't outright joining in with the bosun's game knew better than to acknowledge him. He saw Derrin sometimes but avoided him if he could, not wanting to cause the boy trouble – more than that, he didn't feel like answering questions about himself.

The hardy aryx still followed the ship. Cale wondered if they slept on the wing. Watching the sea and the clouds in silence calmed him and he welcomed the monotony. Derrin had been right: keeping his eyes on the distance helped, though he didn't think the discomfort would ever completely fade. The problem was that when the sickness went away the fear came back, a smouldering ball of worry in his gut. If he concentrated hard he could go without seeing the images in his head for whole minutes but he wished there was some way to make the big ship go faster.

One day, on one of his walks, he passed by a tarp that had slipped, revealing a mouldering pile of wood. A small chunk caught his eye – something in the grimy, rain-soaked grain grabbed at him, though he didn't quite know what. He snatched at it before anyone could see and carried it to the bows, running the pad of his thumb along the ridges of the wood. The next day, with the old folding knife from his kitbag, he stood at the rail where he'd shared grog with Derrin and whittled shavings into the sea, working towards the hazy shape from his memory. The next day, he did the same. Bark gave way to wet fibre gave way to dry heartwood and the work got easier. He was just an observer as his hands worked, following their own plan.

On the fourth day, he saw what it was he was making. A wooden doll with a bulbous head and narrow shoulders. A toy soldier with a rifle over one shoulder, the bend of the wood suggesting a raised knee, as if marching. Bowden had owned a toy like this. It had been his favourite. Cale's hands had remembered what memory had thrown away.

Even then, when his knees knocked together, he wanted to be a soldier. And look where it got him.

He felt a surge of nausea. He went to the rail to throw the unwelcome reminder into the sea, but at the last instant held back. Perhaps it was the hours his hands had put in to shaping it. Or perhaps it was the memory of the look on Bowden's face as he'd played General in a sun-dappled garden, manoeuvring his pieces in an endless stratagem only he understood against an enemy of leaves and stones.

Later, he placed the toy on the small shelf by his bunk and let it watch over him as he slept.

Three weeks out from Endeldam the sky darkened as a big storm cut across their course and the hatches were sealed. Trapped below decks, his days felt like an eternity. The tiny portholes showed either black or iron grey, the only sign that time was still passing outside. The whole ship rang like a bell when a big wave hit and at times he could feel the rhythm of hail and rain as it hammered on the deck plates far above his head.

The cabin began to press in. Sleep wouldn't come, only a

kind of half-doze that left him feeling gritty and irritable. He dreamed sometimes, always the same thing, ugly and hazy. The clanging of the hull became a pounding of artillery; the patter of rain, bursts of small-arms fire. Hospital monitors beeped and clicked and Bowden's face stared up at him with eyes that bled dark, rich cherry. He'd wake with a scream trapped in his throat and bang his head on the bunk above, drawing muffled complaints from his bunkmate.

To make matters worse, the queasiness came back. The ship was so large that when it moved it was as if the world itself was lurching, a titanic shifting of mass that turned his stomach. It was worse lying down, so he set out to explore the ship's maze of deserted rooms and corridors. He barely saw anyone, the crew doubtless on watch or drunk in their bunks. After only a short while wandering he could have convinced himself that he was alone on a ghost hulk, adrift.

The *Alec IV* was old and very big. Six hundred metres of dead steel and rusting iron, the rails of her main deck stood a full hundred above the waves on a calm day. Everywhere he went there was the same smell of aged metal and lingering sweat, engine grease and fish. The hab section made up a quarter of the ship's length by the stern, topped by a conning tower that contained the bridge. As he explored, he passed cabin after cabin clogged with debris, some carpeted with a thick oil and fungus ooze that shimmered in the weak light from the corridor. Other doors were sealed – by age or by design, he couldn't tell. Entropy had pushed the crew to huddle on just two decks, leaving the rest to decay.

The captain lived alone atop the conning tower. The

man reeked of drink but, unlike the rest of the crew, seemed oblivious to Cale's outsider status, even inviting him into the wheelhouse. As he was shown around, Cale saw the man was isolated out here at sea, a nominal leader only. He feigned interest as the captain showed him his most prized possession, the navigational computer.

'Links to the beacons,' he slurred. 'Means I don't have to do a thing 'cept put my feet up.'

'But you can still steer the boat?' asked Cale.

'Ship!'

Cale raised a hand in apology. 'Ship. You still steer the ship?'

'Nope,' replied the captain, patting the box's grey casing. 'This baby takes care of it. I just punch the numbers in and let 'er go.'

Cale became absorbed in a large chart on the wall where their course had been scrawled in red pencil – the marks were old, faded. He traced the outline of the Medels Peninsula with his finger, wondering if this was the only course the *Alec IV* ever sailed any more. He turned to ask but the captain was asleep in his chair, slack mouth hanging open. Cale left quietly.

Forward of the hab section was the cavernous emptiness of the holds. Only one was in use, barely a quarter full of cargo while the others sat empty and echoing. Cale had seen ships like this long ago, remembered seeing cargo crates lashed to the decks and the vessels riding low in the water. This floating hulk could have carried an army; now it had to make do with several hundred tons of ice-packed fish.

•

On the third day of the storm Cale was passing the time by mentally mapping the maze of alleys and dead ends formed by the big cargo containers in the hold. It was then that he heard voices.

'Keep your voice down, cunny. I told you already…' said one.

'You leave me alone!' replied another.

Cale paused, alert. His breathing slowed. The second voice was muffled but the first was a deep bass note he recognised. Tension crept up his neck.

Moving on the balls of his feet he crept along the side of the container, stepping between piles of rubbish. He reached a large clear space that seemed to be a kind of loading area and spotted two figures at the far end. The bigger of the two held the other against the bulkhead. Cale saw a flash of red hair, then heard again the bosun's harsh rumble.

'I seen you lookin' at me, boy,' he said. 'Pipe down now.'

Derrin's reply was muffled by the meaty palm.

Walk back to your cabin, Cale told himself. *Leave it be. This is not your affair; you have your own problems already.*

Bowden wasn't much older when he left home.

Before he knew it, he'd rounded the corner and was darting across the gap.

Derrin's eyes widened and the bosun began to turn, but Cale was already on him. He clapped a hand over the big man's mouth, jamming the edge of his fingers up under his nose and yanking his head backwards as he punched hard into the lower spine. The bosun grunted in surprise and pain and tumbled backwards. Cale let him fall, then turned the pull into a shove and slammed him onto the deck – the bosun's skull hit the metal plate with a hollow clang. Before the sailor could rise he hammered home two heavy punches; the nose flattened to the side with a wet crunch and began to stream blood.

The bosun's eyes rolled back into his skull.

Cale checked for a pulse, found it flickering. He rolled the bosun onto his side and propped him up. Derrin was watching with wide eyes.

'Don't want him to choke on his own blood,' said Cale, just to fill the silence. Derrin stammered something, but he shook his head. 'Just breathe. You'll feel better in a moment.' He spotted a yellow windcheater on the ground and picked it up, handing it to Derrin. 'Here.'

Derrin pulled the coat around his shoulders with shaking hands.

'Has he done this before?' Cale asked.

Derrin shook his head. 'He looked at me sometimes; I just thought he didn't like me.'

'What were you doing down here?'

'He sent me. Said I was to check the freshwater tanks for leaks. Must have followed.' He closed his eyes and shook his head. 'I heard about him, what he likes. I thought they were only stories.' His eyes swam. 'Thank you.'

'You might not thank me later.'

'As soon as we make port, I'm gone.'

Cale nodded, and held out a hand, indicating they should leave. They left the bosun on the floor of the hold, breath wheezing through twisted nostrils.

•

77

For all its size, the *Alec IV* was not a place a person could hide for long. The day after the event in the hold the storm passed and the hatches were reopened. Cale went back to his walks, and it was there that the bosun found him.

The sailor's huge hands clenched and unclenched with fury, like he was rending two necks at once as he spoke through gritted teeth.

'You mark me, fucker. I didn't see your face but I know it were you. I'll take a dear price for this.'

Cale kept a neutral expression. 'Sorry about your nose. Did you fall?'

The bosun's face reddened. 'I'll break your spine, maggot!'

Cale leaned in close. 'In a few days I'll be off this tub.' He pointed at the broken nose and black swollen eyes. 'No one needs to know I did that to you.'

'You'll be dead before we ever make port,' hissed the bosun.

'No.' He felt some of the old steel creep back. 'You come at me again and I'll do worse. I'll do it in public. Think they'll look up to you again after that?' He made a show of looking around the deck. A number of nearby hands were pretending to be busy.

The bloodshot eyes bulged and the bruised face went crimson. For a moment it seemed the bosun might take a swing.

'Landy *cunt*,' he growled in Cale's face, then turned and stalked away. A few moments later, he heard him screaming at someone at the other end of the deck.

He leaned on the rail, letting the tension seep out of him.

The sky was still overcast in the wake of the storm and there was a fine rain pattering down, but anything was better than the metal coffin below. The aryx reappeared, screeching and diving. Even they were a welcome return.

He'd got to the bosun, made the man realise he was outmatched, but that only made him more dangerous. The stories behind those bruises would already have spread and a man who ruled through fear couldn't allow that. When the reprisal came it would come hard, somewhere quiet, and unless he kept his eyes open it would likely be final. He'd seen the animal behind those bloodshot eyes.

He ate in the galley that evening, ignoring the stares. The sailors gave him the usual wide berth, but the sniggering had been replaced by a nervous hush. When he asked for grog, the cook gave it to him without a word. Derrin came to sit with him but he stopped him with a shake of his head. It would be safer for him to stay away, so Cale spooned more fish into his mouth and ignored the hurt look on the boy's face.

That night, when he left his cabin to visit the head he heard the scrape of a boot behind him on the metal gangway and knew the time had come.

The knife was old and rusted, a heavy cleaver that whistled as it sliced through the air where his neck had just been. Cale recovered from the roll and spun to face the attacker. The bosun was shirtless and filled the corridor, lips drawn back over his teeth. He surged forwards, swinging the knife in a murderous slash; Cale stepped in and jammed the arm before the blade could reach him, trapping it against the sweaty chest, then butted him square in the face; the bosun bayed as his nose snapped again.

Cale hooked the free arm and flipped the bosun over his hip and down hard onto the deck, then, before he could recover, twisted the knife hand round until he heard bones snap.

The bosun screamed and the knife fell from nerveless fingers, clanging on the deck. Cale kicked it away.

There was pain, sudden and blinding, erupting white behind his eyes. He was face-down on the floor.

'He broke my stinking hand!' he heard the bosun roar, then heard the scrape of another set of boots. Someone kicked him hard and he felt something break. He curled into a ball to try to protect himself, but the kicks kept coming.

'Good lads,' he heard the bosun say. 'Knew I could rely on my mates. Now kick the fucker to death while I get me breath back.'

Cale braced himself but knew it was pointless. He'd underestimated the depth of fear running through the crew. He'd seen it before, the kind of sustained terror that slowly warps into something like loyalty. He'd not prepared for it and now he was going to die.

Bowden's face filled his mind and he breathed a silent apology.

'Stop it, you're killing him!' shouted a voice.

Then the world pitched on its end. There was a loud bang and a shriek of iron, then everything was full of salt and water.

ii. Quincentennial

'Build walls of the soul and strengthen the Walls of Nation. Only from within can we find the strength to conquer what is without.'

The Seeker's wisdom was inescapable during the Quincentennial, especially on the day of the joint military parade. Passages from *Path to Internal Victory* resonated from every speaker post, louder and more piercing than the usual background drone. From the rooftops, sending walls of sound reverberating, building to building, all along the canyon of the avenue, huge speakers boomed.

'Where once there was waste, there shall be Freedom. Where once there was vanity, there shall be Unity.'

The voice reading the ancient maxims was shrill with passion. Kelbee knew the words off by heart, had done ever since her village's narrow-eyed schoolmistress had put them there with a switch of her cane, and could never be allowed to forget them: to live in Karume was to negotiate a daily wash of tinny reminders that piped from buzzing speaker posts lining every street. Her lips moved in time with the words without her realising.

Gravity ringing from every syllable, the woman on the recording read, pumping every ounce of verve into her words. As the winner of a capital-wide ballot she'd been coached for the occasion by State dramatists; posters announcing it had been put up in every workplace and communal area. But despite her strident efforts, the acoustics of the towering walls of the avenue made a mockery of her, jumbling phrases into one another, obscuring some while others rang out with a screeching intensity. It was enough to make you wince, though Kelbee was careful to disguise it under a sneeze. Looking around her, many others were doing the same.

From her spot on the bleachers of the wives' enclosure, Kelbee could see around half a kilometre of the parade route. Crowds lined the avenue, some in enclosures like this one, others milling behind ropes. Many tower blocks had been draped with giant red-and-blue banners, unfurled from the rooftops and hanging all the way down to the road; some were emblazoned with the words *Balance, Loyalty, Victory*; on others, His face beamed, perfect teeth in a fixed smile as white as snow, eyes beatific with wisdom and love.

The mid-morning was bright and unseasonably hot. The trees were barely in bud, the skeletal branches caught off-guard by the sudden heatwave that had the women around her muttering and sweating in their heavy formal clothes. Some shielded their eyes with their hands, some wore dark glasses against the glare; Kelbee contented herself with squinting. Her eyes followed a banner from its tasselled tip up to the roof of the opposite building, coming to rest on a soldier who stood there, watching. She couldn't see his face, but his body was alert. One foot rested on the parapet, his hand gripping the strap of his rifle. There was a speaker not far from where he stood, a monstrous black-and-yellow stack. The noise up there would be deafening but he was still, shielded from the din by his helmet. The long barrel of his rifle was a razor-cut silhouette against the bright sky.

Crimson and sky-blue were everywhere, on every corner, flag pole, arm and throat. Yellow felsia petals had been strewn a fist deep along the avenue. Every speaker post was hung with a striped tabard: the blue of mourning, the red of victory. The crowds jostled for the best view and everyone was turned out in their finery.

Kelbee felt the weight of her sash on the back of her neck, the heavy two-tone silk rubbing uncomfortably. It was hung with rows of medals, a proud testament to the Major's career. All the wives wore them, some hung with only a couple of commendations, others sagging under the weight of metal, the blue and the red beneath barely visible; some of the frailest ones had brought a daughter or niece to bear the burden of glory for them. Kelbee rubbed her fingers together inside her sleeve – she'd been up before dawn, burnishing the medals to a mirror sheen and the smell of the polish still clung to her.

Every year the people of Karume gave thanks to the Father of the Nation on his birthday, but this was different: five hundred years of peace and joy inside and outside the Walls. Instead of a single day of celebration there would be a whole month. Alcohol rations had been increased, as had the number of police in the streets.

Attendance at today's parade was obligatory, of course. More than that: it was duty. It had never even occurred to Kelbee to do otherwise, though she'd been surprised to see police roaming the corridors of her apartment building that morning. Even if the parades were long, they were all anyone had discussed for weeks – surely everyone knew absences would be noted? And yet there they'd been, all in black caps, eyes intent, running their scanners over the walls and checking for absentees. One of them had glanced at her as she passed, and she'd felt her cheeks go warm – it earned her narrowed eyes but nothing more. It was only later that she realised what had made her react that way.

A gap in a chain-link fence. Dusty stairs. A warm place hidden away, where dangerous and beautiful things were born. She'd never had anything to hide before.

Kelbee mopped her brow and waited for the parade to start. The Major would be there, alongside his soldiers, and as his wife it was her duty to bear witness. In the close press of the enclosure she was five rows from the back. Up here her view was better than those at the front but carried less prestige: the higher the husband's rank, the further forward you went. Her calves were already aching, and it was still early, so she flexed them under her long dress, stretching up on to her tiptoes then back down again. To pass the time, she ran her eye over the other wives, starting at the back and working her way forwards.

Once, when she was very young, she'd come across a tree stump in a grassy field, its ringed surface polished smooth. She'd shown it to Mother, who'd told her the layers were built up over time, each ring the passing of an age.

84

They reminded her of that stump, these women, age and prominence accumulating as the years went by, every one of them leaving its mark.

Behind her were the junior officer's wives, little more than girls, looking new and afraid. Then came her peer group: slightly older, quiet and watchful, some with gazes downcast, others throwing quick glances around as though checking the world for sharp things. A few rows on, the women became notably older. One row from the front were bowed, frail-looking creatures, hiding their years with bangles and piled-up wigs, their withered faces in stark contrast with the freshness of the girls they'd brought to carry their sashes.

By contrast, the entire front rank was full of perfect young women. Fresh-faced, with exquisite features and dressed in garments worth a year's cloth ration. Younger even than Kelbee had been when she'd first come to Karume, each one a true marvel of wide eyes and glossy hair.

What a miraculous regeneration, she thought, *a promotion can have on a man's wife.*

Where did they go, those women who'd shared their whole lives with great men, when newer flowers came along to replace them?

And will I go there too, when the time comes?

The thought came as a shock, as if another person had spoken inside her head. She lowered her gaze, hoping it hadn't shown on her face.

She made out snatches of conversation from a few rows in front. Oblivious to the silent ranks behind, the middle-aged wives seemed content to swap gossip; everyone wanted to know everyone's business.

Meli loves the new school...

...And Sardum is vice-captain of the Squares team...

Did you see what she was wearing? *I'm not surprised...*

Kelbee almost envied them their bubble, a little world they'd created amongst themselves. She didn't have much of a social circle, not yet. She watched them as they complimented, sniggered and pointed fingers. A casual observer might think they hadn't a care in the world, though she knew how to spot the signs: a worried frown when they thought no one was looking, a furtive glance towards the children's enclosure further down the route. Even buried under years of socialising and flattery, the fear remained.

There was a clarion of trumpets and the shrill voice on the speakers faded away. A roll of drums came rumbling down the avenue. Kelbee looked up and saw that the soldier on the rooftop had turned towards the new sound, his rifle ready at his shoulder. A hush fell over the crowd and the air grew thick; feet shuffled, the heavy emptiness of the masses holding their breath. In the distance, there was a retort of gunfire, three volleys in quick succession followed by the deep boom of an artillery piece. A voice drifted over the silent crowd, the clipped roar of an approaching drill sergeant. The drums grew louder and were joined by another sound; rhythmical, sharp, the tramp of thousands of feet approaching in perfect step. The stands began to vibrate.

Kelbee felt a sickening lurch in her stomach.

The cheering started in patches and grew to an all-enveloping roar as the head of the parade came into view. Marines in crisp white uniforms, each in perfect time, rifles held slanted over shoulders, peaked caps pulled down low over their eyes. The other wives were cheering and Kelbee joined in, though she felt like a bird was trying to escape from her chest. They filed past, the red and blue of their armbands stark against the glaring white of their dress jackets. Every dozen or so ranks came bannermen holding gilded regimental crests high above their heads. They all looked so similar, right down to their severely cut hair; all the same height, stern eyes fixed on the man in front. Something about the precise, pendulum-like swinging of those hundreds of arms moving up and down in time made her feel even more nauseated. She swallowed hard.

Following the last row of Marines was a slow-moving skimmer-car carrying a colonel in an elaborate white-and-gold uniform. He held himself steady on a raised handrail and every so often the other arm would flash up in a salute to the crowd, though Kelbee wondered if it was to stop his large round hat from blowing off. As he came closer, she saw that his eyes were bored. Seated around him were his staff members, captains and majors with stern expressions. She wondered how it felt to be there, riding through all that noise. Not one of them looked like they were enjoying a single minute.

Kelbee rubbed at her aching eyes, hoping it would appear as if she were overcome by emotion and not simply tired and irritable. Her vision fogged for a moment, and when it returned it was to a pair of huge, dark eyes staring at her, great black pools of depthless nothing. She tensed, her breath stolen. It took her a heartbeat to realise it was only the screen mounted on the other side of the street. It had been nothing but a dulled mirror but was now filled with a close-up shot of the Venerated Guide herself; as the view pulled out it showed the tall, elegant, bald woman standing in an ornate box, surrounded by generals. She raised a gloved hand in casual salute and the soldiers marching past responded, hands flashing up in salute, never missing a step. The Guide's face was impassive, her mouth a thin, pale line. The stillness in her shoulders, her height, commanded those around her into subservience – the Seeker's chosen representative, commander of His armies and holder of His sacred trust. Kelbee wondered what it would be like to meet that adamant gaze in person and shuddered.

She took a breath. For a moment, she could have sworn those bottomless eyes had bored into her, seeing everything she had to hide.

Pull yourself together.

After the Marines came the infantry in night-black fatigues. Their timing was different, their feet moving two steps for every beat. They seemed to bob up and down on the spot, the tramp-tramp of their boots cracking on the road. Women cried out as they spotted husbands, brothers, uncles.

Kelbee's legs throbbed with fatigue; she wondered how long it would take for the mechanised divisions to make it this far, her husband with them. The sudden thought of him made her stomach lurch again, and the rolling stamp of boots on the avenue rumbled right through her, shaking her inside. The cheers of the crowd assaulted her; the heat was like a physical weight. She shut her eyes for a moment, feeling the vibrations through her eyelids, then forced herself to open them again. She knew she couldn't risk missing something important. She had a duty to observe.

And in the centre of this crush of bodies and noise and heat, she herself was being watched.

The infantry battalions tramped past, and in their wake came war-walkers, each one towering ten metres above the road. Their heavy gun-arms were hung with yellow garlands and the pilots' heads poked out of the open cockpits between the machines' hunched metal shoulders. Their legs were reversed like those of a larg and as each heavy foot fell the ground trembled. There were gasps amid the cheers and as the hulking machines came closer Kelbee caught the sharpness of burning fuel and the growling of engines. Pebbles popped under massive metal feet; each step brought a whine as servos fought to keep the lurching tons of metal upright. As they drew level with her, she felt a rise in her throat and that terrible, uncontrollable tightness in her jaw that told her she had only moments before it happened.

She pushed past her neighbours and bolted for the steps; just before she reached them an older woman with mousy hair took a step backwards into her path. Kelbee bounced off the woman's shoulder, her momentum carrying her on towards the metal stairs that led down the side of the bleachers. She heard the woman give a surprised gasp, but she was already headlong down the steps, her hand clamped over her mouth.

There was a guard on the gate, facing away. Before he could turn she'd ducked under the metal frame of the stand. Underneath, the light came through in dusty beams. The noise from outside was muted. Ordered, well-mannered rows of ankles and heels stared back at her and the air was musty. At the back was a corner with enough room to stand, but her legs gave out and she had to cling to a pole, the metal cold against her palm. There was a great roar from the crowd outside, and then she vomited.

There was mud on her skirts, a dark brown stain on the pale yellow. Her throat felt raw and her stomach felt like she'd been kicked. She stepped away from the foul puddle and sat on her haunches, gasping. Thank the Seeker she'd managed to keep her hair out of the way, and her sash. Through blocked, burning nostrils the stink of metal polish reached up and made her retch again. Outside the parade boomed and trumpeted but all she saw were snatched, washed-out splinters between the steps. She waited for a swell in the drumming and bugle calls to cover the sound of her clearing her nose.

Her dress was stained. Her hair was a mess. She thought of the looks of disapproval she'd get if she climbed the stands to take her place. To do so would be to bring shame on the man she was there to represent – better to risk her absence being noticed than to endure that.

Two hours under the stands felt like a lifetime, until the last troops filed past and the music began to die down. The ankles began to shuffle. Kelbee pushed through the covers at the back of her hiding place and into the open air, then rounded the corner and joined the throng leaving the enclosure, knowing that to pause for an instant would be noticed. A woman walking alongside brushed against her as they went through the gate; a throat cleared. She looked over and saw the mousy-haired woman she'd knocked into. Older, with eyes that looked tired but kind. Kelbee smiled at her, a mute apology.

The woman smiled back. She took her arm as if they were old friends out for a stroll. A little further on, still pressed by the crowd, she leaned in close and spoke.

'Always takes me by surprise too, the sickness.' She winked. 'Gets you at the worst possible time, doesn't it?'

Kelbee did her best to keep a straight face. 'I don't know what you mean.'

The older woman covered her smile with a theatrical hand. 'Oh my! My dear, you don't, do you? This must be your first then?'

Kelbee shook her head. 'No, I'm not... I just felt... that's not what it was.'

The woman patted her hand. 'You can't fool me. I'd know that look anywhere. What a wonderful thing to happen, and on such an auspicious day! He'll be delighted.' She gave Kelbee a conspiratorial look. 'They always are, you know. Strong men in their uniforms and medals, they go to mush when they hear they're about to be fathers.'

The Major came home in the late evening, well after Ras had passed behind the Tower and below the horizon. Kelbee heard his heels clicking off the polished stone of the corridor outside the apartment before he opened the door. She was ready to greet him as he came in, head bowed. He didn't acknowledge her as he walked past, tossing his hat off to one side. He walked straight to the living area and sank into his favourite easy chair with a sigh. Still without looking at her, he held out a leg for her to pull off a boot, then the other.

'Bring food. It's been a long day.'

'Your supper is ready, sir.'

He undid his high collar and let it droop open. It was his most formal dress uniform: a black jacket that hung past his waist and was gathered by a wide stable belt, the round embossed buckle polished to a high sheen. The puffed black trousers were split by a thin red line running down the side of each leg to the knee, where they met the top of the high boots. She'd bulled those boots for hours, applying the polish in layers and alternating between brush and cloth until she could see her own face staring back at her – now they were speckled with grime from the parade, grease and dirt dulling the leather. She realised that she'd not seen him pass by with his unit and her breath caught in her throat. What had he looked like? Had he been riding with the head of his regiment? What if he asked? She tried to compose her face, but he saw her hesitation.

'What is it?' He sounded more tired than irritated.

'Nothing, sir. I found some palma-bean at the market, the kind you like. And strip steak.'

'Bring me beer first.'

Kelbee went to the kitchen to get a bottle of the brown brew the Major liked. As she flicked open the cap, she caught a glimpse of the Tower outside the window. It sparkled against the darkness with the lights from a thousand windows.

Nebn was out there. Eating, drinking, sleeping. Perhaps with a wife of his own, perhaps alone in the secret place they went to be together. She knew so little about him, despite knowing so much.

'Sky, woman! Stop your daydreaming.' The edge had returned.

'Sorry, sir. Coming.' She returned to him and poured his beer into a tall glass. As the brew frothed up to the lip, the question finally came.

'How did you enjoy the parade?'

'It was magnificent.' The words fell from her like water. 'How inspiring, to see all the soldiers all lined up like that, going past.' She thanked the Seeker for not letting her voice tremble. 'I thought you were wonderful, sir. So handsome.'

He seemed content, even smiled a thin smile. He took the tall glass, draining most of it in one long pull. He nodded, eyes fixed on the tapestry that covered the far wall. 'A great day. Good to remind the people who looks after them.'

'We are very lucky, sir. I'm very lucky to have you. I mean… to be with you.'

'Mmm.' He took another sip of the beer, then leaned back, closing his eyes. He looked weary, the bones of his face sharp under his skin. After a moment of dead silence, his dark-ringed eyes opened again.

'I was promoted this morning,' he said. 'I am to be a lance colonel of the Intelligence Division.' His voice was flat.

'Wonderful news, sir, wonderful. You must feel so proud.'

'Yes. I suppose it's… still to sink in.'

'You've worked hard, sir. You deserve your reward.'

He drank his beer. 'You don't have any conception of hard work.'

The rim of the glass was half in his mouth. Kelbee wondered what it would feel like to hit the back of his head, saw a ghost of herself do it: one moment, just a little sharp push and there it would be. Maybe his lips would get caught

93

between teeth and glass? Would it shatter? Would he bleed?

He seemed irritated with himself, but still didn't look at her. 'That was unnecessary of me. It's been a long, tiring day. I'll eat now.'

The meal passed in silence. The darkly sauced steak was his favourite and hers. In the early days, when she still hoped affection might grow, this little bit of common ground seemed the key to more between them, a doorway to things other than brief comings and goings that bookended the day, brusque words and rough, dismissive sex. She'd hoped marinated pieces of meat might be the way in to a loving marriage, but he'd barely responded when she'd told him of her liking for it. She was so new to it all, still young, and had cried without knowing why. That was the very first time he slapped her.

When he was done she took the plates away while he finished another beer at the table. Something had changed in the air: she could feel his eyes on her as she cleaned the dishes in the sink. When she returned to gather the place mats, he took her by the sleeve. It was a firm grip, meant to hold her in place.

'This means you won't be able to work any more. You will have other duties.' He reached up and stroked a single finger along her hair, pensive.

'If it's what you want, sir, of course.'

'And, in time, we'll have better than this place.' His hand travelled down to the swell of her breast. She could feel the cold from the beer glass through the material of her dress. Could he feel her heart pounding like it might break free? She battled to keep herself still.

94

His fingers circled, cupped. Her stomach squeezed like a knot. 'A man of my rank should have a family.'

'I wish I could give you it, sir, more than anything.' The lie came easy. After all this time, was it not obvious there was no chance?

What if it's true? What if the old woman was right? Will he know? After so long trying, he'll guess it's not his. The thought made her stomach tighten, and her vision blurred at the edges.

The Major didn't notice her discomfort – she could smell the arousal on him.

'Here.' He nodded to the table.

'Sir?'

'I want you here.'

'I don't—'

'Now,' his voice was choked. He was on his feet and spun her to face the table before she could move. He crushed close, near enough to swamp her with hot breath.

'I… don't think we should… make a mess,' she said, every muscle in her body taut as wire.

In response he pushed her forwards over the table; her foot slipped and she banged down hard, her face barely missing his empty glass.

The Major didn't notice the slip, instead held her down by the neck. The wood was rough against her cheek as he scrabbled with his belt, then with her dress, pulling it up over her hips. Her eyes stung, her throat was dry, and she could see herself reflected in the surface of the toppled glass, eyes and mouth distorted. His breathing became louder and his buckle clanged as it hit the floor; then she felt him probing, seeking her out, felt him pressing up against her, a coarse, dry invader, then out of nowhere the words exploded from her.

'There's a child!'

He froze. He was so still she dared to hope that he'd died on the spot.

'What did you say?' he grunted, his voice still thick.

'I'm already pregnant.'

His breath rattled in his throat. Then she felt him pull away. The sound of his belt being buckled. She didn't dare turn around.

'Why didn't you... When did you...'

'I wanted to surprise you, after I'd been to the medicos. I felt the sickness this morning at the parade.'

He was silent. She stayed where she was, feeling the moment stretch thin between them.

Then, his hand on her shoulder, like a pat of encouragement for a favourite larg. No words followed.

Then it was gone, and he was gone, shuffling into the bedroom.

She waited until she heard the door close before she dared to stand. She straightened her clothes, wiping away the moisture that had run down her cheeks. Her breathing was as rough as his had been; she closed her eyes until she felt herself unwind like a coiled spring. She let the tears come.

She touched her belly, thanking the flicker of life inside her. Through her tears, she found herself smiling at the absurdity of it. Then her heart sank again.

What will he do if he finds out?

The Field

Green and yellow from trees in full Bask leaf – a light
breeze that brushes the branches and makes them whisper
to one another. Aquamarine sky, whitening at the edges of his
vision, the brightness contracting his pupils and causing him to
squint, washing out the world as though bleached.

Grass smelling of pepper and hay, long and uncut, with a
sweetness from wild flowers that speckle the open ground.

Iron and copper of the blood-stench from the body. The funk
of bowels loosened by a bullet.

Gun smoke, raw and piquant.

The corpse lies face down, legs outside the rim of the crater
with its trunk following the incline down into the hollow. An
old crater from another war, furred with short, scrubby grass,
perhaps two metres in diameter. Blood from the shattered skull
has pooled at the bottom, a berry-dark soup flecked with white
fragments of bone. The smoke from his sidearm has coiled away
to nothing, leaving just the ghost of its scent hanging between
him and the dead man. Soldiers – his men – shift behind him,

appalled yet glad that it is over. Their relief is a thing of mass in the air at his back. Relief that it had been him, their colonel – not them – to stamp finality on that twisted man with the sharp retort of hammer igniting powder. The tongue that had sent their friends to die, that had condemned them all too, was still.

He realises it had to have been him. The sorry story was of his own making.

The Commissar had been new to the regiment: one of a new wave of political officers brought in to ensure seeds of sedition did not take root. This one was ambitious, connected, an idealist – he claimed his authority from the Venerable Guide herself, bypassing the chain of command.

Lists of prohibited materials were circulated, weekly 'briefings' set up: mandatory two-hour reminders of the Hegemony's might and of the dangers of enemy propaganda. The disaffected and petty-minded that were the boils on any regiment were seduced by calls for 'right-thinking men to help promote purity'. Given new uniforms and badges, they strutted about settling minor slights and old disputes with the weight of their new authority.

At first, the headquarters staff ignored the Commissar and his growing band; just an upstart, a flash-in-the-pan inconvenience. If he became a real problem, he could be burned out easily enough.

While they turned a blind eye, he burrowed deep into the flesh of the regiment.

The first summary execution had been of a young private, barely out of his teens, seen by an informant reading a book that was on the list of banned texts. He protested his innocence; his sergeant stepped in, told the club-wielding mob the matter would be dealt with within the squad, as such things always were. It was the right thing to do.

Not so, replied the Commissar. An example would have to be made, to root out the lurking tendrils of ruinous corruption.

At sunrise of the following morning the boy was dragged from the stockade to the parade ground, his face black and yellow, broken jaw hanging slack. He was flogged bloody as they watched; the Commissar's eyes were bright, lips parted. Then, when the boy lay mewling on the ground, the hunched little man put a bullet through his head.

Complaints to the General's staff and the Ministry were rebuffed. The Commissar's was the discretion to mete out justice, his authority inviolable. They all felt it then: the slow creep of fear. They were in the hands of a madman.

Soon, bodies began to turn up every few days on the new gibbet at the parade ground. None saw them die: men would disappear from their barracks in the dead of night only to be found with the dawn, their corpses mangled, the life cut from them, some with ragged words burned into what skin remained.

Propagandist. Insurgent. Traitor.

The eyes of the soldiers turned to him, their colonel. Their gazes pleaded and accused all at once. How long can this carry on, sir?

The end came in a small village, a nowhere place swallowed by another shifting line on a map. The enemy had withdrawn behind their lines and left the hamlet undefended. The inhabitants had submitted peacefully – resigned gazes said that they'd known more than one invader. The mayor, a ruddy-faced farmer with *an old copper pocket-watch and a red waistcoat, said they only wanted to be left in peace. Surrender was accepted with minimal formality, a platoon left as a nominal picket.*

Later, when they were able to speak of what had happened, most men said the place reminded them of home. Local men sat outside the shop, indolently playing some tile game and smoking their fat black cheroots. Streets were worn but lovingly swept. Children played in the open grass field with old craters from another war.

'Burn it. Burn it to the ground', said the Commissar, newly arrived with his gang of lickspittles.

The picket had unconditionally refused, so the order had rung out to execute the 'malcontents' and 'mutineers'.

'Kill them, then burn the village', he said.

The men fought for their lives with rifle, bayonet, teeth and nails. An ugly skirmish that stretched into a running battle as the Commissar's enforcers realised their miscalculation: these were not lone men snatched in the night, but armed, angry soldiers in battle trim and with nothing to lose. The fight became a rout and the men could not be held back from their revenge for every scar, bruise, every toothless skull that had adorned that unholy gibbet. When the Colonel arrived and managed to establish some order only the Commissar was left alive, badly wounded but unbowed.

He screeched from frothing, blood-flecked lips. They would all pay. He tottered on unsteady legs as he described how their children would be transported to mines to live short, back-breaking lives in the darkness. Their wives would be given to the lowest, filthiest brothels to be used as playthings by criminals. Their names, their relatives' names, would be burned from the records. He turned his gaze, alight with madness, on the Colonel and screamed bile at him. This and more would be laid at his door, he howled. The pools of his house would run red.

A pistol shot, bell-clear in the crisp air.

Had he even fired the weapon before? The retort that echoed off the nearby houses for a lifetime still hums somewhere behind his eyes, perhaps there for ever. The body that thumped onto the ground hugs the little grassy crater with dread finality.

The men are silent for a long while. He stands steady, eyes locked on the corpse. The awful moment stretches into infinity. They see then that he, their Colonel, has taken their sins onto his own broad shoulders.

iii. Stakes

The Grand Arena was packed, the roof closed to keep out the heat of the day. Despite the cold air being pumped into their glassed-off box – high up on the third tier – a bead of sweat formed and began its slow journey down Kelbee's spine.

Her new formal dress was long and heavy and felt like a tent. The medal sash only made it worse. As was proper for her first outing as a senior officer's wife she'd caked her face with powders and oils – the stuff was thick as a mask and she felt like a doll. Even her hair was trapped in a pinned, conservative style.

The load of tradition had only become greater, in the amount of metal clinking on her sash as well as the attention. How she looked and behaved was under more scrutiny than ever before. As she shifted her shoulders to stop the heavy cloth from rubbing, she thought of those bent, hollow creatures from the women's enclosure at the parade and saw with perfect clarity how they'd been smothered and sucked dry by this life. And now it was hers.

The Major – no, Lance Colonel now! She had to get used to the change – sat by her side in a double-breasted tunic of the deepest black, a new rank bar gleaming on his shoulder. He chatted absently with their host, a colleague of his who'd invited them to share the box. It was mostly military matters and she maintained a polite look of attention while her mind wandered. Beyond the thick glass she could hear the muted hubbub of the crowd.

The arena, like everything else, was draped in the red and blue of the Quincentennial, now in full swing. High above the thousands, hanging from the centre of the closed roof, hung a giant mandala of yellow felsia blossoms. Every so often a stray eddy would catch the wheel, shaking a few blossoms loose; a slow-motion yellow rain that was gradually turning the grey floor the colour of butter. Some of the petals came to rest on the five prisoners kneeling in a line and the soldiers standing motionless behind them.

Her husband snorted at some quip and she dragged her eyes away from the condemned. He turned to her and rested his hand on her arm with a light touch. He was in a good mood today, better than she'd seen in a long time. Ever since that evening a week ago he'd acknowledged her more than ever before and his voice had lost most of its bark. His manner was still, on the whole, rigid, and his face still creased with occasional irritation, but it was as if more had become permissible, small faults turned forgivable. He made eye contact with her – which still unnerved her – and asked her about her day.

It was the child, and only the child, she had to remind

herself. After six years, she was finally giving him what he wanted. Perhaps this was a marriage after all.

Outwardly, she smiled, reassuring him that she was all right.

He gave a satisfied grunt and turned to the small screen mounted in front of them on the floor, angled up so as not to impede the actual view of the arena. It showed a close-up image of the prisoners, two older men and three young women around Kelbee's age. One of the men was particularly frail, his skin like parchment and blotched with discolorations. This one had been a general. Stripped of rank and decorations, he reminded her of her grandfather just before he'd died, as if time had drained him of bulk and vitality.

The prisoners' ill-fitting uniforms hung ragged. Their heads were bowed, their hands tied behind their backs. On the screen, Kelbee saw one of the women was crying.

'You were attached to that one's staff at one time, weren't you?' This from the colleague, also an officer in black. His wife, cocooned inside her heavy robes, kept her eyes forward and made no attempt to interact with anyone beyond a vacant, fixed smile. Her husband repeated his question, indicating the other male prisoner, this one wide-shouldered and with a week's stubble on his cheeks.

Kelbee felt the Lance Colonel hesitate. His reply was terse.

'Briefly, a long time ago,' he said. 'I never answered to him directly.'

The other officer changed the subject. 'That other one though, eh? Borunmer's uncle. Quite the thing. They say the bastard was set to be no more than a captain for life until she came to power. Wheedled his way up the ranks using her name.'

'That's what this is about, it's obvious,' replied the Lance Colonel, his irritation forgotten. 'It has to be public. She's cleaning house.' He picked up his iced drink and took a sip. 'So damned hot in here.'

'Turn the sound up,' said the other officer, gesturing at the screen. 'It's starting.'

A flick of the controls and the noise from the arena came rushing in. In the background, an announcement was playing over the loudspeakers; as the crowd became aware of it their shouts and cheers died away.

The message repeated: 'Attention. The Seeker's Venerated Guide, Fulvia arc Borunmer, will oversee the giving of justice.'

The message played twice more, echoing around the now hushed arena. Then the guards behind the prisoners snapped to attention and a lone figure came striding from the stands.

Kelbee recognised her at once – tall, straight-backed and filled with supreme confidence. Every sure step, every precise swing of her arms spoke of authority. She seemed utterly disinterested in the thousands of murmurs that followed her as if they were nothing more than the chatter of birds. Her head was shaved close to the scalp and her neck was long and elegant. She was dressed in a soldier's uniform, dark trousers and boots and a fitted tunic. At her waist was the sign of her office, a heavy golden chain.

The Guide reached the centre of the arena and lifted her chin to address the people. Kelbee repressed a shudder as she saw those eyes on the screen, the irises acid green and pupils that flashed crimson as they caught the light. She had the same feeling she'd had at the parade: that those deep wells that swallowed the light somehow *knew* the things about her she dared not say aloud. Cheekbones high and proud, the only signs of age were a few lines at the corners of her mouth. It was a terrifying kind of beauty, like a glint of Ras on an axe blade.

'The Seeker sees all. His wisdom guides us.' Picked up by microphones, her voice was as deep as a man's and boomed across the arena.

The crowd held its breath as the Guide continued. 'He has brought us His love and guidance for half a millennium. We thank Him from our hearts' hearts. We honour Him with humility and praise.' She turned to face the line of prisoners.

'She's going to do it herself. Stone cold,' said the other officer.

The Lance Colonel quieted him with a curt flick of his fingers.

The Guide motioned at the soldiers, who in perfect unison brought their rifles to bear, the snub barrels aimed at the backs of the prisoners' heads. On the screen, Kelbee saw the crying woman's shoulders trembling, tears streaming down her face. The others stared down with blank expressions.

Undeterred by the weapons pointing in her direction, the Guide approached the old man in the centre of the line. His face was peaceful, as if he was somewhere else entirely; he seemed more interested in the pattern of blossoms before him. At a gesture from the Guide, the soldier behind him withdrew.

The Guide paused, watching the old man watching the petals. She arched an eyebrow, then stamped down on them, grinding the blossoms under her boot. The old man closed his eyes. Kelbee thought he looked sad.

The Guide spoke, addressing the arena again. Her deep voice became chant-like. 'Celmis-rey, former General of the Righteous Army of the Seeker. You have been found guilty of treason against the People and the State. You and your co-conspirators have undertaken and perpetrated thrice-cursed acts of betrayal. You have spat upon the profound trust and warmest paternal love of the Seeker. You have desperately worked to subvert the harmony of our Hegemony, the Seeker's greatest gift to the world. You did this out of selfish lust for personal gain and power, using the most cunning and sinister of means.' She paused and looked down at her uncle. 'With His grace, I condemn you and your affiliates to death.'

The crowd erupted.

The Guide looked up at the throng and silenced them with a sweep of her arm. 'You are all witnesses to this justice. See it done in your name. May the Seeker's light be with you.' Then, in one smooth motion, she drew a pistol from her belt and shot the old man in the face.

The crack reverberated around the arena and the body flopped onto the floor. Blood seeped out from the ruined skull in a slick pool; some of it had spattered the Guide's face and she wiped it away with the back of her hand. Then, a nod, and the soldiers leaned into their rifles. Kelbee looked away as the volley rang out.

The Lance Colonel's face was flushed, his eyes bright. She saw the tip of his tongue dart out and trace a wet line around his lips. Something about this horrified her even more, and she turned back. The Venerated Guide was already striding away towards the doors, her business concluded, while the whole arena was caught up in an ecstatic howl of bloodlust.

The Lance Colonel slapped the side of his chair with his palm. 'That'll do for traitors!' He turned to Kelbee, his eyes wide, and she forced a smile to keep her revulsion from showing.

A chime sounded, and the other officer pulled a black comm unit from his pocket. He listened for a few seconds, nodded twice, then gave an affirmative and put it away.

'I need to go,' he said. 'They've found more of the families in hiding and I'm to lead the collection.' He stood and put on his hat, tipping it at the Lance Colonel, then, trailed by his mute wife, swept out of the box through the rear door.

Her husband flicked the controls for the speakers, silencing the roar. He took Kelbee's hand, the contact of his palm on hers an alien thing. Down on the arena floor, the bodies were being loaded onto a trailer, thick black puddles oozing away into a drain.

An abandoned building near the edge of the industrial district was where they went to be together. It was just one of a dozen half-finished, medium-sized tower blocks, a concrete and steel skeleton behind a rusting fence. It backed on to some parkland, left untended and grown wild; a row of spiny bushes concealed a gap in the chain-link through which one person could squeeze at a time. Inside the fence the scaffolding rose like bones around the building's

He came over and held her, laying a small kiss on the crown of her head. She could feel his heart on her cheek. He was also relieved, flushed with his usual excitement. Her own arousal flickered when she breathed in his scent and when he kissed her lips she almost forgot everything she had to say.

She saw them then, flitting across her mind. Bodies on a cold arena floor, an old man with his life dripping into a gutter. It had been just hours before. The shock of the memory was like cold water on her face; she pulled away but kept hold of his hands.

'I need to talk to you,' she said. 'It's important.'

'What's the matter?' His eyes held hers, questioning.

'I'm pregnant.' She watched his face, feeling like she might split down the middle.

Nebn let go of her hands and took a step back, his eyes wide. His mouth formed a word, then another, but finally gave up. Then his face broke into the lopsided smile she loved so much. 'That's wonderful,' he said.

Her heart leapt into her throat and relief washed over her, but she found herself speaking through clenched teeth. 'No, it's not! It's a disaster!' Her eyes began to water and she cuffed at them, annoyed. Nebn held her again, then guided her over to a chair. He sat facing her on the mattress, looking up, elbows resting on his knees.

Kelbee took a deep breath to gather herself. She noticed how warm the room was, though the small, stubborn heater in the corner was switched off. He'd brought it here for her, to banish any chills – he loved to look at her, her body, loved tracing her lines with his fingers and knowing that the bumps that rose on her skin were nothing to do with the temperature. He'd banished the bare concrete floor with a mad assortment of rugs, the overlaps creating a thick-piled geography of their own. Every time there was something new: a wall-hanging, a lamp, a shelf with more books. He'd been sneaking things into this abandoned place for two years. He'd told her it was where he came to think, to be at peace, though when she'd come into his life it had made a different kind of sense.

Nebn was looking at her, waiting for her to speak.

'Have you got anything to drink?' she asked.

'I can make you tea.'

She nodded. 'That'd be nice.'

Nebn went over to the kettle. Like the small hotplate and most of the lighting, it was wired into a small junction box that led to a generator concealed inside an old cupboard. That had been the hardest to get hold of, he'd said. He poured the boiling water into a chipped cup and dropped in a little muslin bag, stirring once before handing it to her. The steam was spicy and pungent and reminded her of the countryside. At first she simply breathed in the aroma, feeling the warmth of the mug against her palms. When it became unbearable she pulled her thick woollen sleeve down over her hand and cupped the mug in her palm. She blew on to the surface of the tea, then took a sip. Nebn was watching her closely from the mattress.

'It's yours,' she said in a rush.

Is it? she thought. It had to be; she wanted it with every fibre, and in six years there had been nothing, until him.

He smiled. 'I hope so.'

'What makes you so calm?' The irritation in her voice came as a surprise.

'I'm absolutely terrified,' he said. 'But I also think it's wonderful news. We'll manage.'

'I wish I was so confident.' She took another sip of her tea, then put the mug down. His face was a conflict, eyes narrowed with concern but cheeks flushed with excitement. Seeing the sweep of his grey hair made her chest clench tight, like someone had reached in and grabbed her lungs. 'He'll know,' she said. 'It'll be obvious.'

'You don't know that.'

'What if it looks like…' She indicated his hair, so different from the usual blacks and dark browns of most men. So different to *him*.

His mouth turned up at the corners. He ran his fingers through his steel mop. 'Would you believe it isn't really this colour?'

She'd never heard of a man dyeing his hair. She wondered once more how little she really knew him.

He leaned back on his elbows, eyes intent on her. His shirt gaped, showing the pale skin of his chest, the darker hair disappearing down into shadow. 'You mustn't worry,' he said. 'I'll take care of you.'

She boiled over. 'How? How will you? Don't just say that!' It was as if the words had been torn from her without her choosing. She'd never raised her voice to him before, not in anger. She saw the surprise on his face and instantly hated that she'd made him look like that, but the words continued to pour out.

'How will you look after me?' she shouted. 'He's an

113

officer! He'll know, he'll know it's not his and then he'll kill it, and he'll kill me and afterwards he'll kill you for *fuck's* sake!' She clapped her hand to her mouth, shocked – she'd never spoken like that, not to anyone. Her whole body was shaking.

She held her head in her hands. 'I'm done. He can do anything he wants and there's nothing I can do about it. How can you keep me safe from that? How can you keep *us* from that?' Her mouth was salty from tears and she cradled her stomach as if it might escape. 'It's just... too much, Nebn. I don't know what... what to—'

He wrapped her in his arms and she leaned in, breathing him. It was like the earth just before a heavy rain.

'I should get rid of it,' she said.

That made him tense. 'Don't talk about that,' he said. 'I don't want you to even think it.' He pulled back and held her by the shoulders. 'I promise you now, Kelbee, I promise I will do everything in my power to keep you safe.'

What power? she thought. *What power do you have?*

'We have some time,' he continued. 'Until it's born there's no reason for him to suspect anything. Maybe even for a while after. I know some people who can get you out when the time comes.'

'Who?'

'Just people. Good people, with resources.'

'I don't like the sound of that.'

'Just trust me.' He used his thumbs to wipe the wetness from her cheeks, then leaned and kissed them. 'Do you trust me, Kel?'

She nodded, sniffing. When she looked up, his eyes were

114

more serious than she'd ever seen them. His jaw was set in a hard line. He looked so earnest, so desperate for her to believe him that a soft laugh escaped her lips.

He drew back, unsure if she was mocking him, so she took his head and kissed him to show she meant no harm. He kissed the side of her neck, her throat, her chin, then her lips again. With a gentle press of her palm on his chest she pushed him back onto the thick pile of blankets that served as a bed.

At first, it was like he was afraid she'd turned to glass, a perfect, fragile copy of herself. He undressed her with such slow care that it almost broke her heart. She used her hands to reassure him, to coax him; she straddled him and guided him into her, taking his hand and holding it to the soft skin between her breasts so he could feel her heartbeat. His thumb gently followed the outline of the nipple, which hardened under his touch. His fingertips traced a line under the curve of her breast, then down over the fine hair of her belly. As his hand moved between her thighs, to the place where they were joined together, she let out a gasp.

Afterwards, they slept, the sheets tangled with their limbs.

Wreckers

Dripping, somewhere nearby. Salt in his mouth. And something else; coppery, flat.

Blood. His blood.

With the taste came the memory of the cool ship's deck against his cheek, the shuffling of angry boots. Pain in his head, pain in his ribs. Then the cacophony of shrieking iron, the agony of steel rent from steel. The pitch and sway of terminal violence, leaving his ears ringing and sharp pain behind his eyes. Water, salty and as cold as death.

Then, here.

Only one eye would open, though he found nothing but darkness anyway. It felt gritty, like he'd not slept for days. He was propped up with his back to something solid and the back of his head and face felt bruised. His ribs throbbed with a dull ache, but there was no stab of pain when he stretched. None broken, there was that at least.

His hands were bound behind him with something solid that rubbed into the skin of his wrists. When he moved his feet, he heard the soft scrape of grit on a hard, damp surface. He breathed in the air, trying to gauge the room's dimensions. It felt close and there was a rankness – the stench of shit and old mud, moss and seaweed. There was moisture, but it was stale. He knew then for sure that he wasn't on board the *Alec IV*. The floor under him was as steady as rock.

After a while, his eyes began to adjust. The only source of light was barely noticeable, a sliver of brightness. He gradually made out the shape of a door, the light coming under the jamb and around the edges of what might have been a small, shuttered viewing hatch. The room, as it came into view, was a bare box only a few paces from end to end. Something bulky hung in the far corner over a bucket. Cale guessed that was the source of the worst stink.

He stretched his fingers, brushing the tips against the wall behind him, and felt rough, brittle ridges. Concrete, most likely. The floor under his bare feet was gritty with sand. Maybe he was still near the coast. He shivered; a draft was coming from somewhere and his shirt had been ripped open at some point.

He remembered lying there on the deck plates, waiting for the killing blow. The angry voice of the bosun, grating. There had been another voice, younger. It had been shouting at them to stop.

Derrin, the shy one, the one he'd told to stay away. He'd been there, but not with the others. He'd come to warn him.

Something had happened then, a lurch. Freezing water had swamped his face, flooding his mouth and nose. Saltwater. He remembered dragging himself up. The deck

117

had been all wrong, pitched at an angle. He'd lurched through corridors, searching for a way out, all the while that awful grinding and the shouts of panicked sailors all around. The night air had smacked him in the face; he recalled the whiteness of the cliff as it loomed above him in the darkness. More rending of metal, crashes, screams. After that, everything was blackness.

He tried to sit up, propping himself on his bound hands. The raw skin stung as he did so, and he sucked in a hissing breath through clenched teeth. Everything hurt.

'Awake, then?' came a voice from the gloom.

Cale tensed.

'Good-o. I was getting bored here, talking to myself.'

Cale scanned what little he could make out. The voice had come from the far corner, where the shape that he'd assumed was a sack hung above the latrine bucket. It was suspended from the ceiling by two large chains and rested flat against the wall. As he stared, the shape moved. 'Who's there?' he called out, louder than he meant to.

'Your new roommate, pal. Though I suppose you're mine, come to think of it. Rights of precedence and all that.'

Cale squinted at the shape, which moved again. On closer inspection, it was not shaped like a sack: there was a protrusion on the top that almost looked like a head and neck. Cale shook his head, dismissing the thought as soon as it came to him.

'Nope, you've got it. That's me.' The shape moved again, the head-like protrusion dipped as if nodding. 'And you thought you had it bad.'

'Who are you? What is this place?' Cale asked.

'Who am I? Easy. Where we are, however, I can only hazard a guess. I'd expect we got here much the same way though. Boat?'

'What?'

'You were on a boat.'

'I… yes. A ship.'

'There we have it then. There we bloody have it. Sorry to lay this on you, friend, but you've been wrecked.'

He was right, the ship had run aground. That was why it had been so sudden, so fast. It explained why it had sounded like the vessel was being ripped apart.

'I know what you're thinking,' said the voice. 'You're not, you know. Dead.'

'I'm a prisoner.'

'Got it in one, buck. Banged up. Tossed in the oubliette, with only old Ardal Syn to keep you company.'

'Ardal Syn.' Cale mouthed the name slowly. It sounded odd, foreign.

'At your service, old chum. Pleased to make yours. May I say, it's nice to hear another voice. Been getting samey of late.'

'How did you get here?'

'Took my eye off the ball, that's how.' There was a hawking sound and a plop as the speaker spat on the floor. 'Put my little tub on autopilot, let the box do its thing. Counted the bars of the Lattice, cracked a beer. Had a snooze. Next thing I know, I'm here. Though – has to be said – with more to me than there is currently.'

Cale pulled his feet in and used the wall to push himself to a standing position. He peered into the murk, trying to match the voice with the shapeless lump. Perhaps the man was bound behind his back too? But why suspend him in that way? Was he resting in a sack? In the poor light, he couldn't tell. It appeared, however unlikely, that his cellmate was little more than a limbless trunk.

'Cheeky sods have been messing with the beacons,' continued the voice from the shadows. 'Playing tricks with the shipping lanes.' A pause. 'What about you, then? What do I call you?'

'Cale.'

'Just Cale?'

'Yes.'

'Hello, Cale.'

Cale shook his head, trying to shake off the dull fug. 'Who are they?'

'You must mean the management. Lovely folk. Salt of the earth, brine of the sea, murderous fuckers to a man. They wreck ships for a living.'

'Pirates?'

'Mmm, not exactly pirates from what I can tell. And I would know, having drunk with some of the best, and they wouldn't have anything to do with this lot. More like professional scavengers.'

It had been years, but Cale remembered hearing of gangs who'd found a way to tamper with the shipping beacons and made a living from the spoils. It was hit and miss: vigilant pilots would simply assume a malfunction and correct their course, but there were always the unwary and inattentive – or drunk, like the most-likely-late captain of the *Alec IV*. Those would find themselves sailing onto jagged rocks, and by the time anyone came looking the scavengers would have picked the carcass clean. Sometimes the Fleet caught a few but most of the wreckers just melted away into the uncounted coves that pockmarked this part of the coast.

Cale heard footsteps approaching.

'Oh, goody,' said Syn. 'Sounds like you're about to be introduced.'

There was a squeal of metal, then the door swung wide. Piercing light flooded in and stung his eyes. Through the shadows of his lashes he saw two men enter. They left the door open.

'Awake then, cunny?' said one. 'Keeping the animal company, are we?'

The speaker walked up to Cale, bringing a faint odour of mould. The other stayed by the door. The rifle in his hands was stubby, the stock sawn off, little more than a pipe protruding from a rough wood block. The man holding it shifted from foot to foot. Cale didn't doubt the weapon worked.

The man in front of Cale came up to his shoulder. He was skinny, with hollow cheeks laced with old scars. A dirty shirt draped his bony shoulders, gathered by a wide leather belt. Small eyes darted about as if afraid to settle on anything for too long.

He frowned up at Cale and clicked his tongue in disapproval. From his belt he pulled a thin cylinder which he flicked outwards. The baton extended with a snick. 'Down where you belong, filth.'

The blow took Cale behind the knee; he grunted in pain and sank to the floor.

'Much better,' said the skinny wrecker, a grin in his voice.

'Now, let's take a look at you.' He grabbed Cale by the hair and pulled his head back. He examined the swollen eye, fingers jabbing at the bruised tissue; when Cale tried to pull away the bony hands held him fast. The man was stronger than he looked. 'Lean forwards,' he rasped, letting go.

Next, he crouched down and checked the binding on Cale's wrists. He made a sucking noise, then stood up, pushing Cale back against the wall with the toe of his boot.

Cale felt the tip of the baton under his chin. The cold metal tingled.

'I'm going to cut your hands free,' said the scarred man. He indicated a nub on the baton's handle. 'Try anything and I hit this. It'll put enough juice through you to floor a mastodon. Understood?'

Cale nodded slowly.

A thin blade appeared from the wide belt and Cale felt it slip between his wrists. Warm breath was in his ear.

'Remember,' said the wrecker, 'Jerbo over there is the nervous type. He's just waiting for an excuse to put a slug in you.'

After a moment's sawing the rope gave way with a crack. Cale gasped as his hands came free and cradled them to his chest. The skin felt like it was on fire. The baton withdrew.

'That'll hurt like a bitch when the blood comes back. You'll likely wish I cut the buggers off.'

Cale looked up and saw the sallow face twisted in a smirk.

'Get the food,' said the scarred wrecker. The younger one lowered his rifle and returned with a tray which he set down on the floor. Cale made no move to pick it up.

The scarred man put away his weapons. 'Eat up now,

boys. Got to keep your strength up for when we ransom you.'

'And how am I meant to do that, you dumb fuck?' came Ardal Syn's voice from the corner. 'Does it look like I can reach?'

The two wreckers swapped an amused look.

'I guess you go hungry, punchbag,' said the gunman. The scarred one guffawed.

'Oh, I see,' said Syn. 'Clever. And what do you expect to ransom if I starve? Thought of that, pricks?'

The younger one with the rifle spat on the floor. 'We took your limbs already. Keep up that lip and maybe I'll take your balls, eh?'

Scar-face cut him off with a snarl. 'Shut your mouth. You're not cutting anything unless I say.' He kicked the tray towards Cale, spilling the contents onto the floor. 'You feed the horrible fucker. I won't have any more lads walk out of here with bite marks, so you can take your chances.' He slapped the door with a loud clang, barked a laugh and left the cell.

The other one followed him out, keeping his weapon levelled.

The door slammed shut, bringing back the darkness. The viewing hatch slid open, and from the tiny square of light came the sneering voice. 'Watch your fingers, you hear? The teeth!' Another laugh and the hatch clanged shut.

Two sets of footsteps receded.

In the black, Cale felt his way to the tray and lifted it with hands that felt like they belonged to someone else. Some of the contents had clung to the surface and he poked at them: a kind of thick, cold gruel. He made out a shape on

123

the floor; picking it up he found it was a chunk of stale bread so hard it could have been a stone. A jug of water had fallen over, spilling most of its contents, though some liquid still sloshed in its belly.

'I won't,' he heard Syn say.

'Won't what?'

'Won't bite you. I did bite them, but only the once.' He paused. 'Well, maybe more than once.'

Cale's hands began to prickle as the fire of the returning blood flowed down to his fingertips like a thousand jabbing needles. He grunted and quickly set the tray down, clenching his fingers until the pain waned, squeezing his eyes shut. When he opened them, his night sight had returned.

In the corner Ardal Syn hung above the filthy bucket. Holding the tray, Cale approached, seeing a bald head and pale skin that seemed almost luminous against the concrete wall. The bony ribs were marked with a livid spread of bruising.

His guess had been right: the man was just a torso, armless and legless and nude. A crude yoke around his chest attached him to chains hung from the ceiling.

'They took your arms and legs?' Cale asked.

'Said I couldn't be trusted with them.'

'Why haven't you bled to death?'

Syn laughed. 'Don't stand on ceremony, do you, buck? They were neticks. Expensive ones too. I expect they've sold 'em by now, the shits.'

Now that he was closer, Cale could see the dull metal ball joints sticking out from Syn's shoulders and hips. He'd heard of a few amputees who'd risked sourcing

124

artificial replacements, a leg or hand. Never anyone with all four limbs replaced. The cost – and the risk – would be enormous: Aspedair products, advanced tech from the Free City where the Hegemony held little sway, were expensive even before the black marketeers took their cut.

'How did you come to be here, Ardal Syn?'

'Now there's a tale. Tell you what, I'll swap it for a mouthful or two of that bread.'

Ardal Syn was good at finding things. Things people had lost, people that didn't want to be found. Sometimes he brought them back. Sometimes, he was nearby when accidents happened – a fire, a fall, a sudden illness. He took cash and didn't discriminate. He even claimed that the Hegemony itself had chartered his services once or twice, though Cale thought this unlikely.

'A bounty hunter.'

'I'm the quiet alternative. I'm deniable. And I'm good.'

'Not good enough, clearly.'

'Touché, buck. Right in the kisser.'

The story of how he'd come to be hung up on a cell wall was an elaboration of what he'd already said. On his return from a job in some back-end town, he'd switched on his hired boat's navigator and gone to sleep.

'I'd kick myself up the arse, if I could,' he said, crumbs flecking his dry lips. 'You get comfortable around machines when they're so much a part of you. I got sloppy. Give me a sip of the water, if there's any. Ah, you're a saviour.'

Cale listened to him talk for a long time with his back

pressed against the cold concrete. Ardal Syn was still alive because he was a good liar. He'd convinced the wreckers that he came from a rich Aspedi family who would pay his ransom, though, not being the trusting sort, they'd taken his expensive netick arms and legs as a down payment. After the biting episode they'd kept him fed by shocking him senseless, until chewing a mouthful of rank gruel was the most he could manage. Sometimes, they came in and pounded him with fists and boots, only just holding back from puncturing a lung or bursting an eye.

If he could keep them guessing long enough, he told him, keep them searching for this phantom family from the Free City, he'd find a way out. Cale asked how he planned to accomplish this, slung from the wall like a side of meat.

'Patience, buck. Patience and a little luck.'

Food had been pushed through the door four times since the first encounter with the wreckers and Cale's hands would not stop shaking. Four days, though it felt longer. From what Syn had told him, he knew his captors would be sending out feelers about him, using the *Alec IV*'s manifest. As the days ticked past, the inevitable came closer: they would find him to be nothing more than a shadow. His accounts were held by Brabant under an assumed name Cale didn't even know – when his friend had offered to help him fade away, he'd been diligent about it. Cale had little doubt of what they'd do when they summed his worth and found it to be nothing.

'I need to get out.' His gut twisted, and it wasn't hunger.

'You and me both, buck.'

'You don't understand. I need to get to my son.'

Syn's face softened a fraction. Then the grin returned. 'You seem like a clever fellow. If you and I put our pretty heads together, maybe we can come up with a plan.'

Despite the dank cell wreathed in shadows and the cold, congealed streaks of old food on the floor, there was something comforting about the mercenary's optimism.

If he can hang there like that and still believe in freedom, what excuse do I have? Cale forced a thin smile. 'Perhaps. If only to get you some clothes.'

'Sorry about that,' said the mercenary, looking down. 'It does rather dangle, with nothing else around it.'

'Here,' said Cale, pulling off his tattered shirt. 'Have this.'

'If you wouldn't mind…'

Cale tied the shirt's sleeves around the other man's waist, fashioning a crude loincloth.

'Ah, modesty. There you are, old friend.' Syn's face scrunched and he shifted in his harness. 'I'd give anything to have a good scratch. The nooks and crannies do *itch* so.' He looked up at Cale, hopeful. 'I don't suppose—'

'Don't push it.'

Steps in the corridor, coming closer. Cale stepped away, his back to the wall, one hand ready to shield his eyes. But the steps continued past their door, and they heard metal shriek as the next cell was opened.

'Guess the neighbours are alive after all,' said Syn. 'Unlucky for them.'

Cale crouched and pressed his ear to the wall, trying to listen in, but the thick concrete revealed nothing. He crept closer to the door, heard the faint *thwack* of flesh being hit. There was a faint whimper, almost too quiet to make out, immediately covered by coarse laughter. He jumped away as he heard the other door slam shut and retreated to the far corner until the sounds of their captors were gone.

'Sooner rather than later, I think,' said Syn. 'They're getting playful.'

In the gloom, Cale nodded to himself. 'I have an idea.'

The door crashed open, spilling light into the cell.

'Holy shit, what a stench.' The guard pulled his collar up over his mouth. 'What's all this hollering?' The wrecker's scarred face twisted with annoyance and he brandished his shock baton, his face a furious scowl. He spotted Cale curled up in the corner, moaning. 'Oh, for fuck's sake,' he breathed, then pulled out a torch. He crossed the cell and poked the recumbent form with the toe of his boot. 'What the hell's wrong with you? Sit up! Now!'

Cale only groaned louder and pulled his knees tighter to his chest, one hand cupped around the opposite shoulder. The wrecker shot a look at his partner, then stalked over to Ardal Syn and shone the light in his face. 'What's that on your face, punchbag?'

Syn squinted away from the light. 'Nothing.'

'Don't give me that! What's that on your chin?'

'He started it!' There was outrage in the mercenary's tone.

The wrecker rubbed a hand down his face and groaned. 'You bit *him* too? What the hell is wrong with you, animal?'

Syn spat a red-flecked wad onto the floor.

'You did! You fucking bit him!' The wrecker pointed at Cale. 'Why's he like that?'

'Bastard got fresh, so I showed him,' replied Syn with relish. 'A while later, he collapsed. He can choke for all I care.'

Scar-face gestured to the other guard. 'I'm not losing another one. The young cunny next door is on his way out as it is. Mal will have our knackers in a vice if we let more go. Check him while I go get the medkit.'

The younger man nodded and went over to Cale. He leaned over and prised the hand away from the shoulder. Beneath the ripped shirt the skin was marked by a raw, bleeding semicircle. 'Animal,' he spat.

As Scar-face turned for the door Syn coughed twice.

Cale moved.

He grabbed the front of the guard's lapel and yanked him forwards, slamming his face into the concrete wall with a hollow clunk. He went limp as Cale pushed himself to his feet. Scar-face was almost at the door, turning as he heard the noise. Cale launched himself across the cell in a headlong tackle and cannoned into his ribs. The man's spine rammed into the metal frame of the door but Cale's head smacked concrete, dazing him for a second before he shook it off, reared up and backhanded the wrecker senseless to the floor.

'Well done, buck,' said Syn. 'Took a bit of a knock there. You all right?'

Cale nodded. He took two deep breaths to steady himself, then set about searching the downed men. The one he'd put face-first into the concrete had red bubbles coming out of his nose as Cale frisked him, turning up a bunch of keys. There was no rifle today, so he stripped the man of his baton.

129

'Tick tock, chum,' said Syn. 'Let's get the jolly fuck out of here, shall we?'

Syn would have been a light carry even with his limbs attached. Cale fashioned a harness from belts and the yoke that had secured the mercenary to his chains. He wrapped one of the guard's shirts around the naked torso, then hoisted him like a backpack.

There was a small antechamber outside their cell. The walls were as bare as the cell had been, lit by a single bulb hanging from the ceiling and furnished with a small table and two rickety chairs. The table was littered with bottles and a game of knucklebones seemed to have been abandoned halfway through. The air was different – after the dank staleness of the cell it was like standing in the freshness of an open field. Cale caught a hint of salt, almost imperceptible, and a distant crash of waves. His hunch had been right: wherever they were, it was near the shore.

'Come on, you need to move,' said Syn in his ear.

'Wait.' Cale went to the other cell that faced on to the antechamber and began sifting through the bunch of keys.

'Buck, we haven't got time to stage a jailbreak. Either we go now, or no one gets out.'

'He said something about another.'

'Who said? Other what? Come on, turn it around. Out we go, quick as birds.'

'The one with the scars,' said Cale, trying another key in the lock and failing to open it. 'He said there was another. I'm not leaving them if they're alive.'

'I'm sure that's very fucking good of you. Just put me down and I'll nod my way out of here.'

130

Cale ignored him and tried another key. The heavy lock clicked. He swung the door open and the stench from the dark room made him recoil.

A body lay before them in the middle of the cell. A big man, dead for some days going by the smell. He lay face-down, a drying pool of blood surrounding his head like a glossy halo. The face was turned towards the door, and Cale saw the tongue had become swollen and purple, bulging from the open mouth like some fat worm. To make matters worse, the corpse had voided its bowels.

'Don't you go in there,' said Syn. 'Nothing for us.' Despite this, he seemed to know what was coming and held his breath.

Cale found the other occupant against the far wall, hidden from the door by the pile of decaying flesh. The boy's head was cradled between his shaking knees and his bare chest was streaked with grime and blood. His red mop of hair hung in lank ropes over his face. He looked up at Cale with hooded eyes.

'Am I dead?' he said.

Cale helped Derrin to his feet. 'Come on, we're getting out.'

Derrin swayed on unsteady legs, his gaze bleary. Cale kept hold of one skinny arm and guided him out to fresher air. He shut the door on the grim cell, then turned to find Derrin staring at him with fogged surprise.

'Why do you have another head?' he asked, his voice fuzzed by thirst and exhaustion.

'This is Ardal Syn. He was with me in my cell,' answered Cale.

'Would shake your hand, if I could,' said Syn.

Derrin took a step back, overwhelmed. 'But—'

'We'll explain later,' said Cale, taking Derrin's arm again and pushing him towards the wooden door where the draft was coming from. 'The longer we stay here the more chance we'll be caught. Understand?'

Derrin nodded.

As soon as they were outside, Cale saw where the sounds of the sea were coming from. The cells had been dug into the face of a tall cliff that ran straight down into the waves. They emerged from the man-made caves onto a wooden platform with a flimsy handrail; looking up, Cale saw that the entire place was a cobbled-together network of walkways and platforms bolted and slung off the cliff face, some carrying huts and shelters. It was dark, Marna hidden by low clouds.

'Looks like we go up,' said Syn.

'Agreed.'

Creeping slowly, they made their way up ladders and rickety stairs, keeping low. The wind played through the wooden structure, filling the night with groans and clicks that had them freezing every few steps. They saw no one, passing several darkened huts on their way.

'Do you think they're asleep?' Derrin whispered.

Cale held a finger in front of his lips and shook his head.

The air changed as they neared the top of the cliff, the smells of earth and vegetation overtaking the brine. It was then that they heard noises that were not made by the wind, the noise of many people gathered in one place, laughing, talking, singing. The sound was coming from a large construction on the widest platform – it looked big enough to be a meeting hall. Light spilled through the cracks in the walls and pipe music snuck under the door jambs, reedy and flat. Every encampment he'd ever known had a place like this, where men could shut out the cold with warmth and drink.

As they crept closer they heard a roar of laughter and men shouting at each other over the music. One slip and the whole camp would be on them. From the way Syn's breathing had quickened, Cale knew he understood.

At the far end of the platform was a large ramp leading up, and beyond it the ramshackle buildings seemed to end. He saw the sky's pinprick lights peering through gaps in the cloud. The top of the cliff was just a dash away but to get to it they would have to sneak past the front of the hall, using the scattered cargo crates as cover.

Cale turned to tell Derrin but saw understanding on the pale face. Moving with even more care, they crept between cover spots. When they reached the double doors that led into the hall Cale sent Derrin across the gap first, directing him to hide behind a pile of thick rope.

The youth made it just in time; with another roar from inside the hall the doors banged open, pouring bright yellow light onto the platform. Two men came reeling out, trading punches. Cale hunkered low, hoping they would be too caught up to spot him.

It was a short fight. The bigger one, with a long beard and a huge belly, managed to grab his opponent's neck and hammer a meaty fist into his jaw. The smaller man dropped like a stone and lay still. The victor rubbed at his knuckles, belched, then walked over to the edge of the platform where he proceeded to unlace his trousers and piss into the sea far below. Cale held his breath, willing the man not to turn towards him.

The wrecker finished, farted, then walked back over to his stricken opponent. He grabbed an ankle and dragged the comatose man inside. There were shouts and more laughter, then the doors banged shut.

'I think we can agree, that was too bloody close,' said Syn in a low voice.

Cale found Derrin cowering behind the pile of rope as they made for the ramp.

It could have been a few minutes or an hour since they had escaped from the cells, but by the time they made it to the top of the cliffs both Cale and Derrin were exhausted, fear and weakened bodies making every step feel like a struggle. The edge was fenced off in a semicircle, with a single gate and guard hut. A man stood on watch, the tip of a smoker glowing against the darkness beyond the gate.

Cale wasted no time, forcing his tired muscles to move. He pulled out his stolen shock baton, clapped a hand over the sentry's mouth and jabbed him in the back, letting him convulse before lowering him to the floor. He stripped the man of his filthy smock and handed it to Derrin to wrap around his naked shoulders.

The guard hut held meagre supplies – a canteen half-filled with brackish water and some hard biscuits was the best they could find. Derrin picked up the guard's battered rifle, but Cale shook his head.

'Leave it. Too noisy, too heavy.'

'I'll carry it. I don't mind.'

Syn clicked in irritation. 'You'll mind in an hour, kiddo. Leave the gun.'

Derrin stuck his chin out and looked like he was about to refuse, but then relented, leaning the rifle against the wall of the hut.

'Help me with him,' Cale nodded at the unconscious guard. Between them, they propped him up onto a chair, draping a limp arm over the rifle. 'That might buy us some time.' The sentry's head lolled and drool trickled down his chin.

There was a scrape behind them, and a cry of alarm. Cale spun and saw another guard at the top of the ramp, a rifle slung over one shoulder and an unlit smoker drooping from his lip. He was already reaching for the rifle but fumbled in his haste. It fell to the ground, he dived for it, Cale tore the shock baton from his waistband and coiled to go for him, then there was a bang; a concussion wave blasted past his face.

The top of the wrecker's head shattered in a bloody shower and the smell of gunpowder filled the air. Cale ignored the squeal in his ear and turned to find Derrin holding the sentry's smoking rifle, his eyes wide with terror.

'I just... he... I didn't...'

Syn's voice was just audible over the buzz. 'Go. Go now, or we're as good as dead.'

Cale knocked the weapon out of Derrin's hand and pushed him into the night, heading inland.

Sleep 28 – 498

Finally, they send me someone. I am not impressed.

The young man came in on the last supply caravan before the cold. I was at the landing pad to supervise the arrival of some high-sensitivity spectrometers – the knuckle-dragging loaders had no concept of their fragility – and assumed the new arrival was one of theirs and was taken aback when he introduced himself as my new assistant.

I resolved to begin filling in some pre-emptive transfer paperwork: someone with that kind of wan boniness seems unsuited to this kind of environment. I give him weeks at the most. He has very odd eyes, one green and one blue, which I took for a defect, but he assured me his eyesight is normal.

He was alert and confident at least, though the look on his face when I showed him the administrative backlog he needed to clear almost made me feel sorry for him.

He told me his name is Mason and that he is from the Home Peninsula, though he doesn't seem to have the maddening air of superiority that comes with growing up in Karume. I've had to deal with it my whole career – unimaginative, tunnel-eyed, third-rate scientists elevated to positions beyond their ability because they know the right people. Fermin's greasy face springs to mind; I wish it wouldn't.

On the contrary, he is polite and quietly set to work with a minimum of orientation. Perhaps he can be useful, if only in sparing me from the baser tasks.

Sleep 38 – 498

The de-icing is proceeding. The diggers still witter on about density and drainage and other such things, but I have become very good at redirecting them to my new assistant. They seem to like him better anyway.

The level of the ice has dropped considerably, and we have access to roughly two-thirds of the chamber. The curvature continued as I predicted, but what I had assumed to be an unusually even ice stalactite has turned out to be part of the structure itself, a kind of tapering pillar in the exact centre. This makes the chamber a toroid, not an oblate spheroid. I have had a platform anchored at the equator which will give us an excellent vantage on the rest of the chamber.

Sleep 50 – 498

I am having trouble sleeping. Perhaps setting down the figures that keep running through my head will clear it. It feels like the lowest kind of psychobabble, but there you have it. I must be getting old.

The toroid chamber has a radius of exactly 10 metres from the inner skin to the assumed centre inside the pillar, which itself has a radius of 2 metres at its thinnest point. This makes the rounded volume of the whole chamber 1,985 metres cubed and the surface area 947 metres squared.

The inner skin is a composite of tungsten, steel and some other material we have yet to identify, though even the basic tests have shown behaviour different to that of any other known metal. Whatever it is, it is both very hard and highly pliant as well as having very low conductivity. This explains why even the plasma lance struggled to cut through.

I have no idea yet what it could be, so my mind wanders into the realm of guesswork. The thing is well made, enough to keep it intact for all those cold centuries. It is isolated, buried underground even before the ice shifted over it. Was it hidden? There is no obvious access point, as if human ingress was not a part of the design. It's as if the place has been locked away, never meant to be opened.

I remind the little, irrational part of my mind not to jump to conclusions. The reality is that the place is impressive but has no more life in it than any other pre-Ruin site (most of which are little more than a series of walls and ditches).

I remain optimistic. I have to believe my vindication lies under the ice.

Sleep 52 – 498

Despite my initial reservations, Mason acclimatised fast to his position, and I can admit in private that he has made life here more bearable. He has a talent for organisation and a strong work ethic – rarely do I finish for the day and find him not at his workstation or waiting at my door for a signature on this order or that invoice. I don't let on that I am impressed to avoid complacency. I don't want a rerun of the Melthum debacle.

When we speak, work is the only subject and this arrangement seems to suit both of us. He keeps himself private, for the most part, though the few times I have seen him interacting with others he has shown an easy manner that people warm to. His face is, I suppose, of a pleasing cast, and despite my initial assessment of him as bony, his body has a wiry fitness to it. He moves well; I suppose you could call it poise. I have caught myself watching him a few times, though he hasn't noticed.

Both of my researchers seem to like him – the male one sees him as a source of good old-fashioned bonhomie and dotes on him. This amuses me no end: from the misty looks the female one throws at my new assistant, the two of them are doubtless fucking. The blind idiot has no idea his new friend is helping himself to the goods!

Let it continue, for now – *her* work rate has improved, at least – but if it turns into a saga, I'll have to put an end to it.

Sleep 56 – 498

Insufferable meteorologist! Cease my work? The gall of it!

I'm sure I had a reason to include him on the team, though I struggle to remember it. He has an official position at the Elucidon and does not fall under my authority, so I can't just swat him away. The man has become insufferable as the days have grown colder, his protestations about continuing with the work growing from notes to letters and through to verbal altercations.

The Death is on its way. I am not a simpleton; I know how the seasons proceed. I reminded him that the base was built to deal with the cold, and besides, the object of study is well below the surface, away from both wind and precipitation. With the new sealed tunnels no one would need to be outside at all.

It wasn't enough. He persisted in his whiny, pathetic voice, so nasal I kept checking around to see if an insect had somehow survived the trip and was buzzing around in the corners.

To shut him up (if only for a while) I agreed to call a meeting of the research staff, who I am sure will want to persist with the task at hand.

ADDENDUM

I am to be abandoned, it seems, by ungrateful wretches who have no loyalty.

I called the little meeting and asked my staff if they would stay through the cold months. I thought I knew my people, thought they valued discovery and knowledge as highly as I do. A little weather wouldn't be enough to scare them.

I was wrong.

They overwhelmingly voted to leave, and I had to concede – what option did I have? To do otherwise would only have ended in either mutiny or apathy, neither of which would get us anywhere. The meteorologist with the voice like a beetle stood off to one side with a face that made me, a woman not given to violence, want to slap him senseless.

They are packing up now, ready to leave in three days. Good riddance to them. The two idiots even deigned to look guilty when I told them I was staying – obviously not guilty enough! They changed their tune when I assured them I would withdraw my endorsement from their respective theses and notify the faculty that they were unfit for further advancement. The outrage on their faces was worth it.

Mason is staying. He came up and told me so. I replied that I expected no less, though inside I was glad that I wouldn't be completely devoid of human contact for the next few months. I asked if he would not rather follow his new 'friend' back to Karume, to shack up there with her, but he shrugged as if it were nothing important.

Death 20 – 498

The cold seeps into everything and I haven't seen Ras for an age. The constant whistling of the wind hitting the side of the outpost is driving me to distraction. When we are not down in the chamber we play music over the intercom (the usual, State stuff: tinny, dull, but better than nothing). I have taken to wearing furs even when in my room and office; even more layers go on if we venture down.

I'm afraid I am prey to base superstition. Since I was abandoned I've found something disquieting about the empty corridors. The torus chamber is the worst, despite the extensive lighting I had installed. The shadows skeet unnaturally over the surfaces and the sounds are odd, muted. I do not like it. I spend the minimum possible time there and never go alone.

I was trying my best to avoid outright asking Mason to come with me every time, but somehow he always seems to find a reason to come along, as if a break in his duties always crops up at the right time. Does he know I don't want to be alone down there? If he does, he never mentions it. He makes this strange place easier to deal with, and I take comfort from the fact he is either untroubled or knows how to hide it.

At first, I was worried I might betray my unease to him, but over time this has lessened. Perhaps proximity and isolation makes me more comfortable around him. He is pleasant when he needs to be, and, more importantly, silent when he does not.

Death 42 – 498

Something has happened, and I am struggling to put it into a logical context.

Last night I woke in the small hours and was unable to get back to sleep. I dressed and began work. Maybe an hour later, Mason found me in the office and, without a word, set about his own tasks. We worked like this in comfortable silence for perhaps another two hours.

Around the time when Ras would normally be rising, I found a sample missing from the metallurgical file I was analysing, specifically a fresh scrape from the base of the central pillar. This had been the last part to be uncovered, shortly before the rest of the team left, and no one had thought to add it to the schedule. I signalled to Mason that I needed to visit the chamber and we put on our outer layers before taking the funicular lift down to the chamber, then down the ladders to the 'floor' of the toroid.

Mason found something to occupy him while I took fresh scrapings. The material here was brittle, flaking away in small jagged shards. I had taken off my heavy gloves to operate the tool and must have missed a stray patch of ice, because the next moment I found myself flat on my face.

I didn't fall hard, seeing as the floor was sloping upwards away from me, but my instinct was to throw out a hand to stop myself and the flesh of my palm caught on a jagged edge. The metal dug deep into the meat of my hand, so deep that at first I didn't feel anything. Then the painful sting registered, and I cried out. Reflex snatched my hand back, ripping more skin.

Mason came over to check I was all right. I was embarrassed, both from the fall and the fact that my eyes had started to water; I gave him a short answer and turned away. He insisted on checking my hand. The edge of the cut was ragged and bleeding. He fished a bandage from somewhere about his person and started to bind the wound. That was when the lights went off.

For a few seconds there was the deepest darkness I have ever known, an all-enveloping blackness like a cloud that wrapped itself around us. All there was in the world was the sound of our breathing and the warmth of his hands holding mine, the distant hum of pain all but forgotten. Then the air lightened, gradually, as if someone was turning it up in increments. The light was a hazy blue and it filled the chamber. I could see my own surprise in his face, and I must have blurted out something like, "Where is it coming from?" Nothing appeared to be generating the strange illumination, though a low humming was coming from somewhere.

As quickly as it had appeared the blue light flicked off, and after a few seconds of darkness the floodlights came back to life.

Something in the chamber had activated – I can think of no other way to describe it. Just for a moment, what had

143

been dead and bare had come to life around us and I was rejuvenated. Boredom and frustration and the pain in my hand, gone in an instant as I realised we were not simply scratching away at some lifeless ruin, but on the cusp of discovering the workings of an ancient and complex apparatus. This would change everything.

I realised that he was still holding my hand and he was smiling at me. I asked him why, and he told me I looked alive.

Perhaps it was that, or simply because it was the best way to celebrate, but I took him to bed.

Hollow

When the three of them reached the small hollow, it was already dark under the trees. Derrin's limp was so bad that when they came to a stop he simply dropped to the ground and lay there. Cale was spent. Already unfit, he'd withered in the cell. The flight from the hunters had almost finished him.

Only a few hours into the wide sweep of evergreen woods, they'd heard the pursuit – small bikes with old, coughing engines reverberating through the trees. The trail they'd left in the thick needle carpet would have been easy to spot and easier to follow; the wreckers had had the sense to sweep the bikes from side to side, spreading a net to catch a lame quarry. Then, as the pursuers had closed, another sound that stirred the primal fear in all of them – largs. Big ones, braying and straining as they closed in on their prey.

At one point Derrin had gone down, hitting his knee on some hidden stone, and his limp had slowed them. Syn's harness wore livid welts into Cale's shoulders. He'd barely kept his balance on the uneven terrain under the thick canopy that filtered the light a deep olive and made potholes and gullies invisible. Syn encouraged at first, until his own agony silenced him. Cale had kept Bowden's face clear in his mind, knowing that to fall was to be ripped apart by the largs or put back in his cell; either way, his son would die alone.

Then, it had happened, quick as the slash of daylight through the trees. They'd struggled up a bank, every pore feeling the clear air ahead – perhaps a stream, some way to mask the trail. They hit the crest and an engine roar made them turn. A wrecker was at the base of the rise, close enough that they could see the holes in his ragged shirt. Cale had felt Derrin stumble beside him, a hand shooting out, a reflex that almost killed them all. Down they'd tumbled, spinning, sliding, loose earth and pebbles under them and the brush and saplings of the cliff whipping them as they fell. Cale had the wind knocked from him by something large, his ribs screaming.

The bottom of the gorge had been soaked from a recent flood – the only reason they survived. How they'd avoided being brained on any of the rocks and trees on the way down was a miracle. They lay there amid the long grasses and moss, buried under ripped earth and foliage, too exhausted and shocked to move, Syn unconscious. There were shouts from the top of the gorge, but no pursuit. The engines had roared off, doubtless heading upstream where the gorge was shallower.

Cale found a dead tree that had splintered in half on a rock, its spindly fingers dragging in the current. He and

146

Derrin stripped the twigs from it even as they waded out into the stream that was deep and cold and fast. It carried them on, away from the hunters. Syn had woken up just in time to be hit in the mouth by a wave.

Then, floating. All of them quiet, listening to the birdcalls from the canopy as it closed back in overhead, the gorge walls receding. They dragged themselves from the river above a set of rapids and headed in the same rough direction as before. The trees behind them had been silent as they'd trudged on, soaked to the bone, each step a battle. The light under the canopy was gloomy, Ras edging the horizon, when Syn sighted the mossy hollow, sheltered by a rock intrusion and ringed by thick-trunked mirins.

Cale propped Syn with his back to the rock wall then gathered up some dead wood from the ground. With a lighter he'd taken from the wrecker camp he set fire to the kindling pyramid, and after some nursing the blaze crackled to life. He added some larger pieces, building it higher until the hollow was lit with a warm glow. The wood popped and whistled as the fire caught pockets of moisture, throwing shadows against the surrounding trees.

Derrin's head lifted as he felt the warmth. Groaning, he dragged himself over. 'Won't they see the flames?'

'Maybe,' answered Cale. 'But without it we'll be dead by morning.'

Derrin shivered as he held his palms up to the blaze. 'Maybe they'll wait until tomorrow before they carry on searching.'

'Maybe.'

Cale sank down against the rock next to Syn and felt some of the tension uncoil. His shoulders were raw from the straps and his ribs ached. They were out of danger, for now. The wreckers might just give up the chase – they were scavengers, not hunters. He had to hope that staying at large until dawn would make the pursuit more trouble than it was worth.

The three of them split the last of the waterlogged biscuits and nibbled them slowly, measuring each mouthful. At least they had water – Cale had refilled their canteen at the river. Welcome at the time, the icy meltwater now chilled him to the core and he huddled closer to the fire. He felt Syn looking at him.

'Goes without saying, buck,' said the mercenary. He nodded slowly, holding Cale's eye. 'I mean it.'

Cale nodded. 'Try to get some rest. I'm going on watch.'

Syn rested his head against the rock and fell instantly asleep.

Cale fed the fire with more logs, hoping to dry their damp clothes. He didn't know if the mercenary would survive the night in his state, though he reminded himself that he'd lasted this far. Stoking the flames one more time, he saw that Derrin was also asleep.

He walked a little way off into the trees and found a small copse where three trunks grew close together. He sat down against the bole of one of them and settled in for the long watch.

The cold spread as the night deepened. Old habits came back to him from a lifetime ago. *Don't focus. Ignore how the leaves shift. Trust your ears first.*

They were not far from Keln, he was more and more sure of it. When they'd escaped he'd made a snap decision about where to head and the gamble seemed to have paid off. The river, the downward slope of the land, all of it pointed towards them being past the spine of the Medels Peninsula. He'd seen their course while on the bridge of the *Alec IV* and knew the ship would round the spear-like headland before making for the harbour at Keln. Tomorrow they would press on in the same direction and the trees should thin out into meadow, then grain fields, then the city. It had been a long time, but something about the terrain felt familiar.

His time in Keln was hazy now. He'd not lived there long; it had been just after Aime had died. He and Bowden hadn't spoken in months – the sting of their angry parting was still too raw. He'd left everything behind, save his tools, hoping for a simpler life. It wasn't long before he realised that the port town, though far from the Home Peninsula, was not remote enough. Keln breathed trade; every day reminders of what he'd left behind – Karume, the Hegemony – flowed through the city. He'd walked the countryside and explored the forests, spending barely any time in his rented house. Perhaps that was why these trees felt familiar.

He'd met Brabant back then, an accidental acquaintance, then a drinking companion, finally something like a friend. When Cale had decided to move to the remote north, Brabant had sourced equipment for him and for the last nine years had been his only contact on the outside world. The memory of the last message flashed in front of him and the ball of worry returned like a kick in the gut.

I can't waste any more time.

149

He could unburden himself of Derrin and Ardal Syn once they reached the city, but getting in with them in tow would be tricky. The three of them made a strange group, something checkpoint guards were unlikely to dismiss. The Factor back in Endeldam had been one thing, but he didn't have time for another entanglement. They would have to sneak in.

Fatigue began to overtake him, and he realised from the shards of Marna's light that it had been several hours since he began his watch. He shook some life back into his limbs and made his way back to their makeshift camp. The fire had burned to embers, so he stoked it and added more wood. Derrin was curled up and fast asleep. As Cale went to wake him he heard a low voice from the other side of the fire.

'My watch.' Ardal Syn was awake, his eyes glimmering.

'You don't need to,' said Cale.

'I won't be baggage. Besides —' white teeth flashed — 'I still have eyes.'

Cale carried him out to the sentry trees and seated him facing their trail. 'If you see anyone, whistle,' he said, and made to leave.

'Care to sit a while?' said Syn. 'Peepers need to adjust.'

Ignoring the call of the campfire, Cale eased himself down against the trunk of another tree. 'What's on your mind?'

'A few things, buck. Whether those largs will catch our scent again. How much I'm slowing you down. Where the hell we are. That sort of thing.'

'In a few miles we should clear these trees, then Keln.'

'That's where I was headed before all this unpleasantness. I have an arrangement with customs, shouldn't be too hard to get them to let us in.'

Cale shook his head. 'No contact with the authorities. I don't have time.'

'Fine, we go sneaky-beaky. I suppose you've thought about that too?'

'I know a way. We could be there by nightfall tomorrow.'

'For the boy's sake, I hope we are. He's not built for this.'

'I was more worried about you.'

Syn's face creased. 'I'm an old mutt.'

From the faint light filtering through the leaves above, Cale judged Marna was at her height. His hand settled on a twig and he began to worry the bark with his fingernail. All around was the sound of the forest at night: small animals moving through the underbrush, insects burrowing under the bed of needles. No footsteps creeping up on them, no ranging pack of largs sniffing them out. A light breeze made boughs creak.

'I owe you for this,' said Syn.

'You don't.'

'You can say that, but it doesn't make it true. I pay my debts. Tell me where we're headed after Keln.'

Cale was silent.

'You don't know how much I charge, so I'll forgive the lame gratitude. Think on it and we'll talk once we make the city.'

'All right,' said Cale, hoping to change the subject.

'What's his name? Your boy.'

Cale dropped the twig between his knees. 'Bowden.' Saying the name aloud squeezed the air from his lungs and he was glad of the darkness.

If Syn noticed the pained expression, he ignored it. 'Not seen him for a while?'

'I don't want to talk about it.'

'Parted on bad terms.'

The certainty rankled, worse for being right. 'You know nothing about me.'

'OK, buck. None of my business. Put your teeth away.'

Cale let out a slow breath. 'I'm tired.'

'Boys fight their fathers. When they're grown, they're surprised when their own cubs start biting back.' Syn raised an eyebrow. 'No extra charge for the wisdom.'

Cale nodded and was quiet. In the silence, the tension dissipated.

After a while, Syn said, 'Go sleep, buck. Don't want you dropping me on my arse tomorrow.'

Cale brushed himself down and left Syn to his watch.

He built up the fire before sinking into a bed of moss and needles, his back resting against the gentle slope of the hollow. He tried to sleep but the images of a younger Bowden's face, his mouth twisted with rage, kept swimming in front of him.

Derrin's sleep was fitful. Sitting up, Cale saw him lying on his front and whimpering softly. His legs gave a sudden jerk and his hands splayed out, as if trying to stop himself from falling as he cried out, the sound muffled by the leaves and moss in his face.

Cale's legs were unwilling as he rose and gently shook the boy awake. 'Shh,' he said. 'You were having a nightmare.' The words sounded absurd in his head.

Derrin's eyes were wide. He shivered. 'It's so cold out here.'

'Tomorrow this will be over.'

'I hope so. I just want to be somewhere warm.' He rubbed his shoulders under his thin shirt. 'Thank you. Sorry if I woke you.'

'Don't worry, go back to sleep. Try lying on your back. I always have better dreams on my back.'

The boy nodded and lay back with his feet to the fire. 'We don't have trees like this where I'm from. And it never gets this cold.'

'You should go back.'

Derrin shook his head. 'I've nothing there any more.' He looked up at Cale. 'I never thanked you. For the *Alec*.'

'Think nothing of it.'

'No, I mean it. I owe you everything.'

Cale smiled at the earnestness. 'Have better dreams.'

'You too.'

Keln's docks were its ravenous mouth. A floodlit, cacophonous arc of warehouses, cranes and flat concrete, slashed out of the darkness of the bay. The backdrop to industry was the blocky skyline of mid-level buildings, all neon and pinpricks of light. The city itself was the furnace, the belly of civilisation. Ports like Keln took the trade of ocean, ate it up, digested it in a smattering of freight terminals, markets and storehouses before excreting it out along the many rail lines that radiated out into the plains. The main roads were filled, even at night, with convoys taking munitions to the Army depositories in Bala, cloth to the factories in Lenis, salt to the capital, Karume. Keln did not rest so long as the Hegemony hungered.

The breakwater beacons blinked in the night, almost invisible from the shore under the glare of the lamps that illuminated the cargo aprons and a dozen unloading ships. There was unceasing motion and bustle. The calls of dock workers echoed down the endless lines of cargo crates. In each metallic box, small pieces of the greater puzzle that was the Hegemony: food in some, alcohol in others; clothes, medical supplies, furniture. Larger crates contained ground cars and skimmers, everything from simple utility vehicles to the sleek, dark executive cars from the luxury factories in Aspedair, bound for high-ranking officials in the capital. Aspedair did good business in Keln. It was not the largest of the Circlesea ports, but it was the oldest and the ties to the Free City were strong, meaning it was the prime entry point for illegal goods.

As the night reached its darkest point a consignment of containers that did not appear on any manifest was unloaded from a cargo ship and taken straight to one of the smaller exits. Hegemony officials were absent, off conducting an inspection at the far end of the docks, a distraction paid for in unmarked envelopes. A rusty old gate, marked as sealed on official plans, creaked as it slid open, pushed by silent men in dark clothes. A single guard watched, unmoving, as it yawned wide.

Waiting nearby were several empty trucks, and beyond, in the darkness, was the open countryside. The lights in this part of the port were badly maintained, those that still worked emitting a muddy brown glow that cast sickly shadows. Others blinked on and off in a mad rhythm, illuminating the approaching cargo hopper with flashes of stained yellow. The small, one-man vehicle's tyres squeaked under its burden as it turned the corner into the loading area by the gate. As he saw it come near, the guard hit a switch and plunged the area into darkness.

The quiet men moved like ghosts, their motions practised and assured. Each wore a set of goggles and worked quickly to transfer the crates from the loader to the trucks. Engines fired and the men jumped on board. The small convoy moved off through the open gate, taking a dirt road that led away from the city.

The lights flickered back to life and the driver of the loader climbed from his cab to help the guard with the heavy iron gate. As he dropped to the ground he saw a flicker of motion. Two shapes, one slight, one odd-shaped and bulky, running in from the darkness and heading for the nearby alleyways. He called out to the guard who scrambled for his rifle, knocking the magazine from its housing. He swore as he scooped it up and jammed it back in, taking aim just as the fleeing shapes reached an alley mouth.

The shot rang out, echoing off the containers.

When the guard checked the alley mouth, there was no sign of a body, just a spatter of fresh blood on the wall. Not wanting to attract attention – to the gate or his extra income – he decided not to file a report.

A hulking bodyguard stopped Cale outside the door to the office. He heard voices coming from inside, one pitched so low it almost sounded like the rumble of an engine. After a few minutes the door opened and a sharp-nosed man in a dark hood stepped out. He flicked a nervous glance at the neckless, bald bodyguard before making off down the stairs. Cale was ushered in by a meaty hand.

The office above the warehouse was plush. Walls were lined with leather-bound books and gilt-framed art, most of it likely illegal. In one corner a ring of chairs surrounded a low glass table and a large arched window took up most of one wall, lightly frosted and looking out over the twinkling night-time vista of Keln's docks.

The room was dominated by an enormous hardwood desk and the equally enormous man who sat behind it. Brabant had been a pile of muscle when Cale first knew him and that size had now run to fat; sheathed in a caftan of light yellow silk, he sat back in his high-backed chair and watched Cale as he entered. His head and many chins were shaved clean and one ear was hung with a large inset jewel. He looked like a man who'd lived life well, perhaps even gone soft, though Cale knew better than to be taken in. A closer look beneath the many rings and bracelets showed flat, callused knuckles and the fine nose had, on closer inspection, been broken and reset. Underestimating a man like Brabant was all the better for his margins.

'Sit down, Cale,' rumbled the mountain in silk. 'Please, have something to drink.'

Cale waved the offer away but took his seat in a plush chair, grateful for the thick cushions. His many cuts and bruises had been seen to by a sullen but competent medico and his head wound bandaged, but the painkillers only dulled the aches. On the desk in front of him he noticed a paperweight and recognised it as one of his own make – a small bird, carved from the same white polished stone as his Faces. He didn't remember sending it.

'The bullet only grazed your skull, my man tells me,' said Brabant. 'Just a fraction over and you'd have been someone else's mess. You always were a lucky one.'

'Thank you for taking us in,' said Cale.

Brabant waved his hand. 'Unimportant. You know you're welcome here, at any hour.'

'The man at the docks, the guard—'

'—has been taken care of. Don't worry, Cale. I'm just glad you made it this far.' Brabant leaned back and steepled his fingers under his nose. 'I didn't know if you'd even received my message. That's the problem with this system of ours; it is somewhat one-sided.'

'I came straight away. I ran into some problems.' As if on cue, his ribs throbbed and he winced.

'So I can see,' said Brabant. 'Pardon me, old friend, but you look like shit.'

Cale managed a narrow smile. 'It's good to see you.'

Brabant clapped his hands together and rose. He rounded the desk and took the chair next to Cale. He placed a hand on Cale's arm.

'I'm truly sorry. About Bowden. Anything you need, just name it. If you need somewhere to stay—'

'I'm moving on, Brabant. Immediately. I've lost enough time.'

'You've been hurt. You're not as young as you were, these things take time.'

Cale fixed Brabant with a look and shook his head.

The fat man held his gaze for a moment, then looked

away. 'If you think it best, I can't stop you. At least stay for tonight, give me a chance to gather some things for you. Clothes, patches for your wounds. You'll need weapons. I can have them ready by morning.'

Cale nodded. 'Thank you again.'

'I told you, it's unimportant. One thing though – your arrival has caused some echoes. I can make them go away, but I need the three of you gone quietly and at the same time.'

Cale shook his head. 'This is my problem, not theirs. With a new set of limbs, Syn can handle himself and Derrin needs a contract on a ship. Neither would be a stretch for you to arrange.'

'Normally you'd be right, but as I said,' Brabant waved a glittering hand, 'echoes. For their part they seem very keen to come along. Both of them feel they owe you.'

'They don't.' Cale shut his eyes as his head throbbed. When the wave passed he opened his eyes and saw Brabant looking at him with a worried expression.

'You know where he is,' said the fat merchant. 'You know this might not work.'

'I have to try,' said Cale.

Brabant nodded slowly, then rose from his chair. 'I'll arrange for transport. It won't be comfortable but once you get to Debrayn you'll be in the clear to do what you need to do. It's not too far from the coast; you can offload your young friend there if that's what you decide to do. As for the other one…' Brabant paused, playing with a thick golden ring on his middle finger. 'What do you know about this Ardal Syn?'

'Nothing, other than what he told me. He's a mercenary.'

'He's dangerous, I know the type.' Brabant leaned in and his basso voice rumbled. 'Watch yourself around that one, Cale.'

'He's gone as soon as I get to Debrayn.'

Brabant nodded. 'All right. Good. I will say this for him: he's good to his word. He bought some second-hand neticks from me and credit was good.' The fleshy face lit up with a grin. 'So at least he won't try to rob you.'

iv. Underworld

Kelbee had always imagined subversives would hide underground. When it turned out to be true, she was almost disappointed.

Nebn went down first, his hands steady on the rusted access ladder. His head disappeared below the surface, then there was silence. After some minutes she heard his voice calling gently to her, the sound funnelled by the manhole. She took another furtive look around her at the underside of the overpass, sure she was still being watched. Apart from a few mangy krits that scurried amid the piles of refuse and broken concrete, the place was deserted.

Taking a breath, she placed her foot on the first rung of the ladder, which hummed as it took her weight. She felt around below with the other foot for the next one and found it. Slowly, like he'd said, she descended until her eyes were level with the ground. One more step down and she was in darkness.

The smell was thick and cloying like she'd dived into a

noxious pool. She could feel it on her skin and intruding up her nostrils. She pressed her lips tight and let go of the ladder with one hand to pull her collar over her mouth. Her eyes began to water.

'It'll pass,' she heard him say from somewhere below. 'Breathe through your mouth, it helps.'

She shut her eyes, as if that would help, then opened them again, annoyed with herself.

'It's on your left.'

She looked over and saw something on the wall glowing through a layer of dirt. She reached out and felt the tackiness of old rubber, then pushed the blister-like protrusion in. It gave a faint click. Above her the manhole irised shut with a groan, making her duck in spite of herself.

Kelbee edged down, stopping once to cuff at her eyes. Her sight adjusted as she went; it was not total darkness, there was brightness below her feet where the ladder bottomed out. The shaft around her was rough concrete, dark with layers of age and dirt. A few more steps and she was through into the tunnel, then his hands were on her waist, steadying her.

There was a pool of light around the base of the ladder, but beyond only echoing gloom. The sewer was old but, judging by the stream of brownish sludge that ran by the concrete walkway, still in use. There was no handrail; just the thought of stepping off the edge into the stinking flow made her throat tighten, so she kept her eyes up. What little she could see of the tunnel was clad with grimy green tiles. Light came from a single recessed bulb in the ceiling; the darkness beyond was so absolute that she welcomed even its sickly glow.

As if hearing her think, he said, 'I have to turn the light out. It's a precaution.'

Her eyes widened, but she nodded.

He took her hand and squeezed it. 'Just keep hold of me,' he said, then found a button by the ladder and pressed it. The light clicked off.

He held her hand tight and led her through the tunnels. Occasionally, he would pause for a moment before continuing down this or that side tunnel. Their footsteps echoed off the curved ceiling, rasping concrete mostly, sometimes the clank of metal catwalks. She shuddered to think what was washing under their feet in the darkness. Just one misstep away. The smell didn't get any worse, which was small comfort.

After what felt like an age, he stopped. 'We're here,' he murmured.

She heard him press his hand against the wall and there was a click. Then the wall split down the middle, a line of brightness that widened into a doorway. She covered her eyes, felt him draw her forwards through the opening. She heard a door slide shut behind her and felt clean air on her face.

The room she found herself in was cool and dry. It was well lit, a kind of antechamber with several doors leading off. Nebn was greeting two people, a man and a woman. The man was older, with a diagonal scar running from above his right eyebrow and down across his nose to his jaw, the eye hidden behind a black patch. She noticed the hair of his beard had turned white where it met the scar, then he turned and she found herself transfixed by a single violet eye.

'This is Kelbee,' said Nebn.

The scarred face was expressionless. 'Yes. Welcome,' he said in a deep, rolling voice.

Nebn seemed about to continue but was cut off as the other person, a tall young woman, wrapped him in an embrace.

The woman looked to be a little older than Kelbee, with long hair that was an unnaturally bright yellow. She let Nebn go and turned to look at her with a face that was fine and proud, with high cheekbones and full lips. She was as tall as the men. Kelbee didn't like how her hand rested in the crook of Nebn's arm, casual and familiar. Then the woman grabbed her hands as a warm smile crinkled the edges of her mouth. Her movements were confident and her long legs and lithe shoulders made Kelbee feel small and clumsy.

'Hello,' she said. 'I'm Tani.'

Kelbee smiled through pursed lips, but the woman's smile widened into a grin. She wrapped her arms around Kelbee's shoulders, giving her a squeeze. Kelbee tried to mumble a greeting of her own as her face was pressed into soft yellow hair that smelled at once of flowers and engine oil. Tani released her, even white teeth beaming.

Nebn shot her an embarrassed look. 'Sorry about her. She's never understood about personal space.'

Kelbee lowered her head to cover the redness in her cheeks and managed to croak out, 'Glad to meet you...'

'She's a beauty, Neb, you were right,' said Tani.

The flush spread behind Kelbee's ears. Somehow this willowy woman made the utility shirt and heavy-duty trousers she wore look glamorous; perhaps it was the length of her legs. She realised she was staring and snatched her gaze away.

The scarred man spoke. 'Let's get out of this hallway, shall we? You men can stand down.'

Kelbee heard a soft movement. Two men moved from behind her; both were hooded and masked, armed with compact machine guns. She hadn't heard anyone even though they must have been there the whole time, close enough to reach out and grab her. A chill ran up her spine.

What had he brought her to?

It was a section of the sewer network, Nebn told her as they walked, sealed off because of flooding and collapse. A helpful hand in the right department had declared the tunnels condemned, then they'd come here and made it their own in secret. The waste had been drained, the tunnels cleaned and lit and soundproofed. Generators kept the place aired and dry.

'It's small, only two dozen of us, though there's room for more,' said Nebn. 'We can live and sleep and work in relative safety.'

The man with the scar turned. 'Perhaps the tour can wait until after I've had time to speak with our guest.'

Nebn inclined his head. 'Sorry, Brennev.' He gave her a smile that was meant to reassure, but only made her feel more nervous.

They came to a panelled door in the tunnel wall and stopped.

'Kelbee,' said Brennev, opening the door. 'This will only take a moment.'

Nebn gave her arm a squeeze and Tani smiled at her.

'If you would,' said Brennev, his voice low and soft.

Kelbee stepped through the door into a small, functional office. Just a desk, two chairs and a small couch facing a low table. In one corner, near the ceiling, a small ventilation fan whirred in its plastic housing. She heard Brennev close the door behind her. He indicated the couch with an open hand and she sat, expecting him to take the large chair behind the desk; instead he picked up another made of light wood and set it down opposite her. He sank into it, holding his hands together, elbows resting on his knees.

'Can I get you some water?' he asked.

'No, thank you.'

He cleared his throat. 'You must realise that what we're doing down here is very illegal.'

She gave a small nod.

'Nebn has brought you here because he thinks you can be of help to us.'

She frowned. 'He told me you could help. I – *we* have a problem.'

'I know about that, Nebn told me. He's also said how sharp you are, how resourceful. He's very attached to you.' The lone violet eye held her. 'This may sound unkind, but we aren't a refuge. We are doing serious work here and a slip-up could see us all killed. I told him he could bring you here, but it wasn't out of charity.' He laced his fingers. 'I'm interested in you, Kelbee. More specifically, I'm interested in your husband.'

In the silence that followed, she became acutely aware of the whirring fan in the corner. There could be a camera there, or a recording device. Were they watching even now, assessing, waiting for her to say something?

Brennev saw her glance over. 'You're thinking this is some sort of test. That you're being set up. That's understandable. You've been taught to feel that way your whole life.' He smiled, a bitter parting of the lips. 'I suppose we all felt like that at one time.'

He leaned forward. 'People disappearing in the night. You must know what I mean? People who showed a lack of respect, who talked or thought too much. You never saw them again, did you? It's a powerful tool, that quiet kind of fear.'

He reached across the low table and took her hand; it was big and warm, but she wanted so much to snatch her hand away because of the single eye boring into her.

When he continued his voice was almost gentle, lulling. 'I want you to believe what I say, so I will give you something now, Kelbee. Just a little thing, just some words. But words that could kill me.'

Her pulse pounded in her ears and she found herself transfixed.

'I hate it all, Kelbee,' he said. 'This city, this world. What it has been made to be. The watchers in the streets, the checkpoints. Neighbours reporting on each other for fear of being under suspicion themselves. Power rationing, though the mausoleum of a mummified corpse is lit and heated every hour of every day. Men deciding the fate of millions with the stroke of a pen.

'This world is a cruel joke, Kelbee. A running sore, made so by a five-hundred-year-old hypocrite.' His grip tightened. 'Let me tell you, if I had one chance to go back and meet the Seeker, just one, I would choke the life from him.'

She gasped and ripped her hand away. She looked around at the door, expecting at any moment for it to be kicked in. Those words were unthinkable, criminal! Sedition of the worst kind!

The room stayed quiet and the door stayed still. The only sound was her breathing and the fan in the corner.

Brennev's voice was wry. 'That appals you. That's because they've done their work – on you, your parents, everyone going back half a millennium. But the truth is, Kelbee, some of us have had our eyes opened and we see the Hegemony for what it is. A broken, unjust tyranny that has stagnated a whole world. It is a lie and I'll die to bring it down.'

He stood and walked over to the desk where he pulled a file from one of the drawers.

'So, there you have it. My gift, a little bit of power over me. Even a senior official caught saying such things would disappear.' He returned and placed the file on the table between them. 'I've done this so that you'll believe me, maybe even trust me a little. That's all it takes to begin with.'

Her eyes were drawn to the file on the table. A thick manila folder of loose sheets, scuffed and crumpled at the edges. She felt his eyes on her as if he were waiting for some sign to continue. She reached out and flipped the cover, setting the first leaf fluttering.

It was a picture of her. She was leaving her apartment block. The image looked recent, made in the last year. It had been taken from close by, at street level.

She flicked through the file, finding more photos, ID documents, certificates of employment, tithe records, permit applications. All with her name. Someone had gathered the paper trail of her life in Karume. She came to the last page, another picture. It was her, much younger. Her mouth was drawn in a serious line, but her eyes were alive. She remembered when it had been taken: six years ago on her first day in the city. The processing had taken hours until she was tired and hungry, but she'd been so full of excitement.

'This file is you,' said Brennev. 'We make sure to watch your kind.'

She flushed. 'What "kind" would that be?'

'When officers apply for a wife, we open files on the girls they bring in. It's sensible intelligence. Most of those files just sit gathering dust, but sometimes we get someone like you.'

Kelbee looked him in the eye. 'I don't know what you mean. I didn't mean to come here. I don't know who you people are.'

'You're valuable.'

'I don't like any of this. I want to leave.'

He held up his hand. 'Before you do, tell me what you know about your husband.'

That caught her off-guard. He relaxed into his chair as her head spun.

What about him? This had to be a trap, an elaborate construction in which she would incriminate herself.

'I'll tell you: you know barely anything. We, on the other hand, do know some things. Where he works, where he was born. Where he goes after work, the men he drinks with.'

She glared, but said nothing.

'We know you have been married for six years and have no children,' he continued. 'We know he spends much of his time away from home, but that he has no mistresses.' The eye speared her. 'I know what he does to you.'

168

'That's enough,' she snapped. 'I don't want to do this any more. I thought you were going to help.'

'I want to. Both you and Nebn. But this man, whom you live with, who beats you—'

'Stop it. Just stop.'

'—who treats you like meat, you know nothing about him.' His voice had dropped even lower, rumbling in his throat. 'He is worse than you know. Far worse. Where he works, the operations he runs, what his orders do to ordinary people. I want you to help us to stop him, and others like him.'

Her breathing was sharp and rapid. Her eyes had started to water and her throat felt swollen, her tongue thick. 'What the hell can *I* do? Poison his... damn soup?' As soon as she'd said it she clapped her hand over her mouth.

'No. We just want the little things. We know he's been promoted and permanently attached to Intelligence, though he's been their creature for some time. We have no eyes inside his new posting – the security level is too high. I don't like to have blind spots.' His hands were clasped, his face serious. 'I want to know what he brings home with him and which people he talks to. Things he would only let slip at home, with a drink in his hand.' He leaned in. 'In return, I promise I will help you when the time comes.'

He doesn't talk at home, she thought. *He never discusses anything with me. This is madness, just all a huge mistake.* For all that he stirred her blood, Nebn was a stranger to her and now she was being asked to commit treason. It was all too much.

She found her hand had drifted to her bump. She needed help, and she knew it.

169

'I turn traitor and you keep my child safe. That's your price, is it?'

'Look at him, Kelbee.' He held up a picture of the Lance Colonel in his everyday uniform. He was standing on a balcony, talking with another officer, a drink in his hand. 'Look at this man. For all the times he hurt you, I'm giving you a chance to hit back.'

'I want to see Nebn.'

Brennev's shoulders rose, then fell. He replaced the photograph and closed the file. 'I understand. This is a lot to take in. You're right to be scared and smart to be sceptical.'

He left the file on the table and stood. He held out his hand with a face that was half-apology, half-question. After a beat, she took it.

'Nebn is a good soldier. He's risking a lot. I hope you make the right decision.'

'I just... there's so much. I don't even know what I could do for' – she waved a hand in the air – 'all this. I just want us to be safe.'

'You can do more than you give yourself credit for.' With that, he opened the door.

Nebn was waiting for her in the corridor. When he saw her, the boyish relief on his face made her smile.

'You're all right?' he asked. 'It's a lot to take in, but I knew you were up to it.'

Kelbee held his hand, kissing him on the cheek, feeling an urge to reassure him though her mind was whirling. 'I'm not so sure.'

'Don't you see, though?' he said, his voice low. 'You're perfect. You've never put a foot out of place; you blend in.

And you'll be helping so many people.'

Kelbee looked at his wide eyes. She heard Brennev shut the door behind her and again saw his questioning look.

She took a deep breath. 'I'd like a little while to think.'

The scarred face was unreadable. 'Of course. I have to be going,' he said. 'Nebn will see you out. Goodbye, Kelbee, I hope to see you again.' He turned and walked off down the corridor.

Tani was leaning up against the wall, chewing on the end of an elegant finger. She caught Kelbee's eye. 'How long do you have?'

'The Lance Colonel's away until tomorrow,' answered Kelbee. 'Outside the Walls; an inspection, I think he said.'

'You see, you're already useful,' said Nebn. 'I want to show you something; come with me.'

'Mind if I join?' said Tani.

Irritation skittered across Nebn's face, but he nodded. 'Fine.'

'More secrets?' said Kelbee.

'Just something that's important to me.'

Nebn led the way through twisting corridors until they came to a heavy metal door. It didn't look part of the sewer, more like a hole had been punched through the tile and concrete. Nebn entered a code into a keypad and led them through.

The room beyond was circular and low. The walls domed up to form the concrete ceiling and the air was ancient, tinged with something like copper.

'We found this place by accident. It's my favourite place to come and think.'

Kelbee felt the rough surface. It was like standing inside a large bubble; the floor was made of perfectly fitted stone flags that curved downwards in a shallow bowl. Inset, the metal gleaming like new, were concentric lines running around a stone hemisphere in the very centre of the bowl, each track carrying its own, smaller dome.

Tani's voice echoed. 'It was bigger, but whoever built the sewers wanted to bury it, so they poured in tons of concrete. They did it too fast and a bubble formed, leaving this.'

'It feels... old.'

'It's from before the Ruin.'

Kelbee shot the other woman a look, wondering if she was being mocked.

'It's true,' said Nebn. 'It has to be, look.' He crouched and tapped the largest dome, the one in the middle. 'This is Ras, we think.'

Kelbee shook her head, not understanding.

'All of these,' he continued, 'are meant to be other worlds. They move around Ras in circles. Some slower than others.'

'Ras runs on a track set in the sky, the same as Marna. Everyone knows that.'

'That's how I know this is so old,' he said. 'They used to believe ours was just one world of many, all circling around Ras in a great black emptiness.'

The thought of all that emptiness, the idea of hanging in nothing, made her feel dizzy.

'It's something that was lost and then found by chance – I like that,' said Tani. 'All this about other worlds, it doesn't make much sense. But then, our boy's a sucker for anything pre-Ruin.'

Nebn's face clouded. 'They were ahead of us in so many ways. We should learn all we can.'

'That's what destroyed them,' Tani countered. 'Their decadence brought the Ruin down on them. It's why we're in this mess.'

He snorted. 'You sound like a Teller.'

'Suppose you're right, suppose that crazy old witch at the Elucidon is also right and it was some kind of milk-and-honey wonderland before the Ruin: all plentiful food and automaton servants. It doesn't matter. They still wrecked the world, for all their magnificence.'

'We could learn from them.'

'What could they have that's worth knowing, if all it did was smash the world?'

Kelbee looked down at the globe at her feet. Unlike the others, it wasn't smooth, but was covered in a fine grid of lines that stood out a fraction from the surface.

'What's this?' she asked.

'Us,' said Nebn.

'So, these are…'

'Map lines, maybe. Or what the Lattice might have looked like before it fell.'

Tani sighed dramatically.

Kelbee saw this was an argument that had run, so she headed it off. 'It's very beautiful in here.' She took his hand and smiled. He held her by the waist and she felt the heat of him through her clothes.

'I'm getting that third-wheel sort of feeling,' said Tani. 'See you outside.'

When she'd gone, Nebn kissed her. 'I remember the first

173

time I came here. The first time I tried to swallow the idea. It's scary, I know, because it makes you wonder… what else could be different from what we think is the truth?'

'Who's this woman Tani mentioned?'

'Sulara Song. She does research at the Elucidon, but they starve her funding. They'd like all talk of the pre-Ruin to disappear, and maybe it will – not many seem to care any more. I know of only one other person who does, and he's with Professor Song now, keeping her safe.'

She kissed him softly and he held her for a while. The place didn't feel so stark now, the walls holding them like an embrace.

'Tell Brennev I'll do it,' she said.

He pressed her to his chest. 'I'm sorry it had to be like this.'

'I don't have the first clue how, though.'

'I'll show you.'

Debrayn

The train rumbled along, heading out from Keln and hugging the coast. Corrosion from the salt spray had eaten at the joints in the track and made it uneven. At every kink or turn the great caterpillar would shift to one side with the squeal of steel on steel. The engine car couldn't be heard from where Cale and the other two were hidden, in a box car near the very end of the long line of carriages. The only sounds were the groans of the suspension and the regular *snicker-snack* of wheel on rail.

They'd cleared a space between cargo crates by the rear doors. Brabant had assured them the carriage was marked with his private seal and wouldn't be checked, but Cale wanted to be able to get out fast if he needed to. Derrin lay stretched out on his bedroll, fiddling with a knife he'd claimed from the bag of clothes and equipment Brabant had provided. Cale was helping Ardal Syn with his new legs.

'Pink, I ask you!' said the mercenary, puffing out his cheeks. 'Just look at me. I look like an Aspedair sex doll!'

'Keep still,' said Cale, his eyes level with the mercenary's hip. With a multitool he tightened the bolts and rods that secured the artificial legs to Syn's hip joints. All four limbs had turned out to be sheathed in synthetic coating of garish pink that glistened like oil under the lights. Brabant had stated, quite unapologetically, that this was the best he could do at short notice. Syn had plumbed new depths of profanity, but eventually relented in the face of Brabant's wide smile and impassive bulk. Not long into the journey to Debrayn, they'd discovered that the hip joints made a high-pitched squeal at anything faster than a slow walk. Cale agreed to help with the calibrations.

'Not exactly subtle is it, buck? This delightful shade of death-sick? Oh fuckadee-dee, I'll never get laid again.' He scratched a patch of raw skin over his collarbone. 'You should have seen me. Oh, the dash I cut in my old gear. Magnetic compensators, carbon-fibre gyros, the works! Girls go mad for that sort of thing, you know. I could pick four of them up at once, and I mean that literally.' He affected a wistful look. 'Grand times.'

Cale kept his eyes on the screw he was tightening. 'Maybe save it for when I'm not down by your crotch.'

'Message received, buck. Strictly business.' Syn rubbed at his forearm as if trying to dull the sheen. 'Maybe we could put some boot polish on it or something.'

'You're not coming with me, Syn.' Cale finished tightening the joint fasteners and closed the access port. 'Try them now.'

Syn set off up the narrow aisle between the crates at a jog. There was no grinding noise. Cale heard him lope up the carriage and back, reappearing with his usual smirk. 'It'll do. Not as good as what I used to carry, but a fuck sight better than nothing at all. They'll serve.'

He accepted the trousers Cale held out, then went over to where he'd dumped his gear and pulled on a black shirt and a khaki gilet. 'Now that you bring it up, buck, a word in your shell-like.' He snapped shut the fasteners on the front of the gilet. 'I'll do what I damn well please, even if it's following your substantial backside on some ill-advised rescue. Have you ever actually set eyes on this place?'

'Yes.'

'Well, then, you'll know it's surrounded by fences, guards and turrets. As hospitals go, it doesn't scream about the healing part.'

Cale didn't reply, instead stowing the multitool in a kitbag.

'That band of toothless, salty inbreds would have figured out I wouldn't be ransomed, and then I'd have spent the rest of my short life as a meat punchbag. You got me out. I intend to settle. It's just good business.'

'You don't owe me.'

'Yes, I do.'

Cale went to his bedroll where he sat with his back to the wall. Syn grabbed length of rope. 'Think on this, buck, while I go get used to these new appendages. I am *very* good at being where I'm not wanted, I know where we can get a good driver and I have an exit already in mind.'

'Why do we need a driver?'

'You'll find out soon enough. Also, I think I know where we can offload our young flame-haired friend here.'

Derrin glared at Syn.

'I'm getting you in, I'll get you and your boy out, and if you still feel bad you can buy me a drink. Several drinks. Then we're even.' Syn hefted the rope and walked away up the carriage. From the other side of the stack of crates, Cale heard the swish of the skipping rope. After a few seconds there was a crash, followed by a burst of colourful invective.

'I don't trust him,' said Derrin.

'He may have a point.'

Derrin propped himself up on his elbow and lowered his voice. 'I mean, he just pops up, this... freak, out of nowhere, then he won't leave you alone. What's he after?'

'Should I worry about you too?'

'That's not the *same*! I don't have anywhere to go! You know I—'

Cale raised a hand. 'I know. But he's right about one thing: I do want you to be on your way once we reach Debrayn. Brabant said we could make arrangements, maybe get you a contract on another ship.'

'I hated working on that ship.'

'I can't take you where I'm going.' Cale fixed the youth with a steady look and held it until he looked away. He knew it wouldn't be the end of it. 'Let me worry about Syn.'

Derrin sighed and hunkered down on his bedroll. 'What's your son like?'

Cale paused and thought for a moment. 'Now? I don't really know. It's been a long time since I last saw him.'

'Why?'

'We had an argument. About my wife. My second wife.'
Sounds so simple, he thought, *when it was anything but.*

178

'I used to fight with my guardian. Over the stupidest things.' Derrin rotated the blade in front of his eyes. 'Most of the time it just opened the door to the bigger stuff, things you keep bottled up.'

Cale considered this for a moment. 'He was a very angry boy.'

And whose fault was that?

'I hope you know what you're doing,' said Derrin.

'I do,' he lied.

Derrin turned to the wall; after a few minutes, his breathing deepened. Cale watched him sleep. He was the age Bowden had been when they'd last set eyes on each other. The fight was hazy, just jagged flashes of accusation and anger.

I'm your son, but we're strangers.

He'd been right, and that had hurt the most.

Banners and garlands from the parades still hung from the roofs and lampposts, a fading, frayed hangover. No one had seen fit to remove the planters that ran along the main avenue and the yellow and blue flowers that had bloomed just in time for the start of the Quincentennial had now withered, leaving brown stalks spiking out of the dry dirt. The cooling air of early evening brought with it dust eddies that scurried around the pavements, stirring up litter in tiny dances. Debrayn echoed quiet – curfew was not far away, and the locals had learned to be off the main streets in good time.

Syn led them off the main avenue and into the back alleys that wormed their way deeper into the city. It was close and dark between the blocks. The dryness of the main streets gave way to damp earth and decay, the smell of people living close together. Pipes and cables twisted along overhead, forming unnatural overhangs slung from the face of concrete cliffs. It felt like hundreds of windows above them were watching; occasionally there was movement, a head or arm silhouetted against the darkening sky before darting away.

Debrayn was a large city, the largest outside of the Home Peninsula. It squatted on the plains, dark and spreading, consuming the surrounding landscape a little more every year. It wasn't the centre of anywhere, had no strategic value and no major resources but it had a gravity that drew people in droves from the wasted countryside to live, work and multiply. The middle of the city had been razed and restructured in a style that suited the Hegemony – wide avenues and clean, brutal facades, even a diminutive copy of Karume's Tower – but outside the inner precincts spread overcrowded warrens where light and law were only occasional visitors. The hives, Syn told them, grew by the year.

Their path wound downhill, a spiral of passages that grew closer and hotter. As they penetrated deeper they began to hear signs of life: a man yelling overhead, a woman bawling back. From nowhere a gaggle of children in ragged trousers scampered past, skidding around the legs of the three strangers like a stream around rocks, chittering amongst themselves.

'Watch them,' said Syn. 'Little shits'll have your teeth out.'

Derrin tripped over something, gasped when he saw the shape of a jawbone. Syn poked the stripped human skull with his toe. The rest of the body was half buried in a subsided pile of refuse, still trailing the rags it had worn in life.

'Must have been caught in the last purge,' he said.

They began to hear a thump-pulse of music, faint but rising. They came upon an alley mouth, where overhead pipes completely hid the sky and the heavy beat made the air throb, light thrown from sparks and lit signs scattering over the mud and water and grime that slicked every wall and doorway. The smell of frying meat and stale urine came at them all at once, and somewhere a man roared with laughter just as another screamed.

'They used to call this Piss-Gutter Road,' said Syn. 'Mind you don't get stabbed.'

The alley was crisscrossed with strings of blinking coloured lights. Drops of water caught the wires and sent showers of sparks racing down the walls. Bunched tight, wall to wall, were grilled-meat stalls and drinking dens, each one little more than a room with a lit sign, three walls and a counter at which men sat, drinking and chewing on skewers.

Cale stepped carefully over the sodden ground, avoiding the milky stream running along a central culvert. Somewhere ahead there was a roar and the sound of breaking furniture. 'The Factors allow this?' he asked.

'They raid it once in a while, hang a few. It springs up again soon enough.'

'You called it a purge.'

'Keep your voice down,' Syn cautioned. 'No. Purges are far worse, when the homeless spill over into the nicer parts of town. The military comes in. The locals don't like to be reminded.'

They came to a small doorway with a red sign blinking weakly above it, a filth-encrusted, stylised depiction of a growling patchkrit. Half of the tubes had died and it didn't look like anyone was bothered enough to replace them.

Syn banged on the metal door. After a moment the view-slit slid open and a set of narrow eyes glared out. Syn said something in a low voice and pushed a crumpled bill through the hatch, then the door creaked open, revealing a set of steps going down. The mercenary waved them in.

The door clanged shut behind them and Derrin gasped in alarm. Cale hoped Syn was right and they could find some way to send the boy on his way.

The stairs opened out onto a low vaulted room lined with curtained booths and a bar at the far end. The place was half full, drug smoke wafting in blue clouds over the heads of the patrons. Cale felt rather than saw them size him up and knew better than to make eye contact.

Syn waved over a server and leaned in to whisper in his ear. Money changed hands, then they were led to a booth along the back wall.

'Bring a pitcher of whatever's drinkable,' Syn said to the server, who disappeared off into the crowd as Cale and Derrin settled into the splitting leather couch.

'What now?' Derrin said with a crack in his voice. His eyes darted around, unsure.

'We have a drink. Like civilised people,' answered Syn.

The server came back with a clay pitcher and some cups. The dark liquid sloshed over the rim as he banged it down on the table, then left without a word.

'I don't like it here,' said Derrin. 'We should leave.'

Cale shook his head. He held out his cup for Syn, who filled it. 'We stay. There'll already be eyes on us.'

Syn poured Derrin a drink, then took a chug of his own. 'Oh, that's just awful. Should've tipped. This calls for something stronger – wait here while I get us some rakk.' He scooted out of the booth and waggled a finger at Cale and Derrin. 'Don't start anything.' He wandered off in the direction of the bar.

Derrin considered the foaming ale in front of him, unsure. Cale took a sip; it was acrid on the tongue and smelled like a bag of wet hay. He'd had worse.

A crash from a nearby table made him crane his neck. The remains of a card game lay scattered, two men yelling at each other while the other players scrambled to recover their spilled chips. A louder shout from the direction of the bar revealed a fat bald man in a stained butcher's apron. The barman hefted a hand-cannon and rumbled something that didn't need to be heard to be understood. The opponents swapped murderous looks but backed away, to the disappointment of the crowd of onlookers, who'd smelled blood in the air. The table was turned over, the cards dealt, and the game continued as if nothing had happened.

Derrin looked like he might bolt. 'This place is full of scum.'

'I'd keep that to yourself. I don't think Syn was joking about the stabbing.'

The boy lapsed into a sullen silence. He tried the brew, recoiled. 'It's worse than the shit they used to serve up on the *Alec*.'

Just then Syn reappeared with another man in tow.

183

Cale looked him over as he approached: short and heavy-browed. One eye was milky-white and he had a tradesman's rough hands.

'This is Dar,' said Syn. 'He tells me he can drive fast and away from things.' Syn indicated the space occupied by Derrin. 'Little crowded?'

Cale turned to the boy. 'Now would be a good time to go looking for work.'

'I noticed a group of cargoers talking over the other side of the room,' said Syn.

'Why don't you go talk to them?' Cale held Derrin's gaze without blinking. The boy's face went red and Cale thought he might argue, but he scooted out, giving the newcomer a glare before pushing into the crowd. Dar, for his part, gave no indication he'd seen the poisoned look and wedged himself into Derrin's seat.

'What's the job?' he asked, his good eye looking Cale up and down.

'Getting someone out of Sessarmin.'

Dar shook his head and made to leave. 'Too risky. Bad place.'

Syn dropped a hand on his arm. 'Not so hasty there, Dar. You haven't even heard the details. Five hundred in cash just to sit on your arse and wait. Get that kind of offer every day, do you?'

Dar paused and looked between Cale and Syn. Cale caught his good eye and nodded. 'You just need to keep the engine going. No risk.'

The bald man sat back and thought for a moment. 'A thousand,' he finally said. 'And I can keep the uniform.'

184

'Seven hundred and you can have both of ours as well.'

Dar nodded and spat on his palm. 'All right.' He shook Syn's hand. 'Where and when?'

'Tomorrow, early,' said Syn. 'We'll meet you here a half-hour after curfew ends.'

Dar nodded. He gave Cale another searching look before sliding out of the booth and heading for the bar.

'You've done that before,' said Cale.

'I know how they work. People like that don't want complications, they want a price and a time and little more. Actually, I rather like Dar's sort. There's rarely a dull moment around the saltier types.'

Syn filled their cups. The bar was bustling now; all the booths were taken and standing patrons were pressed up against the walls. The music had been turned up and the sound of a thousand conversations, arguments and seductions all mingled together, a pulsing pool of sound. They sat in silence, watching the ebb and flow of the crowd. Cale knew there was planning to be done and details to settle but just for these few moments he'd take the peace of a crowded room.

Something in the soundscape of the room shifted, as sudden as a thunderclap. Someone killed the music and in the vacuum conversation died, just for an instant, before a chorus of shouts rose from the centre of the barroom. Syn shot Cale a sharp look and the two of them got to their feet.

Pushing past a couple of drunks they found a circle had cleared in the middle of the room. A table lay smashed and a man was sprawled on his back, the handle of a large knife sticking out of his chest. Next to him was another on his knees, eyes wide, face dark with blood. Red hair slicked back on one side by gore. As Syn and Cale approached he looked up and mouthed something over the roar of the crowd.

'Little idiot!' Syn hauled Derrin up and lifted him off his feet. Cale turned to cut a path to the door, pushing past a sea of angry faces.

He saw the first punch swinging his way. He ducked and threw a kick in the direction it had come, feeling it connect. A heavy blow landed in his side and he winced. Syn put his shoulder in and a man went flying over a table, then they were clear and rushing up the narrow stairs. The bouncer took one look at them, weighed the options, then yanked the door open. The three of them burst out into the alley.

A little later, when they were far enough away that they could no longer hear the shouting, they stopped. Cale leaned against a wall, his breath wheezing as he gulped the air. Derrin slumped to the floor. He opened his mouth, but before he could get more than half a word out Syn grabbed him by the collar and pushed him up against the wall.

'What the fuck happened?'

Derrin tried to push the mercenary away but the pink netick hand was unyielding. 'I was... just... came at me,' he spluttered.

'And you thought you'd stick a knife in him? The very man we'd just hired for the job?'

Cale straightened and looked him in the eye. 'You're sure?'

Syn nodded, his face thunderous. 'Bald. Ugly. Gammy eye. Pissing blood, thanks to our buddy here.' His fist tightened with a whirr of servos and Derrin's feet left the ground. 'What's your game, boy?'

Derrin's feet kicked the empty air as he gasped. His eyes pleaded.

'Don't make me get professional,' said Syn, his voice dangerous. 'Tell me what happened.'

'Put him down,' said Cale.

The mercenary gave a snort of disgust. He held on for another second, then let go. Derrin crumpled into a heap and sucked in a few breaths.

'I was just coming back over,' he gasped. 'I bumped into him, spilled his drink. It went all down him, and also another man. Big, with tattoos. There was shouting and pushing... I couldn't see. Then there was this big knife and the one with the tattoos he stabbed the other one, the one you were talking to. He fell but he grabbed my shirt; it was slippery, I fell on him. Skies, there was so much blood... I didn't know what to do.' He shivered, then looked up at Cale and Syn. 'I didn't mean it. I know how it looks. You have to believe me.'

Cale watched him, waiting. 'Get up,' he said.

Syn rounded on him. 'Tell me you're going to pack this gobshite on the next train. He's a fucking liability.'

'You said it yourself,' said Cale. 'We need another hand. I don't have time to wait for this to die down.'

Derrin looked like he was about to cry.

Syn kicked over a crate with a grunt of frustration. Then he stomped over and dragged Derrin to his feet. 'One more balls-up and I'll show you why I'm not a very nice man. Get it?'

Derrin nodded.

Cale turned his back on them and strode off into the darkness of the rat-runs.

Wake 20 – 499

The more time I spend around this thing, the more I fear it.
There are days when I wish we'd left it alone – that I'd had
the sense to leave before the bad snows set in with the rest
of the imbeciles. Oh, to be languishing in obscurity along a
dusty hallway in the Elucidon!

I would go mad if it weren't for Mason. The cold months
have brought us close, much more than I could have
anticipated. At first it was the rush of exultation that threw
us together, and it was fine. But then it kept happening,
time and time again – he'd lean over me while I was
working on a sample and I'd smell his neck and before
I knew it we were naked and coiled around each other,
and damn the scattering of notes on the floor. Then – the
greater surprise – came tenderness. Little things like his
palm resting between my shoulder blades, a squeeze of
the hand or a light kiss without expectation, that carried
with it nothing more complicated than companionship. He
was better at it than me at first; he must have thought me
dreadfully buttoned-up in those early weeks, but the truth
is this: I had never truly *done* affection before. I can hear my
old self snorting with derision even as I write those words,
but the old me was a cold fool.

It's not just the solitude and the ice storms (endless, even after the Death passed!) that pushed us together: it is the very fact that we are not alone. It squats down there like a leech-thing, waiting.

My journal has been patchy these last months, so I will attempt to sum up events, if only to give my own thoughts some kind of clarity.

After the headiness of that first time, when the chamber seemed to activate around us, there was nothing for a long while. We tried in vain to repeat each step of the process that had led us there – scratching at the same spot where I had collected samples, setting the brightness of the lights just right. I even had Mason stand in the exact place he'd been, then walk over to me in case he'd stepped on something that had caused the event. Nothing. In desperation I even extracted a vial of my blood and poured it over the spot like a twisted libation, yet the torus remained cold and dead.

Mason was the one who came up with the solution. It was not the blood, he said, but the fact that my bare hand had touched the surface. Heat, perhaps. Before I could stop him he'd unclipped his glove and placed his palm on the surface. There was nothing for a moment, and I was getting ready to tease him, then it happened again! Lights dipped as though drained of power, then the source-less blue haze lit the chamber.

Mason kept his hand pressed down and shrugged off the other glove, laying both hands flat against the surface. There was another delay, but this time my breath was caught in my breast. A low hum began that seemed to emanate from the very air itself. The pillar pulsed, imperceptible at first, then increasing in frequency as it began to glow. I told him to stop, felt fear overtake my curiosity, but he held on as the glow running over the pillar seemed to concentrate in a single bright blue dot halfway up. It was so bright that I couldn't look directly at it, then the glare subsided. Mason came to stand by me; I took his hand, barely daring to breathe.

It spoke then, for the first time.

It was unintelligible, an insane jumble of words pouring out at first, some comprehensible, others gibberish. The voice sounded like the grating of a hundred engines running behind a thick curtain, a choir of unnatural voices all speaking in synchronicity. I tried to address the thing but it continued, oblivious to either of us. Then it shut off, the silence deafening.

When it spoke again, it was like being addressed by someone who'd heard language once, from afar, and was trying to ape the sounds as best it could. It asked *when* it was. Not where, but when, the year. I replied, but it said it didn't understand. Then it asked a perplexing question:

Had we come to join?

I asked it what it meant, but it only repeated the question as many times as I asked for clarification. I looked at Mason in frustration, expecting the same, but his face was lit with curiosity. He took a step forwards and asked what it was.

Spark, it replied. Then it went silent.

We discussed what we'd seen at length before returning to the chamber. I'd overcome my initial shock and was keen to return, but he advised caution. He noted that physical contact with the surface of the torus had caused 'activation' of whatever it was – the Spark, we began calling it, for want of a better name – and that we had no way of knowing if prolonged exposure could be harmful – either to us or the thing itself. There were too many unknowns, so we resolved to go back to the basics. We'd rigorously document each contact, starting small and increasing the time spent with it, checking ourselves over for signs of injury afterwards. In the face of such an unknown, we would need to be painstaking.

Mason set up recording devices all around the pillar, so we could play back and analyse our interactions, and we would run a comprehensive debriefing after each. I'm glad we chose to do it this way – taking a slow, methodical approach – because the scale of what we were about to experience dwarfed any expectation, terrifying and intoxicating all at once.

I need to rest now. Trying to make sense of it all drains me.

Wake 37 – 499

Once we understood how to move beyond simple question and answer came the moment of revelation. I can think of no better way to describe it. The data corpus is vast.

On perhaps our third visit, when we'd dared to increase the duration just a little further, I asked it who had built it, expecting another cryptic answer. Instead, it told me to close my eyes and then I was somewhere else, a nowhere place. I saw a man's face in front of me, bearded, tall, dressed in an odd suit of white clothes. It was as if I *knew* him, his life rushing in like a torrent: where he was born, where he trained, his wife and children, his field of study. A neuro-cryptologist with a specialisation in synthetic logic – words that were meaningless mere seconds earlier but now seemed as normal as my own name. This 'Dr Eales' had been in charge of the construction of this facility and had died not long after its completion. Then he was gone, and I opened my eyes, breathing fast, the knowledge a ghost in my mind. In just a few seconds the details of what I'd learned (no, not learned – what had been forced into my head!) faded, leaving behind only the outline points. One look at Mason told me that he'd seen it all too.

That was our first true foray into this 'archive'. There was so much of it, so many centuries of knowledge just waiting for the right questions. At first I was aghast at the way it worked, how the information seemed to pump itself into my mind (it felt like an invasion) but soon that feeling was supplanted by elation. Here I was, a woman whose life's work amounted to a few papers on dusty ruins, now sitting on top of a reservoir of ancient knowledge that shattered all my preconceptions.

We were bred for it, we discovered – not just me or Mason, but everyone. Our ancestors had tinkered with themselves, with the brain itself, back before the Ruin. Every newborn child inherited its parents' ability to connect with the data corpus, not limited by proximity like we were, but able to do so anywhere on the planet.

Planet – another new word. So much of which we were certain, now overturned in such a short time! My head ached from it, still does; at times I thought I might be sick. Imagine the sense of disorientation to find that the sky is not a domed barrier but just empty space, each light that pricks it another Ras! That we are not the only globe that spins its way around our 'sun', that comforting warmth now revealed as a monstrous, violent gas furnace.

A small part of me wants to rail against this usurpation of the fundamentals – that our base notion of reality is so flawed – but I know it is the truth. The evidence is there; all enquiries are circular and mutually supporting, no matter how terrifying or vertigo-inducing it is. And for some reason I can't substantiate (perhaps this biological link at work) I just *know*.

Mason is good at dissembling but I can spot the little nuances of him now; it's plain that he's also afraid of the implications. How will the masses cope when the veil is ripped away from their eyes? Worse still, what if the Hegemony simply bury this place and everything in it? It is too vertiginous to grasp all at once, so, as with all the great problems, we must take our time.

Mason murmurs in his sleep sometimes. The wind roars beyond the walls and we hold each other a little tighter at night.

v. Hush

They sat side by side in the waiting room. The Lance Colonel's fingers drummed an impatient tattoo on his knee. Kelbee kept her eyes on the bolma wood wall panelling, trying to shut out the faint odour of disinfectant. The dead-eyed receptionist had taken their names with disinterested formality and waved them towards the rows of plastic seats. Every so often the door to the clinic proper would open and nurses would call patients through. None of them returned, so Kelbee assumed there was an exit somewhere else.

After the best part of an hour the Lance Colonel's patience was almost up. The rhythm of his gloved fingers had sped up and the furrow in his brow had deepened with annoyance. At least it wasn't directed at her. He didn't dare, not any more.

He'd not tried to take her since that night – she'd become something else, something he was afraid to break. His attempts at affection were as awkward as they were surprising; she felt more like a precious vase than a person.

Not that being treated with such attention was entirely without benefit – it was better than wondering where the next bark, the next slap was coming from. More than this, she wouldn't be returning to the clothes manufactory, it not being seemly for a man of his rank to have her ordered around by monitors and mixing with the common folk.

This was only the latest of his self-conscious gestures, meant in his mind to spoil her, no doubt: this quiet waiting room – and what lay beyond the door – was all for her.

He'd sprung it on her the day before. She'd only been home a scant few minutes after a trip to see Nebn – via the food market – before he came bustling through the door, waving papers. She arranged her face in the usual bland smile, but it had been too close for comfort. He announced he'd pulled some strings and got an appointment with one of the best birth clinics in Karume – she could tell that he thought this would please her, but more that he was delighted with his own ingenuity. Her thanks had been toneless, unnoticed.

A real privilege, he'd said, to be using the Galamb clinic. Just to be *seen* there was proof of his rise. People would notice, the right people. Not long until better living quarters, more room. One day, maybe, even a house in the Galamb itself! He only needed to bend the right ears, show them he was their sort of man. And the child, only the best for his child, he'd said. He'd rushed her out of the door the next morning and they took his newly assigned, gleaming black chauffeured car.

The clinic was on the very edge of the Galamb. The women back at the garment factory had occasionally gossiped about the area, always hushed, full of admiration for the great houses, some with their own parks. Reserved for the select few, the highest of the Seeker's servants. It had sounded like paradise. The streets were swept and in good repair, bordered with well-tended grass verges. Over trimmed hedges, mansions showed their steep, red-tiled roofs. They passed one with its own lake; gardeners with wide hats and rucked-up trousers waded in the shallow water, scooping up weeds and twigs with long nets.

The clinic was an impressive pile of steel and glass; the interior was cool with floors of polished stone, a welcome relief from the heat. She'd watched as the Lance Colonel tried to maintain reserved detachment, but the excitement shone through in the wideness of his eyes and the briskness of his step, his hands clenching and unclenching.

The long wait had brought him back down to earth.

She could tell now, even without looking, that his body was stiff. His breath had begun to rasp in his nostrils. There were two other couples quietly waiting in the room with them, minding their own business, and she hoped he wouldn't make a scene. Just as she was about to say something quiet and soothing to him the door at the far end of the room swung open and a woman in a white tunic peered through.

'Lance Colonel,' she said, 'the medico will see you.'

'About time,' he huffed. He stood and took Kelbee's wrist.

Beyond the door, wood panelling gave way to artificial lighting and rubber floors. The walls were brushed stone inlaid at waist level with a strip that gave off a soft, pinkish light. The nurse led them down the corridor then turned into a wider passage. They passed other corridors as they went, branching off in all directions; Kelbee saw nurses and medicos in white tunics coming and going, conversing with lowered heads. Orderlies, distinct in scarlet, pushed rattling steel trolleys. No other patients were to be seen. The place was so much bigger than it had seemed from the outside.

The nurse took them around a corner and into another, smaller waiting area. The Lance Colonel looked with distaste at the chairs, but the nurse walked straight up to one of the adjoining doors and opened it, beckoning them over.

Inside, the first thing Kelbee saw was the chair. Bolted to the floor, it was inclined backwards at an angle and was plush: thick hide upholstery laid over a metal frame. The well-kept leather was lustrous even though it showed the cracks and creases of age. Her eye was drawn to the foot of the chair, then to the armrests where she saw restraints. These looked newer, metal and plastic, out of place on such an antique piece of furniture. The buckled straps lay open like jaws and the chair loomed, as if everything else in the room had suddenly blurred out of focus.

Restraints? she thought. *What is this place?*

She shot the Lance Colonel a questioning look, but he didn't notice, staring straight ahead. She followed his gaze and saw a small man in a white coat sat behind a desk, scribbling on a chart.

'Your wife can take a seat on the examination chair,' he said without looking up. 'Then wait over there, if you would.' The little man's voice was thin and reedy, but confident as he waved a hand at the chairs against the far wall. 'Pull the curtain across, there's a good fellow.' The medico stood and pushed his tiny spectacles up his nose with his index finger, his eyes fixed on Kelbee. His thin hair traced a crescent around the back of his head, the bare egg of his scalp gleaming as though polished.

The Lance Colonel stiffened at the order. The medico ignored him and took Kelbee's elbow and led her to the chair. 'This shouldn't take long,' he said.

She sank into deep cushions that seemed to envelop her. She felt the soft resistance against her legs and back, settled, then remembered the restraints. She pressed her elbows against her sides, keeping her wrists as far away from them as possible.

'Make yourself comfortable,' said the medico, then saw her eying the restraints. He gave her a thin smile with no warmth. 'Those shan't be necessary.'

Hesitant, Kelbee placed her hands on the armrests. Her wrists itched.

The Lance Colonel hadn't moved. 'I will stay,' he snapped. 'That,' he pointed to her belly, 'is my child.'

The medico looked over his shoulder at him as if he'd appeared from thin air. 'Ah, you're still with us.' He went over to the desk and picked up a clipboard, his eyes scanning as he continued. 'Do you consider a simple curtain an impassable barrier, I wonder?'

'It is my—'

The medico cut him off with a deep sigh. 'Yes, yes. Rights, duties and all that.' He looked up over the top of his clipboard. 'I'm going to examine her and take some samples to ensure the pregnancy is as it should be. You are in this room for the sake of propriety, but I won't have you interfering with my work.' He paused. 'Or perhaps you'd rather wait outside?'

Kelbee could see the Lance Colonel's face going red, found herself sinking back into the chair and away from the impending explosion. He opened his mouth to bark a retort, but the medico cut him off again, this time his voice cracking like a whip.

'Do as I say, Lance Colonel, or I'll have you thrown out.' The reediness had gained a steely edge. 'In here I outrank you, so you'll damned well take a seat and pull the curtain so I can get this over with.'

That snapped the Lance Colonel to attention. The flush in his cheeks remained but he jerked a nod and did as he was told, pulling the plastic curtain across and leaving Kelbee with the little medico, who was rubbing his eyes as if the force of his words had tired him.

'Let's continue, shall we?' He touched a control on the side of the chair and motors whirred. The brown leather reclined until she was lying flat on her back. 'Lift up your shirt,' he said.

Kelbee did as he asked, pulling her blouse out from the waistband of her long skirt and gathering it up under her breasts, leaving her belly exposed. The medico produced a jar and applied some clear gel to her abdomen; the substance was cold as he spread it with his gloved, efficient hands. From this angle, Kelbee could see how much her belly had swollen into a glistening little hill of taut skin, though the rest of her body had barely changed. It looked almost like the medico's head.

He reached behind the chair and pulled round a metal trolley, each shelf lined with blue towels. From the top shelf he took a plastic box as long as his hand and held it lengthways. The leading edge ended in an opaque bubble which he began to pass over her bump, pressing down gently. Small yellow and green lights on the device winked as he worked. Occasionally, he checked a screen set into the box's side, continuing the slow, methodical pressing. The face behind the gold-rimmed glasses stayed neutral, almost disinterested.

There was a click and a bleep from the device and he withdrew it, leaving a finger on the spot where the machine had made the sound.

He took a square piece of cloth from a shallow bowl of red liquid and wiped around and under his finger – it made her skin tingle and left a stain like a birthmark. Then he was holding a thin syringe with a long needle. The sight made her go rigid.

Irritation flashed over the medico's face. 'Nothing to worry about. Stay still.' He lowered the needle towards the red stain. Her hand moved to cover her belly. He frowned, then slapped it away. His eyes moved over to the arm restraints, lingered, then returned to her face. One eyebrow rose just a fraction.

She rested her stinging hand out of the way and allowed him to continue.

The needle touched her skin and she clenched her teeth. She felt it go in but there was no pain, just the feeling of something alien entering her flesh. It was like waking up with a numb arm, when the skin felt like hers and yet not, distant like an echo of sensation. As quickly as it had gone in the needle was withdrawn and she dared to open her eyes. A red pearl of blood sprang up, but the medico's swift hand wiped it away and applied a small adhesive bandage. He touched the chair's controls and brought her back to a sitting position, handing her a clean paper towel. 'That's it. Tidy yourself and get dressed,' he said.

Kelbee wiped the gummy remains of the gel away and tucked in her blouse. She heard the curtain rasp back.

The medico took a seat behind his desk and opened a file. He made a brief note on the cover sheet, then looked up and spoke directly to the Lance Colonel. 'One to two weeks for the gene test, another for authentication. Any abnormalities and you'll be contacted by Termination Services. Any paternity irregularities...' Kelbee saw the Lance Colonel stiffen and she fought to keep her own expression neutral, '...will be notified at the same time. If you hear nothing a month from now, assume everything is nominal. Good day.' With that, he opened a drawer and dropped the file in, drawing out another. He began to read.

The Lance Colonel cleared his throat, but the medico acted as if they'd simply vanished, so he grabbed her elbow and led her out of the room. Outside, another nurse was waiting and led them to the exit at the rear of the building where she said goodbye. There was a vein standing out in his temple, but he fumed in silence.

Outside, the heat of the day hit Kelbee like a slap. The car was waiting, and they climbed in to escape Ras's glare. As they pulled away, she gazed out of the window, keeping well away from the Lance Colonel, not wanting to set him off. There was a cold lump over her heart, a clawing thing that felt like it might burst black panic inside her. The paternity test. He would *know*. Even before the child grew and looked nothing like him, the Lance Colonel would know. Looking at him now, distant eyes narrowed and his mouth firm, she knew he would kill her before bearing the disgrace.

What if it's not Nebn's child after all? said a small, panicked corner of her mind. *Maybe nothing has to change.*

Fantasy, and she knew it.

Six years of sharing the same bed and nothing had quickened, no matter how many times he'd taken her. It was what had turned an already sullen man even more so, and now suddenly made him something approaching happy.

This is real. I have to deal with it. She pressed a hand to her belly. *For both our sakes.*

Clean streets gave way to concrete and high-rises. After several minutes of silence, she heard him turn towards her. His face had regained its composure.

'We are visiting a colleague of mine this evening,' he said. 'Wear something nice.' Then, most unexpected of all, he smiled. It made him look younger.

Kelbee nodded, forcing a smile back.

Their hosts were the officer from the execution and his bland wife. Their apartment was only a few streets away in a tower block so similar Kelbee felt she could have walked around a corner and found her own home.

The wife was older than her, hair and clothes traditional – she could have been taken straight from an education pamphlet on home values. Her face never wavered from its blank half-smile as she took their coats and directed the Lance Colonel through to the living area where he was greeted loudly by three officers in mid-conversation. Their collars were undone and their manner casual as they welcomed him in, telling him to put his hat down, have a drink, relax. Behind them, a screen flickered with static.

The apartment was very much like hers, only bigger. The place smelled different, perfumed with sandalwood and jasmine. Though the kitchen and lounge were open to each other, like hers, the cabinets were new and the smell of barely disguised rot from the refuse was absent. The taps gleamed under the sole window that looked out towards Karume's rim and the factories that skirted it. Ras had just dipped under the horizon and the dying rays outlined distant chimneys, red lights blinking on and off, smoke stacks trailing in the wind.

The view, at least, is worse, she thought.

The furniture was plush, gleaming leather pin-back chairs and dark wood side-tables. The wall-hangings were elaborate, colourful scenes of the Seeker's life, where hers were frayed at the edges. The Seeker's portrait was gilded where hers was a plain wood frame. She wondered if there were more bedrooms here – space enough for a family, perhaps?

Imagine this as yours, said the little voice in her that had spoken earlier, *if he takes it to be his flesh and blood. A lance colonel and his family in a big, comfortable home with a steamer that doesn't leak and wood floors instead of cold plastic. And one day, perhaps, he'll be a brigadier or even a general in a tall house in the Galamb; there'll be nothing to do but gossip with the other wives of your station and meddle in the lives of your children*

Children? answered the harsher, grounded part of her. *Will you find another man to take his place in your bed every few years? Or will Nebn have to see several of his blood grow up in another man's nest?*

The crowning glory of the apartment, all chairs pointed at it like an altar, was the personal vid screen that flickered on the lounge wall. As much as her common sense told her to remain clear-headed, the appeal of an easy life was like the pull of the ocean. All it would take was more lies.

Her hostess was at her elbow, guiding her towards the kitchen where two other women stood at the central island, rigid like soldiers on parade. They looked on-edge, alert for any sign of summons: dutiful wives, poised and ready. Neither woman acknowledged her. Her hostess led her to her place, clearly expecting her to adopt a similar pose.

No-Face, I'll call you. It's more like a mask anyway. The thought steadied her. She watched the Lance Colonel unbutton his tunic and take a seat. Responding to some unseen signal, No-Face took over a tray of cold drinks; the men helped themselves without acknowledgement.

It was close and hot in the apartment, though no one else seemed to mind. Kelbee wondered if they would open a window. The nape of her neck felt damp; she saw the woman next to her was flushed, with just the hint of a sheen on her forehead.

'It's hot, isn't it?' she murmured, chancing a smile. The woman shot her a glance but remained mute.

There it is, Kelbee thought. *That look of fear. How well I know it.*

'I'm a little warm,' she persisted. 'Perhaps it's my condition.' Mentioning the pregnancy might break the ice. There was no reaction, the other women as still as rocks.

She forced a smile. 'Not to worry, I know my way around.' She turned to go to the window over the sink. She would crack it open, just a little, let some air in. They would all benefit from it, it was so hot.

As she turned her elbow was gripped, and she was yanked backwards. Her hand was pinned to the counter; No-Face's head hadn't moved, the half-smile in place, but her grip was like stone. Her nails dug into the top of Kelbee's hand.

'My husband hates the cold.' The tone was as flat and dead as her eyes, as if different minds were operating head and hand.

Shocked by the sudden violence, Kelbee felt her heart hammering in her chest. The black eyes held her. Something inside screamed to slap that expressionless face, to keep hitting and hitting until it showed some semblance of life even in pain. Instead, she nodded and stayed where she was. The grip released. Neither of the two other women had moved.

There was a crackle and the screen began to flicker. The low hum dissolved into broken sound, speech over music. 'Turn it up,' called one of the men and the host played with a control box by his side. The words became sharper and the picture snapped into focus. The familiar words of the Seeker boomed out loud. A man appeared, looking up at the sky with pride on his face. The music swelled, trumpeting and triumphant.

The man on the screen looked like he had tears in his eyes as he began to speak.

'Today our beneficent Venerable Guide was visiting a re-education park. Even malcontents and troublemakers are not spared mercy!'

Onscreen, the straight-backed figure of Fulvia arc Borunmer gazed out over an ordered grid of buildings. The sun was shining and the pathways looked neat. There were high fences there, though, Kelbee noted, if you looked close enough. Then the Guide was passing in front of a line of men and women in simple but clean clothes, all of them bowed low.

'Damn traitors!' barked one of the officers.

'Look at the mercy she shows these scum,' said another. 'I'd have them thrown off a rock.' Then, after a pause, he hurried, 'Of course, the Guide knows best!'

'The guests all showed their eternal gratitude for the leniency of the Hegemony and its blessed leader. Even outcasts are not forgotten under the Seeker's eternal gaze!'

Fulvia's smile was thin and fixed but her eyes looked deadly, as if at any moment she would smite one of the bowing figures into ruin. One of the 'guests' was beaming, gap-toothed, laughing. Kelbee remembered the cold way the bald woman had drawn the pistol and executed the old man; she remembered the blood on yellow blossoms and tasted copper in her mouth.

A flash of something behind the line of people. A small face at a window. It had gone unnoticed by the filmmakers, she was sure of it, and none of the people in the room made any comment, but she'd seen it. A child, sunken eyes in a dirty, drawn face, peering out; there was pain there that had no right to be on the face of someone so young. It was gone so fast she wondered if it had been there at all but the weight in her chest remained.

Is this the world you want for the life you're carrying, where other children can have looks on their faces like that? She imagined it, her child, still faceless in her mind but so very intimately hers. Would it have her deep black hair? Would it be tall like Nebn? Would she know what to do when it felt sad, or angry, or afraid? She imagined it with tears running down dirty cheeks and her jaw tightened.

The picture dissolved to black.

'Witness the glory of the Seeker's victory over the rank squalor and decadence of the old world. Watch him sunder the Lattice, scour the seas clean. See him carve out the new world, the glorious world of today! Unity through Might!'

The picture dissolved into a dramatic sweeping landscape, a windswept battlefield. On top of a mountain, Ras setting behind him, a rider sat atop a rearing horse, frozen in motion, a great red flag streaming from his raised hand. Above, lights burst in bright flashes of yellow and blue and the music swelled to a crescendo. The men whooped and clinked their glasses together.

It was the story of how the Seeker saved the world from the Ruin. How the corrupted, arrogant world that had gone before had been destroyed by fire and by water. In the film it was the Seeker that swept the world clean for the chosen ones, though the Tellers always spoke of him saving them from the Ruin as if it was an outside force. Which was the truth, she wondered. After all that had happened to her recently, she wondered if anything in her head was right any more.

The film was two hours long. She'd seen it many times before – everyone had, surely? – but she'd never had to stand throughout. She thought about asking for a chair but the memory of those nails digging into her skin and the

207

unmoving women by her side kept her from it. She might be doing her duty as a wife, bearing a child, but always Fortitude, always Restraint, that was the message from her silent, blank-faced hostess.

She watched as a bead of condensation formed at the lip of the Lance Colonel's glass, tracing a slow path down to the top of his hand just as the sweat from her neck meandered down her spine. Laughing, oblivious, her husband swapped his glass to the other hand and licked the droplet away.

Later that night she helped the Lance Colonel through the door of their apartment. He was drunk and affable, an unfamiliar mix. In the bedroom, after she'd pulled his boots off, he touched the side of her face.

'Hope you enjoyed tonight.' He took her hand and laid a sloppy kiss on the inside of her wrist, then placed his palm on her bump. He murmured something under his breath. She smiled, wishing he'd take his hot hands off her skin. He let himself fall back onto the pillows and soon his breathing became deep and regular.

With a quiet sigh, she peeled off her many layers and slipped into a night shift. Leaving him, she went into the bathroom and soaked the corner of a towel under the tap, sponging under her arms and at her forehead, letting the cool water drip. The heat was harder to deal with since the pregnancy had begun, and the weather seemed to conspire to keep her on the edge of exhaustion all the time. The sickness in the mornings had passed but she felt bloated after every meal. At least she had more free time – more than she'd ever had before. It made seeing Nebn easier.

As she squeezed some water onto her neck, she watched her reflection in the little mirror. Were those new lines at the corners of her eyes? She'd never taken much time to look at herself in the past. Her hair was longer than usual, dipping beneath her shoulders. She gathered it up in a fist behind her head, observing the effect.

She'd never liked her neck: too long, stalk-like. As a girl she'd been teased by the village boys for it. They'd called her 'Lyca-girl', like the long-necked, ungainly sea birds that waddled so gracelessly over the beach, searching for shellfish. They'd made up a song about it, but she couldn't remember how it went. It had been years since she'd even thought of it. Where would those boys would be now – farmers, butchers, soldiers, fathers? Had they made good lives for themselves?

Have you? asked her image. *Have you made a good life?*

She let the hair fall back over her shoulders and caught her own gaze. Her reflection stared back, then dipped its head.

Do it. Now's the time.

She left the tap to trickle – to cover the sounds – then padded into the lounge, listening for the regular, wheezing breath from the bedroom. Her footsteps were silent, though it only made her more aware of every other sound, from the drip of the tap to the gentle moan of the wind outside. She calmed herself. Years of creeping about trying not to disturb him had prepared her for this.

As she passed the Seeker's portrait something made her pause. The picture stared out at her, His face beaming, always watching, always mindful. Ever since she'd learned to talk she'd greeted this portrait every morning. The Architect of Unity.

Brennev's deep voice jumped into her head, his words as sharp now as they had been before, as was the shock that nothing had happened when he'd said those terrible, unspeakable things. The world had not ended. No soldiers had kicked down the door.

She looked closely at the portrait, all full cheeks and shining eyes. Is it possible, she thought, that He is only a man? A dead man?

Before she knew what she was doing, her hand stretched out and flicked the glass of the picture, her fingernail pinging off the Seeker's forehead. Her breath caught in her throat.

Why had she done that?

Just to see if anything would happen.

Nothing did, bar a tiny stinging feeling under her nail. The Seeker beamed back at her, untroubled. Just a fat man with a big smile. Kelbee rubbed her hand on her leg, then remembered what she had to do.

It was dark, only a sliver of faint light coming through the kitchen window. The Lance Colonel's bag was by his favourite chair, a square briefcase held shut by two polished clasps. Kelbee picked it up and placed it on the low table. One of the clasps had four rotating cylinders embedded in it, numbers engraved on the face. Each cylinder could be rotated to display a combination of four digits. Kelbee examined the lock for a moment, made a mental note of their positions, then turned the dials to show the number of the Lance Colonel's regimental unit and pressed the metal stud. The lock stayed shut. She flicked the numbers to show the day and month of the Lance Colonel's birth. Again, the stud refused to move.

What numbers would he find significant? Now, more than ever, her lack of knowledge about anything in his life before she'd entered it stared her in the face. A birthday, perhaps? She tried the day and month of his, but the lock stayed firm.

The minutes stretched, every tick of the chrono another moment when he could walk in and find her here. She began to feel sweat pooling, dripping.

She thought of the way he'd looked at her lately, with something like hope. Rigid affection, maybe? She realised she'd seen it only once before, but it had been buried deep under angry words and furrowed brows. Once, six years ago, when her veil had been lifted at the altar and he'd seen her for the first time. He'd been hopeful then, too.

She flicked the dials to the day and month they'd been married and with a dull click the clasps pranged open. She let out a little gasp of surprise, then froze. The apartment was still.

She flipped open the lid.

Inside were papers and a pistol. She pushed the weapon out of the way and pulled out the sheaf. The light was bad and what little she could make out made no sense to her. Columns of numbers in neat rows, names of places she'd never heard of.

Kelbee put the papers on the table and pulled from the waistband of her underwear the device Tani had given her. A small box the size of two fingers pressed together, a lens on one side and a viewfinder on the other. She brought it to her eye and pointed it at the papers, then pressed the little button on top. There was a click, then a faint whirr. She could barely see the markings on the pages but Tani had assured her the device would cope with that.

She continued leafing through the pages, clicking the little device at each one in turn, then put them back. There was a shuffling from the bedroom, and she froze.

Her heart pounding, she pressed the two clasps shut, each click as loud as an artillery battery in her ears. More shuffling – she had to think fast. She spun the dials to their original positions and placed the case where she'd found it, then scooted into the kitchen, keeping low. She filled a mug from the sink and, hands clammy, stepped into the corridor.

He was standing there, half in shadow by the bathroom door. His eyes were groggy from sleep and drink and he was staring at the trickling tap, confused. She caught the alcohol on his breath, her heart pounding. Perhaps he'd not heard anything.

He glanced over. 'What... are you doing?'

'Getting some water. I was thirsty.'

He looked over at the still-running bathroom tap, then back at her and the mug she was carrying. He pointed over his shoulder. 'Tap's on.'

'I'm sorry, sir. I forgot.'

'Why not go to the ba—'

'I like the water from the kitchen,' she said. 'It tastes better.'

His eyes narrowed a fraction at being interrupted, but he was still only half awake and let it pass. He shook his head, then shuffled into the bathroom and turned off the tap. 'Don't waste water,' she heard him say before the door clicked shut and the light turned on.

In the bedroom, Kelbee placed the cup down on the side-table, her quaking hand spilling some water. She rubbed her knuckles into her eye sockets, wishing she could scream. She inhaled deep, then let the breath out.

It had been too close.

Sanatorium

The small skimmer truck was carrying low-priority supplies – syringes, beakers, stationery. The driver and his loader rode in the high cab. A weekly run: boring, usual, slightly ahead of schedule. Neither bothered to make conversation.

They headed out from the depot, bound for the sanatorium and making good time when they reached an underpass on the outskirts of Debrayn, just where the ring road marked the limits of the city. If you looked hard enough you could see where the shanties had begun to creep beyond the boundary, though the inhabitants kept a low profile. The men in the truck didn't look too hard.

The driver slowed the vehicle and pulled up, swearing through the windshield at a beggar who'd wandered into the road and fallen asleep. Drunk, most likely. The loader – big, with red splotches on his bare arms – swung down from the cab. The driver watched him stomp over and shout at the old fool.

Too many of these recently, thought the driver, running his fingers over the tiny brass bust of the Seeker on the dashboard. There was sure to be another purge soon, if the authorities had enough to go on, if more of these poor desperate fools spilled out of their hovels and onto the streets. The Factors wouldn't have it. He shuddered, remembering the last one: huddling behind bolted shutters in his tiny apartment, waiting out the night and trying to keep the children distracted. Just fireworks, he'd told them, hiding his hands so they wouldn't see them shaking.

The loader was leaning over the beggar, prodding him with the toe of his boot and yelling at him to move out of the road. A groggy hand batted at the offending foot. The loader wound up for a hefty kick, then jerked backwards. He slapped at his neck as if swatting an insect, looked back at the skimmer, then crumpled to the ground.

The driver was paralysed for just an instant, then the training kicked in – they were being robbed. He dove for the commset mounted on the passenger side; as he did so his door was wrenched open with a pop-squeal of metal and a hand as cold as stone grabbed his ankle. He cried out in shock as he was dragged from the cab. His face hit the road hard and he smelled burning oil, then he felt a sharp prick on the side of his neck and the world went white.

A few minutes later, the skimmer emerged from the shadows of the underpass and headed out on the road toward the sanatorium, leaving behind two bound, sleeping men dressed like beggars under a pile of discarded stationery.

•

The sanatorium was built on flat scrubland, several square klicks of ground where building was not allowed. Debrayn would one day surround it if it continued to swell, but for now it bordered it on two sides. A barren strip had been cleared all around it to preserve the sightlines from the tall guard towers, a grey-green scar on the landscape. Irrigation ditches, a few skinny pylons and warning signs were the only features, so that when the skimmer truck came up on it the great dark block loomed like a thundercloud. The skimmer slowed and came to a stop on the bridge to one of the smaller, auxiliary gates.

The driver lowered the window and handed over both his and his passenger's ID cards from the breast pocket of his coveralls. The guard's scanner ticked over, then flashed a green light and chirped. He checked the second card, then handed both back. The two jumped down from the cab and accompanied the guards to the rear of the vehicle where they lowered a single large crate using a grav unit. The lid was removed, the contents given a cursory glance before the guard with the scanner waved at the inside of the compound.

'One of you stays here with the truck,' he said.

The scrawny bald driver grunted an affirmative. He set his hands on the crate and pushed it, bobbing on its grav field, towards the entrance to the facility. The guard barked an order and the remaining workman scurried off to the cab of the truck to wait.

The inside of the crate was musty, the light filtering in through cracks in the sides. Cale sat with his knees pulled to his chest, a wooden shelf touching the crown of his head, carrying enough of the crate's original contents to pass brief scrutiny. All he could make out were footsteps and his own heartbeat thudding in his ears.

Doors opened, then slammed behind them. They stopped, and Cale heard Syn and the guard exchanging words, their speech muffled. Syn's voice rose in volume and pitch, the words coming faster, and the guard's rose to match. Then a grunt, an affirmation, and the crate began to move again.

The confined space was straining at his nerves. He hated not knowing where they were, or if at any moment the lid would be lifted and he'd find a gun in his face. He fixed his attention on the guard's steps, listening for any stutter or hesitation or change in pace that might indicate alarm. His stun baton was held ready to thrust upwards. A simple weapon, a flat-ended cylinder with a rubberised handle and a disc-shaped hand guard. A sharp stab would push back the casing and extend a needle carrying a powerful tranquiliser. It was fast-acting; the same they'd used on the delivery men. The stick only carried one charge at a time – if it came to it, he'd need to make it count.

Heavy doors slid shut behind them and he felt the unmistakable upwards jolt of an elevator. He wished he could see the floor numbers ticking up but contented himself with the knowledge that at least they were going up into the superstructure, not down into the warren of basements. After a few minutes, the elevator stopped and they were on the move again. They passed other people on the way; he heard other feet go by and some muted conversations. The commset on the guard's lapel chirped at regular intervals, and once Cale heard the man murmur back, checking in. A final door opened and shut, then the crate was still.

Cale tensed, ready. He heard Syn's voice, then the sound of something large hitting the floor. There were three loud raps on the side of the crate, then the lid was removed. Cale emerged blinking into the light.

Syn was already stripping off his delivery overalls; the guard was lying on his side on the floor, eyes open but glazed. Cale brushed some packing material from his shoulder and stepped out of the crate. They were in a small office, desks arranged in a square, one of them carrying a single terminal with a cracked outer casing. It was harshly lit from strip lights in the ceiling and the sharpness of disinfectant vied with the smell of old dust. Syn pulled the uniform off the guard and began putting it on.

Both men froze as the commset chirped. Syn pressed the send stud and mumbled back in a good approximation of the guard's voice. He turned to Cale, catching his eye.

'The checks are about every ten minutes. I heard him on the way up. I think we can get away with a couple.'

The terminal was old but still functioned, powering on with a cough-whine of cooling fans. Syn handed him a grey oblong with rounded corners.

'Data cracker. Plug it into that access port.'

It clicked into place and the screen flashed a password box, froze for a second, then changed to show a series of files, each one bearing a name and a number. Cale scanned for Bowden's file, found it and opened it.

A headshot. It was him. His russet hair was clipped short – it looked like a recruitment photo so couldn't be too recent. Still… he looked older. There were lines there that Cale didn't recognise.

How will I know this man, who's lived a life without me? he thought. For the first time, he was afraid – not for Bowden's safety, but for the reunion itself. How was he meant to bridge that yawning gap of time?

Syn touched him on the arm. 'Come on,' he murmured. 'Let's hurry.'

Treatment notes took up the rest of the page and Cale skimmed over them. At the very bottom, there it was: Ward Six, eighth floor. Syn snapped his stolen jacket shut and put on the cap, then slung the rifle over his shoulder. He pointed at the guard. 'Tie that one up, if you would?' He handed over some cable ties, and Cale secured the unconscious man's ankles and wrists, then ripped a length of cloth from Syn's discarded overalls and balled it up, stuffing it into the slack mouth. It wouldn't stop him being found for ever, but it should buy them some time.

'Let's be about it, then,' said Syn. 'If we come across anyone I'll have to play to character. There may be harsh language.'

They took the elevator up. The corridor walls were a sterile, slick white and the rubber floor squeaked underfoot. The smell of chemicals was stronger here, sickly sweet, and it was hushed; most of the doors that led off into rooms that they passed were closed, each one numbered. Offices, storage rooms. Small laboratories.

Through a set of double doors they passed a pair of orderlies in red tunics, talking in low voices. The pair looked up but Syn kept his eyes forward and his hand on his rifle strap. The orderlies watched them go, then resumed their conversation.

Cale guessed they'd walked a hundred metres or so when the corridor widened into an atrium. On both sides were more double doors, matte grey plastic inset with smoked glass panes. Ward Six was signposted on their right.

'Here we are,' said Syn. 'Now, hopefully...' He unclipped the ID badge from his breast pocket and held it up to the scanner pad by the doors. A light above the pad shone red, flashed to amber, then flicked off. 'Hmm, let's try again.'

Cale shot a look back down the corridor, feeling the walls getting closer. There were a lot of doors, a lot of places to hide. Who knew how many were waiting behind them, ready to respond to an alarm?

'We need to be quick,' he said.

'You don't need to tell me, buck.' Syn tried the badge again, waving it from side to side. Once more, the light shone red, then amber, then dark. 'It's not working.'

'The guards must not have access to the wards.'

'This one didn't. We'll have to try someone else. Those two we passed a minute ago.' His comm unit chirped.

Cale shook his head. He peered through the frosted glass strip and saw beds. Bowden was so near, just a finger's breadth of plastic and metal between him and his son. He moved Syn away from the doors.

'What're you—'

His heavy workboot bent the doors inwards with a loud bang. They snapped back, quivering but intact.

Cale took a few steps back, squared his shoulders, charged.

He put all of his weight behind his shoulder and cannoned into the doors, heard a *crunch-snap*, then he was through, skidding on the rubber floor, his cheek rubbed raw. The door had sheared away from the frame under the force of the impact, now hanging limp on its hinges.

Cale picked himself up, then heard a gasp. A young man in a lab coat had risen from his desk, tucked away in a nook by the door, and was staring at this intruder that had come hurtling into the ward. His mouth moved, unsure of whether to scream for help or challenge, then Syn's pink hand clapped over his mouth while the other arm snaked around his throat. The mercenary squeezed, lifting the medico off his feet. Eyes bulging, face going crimson, the young man tried to wriggle free but Syn had him held fast. All it took was a few seconds before he went limp.

'Well, that's one way of making an entrance,' said the mercenary, laying the unconscious man on one of the beds. 'No point pretending now. Let's go.'

The two of them ran past rows of empty beds. At the far end were some private rooms. Cale picked the one on the right, found it was unlocked. The door slid open with a whisper.

Bowden was lying on the bed, thin and drawn and asleep. His head had been shaved and his skin was pale. His closed eyes were sunken, encircled with shadows, but it was unmistakably *him*.

Cale's skin felt cold. The inside of him was a void but on the edge of it was a maelstrom of fear and sadness and confusion that threatened to burst in and drown him. He forced himself to take the few steps to the bedside, to reach out and take a hand in his own. A little older, a little thinner, but it was his boy. The hand was clammy to the touch.

The last time I saw you in a hospital, you were yellowed and asleep with blood in your hair. It seemed so unlikely as to be absurd, this trick that time had played on him: turning the little scrunch-faced thing with black eyes, which fit in the palm of his hand, into a grown man.

Syn examined the medical equipment. 'Looks like most of these wires from his chest are for monitors. No respirator, that's good. We'll have to take that drip with us, I reckon.' Syn pointed to the clear fluid bag suspended by the bed, the tube running down to Bowden's hand where it disappeared under some bandages. 'I'll go get a gurney or something.'

Cale nodded. When the mercenary was gone he began to remove the restraints from Bowden's hands and feet. Why was he held down? He noticed how much thicker his fingers had become, the lines more pronounced than he remembered. Age, just age. Two jagged scars marked the heel of his right palm, old ones. Cale didn't remember those either.

You don't know me, he'd said. He'd been so right. Cale should remember every inch of him. He cuffed away the moisture in his eyes and fought to keep the lump from his throat, unhooked the drip bag and laid it on Bowden's legs, then checked the cabinet on the far side of the room where he found two more unused bags of clear fluid. The markings were the same.

'Good idea,' said Syn, reappearing with a metal wheelchair. 'We don't know how long it'll be until we get him help. That's your part of the plan.'

222

He pushed the chair over to the bedside, then opened Bowden's hospital gown at the chest. Four white pads were attached to the pale skin, wires leading off into the monitors.

Syn grabbed the wires in a bunch. 'When I pull these, an alarm will definitely go off.'

Cale nodded. 'Do it.'

Syn yanked downwards and the pads ripped away, leaving behind four red marks as the regular beep of the monitors changed to a high-pitched whine. Cale scooped his son up and found him light as a child. For an instant, he was back there: a moment of home after a long campaign, carrying his little boy to bed after he'd fallen asleep. He placed Bowden in the wheelchair, laid the drip bag on his lap, then made for the door.

Out in the corridor the comm unit on Syn's chest burst with static and they both heard a muffled shout on the other end. Syn leaned in and listened, then looked up at Cale. 'The guard room knows something's wrong. They're sending people in.'

Cale pushed the wheelchair as fast as he could, following Syn through the corridors of the hospital, down the elevator and along the harshly lit hallways. The mercenary had memorised the route and after only a few minutes they pushed through some utility doors into the loading dock.

'With any luck they'll be looking for us back there,' said Syn. 'There should only be a couple of them watching the truck.' He led Cale over to an exterior door. Cracking it open, the mercenary stole a quick glance at the outside.

'Three. Two of them have Derrin against the wall and it doesn't look like a friendly chat. You ready?'

Cale nodded and gripped the handles of Bowden's wheelchair. Syn flung the door open and daylight flooded in. The truck's rear was facing them across a few metres of concrete apron. A guard was in the process of climbing down from the bed of the truck as Syn broke from the building at speed. The guard saw him and shouted.

The two men holding Derrin against the wall turned. Syn's netick legs whined as he sped towards them, launching himself high into the air at the last moment. A piston kick took one man high in the chest, flipping him backwards onto the ground. Syn landed, smashed a fist into the other guard's temple, dropping him. The guard at the truck was screaming into his comm unit as his other hand brought his rifle to bear.

Cale pulled his shock-stick from his belt and hurled it. It spun in the air, then the butt end smashed into the guard's face, knocking the commset from his hands and bouncing him off the metal tailgate. Cale was already moving, covering the distance at a sprint and driving a knee into the downed man's jaw. He slumped and lay still, a thin trickle of blood coming from his nose.

A shot rang out.

Derrin was down, screaming, holding both hands to his gut where blood pumped through his fingers. The guard Syn had kicked had pulled a pistol and was taking aim again, his hand trembling. Syn knocked the pistol away with a roar of frustration, then booted the man unconscious. The mercenary scooped Derrin up in his arms and raced over to the truck. 'Get your boy. You know any first aid?'

Cale nodded and helped Syn heave Derrin into the back of the truck. The youth howled in pain, then passed out. They returned for Bowden, leaving the heavy wheelchair behind.

'What a fucking to-do,' said Syn, helping Cale climb up. 'Hold on tight in there.' The mercenary slammed the rear doors shut, leaving Cale in the dark, smelling blood. A few seconds later the engine fired to life and they took off at speed.

Bask 45 – 499

Today as I looked out of the window I saw a speck on the hills which grew and became a transport skimmer. The cowards have returned.

Mason and I resolved at once to seal off the chamber – or to leave signs that we had. What we know now is just too big to release into the world. What the two of us have learned from our sessions with the Spark undermines the very fabric of the Hegemony, showing it up as the crawling thing that has wilfully kept us in darkness for almost half a millennium. What lives in this place, if used diligently, could change everything – we could catch up with the pre-Ruin, giving us another chance at the stars. Yes, I know it sounds insane – not only is the void a real, quantifiable thing, it is accessible with the right tools. The thought of it makes my fingers itch, then I have to remind myself that there are more immediate concerns. Namely, the thing's appetite.

We'd pushed ourselves, making the sessions longer, exposing ourselves to more and more each time, seeing how far we could go. One would sit and watch from the platform while the other explored the data corpus, travelling that iridescent web of knowledge until called back. I began to develop a migraine, and so did Mason, but we blamed it on lack of sleep, or just the overwhelming,

226

ceaseless breaking of boundaries. That was until one day, when he insisted on staying longer, to dive deeper than before. I tried to rouse him after thirty minutes but he was limp in my arms and his skin was like fire. I broke his contact with the torus and found the strength, somehow, to haul him to the safety of the platform. The Spark made a noise almost like a groan of despair – a deeply unsettling sound if ever I heard one. By the time Mason came to, I knew what the problem was, and the fact that we'd not seen it earlier was our own fault. So entranced by the complex beauty of the sea of knowledge opening up before us, we'd dived into technology, philosophy, history. What we'd ignored was the make-up of the thing that was the reservoir of all of this knowledge, the Spark itself that was administrator and heart of the data corpus. It needs us, craves us, to make sense of its own internal logic.

The damn thing was *feeding* on us.

Little wonder the thing's creators never fully activated it. I don't want to think what would have happened if we'd pushed ourselves any further.

We resolved, on seeing our inbound visitors, to stop anyone else going down there. They'd either kill themselves or run off to tell what they'd found, and I'm not sure which is worse.

I put on my best bored-for-a-whole-Death face and met them at the loading dock. The two imbeciles (who have reconciled – I wonder if he ever found out what she'd been doing?) were accompanied by none other than that oily grotesque Fermin. What he's doing all the way out here, I have no idea – he's cagey, spinning some bunkum about reviewing the geological findings from the original survey. I asked why he couldn't have sent an underling or left it to me, but he shrugged it off.

So, there we have it. All those months of locked-in cold were a total waste, I told them. The chamber below was just an attractive ruin, nothing more. I made sure I laid it on thick about their departure scuppering the enterprise – how we'd been unable to carry out the necessary mapping with only two of us present. They seemed guilty enough to not ask any questions. Fermin looks at me oddly though, even for him. I will keep a close watch.

vi. Overlooked

Kelbee had barely slept since she'd broken into her husband's briefcase. She kept the compact recording device tucked away in her waistband, not daring for a moment to let it out of her sight, though she didn't dare try to sneak away, not yet. On top of this was another looming presence, the words of the little medico that had slipped out so casually but had her heart stuttering every time she heard them back.

Paternity test.

The fear was so consuming she was almost glad to have a more immediate worry to take her mind off it.

Now the Lance Colonel was away again, staying away for a night, and she knew it was time to deliver what she'd found. By midday she'd worked up the nerve to go, checking for the tenth time that the device was secure under her clothes before locking the door behind her and taking the stairs to the foyer.

A woman was up on a stepladder near the doors, close

against the large portrait of the Seeker, cleaning it. Her head was wrapped in a scarf and she was slowly passing a cloth over the glass, each stroke meticulous. Kelbee paused by the pitted message board with its collection of dog-eared notices and bowed to the portrait, as was expected. The cleaning woman ignored her, and she hurried the usual muttering of thanks.

As she was about to walk through the doors there was a prickling feeling on the back of her neck, not unlike what she felt when passing through a checkpoint or one of the controlled areas of the city where the speaker posts were everywhere. It was something primal, a sense of being observed.

It's nothing, she told herself. *Stop acting like a frightened girl.*

She shot a glance behind.

The cleaner looked intent on the portrait, but there had been something just as Kelbee had turned, a flicker of motion, as if the woman had been watching her, then snatched her head away.

Pull yourself together, she thought. *You're jumping at shadows. Keep this up and someone will notice.*

She asked to speak to Brennev, but Nebn told her he was away. He wouldn't say where, and took her to a long room filled with desks. The low light was mostly the glow of flickering screens as a dozen men and women with headsets quietly went about their work, some moving with quiet purpose between stations, others motionless but for the blur of their fingers on keyboards.

'We monitor military comm traffic from here,' Nebn told her as he led her through the desks and to the back of the room where there was an alcove-office with a desk, a terminal and two chairs. He pulled a partition screen across; Kelbee could still hear the gentle thrum of keys, punctuated by the chirps and bleeps of monitoring equipment.

Only the military were allowed long-distance communications, that she knew of. A few weeks ago the idea of being next to people spying on them would have had her quivering, but she felt numbed to it now. She handed the tiny camera over to Nebn.

'Here,' she said. 'This is all I could get.' The hushed industry of the room behind the partition made her want to whisper.

He took it and flipped open a panel in its side, pulling out a black wire which he plugged into the terminal. She sat across from him and watched the light dance on his face as the pictures she'd taken flashed up on the screen. His eyes were intent as he scanned through them.

'I was in a hurry,' she said, feeling like she needed to explain.

'These could be useful,' he said. 'But they all relate to his old job overseeing the labour camp provisions. Nothing about the new posting.'

'What camps?'

He continued staring at the screen, absorbed. Then he seemed to register her question, though his voice remained distant. 'I'll tell you another time.'

She'd never seen him working, so absorbed in something else it was as if she were only an outline. It felt like an age before he finished reviewing the pictures. When he did, he flicked the screen off and unplugged the camera before pushing it across the desk towards her.

'For your first try, you've done well,' he said. 'You'll get more next time, I'm certain of it. We should get you set up for audio too, in case he lets anything slip when he talks.'

'Next... time,' she said in a flat voice. 'Nebn, I'm not doing that again. I was terrified he was going to walk in and find me.'

His eyebrows rose, just a fraction. He rested his elbows on the desk and leaned towards her. 'Of course you can do it. You're a natural. Believe me, it gets easier.'

'You're not listening to me. It's not that I can't do it. I won't.'

'Listen—'

'No!' The word shot out like a bullet, before she remembered the room full of people on the other side of the partition. Her cheeks grew hot and she lowered her voice to a hiss. 'He was *there*, just a few steps away. If he'd been sober he would have seen me and I don't think even the baby would have kept me safe.' She rested her palm on her stomach. 'You have to get Brennev to get me out.'

'Tell me what happened, from the start.'

She told him everything that had happened to her, from the clinic to the moment she found her way into the Lance Colonel's briefcase. He listened in silence, nodding at her to go on when she paused. It felt like she was being assessed, and the fact that it was him doing it made it surreal and worse. She left out the part about the briefcase code being her marriage date, not really knowing why.

'It sounds to me like you did exactly the right thing. Did he know his case had been tampered with?'

'No.'

'Then it's fine. Listen, I know it must have scared you. I was frightened too, the first time I did something like this. But you did really, really well. He was nowhere near spotting you.'

An image skittered across her mind of Nebn, half-naked in a cold apartment, sneaking a glance at stolen documents in the dead of night. 'I don't want to do it again.'

He sat back, contemplating her with a furrowed brow. The expression was alien, so different from the man she thought she knew; a detachment that reminded her of Brennev. This wasn't the man that had snatched a furtive kiss under the shade of a tree, that had run his fingers over her skin. She felt disorientated.

'I don't want to do it,' she repeated.

'Kelbee, many people are risking a lot. For you.'

'Just for me?'

He raised his hands. 'For us, I know. But it's more than that. This is about the greater good.'

'I don't care about "the greater good",' she snapped back. 'I care that somewhere out there a lab is testing a sample that will tell him the child isn't his. It could arrive any day, and you want me to go back to that? Don't you care?'

'Of course I care.' He sounded angry now. 'But Brennev's a hard man, Kelbee. Fair, but hard. He's lived outside the law for a long time and he doesn't do favours for nothing. Either we help him or we're out on our own.' He reached for her hand and scowled when she snatched it away. 'If I told you I had a way to make the lab test go away, would you feel better then?'

She looked away. Tears were creeping up but she used anger to force them back. 'Fine,' she said in a low voice. She wanted to ask more, like how in the world he could make a paternity test disappear, but couldn't bring herself to say any more.

He held her gaze for a moment but then looked away. His cheeks were flushed. 'Thank you,' he said, sounding choked. 'It's for the best.'

The sound of the people typing on the other side of the partition was like a clamour. Nebn took a breath and forced an even tone. 'When will you next have a chance?'

'Tonight, maybe.'

He nodded and tapped the camera on the desk with his finger. 'Hold onto this in case you get the chance, but we'll rig you with a wire as well.'

She nodded, still avoiding his eyes. 'He sometimes talks when he drinks.' She slipped the camera into her pocket.

Nebn pulled back the partition. They left the busy room behind and she hated the idea that they'd been overheard, though as they went every face seemed intent on the screens. He led her along several turns of the tunnel, passing through some heavy doors, the silence hanging thick between them. They took some metal stairs down into what appeared to be a workshop, the walls covered with tools and the benches overflowing with equipment. There was grease in the air and dark marks on the floor.

Tani was at a worktable, leaning over a mad jumble of wires and tubes with a soldering iron when they entered; she saw them and straightened, waving them over. She tucked back a lock of her yellow hair with a grimy hand and flashed a wide smile.

For a second Kelbee hated her, hated her elegance, the way she looked even covered in grime.

'How's it, you two?' Tani arched her back with an audible click followed by a grunt. 'I could do with a break.'

Nebn ignored the question. 'We need Kelbee fitted with a wire. Something discreet.'

Tani arched a perfect eyebrow at Kelbee, who looked away. 'All right,' she said. 'We can do that. Follow me, please.'

She led Kelbee over to one of the other benches and rooted around under piles of gear, at last coming back with a bright orange case made from hard plastic. Nebn wandered over to the other side of the room and poked around in the equipment spilling from a cabinet.

Tani opened the orange case and pulled out a grey disk as thick as her thumb attached to a thin belt. Next, she retrieved a tiny beige nub.

'This is a microphone,' she said. 'This round bit is the control box. Lift up your shirt so I can fit it.' Tani strapped the band around Kelbee's hips and tightened it. 'How's that?'

'A little higher,' said Kelbee. 'It might show if I wore a dress.'

As Tani moved the belt to sit just below her bump, Kelbee watched Nebn out of the corner of her eye. His eyes looked sad. She felt a pang of remorse, but still the anger was there. The sight of him at work – focused, determined – was unsettling, at odds with the gentle hours they'd spent together. Which was the real him?

A bitter little voice whispered in her ear. Did he want her for her, or for her husband? Perhaps that's why he'd sought her out, drawn her away from everything she knew into a danger that seemed so irresistible at the time but now made her sick to her stomach with worry. She looked away as she saw him turn, rather than meet his gaze. Not for the first time, despite everything that had happened, she wished that it would all just go away.

Tani tightened the belt. 'Just a moment, I need to calibrate.' She fiddled with the control box until it chimed. A light on the grey disk blinked on. Tani hummed, satisfied, then helped Kelbee to rearrange her clothes.

'There, all set to go. Touch the casing twice to activate, three times to turn off, like so.' Tani tapped a long finger on the hard shape under the dress three times in quick succession and Kelbee felt the unit pulse. 'Got it?'

She nodded, smoothing her shirt down. The control unit was invisible.

Tani handed her the beige nub, which was sticky on one side. 'Put it where you think it'll get the best feed. Cleavage is good, but make sure it's not showing.' She caught Kelbee's eye and tilted her head at Nebn in a silent question.

Kelbee closed her eyes and shook her head.

Tani sighed but gave her an encouraging smile, reaching out to give her upper arm a gentle squeeze, then called out to Nebn. 'You can leave that alone, you'll break it.'

Nebn put the power drill back in its cradle on the wall. 'This place is a mess.'

'Great minds thrive on clutter. I don't expect you to understand. Now maybe you should walk Kelbee out.' She gave him a meaningful look.

Nebn's brow furrowed; he reddened, but held the door open.

Kelbee shot her a grateful look, feeling guilty for how insecure she'd allowed herself to get. Tani wasn't the problem, Nebn was. The way he'd been with her, like he was her employer instead of the man who'd fathered her child. How could he treat her like a piece to be moved around? She tried to breathe deep, to clear her mind, but the sharp little voice saying terrible things soured the air.

Nebn followed her out and they made for the sewer entrance. After some minutes of silence, she felt a tentative hand in the small of her back. A fresh burst of irritation made her walk faster, pulling away.

The outer door was manned by the usual masked guards. They flanked the door like statues, eyes staring straight ahead. As they approached, Nebn stopped her with a touch on her shoulder.

'Be safe,' he said.

She stared at the ceiling, her voice terse. 'I hope so.'

'You're still angry with me.'

'I'm fine, I just need to get home,' she said. 'There's a lot to do.'

He took a step closer. 'I want to see you again. By ourselves, in our own place. It feels like it's been for ever.'

'I'm sorry you feel so neglected,' she snapped.

He winced, shook his head. 'I know this is hard for you. I wish I could go myself.'

Her smile was bitter. 'I bet you do. Tell me something: have you? Done this before?'

His face went pale.

'How many others?' she pressed. 'How many times have you gone through a man's wife to get what you wanted? Is there always a child, just to hook them, or are there other ways?'

'Kelbee—'

'It's very clever. Get the little mouse into bed, knock her up so she's afraid and then she's yours.' The skin on her face felt tight and drawn. He looked like she'd slapped him, but something inside her snarled for blood. 'What happens then, when they're used up?'

Before she could continue he banged open a nearby door and pulled her in after him. Two men were sat on low bunks talking. They shot to their feet as Nebn entered.

'Out!' he barked. They hurried out of the room and he shut the door.

His pupils were enormous and his face was flushed. Kelbee shut her eyes and waited for the blow to fall, but instead she felt his hand on her belly. His palm was warm even through her clothes and his breathing was ragged.

Then, a sensation inside of her. A ghost-flicker, on the very edge of feeling that felt like something responding to his touch – at once a part of her, yet separate. She opened her eyes and saw his were tinged red.

He opened his mouth and breathed a single word. 'Never.'

Kelbee felt her anger collapse in on itself. She took a deep breath and exhaled, then grabbed him. 'I'm sorry,' she said. Her face was wet.

He stood, rigid as stone, and every second felt like an age. She was paralysed, terrified she'd smashed them both to pieces in that white-hot moment. Then his arms enveloped her, and a deep sob wracked her body.

He just held her for a while, not speaking. Then he pulled back and looked into her eyes.

'Never,' he repeated, soft but with his entire being behind it.

She nodded, cuffing at her tears. He kissed her cheeks, then her lips, then used his thumbs to wipe the rest away. She held on like a drowning woman and kissed him back.

Nebn lifted her up and she wrapped her legs around his hips, crushing him to her. He carried her over to one of the bunks and laid her down, his mouth still on hers. She tore at his clothes, desperate to feel him, taste his sweat. There was salt on her lips as her legs crushed him to her, knuckles white as she clung to the frame above her head.

When she came, she bit down on his shoulder to stop herself from crying out, and tasted blood.

They lay together as the sweat cooled on their skin, their legs laced. He ran his fingers through her hair as she traced the lines of his chest.

'You know, if I had my way no one would have to do this,' Nebn said, staring at the ceiling.

'This? I quite like this.'

He ran his nails through her hair. 'The sneaking, the spying. The blowing things up.'

'You do that?'

'Not me personally, but yes. Brennev calls it active resistance.'

'You disapprove?'

He was quiet for a while before answering. 'Brennev does things the way he knows how. He'd go a lot further if he could. He's building an army.'

Kelbee thought about this. It seemed so unlikely. None of the people she'd seen in the tunnels, save for a few guards, were armed. If there was an army, it must be somewhere else. Her mind went back to the Quincentennial, the endless ranks of marching troops. How could anyone think about taking on that many soldiers?

Nebn answered her unspoken thoughts. 'He's been working for years to build up our reserves, training a corps for open warfare. And the bigger it gets, the greater his influence.'

She thought about what this could mean. Gunfire in the streets. Buildings on fire. 'It scares me,' she said.

'Me too. And it gets us nowhere new. All we do is burn the regime to the ground and set up another, repeating old mistakes. Nothing changes except the symbols the people scrape to.'

Kelbee sat up on one elbow. 'Is it really that hopeless?'

He looked at her, then away, embarrassed. 'I'm sorry. I don't want to scare you.'

She kissed his neck. 'I don't believe you.'

He looked at her, questioning.

'You wouldn't carry on if there was no hope at all.'

He stretched, looking up at the ceiling. 'Remember the room I showed you before? I keep going back there, just as I keep rereading the scraps I have about the pre-Ruin, because I can't help but feel there's something more.'

'How so?'

'If you look past all the warnings, the moralising that's been built into any of the texts we have, you can see that they were so advanced because they kept the information flowing between them freely. One side of the world seems to have known exactly, instantly, what the other was doing, meaning they had some way of talking to each other that makes the Hegemony's relay network look like smoke signals; there's no way they could have been so co-ordinated otherwise.'

'So, talking is the way out of this?'

'I know it sounds crazy, but imagine if you had a truth in your hand, something life-changing. A cure for a disease, or reports of abuse of power. Imagine if, instead of trying to slip that into people's heads through subversion, you could just tell them in a way that couldn't be intercepted. Free information, free thought.'

She thought about it, because she could see how much it meant to him. 'I don't think you can get around the fact that what we tell each other is altered by what we want, even if we don't mean to do it.'

His eyes lowered. 'It's just a fantasy. But I still think Brennev's way is wrong, repeating what went before even though he feels righteous. It's up to me to carry on trying to find another way. I'll shine a light in the dark even if it's inefficient and messy and probably futile. Pamphlets and graffiti. Who knows?' he smiled. 'Maybe it'll catch on.'

She didn't answer, just lay back against him, enjoying the scent of him and her intertwined. His heart had calmed and now drummed a gentle beat inside his chest. He ran a finger over the curve of her shoulder, as if committing it to memory.

'I'm still afraid, Nebn. What if he finds out?'

'I've not forgotten. I have a contact in the central labs; they know which date your exam took place.'

'But how—'

'Accidents happen. Sometimes samples get contaminated, vials break.'

'They'll just do another.'

'For the right price, the result is what we want it to be. He's no reason to push for more tests anyway – in fact it might look bad for him, with his new authority.'

She knew he was right. The trip to the Galamb had been about being seen, bragging rights. Despite this, the unease still ate at her.

'I need to go, it's getting late.'

Outside, the two men they'd evicted stood some way down the corridor with their backs to the wall. Nebn waved them back into the room; Kelbee repressed a laugh.

At the outer door he kissed her goodbye. 'Stay safe,' he whispered in her ear.

Fleet Coast

A half-collapsed warehouse on the outskirts was where they abandoned the skimmer and moved to the ground truck Syn had stashed there. Before they left, they piled rotting wood panels and rusted roof sheeting against the doors. If they were lucky, it should buy them enough time to get to the coast.

The inside of the truck looked like a field infirmary after a battle. Derrin drifted in and out of a fitful sleep. Cale had sedated him as best he could with the meagre supplies Syn had laid in and bandaged his gut wound, but feared that it would most likely have just one outcome. He'd seen it before: the sweating, the clenched jaw, the dark spread of blood through the rough cloth of the dressing. It would not be quick. He could only hope the boy would last the journey.

'You fucked this up, old man,' he told himself aloud.

Derrin's eyes moved behind closed lids and he moaned at whatever fevered dream had him. The skin of his forehead was stretched tight over bone.

Cale went to rub his aching eyes, stopped. His fingers were gummy with old blood.

On the other side of the shifting trailer lay his son. Like Derrin, Bowden's unconscious form lay on a row of canvas seats pressed into service as a cot. A clear plastic line from one arm led up to a drip bag hanging from the roof and every time they hit a bump it swayed madly, sloshing the liquid inside.

Rushed, aimless, stupid. Dumb luck we survived with just one casualty.

He checked Bowden's pulse and found it fluttering, faint but regular. A small mercy. The skinny chest under the blankets moved up and down, almost imperceptible. Under the poor light of the swinging bulb the face was more how Cale remembered it; perhaps just a little gaunter in the cheeks, and there were deeper shadows under the eyes. They would have to find a way of feeding him soon. If only he'd looked for a chart, or some other indication of his condition, he might know what needed to be done; as it was, he was reduced to playing guessing games with his son's life. He lay his palm on the clammy forehead, wishing he could share life through the touch of his skin.

What had he expected to feel in this moment, here, with him? Relief? There was none of that. He realised, as Bowden's faint pulse beat against his palm, that ever since that day on the steppe – when the message had come – he'd been headlong, never pausing. He'd been so sure that once he had Bowden in his care the helplessness would go away. He would know what to do. He'd always known what to do. But here he was, with two young men's blood under his nails and filled with a brand-new fear, one he hadn't counted on. If Bowden died now, it was no one's fault but his.

Everything ahead was uncertain, vague. When they got to where they were going, he still needed to find the way in. The place could be abandoned for all he knew. Perhaps they were not there any more, the people he'd once called friends – it had been so long. If by some slim chance they remained, would they even let him in?

He remembered the machines, the ones that set bone and stitched skin, spindly mechanical arms moving in a blur. He'd seen men left for dead made whole with only pale scars to show for their ordeal. Derrin might live, but Bowden? There was nothing visible, no obvious wound for the machines to work on. Besides a pulse and shallow breath, there was little to show that he was even alive. The fear gripped his heart in its claw and twisted when he realised this might be all there was left.

He ran his fingers through Bowden's short hair, noting how it had started to thin at the temples. At the hairline was another scar he didn't remember.

'Made things worse for you, boy,' he told him.

Not a boy now, he corrected himself. There were lines on his face now, from laughter or maybe anger. The hands were thicker, callused. This was a man, with his own burdens.

Always enough of my boy left in him, though.

He'd had to do it, he pleaded with the jury in his mind. He'd done it badly, rushed it, but he knew there was no other way as soon as he heard that name.

Sessarmin. Shadows hung off it. He'd heard the stories even before he'd joined the underground. Never spoken of above a whisper, as if there was something malevolent behind those grey walls; rumours of isolation, experiments, torture. Pain and fear and no hope of escape. For the few of them in those early days of the movement, when every day was fraught with danger, it had held a special kind of horror.

They'd always been so careful, but sometimes people got caught and when they did they were always shipped to Sessarmin for 're-education'. Instead of covering it up, the authorities advertised it in bulletins, used it to show their benevolence.

Look at our compassion, they said. Taking the time to fix what had gone wrong in subversive minds, shepherding the misguided back onto the path. After those men and women entered the sanatorium, they were never seen again. When he'd heard his son was in that place he knew he had to act fast, no matter how messy it got.

He pulled the blanket higher over Bowden's chest, checking the beat of his heart again. *Better to die out here, under the sky, than buried in that place.*

Something else nagged him, sitting in the corner of his mind. Now that the adrenaline from the escape had burned away it was more insistent. He'd expected more guards, more orderlies. A watch on the wards, even. But there hadn't been, other than the guards by the entrance. Was it possible the whole thing had been too easy? As the thought crossed his mind, Derrin coughed himself awake, blood rattling in his throat.

'It hurts,' he said, squirming. His pale fingers pressed against the rough dressing as if he could squeeze the pain out; Cale had been forced to pry his hands away from the wound to be able to bind it. The cloth was sodden, almost black.

Cale shushed, patting his shoulder. There was nothing else to do, no more painkillers. There was a good chance he might not last the night. 'You'll be all right,' he said.

'I'm going to die, aren't I?' The wide eyes were bloodshot, but his voice was calm.

'No. I'm going to get you help.'

'You can tell me, you know.' Derrin tried a smile but it came out as a grimace. 'Not afraid. Just wish it didn't fucking… *hurt* so much!' He twisted, snorting through his nose as another surge hit him. He grabbed Cale's hand and gripped it hard until the feeling waned, a single tear tracing a streak through the grime on his face. After a while his breathing calmed, and he uncurled a little. 'In the corner,' he said, waving at the far end of the trailer.

Cale looked where he was pointing and spotted what looked like the top of a bottle sticking out from behind an old toolbox. Picking it up, he brushed away a greasy layer of dust. There was no label and the liquid inside was glutinous, leaving outlines on the inside of the glass. In the low light, it was a dark amber.

'Rakk?' asked Derrin, hopeful.

Cale pulled the stopper with a *squeak-pop* and gave the stuff a sniff. He snatched his head back as the fumes stung his nostrils – something like cheap rakk, but more like paint thinner. Whatever it was, it was booze, and it was strong.

'Give it here,' gasped Derrin.

Cale sat on his haunches. Before handing the bottle over he swilled a mouthful of the amber liquid, finding it acrid and harsh but probably not poisonous; he swallowed, feeling it burn down his throat. He passed it to Derrin, who took a deep pull. The boy gagged, doubling up, but waved Cale's hand away and took another swig before handing the bottle back.

Derrin wiped the back of his hand across his mouth. 'Drink with me.'

Cale rested his back against the wall of the cab. They passed the bottle back and forth between them in silence. Cale took small sips, knowing Derrin needed it more and wanting to keep a clear head. Even so, he could feel it seeping into his blood. After a while Derrin lapsed into a doze.

Cale sat back and watched over both of his charges, the murmur of the engine running through him. From the cab, he could hear Syn humming an old marching tune as he drove. The shard of daylight under the door that connected trailer and cab was dimming as night came on.

'It must have been bad, what happened with you two.' Derrin's voice surprised him, and he realised he'd also drifted off. The youth had propped himself up on his elbows.

Cale didn't answer straight away, his gaze fixed on his son's form. Finally, he said, 'We disagreed.'

'About what?'

'Lots of things, as he got older. The last time was the worst.' He rested his elbows on his knees. 'I left his mother when he was young. I saw him, sometimes, but it wasn't enough. He started lashing out. I don't blame him.'

'Couldn't you have stayed?'

Cale shook his head. 'We married too young. It was arranged by our families, but it wasn't long before I got my

248

commission. They kept me busy with little wars, always some insurgency popping up. I found I was good at it, and when I came home to her...' Cale paused, looking at the floor. 'I didn't know how to be married. Always got away as soon as I could.' His eyes went back to Bowden. 'When he was just a baby, something happened in the field. It was bad. They... didn't execute me because of my rank. They just kicked me out.'

Derrin frowned. For a moment, his gaze became clear and intense. 'So, you just went home. After.'

Cale shook his head. 'The regiment was my real home, then all of a sudden it wasn't. I didn't know the woman who shared my bed and I didn't know where I fitted in. I suppose I left to find out where that was.' He worried the edge of a fingernail. 'It was quite the scandal.'

Derrin watched him for a moment and Cale felt like he was being picked apart. Perhaps it was the fever or the wound, but he'd not seen the boy look so... determined. Death was like that sometimes. Before the end came a terrible kind of sharpness.

Derrin coughed and curled up in a ball on his cot. When he relaxed, his eyes were docile again as he gazed at the ceiling. 'I know what that's like,' he said. 'I left home because I didn't fit in. Got on the first ship that would take me. I thought it would be an adventure, you know? Stupid kid.'

'Everyone thinks that,' said Cale.

Derrin took a shuddering breath. 'What did you do afterwards?'

Cale could see the youth's eyes drooping. He'd be asleep

249

soon, so he kept his voice low as he answered. 'I studied. Did things with my hands. Made new friends. Thought maybe I could start at the beginning. I met a girl who liked me back. Got married again.'

'What was her name?'

'Aime. She was a beauty.' He smiled, remembering. 'She reminded me I wasn't as ancient as I felt.'

'Did your son like her?' Derrin's voice slurred.

'He never met her. She wanted to, wanted to make things right between us. We even arranged to meet, just the three of us, but she was out when he got to the house. He wanted to join the Army and I was afraid for him because he was barely a man, so I told him not to. We both got angry; we fought.'

He watched the light play over Bowden's face.

'He called me selfish, a coward. He left and she never got to meet him.'

Cale realised Derrin was asleep. He sat in the silence, feeling the movement of the truck on the road.

I wanted to shield him, he thought. *Was that so selfish?*

It still felt raw, even after all those years. Aime had come to him after Bowden had stormed out and soothed him as only she could. If he closed his eyes, he could still hear the music of her voice, feel her small, strong hands kneading his neck. Soft lips, kissing the crown of his head.

She'd told him it would blow over. She'd always look after him, she'd said.

She was wrong about so many things that day.

Syn's voice came from the cab, jolting Cale into the present. 'We're here.'

•

Syn paid cash to an old fisherman for the motorboat. Under the cover of darkness Cale carried his son while Syn helped Derrin to hobble over the shingle to the boat on the edge of the weak surf. The craft was ten metres long, a thin launch with a covered section in the bows, a stern tiller and single outboard motor. Syn left to dispose of the truck; as soon as it had chugged out of sight behind the scrubby dunes Cale waded into the water and pushed the boat out until he was up to his waist. Clear of the beach, the hull bobbed on the waves, held by a land anchor. He clambered aboard. Bowden was unresponsive and Derrin was hunched in silent agony, clutching his wounded abdomen with bloodied fingers.

Marna was still hidden and the night was black. There was a suggestion of old seaweed on the breeze that flapped at the stern cover; the only other sound was the regular bump of the hull on the shallow beach. Cale stood ready in the stern, one hand on the rope that tethered them to the land, watching the darkened dunes. After a while Syn emerged on foot.

'Salt marsh just over the hill,' he said, wading into the sea. 'Left the truck there.' Cale grabbed him by the arm and hauled him, dripping, over the side.

The old engine gave off a gout of smoke and a roar as it fired. Cale feared they'd have the whole village down on them, but no one came. He revved up and powered them out into the wide bay where the sea was almost pond-flat. Cale looked up and saw the clouds had cleared. The silhouette of the Lattice was etched against the twinkling light clusters set in the surface of the sky, the claw marks of some gigantic wild beast. He found the one he was looking for: the Petty Light – favourite of sailors, always bright in clear skies. He aimed the bows towards it, heading out to sea where the troughs grew deeper and the rollers were capped with spume.

They alternated watches at the tiller. When it was Cale's turn to rest he lay close to Bowden's still body to reassure himself there was still breath, a heart still beating. Sleep was impossible, so he listened to Syn humming a wordless tune as he kept them on their course. After a while he rose and took his second watch, waving away Syn's offer of company. The sea and the pinpricked vault overhead seemed boundless and he felt like its enormity would swamp them in their tiny craft. Not like last time, aboard the giant cargo hulk. That had been different, like being on an island.

A few hours in he realised, with some surprise, that he'd not felt sick once.

When Ras rose it was muted by clouds that had formed in the pre-dawn sky. The wind began to pick up, frothing the crests around them and rolling the little launch. In the distance, the coastline came into view, indistinct in the murk. A steel-grey strip, dark against the low clouds and the green sea.

Syn emerged from under the cover, sitting on the gunwale and watching the cliffs come closer. 'Never seen the Fleet Coast before,' he said. 'Always assumed people were exaggerating.'

Cale didn't reply, keeping his eyes on the approaching land. He began to make out details, patches of light and dark amid the uniform grey. He could now see the ash colour of the Walls, the ancient defences of the Seeker's country that encircled the entire peninsula.

The Walls had kept the monster waves at bay after the Ruin. When those few survivors had emerged, it was easy to see how they might consider themselves a chosen people.

'Skies,' said Syn, 'isn't that a sight?'

The Walls had been built atop sheer chalk cliffs, but that stone was all but invisible now under a jacket of compacted metal. Embedded into the rock face, piled almost to the height of the Walls' base, were ships. Thousands of ships. Mouldering iron and broken, jagged steel slabs, left there by the waves that had followed the cataclysm. Centuries of wind and tide had trimmed and rusted the fleet trapped against the stone, pushing uncounted tons of metal into the surface until it blended with the land. The cliffs for a dozen kilometres in each direction were a honeycomb of caves ranging from the size of a doorway to cavernous arches formed by smashed-open hulls of ancient vessels.

They neared the shore and made out dark windows peering from beneath birds' nests, the red curves of hulls bulging out from the surface of the cliffs like giant rusted blisters. At the base of it all was a narrow pebble beach. Cale ran the launch in close and killed the engine in a splutter of smoke, then he and Syn jumped into the shallow water and scraped the old boat up onto the beach.

They set up a makeshift camp under the shelter of an arch formed by the collapsed deck of an ancient freighter. Twenty metres above their heads it had snapped off from the bows embedded in the rock, the remainder of the ship coming to rest on the sea bed. What had once been the main deck of the vessel formed a slanting roof under which they pitched their tents and dug a fire pit. The structure whistled and groaned in the mild breeze.

'Looks safe enough,' said Syn, settling Derrin into one of the tents.

Cale considered the overhang. 'If the tides haven't shifted it by now, it'll hold.'

'It'd be just our fucking luck. Come all this way only to die in a rockfall. Or… ship fall.' Syn scratched the stubble on his cheek. 'Either way, shitty way to go.'

Cale checked their position on the old map they'd brought along. The paper was thin and supple from use and marked all over in a dozen different hands.

'What's the plan, buck?'

'You stay here with them,' said Cale. 'Get some food on, make sure they're warm. I'm going to check our position.'

'Right you are.'

Cale set off across the shingle, aiming for a small headland formed by a mishmash of girders and hulls. After centuries the metal had become so compressed and twisted by the elements that it had taken on an organic quality, like the discarded hive of some huge insect. When he reached the point, he set about clambering over the low spine of metal and rock, avoiding jagged holes that dropped away into darkness. The sea echoed within the structure, dripping and sloshing through caverns formed by ancient cargo holds and wheelhouses. As he reached the spine of the rise he stood and looked out over the cove on the far side.

Roughly a third of the way around Cale saw an oblong

protrusion jutting into the sea like a metal tongue. The flat, angular deck of a military carrier vessel; built to last. Unmovable and massive, even against the tides, the ship remained mostly intact and the beach had built up around it, making the cove a rough heart shape.

He remembered this place.

He looked back towards their camp, shielding his eyes as a gust of wind whipped up the spray. There was the overhang and the tiny figure of Syn moving about, though it was hard to see what he was doing; more clouds had come streaming in from the east and the light had dropped. Cale decided to press on before the rain came.

He picked his way down the far side of the metal hill and along the beach towards the old carrier. Redcrumn scuttled out of the way of his boots as he walked, their pearlescent carapaces winking in the light, their tiny foreclaws held up in defiance of this alien invader. Cale heard the growl of thunder and picked up the pace.

The side of the carrier was a cliff of towering red and grey that stretched higher and higher as he approached. The entrance would be here, somewhere near. If they'd stayed, if it was the same after all these years. What if they'd abandoned this place? He would have done, had it been down to him. Too static, too risky. Regardless, he kept walking, hoping to drown out the growing clamour of his doubts.

When he reached the metal wall of the carrier's side, running at right angles to the beach, he followed it back to where it met the cliff face. There, just where the giant ship merged with the amalgam of other vessels, he spotted a large flat section that lay flush against the cliff: the remains of an elevator used to lift aircraft from the bowels of the carrier to the flight deck. He approached the slab and found the edge, green with moss and creepers; a curtain that hid the cave behind. Pulling the moist vegetation aside, he ducked his head and shouldered his way in.

His hand torch was a lonely spot in the echoing darkness. It picked out a circle of the side of the carrier, shimmering off a dozen tiny rivulets running down the metal wall. There should have been a door there, big enough to fit a fighter craft through, with man-sized access ports all around. That was how they got in and out in the old days, but the weak light from his torch found only smooth metal. He pressed his fingers against the hull, hoping for something: movement, a sound, a trick of the light. There was nothing, only the gentle curve of the hull running down to the pebbles of the beach. His fingers came away damp and gritty with rust.

Cale began to search for the entrance that he knew must be there, feeling the rough surface, sometimes knocking and listening for the telltale hollow ring of a concealed door. Other than the seams and rivets where one panel met another, there was barely a mark. He tried to still the pounding of his heart and the rising nausea, checking again and again, becoming more desperate with every pass.

After an hour, at the bottom near the shingle, he found something. Hidden by moss and indistinct in the dark was the faint patina of a plasma torch. Effort had been made to hide the marks but not all had been erased. He took a step back and allowed his eye to run over the surface, starting at the blistering and running upwards. He saw it now, invisible from more than a step away and darkened by oxidisation.

An oval hatchway – not only sealed but erased.

Knowing what to look for now he soon found another three portals, all sealed and disguised. Whoever had done this had gone to a lot of trouble, filing down the seams until the hull appeared unmarked.

Cale stepped back, his jaw clenched tight. They were long gone.

A dam in him burst. Fear, held in check for so long, rushed through him, stealing the strength from his legs. He dropped to the floor, the torch falling from nerveless fingers and shattering on stone, swamping him in darkness. The shingle was rough against his hands and the grit scoured his cheek. Somewhere, in a nearby cave, the wind picked up and howled like an animal.

There was no help here.

Cale stumbled into camp just as the storm hit. The wind whipped across the sea from the west and howled down the coast, making the cliffs moan like a thousand empty mouths.

Syn must have seen the weather coming in because the small camp had been moved back against the face of the cliff, still underneath the broken ship and nestled between two jutting shoulders of rock that formed a sheltered pocket from the crosswinds. Cale heard him shout a greeting but didn't respond. He tramped up to one of the tents and went inside, pulling it shut behind him.

Bowden was stretched out on a thin foam mat, a drip-bag still attached to his arm. Cale couldn't look at him, not yet. There was too much now, regrets and failures all screaming at once, and he had no answers. He slumped down on a spare mat and curled up, shutting his eyes as the wind made the side of the tent crack.

He awoke some hours later, a dream still jabbing at his eyes. Every adversary, every person who'd ever spoken against him had formed a single buzzing voice and a single bitter face. His first wife was there. Men he'd killed. Even Bowden, but he'd been pale and cold and silent.

There was a moment of stillness, then he realised that the nightmare was real. He'd brought his son here to die.

Fool, they said, echoing, laughing. *We always knew.*

His mouth was thick with thirst. Something had woken him, a noise from outside. A shift of gravel, the sound of stone on stone. Syn, on watch, he thought. Holding things together while he wallowed.

Get up, do something. You're not dead yet, and neither are they.

Get up and try.

Cale pushed the flap of the tent aside and the cold night air on his face drove away the last threads of the dream. The storm had passed, though the waves still crashed heavy on the beach. There was scant light to go by: between him and the other tent he could see the outline of their little launch. Syn must have dragged it all the way up the beach on his own.

He ran a hand over the gunwale of the boat, feeling the rough wood under his palm.

Seaweed and fish and engine oil. A good boat, reliable and simple.

There were other places to look, he told himself. A

hundred coves where they might find a sign. And if not, there were other places he could try, all the way to Aspedair if necessary. As long as Bowden was breathing, he had to try.

Another pang of guilt hit him as he remembered Derrin. The wound could kill him in the next few hours, and there was nothing they could do.

I should check on them both, he thought.

As he straightened, Cale felt the hairs on his arms spring up. There was a whooshing sound behind him and without thinking he threw himself to one side and rolled. Behind him, the boat disintegrated in a white-hot explosion. He shielded his eyes and scrambled backwards, trying to put some distance between him and whatever had attacked. His back and neck felt raw, burned. He remembered that sound, that guttural *whoosh-thump.*

Plasma cannon, heavy bore.

He saw the blue-white flash of the second shot hit the burning wreckage of the boat and smash it to splinters. Somewhere, a voice was shouting and he realised it was Syn who'd appeared at his side. He could see the other man's lips moving but could barely hear anything over the ringing in his ears. '—ing walker!'

The ground shook, rhythmic thumps that vibrated all through his body. Whatever it was it was big, and it was getting nearer. Cale looked around, trying to spot the attacker, fighting to clear his head. If he could just get Bowden out of the tent, he might make it to the cliffs, hide in one of the caves.

A spotlight hit him, a white-stark flare in front of his eyes. The glare pierced his eyelids and he threw his arms up as a shield. A noise, deafening in volume, blared and his head rang and he felt the beach rise up and hit him in the back.

He tasted blood and there was something wet in his ears. A voice sounded, metallic and harsh.

'STAY STILL,' it said.

Then another voice, human.

'Wait. I know him.'

vii. Complication

The grand foyer of the Tower buzzed with the chatter of hundreds of dignitaries, officers and functionaries from all over the capital, trailing their wives in ever-shifting mandalas of conversation. The space echoed like a cavern, feet shuffling amid colonnades, the crowd hunkered under a bluish cloud of heavy incense and smoke. Other than the gaudy Quincentennial banners – so common in the last weeks as to almost fade from view – the Tower was sparse, brushed stone and marble. Austere, like the man that had (so it was told) built the whole immense structure in just the first year of his benign rule.

At least it's cooler, Kelbee thought. *The power is always on here.*

A pair of soldiers in ornate domed helmets at the far end of the hall raised their bugles and blew a discordant blast that cut through the chatter. There was a pause, then the patterns unwound, feet shuffling to take their place. In just a few minutes the length of the room cleared, hedged by two lines of dress uniforms and expectant faces.

The Lance Colonel's touch on her arm was light as he directed her to their spot. She'd never seen him this nervous.

The hush became a physical thing, anticipation hanging heavier than the incense. Then the huge doors between the buglers yawned open, and from it came a procession. The Lord Factor, head of his office, seemed not to notice the throng as he chatted in a low voice with another man in Teller's robes of pure, shimmering gold. Behind them were academics from the Elucidon who looked like they would rather be anywhere else but here, faces down in the puffed collars of their robes. Then came the heads of the military – Fleet and Army – two old men who couldn't avoid falling into step with each other as they marched down the aisle.

Last, in the centre of attendants that buzzed like flies, the Venerable Guide herself. Tall, bald, her stride easy and proud. Her gaze was sharp and her expression fierce, like she might punch holes in the walls just by staring.

Kelbee's heart felt like it might escape through her ears. The old man was there again, like a stain on her mind, and next to him the face of a little girl at a dirty window, eyes that were pools of sorrow. She swallowed, hoping her mask hadn't slipped.

The procession was glacial, stopping to speak to this or that person. The Guide herself spoke to few individuals, seeming more content to observe, acknowledging the odd bow with a raised hand or an inclination of the head. Every gesture was contained, measured, as if eking out a finite supply of movement. When she did speak, it was quick and left the interlocutor looking drained.

Kelbee shifted, longing for the evening to be over already. In the last few days her breasts felt like they'd swollen to twice their normal size and had become so tender that even light clothing was uncomfortable. The heavy material of her gown was raw and awkward, finding new places to irritate every time she moved. She'd left Tani's recording device at home – with this much security, she couldn't take the risk.

The Lance Colonel patted her hand. 'Don't be nervous,' he said, though he could have been speaking to himself.

She gave him a dutiful smile. The procession came level with them and Kelbee kept her gaze low, respectful and deferential as was proper. The shuffling throng passed, and she breathed a small sigh of relief.

A long, slender finger touched her under the chin. It lifted her face up until she was staring into striking green eyes. Her breath caught in her throat as the Guide stood before her, her mouth turned up at the corners. Her expression was quizzical, faintly amused.

Kelbee didn't dare move.

'Beautiful,' said the Guide in her deep voice. It was a voice that was felt as much as it was heard. 'Where did you find such a specimen, Lance Colonel?'

By her side Kelbee felt the Lance Colonel snap to attention. 'My wife is from the provinces, Venerable Guide,' he said.

'Which one, I wonder? That hair…' The finger left Kelbee's chin and traced the edge of her forehead, running along a blue-black lock that hung loose.

The Lance Colonel hesitated, and the Guide tutted gently,

the edges of her mouth curling into something approaching a smile. 'You should know your wife better, Lance Colonel. The Seeker places family above all things.' She turned back to Kelbee, and her eyes crinkled at the corners.

She knows me, screamed the voice in her head. *She knows everything.*

'You're doing fine work, Lance Colonel. Particularly with regards to our little northern problem. You are to be commended.' The eyes had moved away from her, though Kelbee still felt transfixed.

The Lance Colonel flushed. 'An honour, Guide. I live to serve.'

'A pity it's taking so long.'

The Lance Colonel tensed and his blush was replaced by an icy pallor.

The Guide gave a low chuckle. 'Oh, I'm teasing. I've seen the progress reports – he's very close now.'

The Lance Colonel stuttered in his rush to get his words out. 'I will notify you as soon as the asset is—'

He was cut off by a low murmur of acknowledgement. The Guide inclined her head and both Kelbee and the Lance Colonel bowed deep, and when they straightened she had moved on.

The Guide's retinue made it to the other end of the hall just as Kelbee thought she might collapse; the balls of her feet were throbbing from standing in place for so long. The Lance Colonel regained his composure.

He looks more scared than I do, she thought. For a split moment she wanted to reach for his hand to reassure him.

The bugles blew again. She saw the Guide and her

entourage mount the private dais and take their seats. This was the signal for the lines to break up; people returned to milling. Waiters in red tunics appeared from the doors that led off from the lobby and began to circulate with trays, offering iced fruit juices and flutes of wine. After the tension of the procession, the room began to relax back into the ebb and flow of conversation, watched over by the chosen few on the dais. Kelbee saw the Guide wave away a drink before she disappeared from view.

'Moving up in the world, Seregad!' The voice boomed from a grey-moustachioed officer in a high-collared uniform of sparkling white. He was older, his barrel chest laden with medals and his belly jutting like a white dome.

It had been so long since she'd heard his name that it took Kelbee a moment to remember that it belonged to the Lance Colonel.

Her husband didn't quite manage to hide his annoyance. 'Brigadier,' he said.

The newcomer slapped the Lance Colonel on the back, jarring the drink in his hand and seeming not to notice the frostiness of the reception. 'I still remember you as a junior lieutenant, all britches and no balls, what!' The jowls turned to Kelbee. 'And now look at you, all grown up and with this fine thing on your arm.' He grinned a mouthful of discoloured teeth. Kelbee bowed her head.

'That was many years ago, sir,' said the Lance Colonel. 'How goes your command?'

'If you can call it that,' said the Brigadier, rolling his eyes. 'Pushing boys with piss-stained trousers through the snow. The north really is the most atrocious place; I don't know how the natives bear it. Low expectations, I have to conclude. I get away as often as I can. The scenery's more pleasant in these parts.' He gave Kelbee a look that made her jaw clench.

The Lance Colonel's face coloured dangerously.

The Brigadier saw the flush and chuckled. 'Come off it, Seregad! Banter between old chums.' He addressed Kelbee. 'We go way back, your man and me. The stories I could tell…'

Her husband's voice was cold. 'Perhaps now is not the time.'

Another look from the Brigadier tried to worm its way through Kelbee's clothing. 'You're very fortunate, as I said. What I wouldn't give for something soft in my bed – it'd make those long Death nights fly by.'

'You forget yourself—'

Ignoring him, the Brigadier raised Kelbee's hand to his lips. His moustache was like a hard brush. 'How are you at cards, my dear?'

The Lance Colonel whipped the Brigadier's hand away. His voice was white with fury. 'That is my *wife*.'

The Brigadier stepped back, startled. Then his face went puce under his whiskers. 'No, *you* forget yourself, boy. That's tantamount to striking a superior officer. I taught you better than that.'

The Lance Colonel paused, then smiled a thin smile. He stepped in close enough so that only the three of them could hear.

'This *boy* will outrank you sooner rather than later. Enough to pick his own staff. Perhaps he'll treat them well. Perhaps he won't.'

The Brigadier spluttered but was cut off.

'Stay away from me, old fool. And from her.'

For a moment the air crackled between the two men. The Brigadier gave in first with a quiver of jowls. He grunted, spun on his heel, and disappeared into the throng.

The Lance Colonel was breathing deeply, but his eyes were wide with elation. He looked at Kelbee and smiled, and for the first time she saw the boy he might once have been. 'Always wanted to do that,' he said.

This time, she did take his hand.

It was past midnight when they returned home. Kelbee lit candles and he sat in his favourite chair, a glass of rakk warming in his palm. As she went to leave him, to go and remove her heavy outerwear, he stopped her with an outstretched hand.

'Have a drink for yourself when you come back.'

Kelbee slipped into her nightclothes and returned to him, pulling off his boots before pouring herself a small tumbler of dark ale from the bottle in the cooler – this invitation called for something other than water. He waved her to the chair by his side and sat quietly while she joined him. She'd rarely tasted the stuff before; it was thick, almost creamy, but with a bitter aftertaste. A polite sip, then she leaned back in her armchair; for once the silence in the room was something like comfortable.

'She was right,' he said, ever so slightly slurred. He turned his glass against the light, watching the candle flames dance through it. 'I should know more of you.'

'My life started when I came to the city.' The words came so easily.

'No, really. Where were you born? Tell me of it.'

Kelbee toyed with her glass before replying. 'It was a small farmer's village. Poor, but very pretty, in the hills.' She paused, then added, 'Though of course the Seeker provided for us, as with everyone.'

The Lance Colonel's eyes crinkled at the corners. 'Perhaps he provides more for some than others.' He picked at a loose thread on his cuff, and Kelbee made a mental note to fix it. 'What did you farm?'

'Father had three fields. For rice. Sometimes he hunted.'

'How many of you?'

'Him, my mother and me. She drowned in a river when I was seven. Then we were alone.'

He sipped his rakk. 'Young, to have to see that.'

'It was a hard life. It's why I didn't mind him selling me.'

A look of discomfort passed over his face, perhaps the first time she'd seen it. Guilt? It was hard to decipher. She felt a momentary pang of remorse for causing it.

'What about you?' she asked, then added, 'Sir.'

He waved a hand. 'You don't have to call me that. Not here.'

'Thank you.'

He was quiet for a while; she decided he wasn't going to answer. When he spoke, his eyes were distant.

'My father was a soldier, just a common private when I was born. It was here, in Karume. I only ever knew buildings and streets before I earned my commission. Sometimes, I wanted to go and live somewhere very like your village. In the green.'

Kelbee thought of the tiny hamlet, dilapidated by the Death's storms and sucked dry by penury. Empty eyes, listless days. 'I don't think you would have liked it.'

'Perhaps not. You always want what you don't have. My father was killed by a sniper and I was educated on his death dues. Mother... was not a kind woman, though she made me strong.'

It was hard to imagine him, Seregad – the name felt so alien – as a child.

He chuckled softly. 'I'd hide under the stairs when she had one of her turns, and pretend to be on patrol in enemy territory, like my father.' The image was so absurd she burst out laughing, then slapped a hand to her mouth.

He didn't scowl, as she was expecting, but smiled back. 'Can you imagine it?'

'I would hide up a tree when Father was drunk. He was very angry with the world.' This was something else, she thought. It felt like the first time they'd ever talked.

'You look sad,' he said. 'Was he cruel?'

'No, I think he was just... lost. Lonely, after Mother passed. Sometimes he could be kind.'

The Lance Colonel leaned forwards and placed a hand on her knee. It didn't feel like it normally did, the lead up to him demanding what he wanted. No, it was amiable; comforting, even.

'I'm...' he paused, unsure, then continued. 'I'm glad I have you. And the child. The last few weeks... have made me think.'

She felt herself go cold inside, though she masked it. She knew this was a shatter-point, an instant that, had it occurred six years before, could have led to such a different life. But it hadn't.

She held his hand as she lied to him. 'I'm glad I have you too.'

He grunted, then drained the last of his rakk. 'I'm going to bed.' He rose and made for the bedroom, his step only a little unsteady. Then he held up, remembering something.

'I had the tests back today, about...' he waved his hand at her. 'It's all fine.'

Her eyes sprang water and she had to force herself to breathe normally. 'That's... good news. Thank you.'

'Mmm.' It was either the drink or the flickering light, but he didn't seem to have noticed her tension. 'Goodnight.'

She heard him pulling off his clothes and collapsing into their bed. He was snoring in minutes while she sat in the silent lounge, listing to the odd ticks and cracks of the building around her. Her cheeks were soaked, her breathing ragged. All fine, he'd said. That had to mean the paternity test as well.

Either that, or he really is the father.

She silenced the thought, daring to hope Nebn had come through as he'd promised.

She sat back and tried to relax, watching the candle flames dance through her closed eyelids. A ghost sensation tickled her, a tiny movement below her navel. Was that a churn she felt, a small vibration inside? Was it just the fluttering of her own heart, bowels, muscles clenching and unclenching? She knew it wasn't, was certain of it. It was new life, the life she'd made, stretching out to touch the boundaries of its close, warm world.

It had to have been Nebn. He'd somehow made the danger go away. Maybe now, soon, he could get them out of here.

A Parting

First days of the Wake, raw as a blade on his skin. Late snow in the front garden, pockmarked by grass that refuses to die, jabbing upwards towards light and air, unbowed by the Death.

Ras, come and make the world new again.

Aime has been a long time at the village – why isn't she back yet? They'd come so far to meet him here but soon he'll be gone. She'll know how to fix this, smooth this, heal this.

So much anger in this small house. There he is, the boy on the other side of the table, arms crossed over a pressed green tunic. The peaked cap is on the table.

The peaked cap is on the hook that he whittled from a branch Aime found in the woods behind the house.

The peaked cap is on the floor where he threw it... Why is Bowden so angry?

Why do you always get in the way? he asks Bowden's stern face.

No, it's all wrong. He is the other one, the stern one, the still one. But also angry, that the boy has learned nothing, knows

272

nothing. As if all those years, all those warnings meant nothing, nothing, nothing.

Bread is charring, unattended and alone in the oven. Aime worked so hard, kneading and mixing and shaping it with care and love. Burning now, all burning.

Hubris brought down the old world. They reached further than they should have and toppled because of it. That is what you're doing. You dream of uniforms and polished boots on parade grounds, but the truth is mud and blood.

I'm a man. I decide my fate. Enough of your stories. Now Bowden's face moves with the words.

The laugh in his throat is bitter.

A little red bird lands on the wall outside. It shivers its plumage, making itself fat for a heartbeat, then it is gone again. Red, white. Blood on snow.

Blood in his heart, veins, eyes, ears; throbbing, pumping. It's fear, he realises now, not anger. The crash and boom of guns, pitter-patter raindrops of bullets; whump-whump goes the plasma fire, blue death to all it touches. It freezes him even as he burns inside, the memory of a war. No glory there, only death.

His boy. His boy. *Running towards that symphony of pain and murder with a heart full of stories told by other men that drowned out his own.*

I'm a man, he says again.

You know nothing!

Bowden is on his feet and words slice the air. Failure, coward. He'd abandoned them. And now there is this little cottage with furniture that barely stands, which he made himself and a young wife in his bed and the past is swept away like crumbs.

He tries to speak but his voice is choked.

What good were you ever, old man? Go ahead and rot in your hovel with your new toy. Leave me to my own life.

He hadn't said anything then, when it was real and the walls were solid and the smell of the bread burning in the oven matted the air, because there had been too much inside him; fear, rage and foolish, foolish conceit, but now he shouts and screams at Bowden's back as it recedes through the doorway. He wants to catch him, hold him back with the painful love that stretches his skin to breaking point, grown from a soft flood of memory. Every half-recalled image of a speck that grew into a pink, wrinkled, tiny creature; a fat little thing that tottered on unsteady legs; a child that was inches taller every time he came back from his own wars and met him at the door with a scratched face and worn knees and a smile that was a mirror that stole age and sorrow away in a golden moment; the angry young man that turns his back on him and walks away, he adores with his bones and his breath.

But his feet are rooted, stuck deep into the ground; his body is fixed in space. Even his voice is stolen away by the thick air.

Aime will be so disappointed. To come all this way, to make everything right. A peace offering, a greeting, an invitation. There had been so much war; she wanted only peace, for all of them.

The green uniform is gone now. It marches on parade grounds and embarks ships and accepts the rifle that is given to it, polishing it over and over, ready for the day when it will be tested in fire and anger.

When it was real, when the oven was extinguished and the black loaves lay on the table like a mockery of their efforts, Aime was there with soft words and softer hands. Her bag of groceries

274

left propped at the door, greens spilling onto the flagstones. There would be another time, she told him, another place for them all to be calm, together. Whole. Her hair had brushed his face and the weave of her clothes had cushioned him, the honey smell of her.

Not now. Now he is alone in the room with the burned bread and there is no rage any more, just emptiness. It had never happened, he'd never come home. One day, neither did she.

The peaked cap is in his hands.

He wants to squeeze it tight, press his face into it, but he doesn't dare crease it, this last piece of the son he drove away with nothing so base as pride. It smells of his hair.

His face splits with his howl and everything shatters all at once.

Bask 59 – 499

Disaster. They did it, the fools. I have never felt such a bone-crushing rage, for what they did and what it did to him.

I am writing this on the way back to civilisation in a dilapidated truck – Fermin took the skimmer when he bolted. I have to get back and stop him from releasing his findings – they will come north, and they will destroy the best chance we have for a better world. And I'll have my due for what that fucker took from me.

Mason and I woke in our bed around midnight three nights ago. Both of us felt the odd sensation, like the walls were vibrating and the air thrumming. We threw on clothes and sprinted for the funicular – which was at the bottom of the shaft as I'd feared, the seals around the door broken. Waiting for it to rise back up felt like an aeon.

When we entered the torus, we saw the two morons standing by the central pillar, hand in hand with the others flat against the surface material, like they were performing some manner of damned ritual! The blue haze was thicker than I'd ever seen it and the heat was unbearable, the pressure making my ears pop. The pair were upright but unconscious – I recognised that look on their faces. They were inside the corpus! Neither would be able to call the other back. The Spark was pulsing like a racing heart and had turned a deep magenta. Then the screaming began.

The male started first, then the female, their mouths hanging slack, an ululating wail that bounced from the walls, though they didn't let go. I watched, paralysed, as the skin at their temples began to darken, then blister, then fire erupted from their mouths and eye sockets. The Spark made that horrid groaning noise, only this time louder than ever before. Then it uttered two words with dread finality.

Unsuitable. Purge.

Before I knew what had happened, Mason had pulled me backwards into the funicular and was slamming the ascent button. The doors began to close just as the temperature spiked. I huddled in the corner as I felt the motors of the car take the strain; the doors were a metre apart, half a metre, a few centimetres, then the gap became a white-hot band as if Ras had fallen on the other side.

The doors closed, the edges glowing berry red, but we were moving. There was a sweet smell like cooking meat mixed with burnt hair, then I heard the whimper next to me.

Mason, my comfort, my strength, was burned in a narrow strip all up his body an instant before the doors closed. A livid line had been scorched the length of him, starting at his knee, running up the leg, his chest, his neck, then over half of his face. One eye was gone, the other rolled back in his skull. His hair was singed and the flesh blistered and blackened. He regained consciousness only to scream in pain.

I did what I could with the meagre supplies we had left. His burns were so severe that he began to go into shock, his body quaking to the point where I could no longer hold him

277

down. The painkillers barely calmed him and all the while the smell of his wounds filled the place, a miasma that still sticks in my nostrils. I will never be able to eat meat again as long as I live.

I tried to calm him, tried to stop my own panic and tears and think rationally, but I was out of my depth. His breathing laboured. In the last moment he looked at me with his one good eye, crushing my hand in his.

He told me he loved me. He told me where to go to find help.

Then, he told me his real name.

Sleep 20 – 499

Karume is worse than I remember it. On one level I think I have become used to my own company and the unpolluted expanse of the glacier – here the soot clouds are visible from kilometres distant, draped over the city like a shield that turns the midday sky purple. It is not being forced to be amongst people again, it is the way they look; their faces are either bovine or skittish from moment to moment. And the smiles: fixed, lifeless, telling the world everything is fine and life is good while inside fear twists their guts.

Did I look like that once? I am most likely projecting – perhaps they are not all tortured inside, perhaps their ignorance is a comfort of sorts. How could they know unhappiness, never knowing anything else but the lives they lead? The only person alive that has any kind of outside context is me, and in truth I don't know if the things I learned have freed or condemned me.

Getting to Karume was not easy and took much of the

money I had with me, but through negotiation and threat and cajoling I made it. Gaining access to the Elucidon was the easiest part – the doorman was likely an undergraduate who'd been stuffed into a uniform and taught to hold a clipboard. A change of clothes at my apartment had me looking like myself and I gave him my most contemptuous faculty stare before striding through the gate, leaving his goggling eyes and hanging pen in my wake. He might have called weakly after me but I had rounded a corner and kept going, heading for my old department.

Fermin had made himself comfortable in the few days he'd had on me – my office was now filled with his clutter and his anaemic staff laboured outside, though he wasn't there himself. One of them tried to stop me from entering and I let my tongue have free rein. I think the woman almost cried. She recognised me then, I think, and stepped aside. Reputation is a useful thing.

They watched through the window as I turned his (my!) office upside down. I broke his trophies, smashed his framed diplomas, scattered his papers. I found his valise under the desk, still stinking of his journey and lying open. Inside, amid the clutter, I found a thick brown folder I recognised.

My elation was short-lived, however. What I held were the co-ordinates of the outpost, a couple of charts of the Makuo glacier, but the accompanying diary (wherein we'd recorded all of our findings from our sessions with the Spark) was missing. The fat idiot had clearly run off to the faculty with it to beg for a pat on the head, leaving the location behind for later.

I made sure the papers were properly alight before I

tossed them aside. The office went up like kindling and I pushed past Fermin's aghast researchers as they ran in to try to stamp it out. I managed to slip out in the confusion, even passing the hapless doorman running the other way with an extinguisher clutched to his chest. Appearing to belong there is just as good as the real thing.

I am sure of two things. First, they know what we found up there, its significance and doubtless the threat it poses to the Hegemony's status quo. Second, they do not know *where*: I have the printed maps and I made sure no copies survived through a short visit to the archives, as well as the geology department. The fire I'd started kept attention elsewhere and I was unimpeded. Each department of the Elucidon guards its finds like a miser; once a source of frustration back when I was just another academic, now a blessing as I didn't need to range far to destroy all records of the early surveys – the ones that had sent me to Makuo in the first place. Once this was done I joined in with the throng being shepherded towards the exits.

Had I found Fermin in his office, I would have clawed the skin from his face, to let him feel a fraction of what Mason – I cannot think of him with any other name, despite what he told me – had felt in his last moments. I didn't get my base revenge, so I will do something else. I will find the place he told me about as the life stuttered out of him and give what I have to his friends. If the world were a bone, it broke five hundred years ago and was badly set by a blind man. The only way to allow it to grow properly is to break it once more.

viii. Knife

By mid-afternoon the heat had lulled, pavements sighing as the warmth bled from them. Kelbee emerged from the sewers after completing another drop and checked around her, as had become her habit, to be sure she was alone. The quiet part at the back of her mind, the observer, noted how much she'd changed. She no longer quivered with fear after sneaking out of bed to gather information; she knew how to blend into a crowd.

Despite this new confidence there was a sliver of doubt that had crept in ever since the night when she and the Lance Colonel had talked – truly, like equals – for the first time. She still couldn't bring herself to use his real name but there was a difference, a shift in the tiny air currents of their marriage. He'd come home one day with a small, hand-picked bunch of orange flowers which he'd placed in a mug on the kitchen windowsill. He'd been embarrassed, but instead of covering it with anger as he normally did he'd smiled like a boy. Later that night, in bed, he'd moved towards her and the old fear crept up again that he was going to take her. Instead, a single kiss, a light brush of his lips on hers, holding for just a moment of absolute stillness where his heartbeat matched hers, then he moved away. She'd not been able to sleep for some time after that, feeling his warmth on the far side of the bed as futures clashed in her head.

The side of her that said it wasn't enough to make up for the bad years still held the field but it wasn't absolute any more; it had been much easier to steal from him, betray him, when he was nothing more than a looming threat.

Sometimes, in her quietest moments, she wondered if she could just walk away from all this danger, back into her old life. There was nothing left to incriminate – she could pass the child off as his for the rest of her life, knowing now how easy it was to lie. Danger would pass into normality. But what of the child inside her? A boy would be thrust into the military and a girl would be married off to a man who would doubtless use her just as she herself had been used. And the most honest part of her knew that it was too late to unlearn what she'd learned, to accept the unacceptable.

No, she thought, *that door needs to close*. When it was time, she would leave.

Just as the hour struck for the workers to go home she arrived on a familiar street. Opposite, she saw the squat pile where she'd once spent the days sewing garments – where she'd met Nebn, where it had all begun. She paused for a while, watching the women on the other side of the street; their eyes were tired and downcast as they trudged along the pavement. There was a face she recognised: the girl who'd cut herself on the shears. Her once-pretty face was worn now, and she walked with an unsteady lurch, cradling her bandaged stumps to her chest.

From around the corner came a large staff car bearing flags. It was travelling at speed and the light traffic moved off the road to allow it through. Some officer on his way home, no doubt, or off to a night's drinking. She watched it pass, then set off again, already preparing herself for another evening aping the quiet servitude of her old life. She touched her bump, as had become her habit. It was stretching the fabric of all her tunics these days and she found more and more that she needed to sit down and take the weight off her back.

There was a screech of tyres behind her, then a bang. The staff car had collided with a small utility van that had been pulling out of a side road; both drivers were out on the street, yelling at each other. As she turned to look, Kelbee caught a flash of motion from the street she'd come from, a person ducking back behind the corner, trying not to be seen. Ice gripped her throat.

The crowd on the other side of the street had grown as more workers left the building, bumping into the backs of those who'd stopped to gawp at the accident. Kelbee rushed over to meld into the crowd. She jostled past people, keeping her head down as she made for an alleyway just up the street that should be a shortcut to the park. If she could make it through she could lose herself in the trees. She came to the alley mouth and ducked in, breaking into a run.

The alley was cast in shadow, a deep snaking trench between two tower blocks. It was narrow, barely wide enough for two people abreast and littered with rubbish. The echoes of her feet pounding on concrete reverberated – and perhaps another, following behind. The terror gave her a boost and she pushed harder.

She came to a dogleg and rough concrete tore at her palms as she fended off the walls, speeding around the kink. Ahead was a slice of daylight, and between her and freedom was a high fence of chain-link.

She swore under her breath.

If she stretched her hands as high as she could she could almost reach the top of the fence. Scanning the alley, she saw an old stack of crates mouldering by the wall. The old wood cracked under her fingers as she hauled them one by one over to the chain-link, piling them into a rickety stair. The wood cracked and splintered under her weight as she climbed, the light at the alley mouth beckoning safety. Then the boxes collapsed.

She scrabbled to grab the fence as she fell. The crates did the rest, the waterlogged wood breaking her fall. A few shards tore through her clothes, one of them slicing a neat gash over her forearm. Her throat closed up and she pushed herself into the corner, waiting for her pursuer to come charging around the corner, gun pointed at her, ready to haul her off for questioning.

There was nothing. No footsteps, no Factors bearing handcuffs, only the sound of her own sobs bouncing from the walls. She heard someone shout from a window high above and flinched, then another answered it and she realised it was only neighbours arguing. The alley was still.

She picked herself up and dusted herself off as well as

she could, using her shawl to hide the tear in her sleeve. She leaned against the wall for a few moments with eyes shut, waiting for the pounding in her chest to quieten, the sweat on her brow cooling in the gentle flurries that set the splinters dancing.

She was jumping at shadows. No one was coming. But she'd seen something, she knew it, felt it in her bones. She had to get out. It had to happen soon.

Back at the apartment, she set about scrubbing, washing and preparing dinner as if work could burn her worries away. She moved from one thing to the next, never allowing herself a gap, knowing it was always there, the fear that someone had been following her.

If it hadn't been for the accident in the street she'd never have seen that darting shape on the corner. But what if it hadn't really been anything; what if it had just been someone dropping something, or changing direction for a reason wholly unconnected to her? She shook her head to try to clear it and set about scrubbing the floor tiles with renewed vigour.

A half-hour later she felt a little better; the gnawing feeling in her stomach had been pushed into the background. She took a few moments to gaze out at the Tower, the way she used to before all this had started. There was a reassuring solidity to the edifice, a still, unmovable constant in her life. Calmer now, she could order her thoughts. No one had come after her back in the alleyway. If she'd been tailed they would have had her plumb, lying against that fence.

Be rational, she told herself, *think logically*. There was nowhere to hide overlooking the sewer entrance – that she

knew for certain; it had been picked for that very reason –
and the streets leading back to the central district had been
wide and empty.

*You would have noticed someone coming after you. Just keep
a grip.*

She rubbed absently at her belly as she gazed out of the
window, fingers tracing the outline. Evening crept over
the city. It was an odd feeling, being able to calm herself
so quickly. She'd changed so much in such a short time –
never a toe out of line in her whole life and now here she was
running with subversives, spying on her husband. And how
normal it all felt!

It was *doing*, she decided, rather than merely existing, that
felt right. Not going through the motions set out for you,
being a dutiful shell. Duty: to father, husband, authority,
the Seeker himself; always at the bottom of the mountain.
Obeisance. It had been the schoolmistress's favourite of the
Principles, repeated over and over.

Obeisance, rotten girl. Above all.

*Would I have remained as I was without meeting Nebn,
stealing away a kiss, a caress, then more? Would I still be
walking that narrow, proper road without being pushed off
it? Or perhaps there was always something inside, waiting for
the chance.*

Was this it, though, the cure to her sickly former life?
Being used to lying wasn't the same as revelling in it, and
for all that she could pad out of their room in silence to steal
Hegemony secrets, it didn't mean the knot of terror went
away. In a room with two doors, each leading to opposite
extremes, she wanted to open neither.

Was that old crone right? Am I rotten?

It didn't matter, she decided. Until Nebn could take her away, she would have to bury her doubts and endure.

Be just another blank face, let the speaker posts wash their toneless mutterings over your head and never look the Factors in the eye.

Karume, the Hegemony, it was such a fragile, cracked thing – she saw that now, but until she was away from it the knowledge needed to stay in the dark place behind her eyes.

A chime from the wall chrono brought her back. She had to get ready for the evening. Kelbee glanced at the back of her hand; the skin was unmarked now but the memory remained of No-Face's nails digging into her. Would she have to humour that strange woman and her boorish husband again tonight? As she put away her scrubbing brush, she resolved to be a gracious hostess, though when she thought of those painted talons pinning her flesh to the counter, she resolved that *that* would not happen again, not in her house. She'd continue to wear the wire Tani had given her, pour drinks, smile demurely. The perfect wife, the perfect liar.

She halted at the bedroom door with a sharp intake of breath. The room had been trashed, her closet ransacked, the bed upended against the wall and smashed in, pieces of foam from the slashed mattress littering the floor. And in the corner, sat like a child with his legs crossed, the Lance Colonel, his head down as if asleep. She saw him cradling something, a grey disc-shaped box.

Her blood ran with ice.

'How long have you been here?' she asked.

He lifted his head; his eyes were red. His uniform tunic,

normally so neat, was torn open at the collar like he'd been struggling to breathe. He watched her for a quiet moment, until she wondered if he could see her at all.

Was he drunk? If so, it was bad – he'd hit her before, but never trashed a room.

'I received a letter today.' His voice was steady, unslurred and eerie in its flatness.

Not drunk. Something far worse. The hairs on the back of her neck stood up.

'A letter from the clinic,' he continued. 'Some problem with samples, a breakage. They salvaged just enough to run the test, after a delay.'

She began to back away from the door. He stood, slowly, as if every motion was weighed down. He looked at the recorder in his hand, turned it over. 'I came home. I was angry.' He waved a hand at the chaos around him. On the floor by his feet lay a heap of her clothes; stark against the others was the yellow dress with flowers around the hem. It was inside out and the extra pouch she'd sewn in herself to conceal the device torn open.

How could I have been so careless?

The Lance Colonel fiddled with the disc-shaped device in his hand as if fascinated. He looked up at her, his bloodshot eyes spearing the distance between them.

His voice was quiet murder. 'Traitor.'

She took another step backwards. He let the wire fall from his fingers. His face was resigned, almost reluctant, like he was performing a chore. He drew his pistol and fired.

Her ears screamed from the sound of the gunshot but the pain on the side of her head told her she was alive and he'd missed. As she scrabbled backwards on her palms she saw the gaping hole the bullet had punched into the wall. He appeared at the bedroom door, gun up, his face a terrifying blank. He sighted again and she kicked a small end table – the dark wood skittered over the floor and banged into his shin. He swore and the second shot went wide, shattering the Seeker's portrait as she scrabbled to get out of the way.

There had to be something she could use; to shield herself, a weapon, anything. She ran for the kitchen but in her hurry tripped over a stool – she hit the counter with her ribs and fell to the floor, the breath knocked from her.

The Lance Colonel was there, the same detached look on his face. She knew it was too late to move, nowhere to go. The pistol came up, hiding one half of his face as he took aim. His finger squeezed the trigger.

There was a dull click.

He held up the pistol, his face quizzical. Impatiently, like swatting an insect, he cranked the action back. There was a grating sound from the mechanism.

Kelbee watched the scene as if separated from herself, rooted to the spot as he took aim again. Another dead click. She felt the burn in her lungs, the cold floor under her palms, the heaviness of her limbs. She tried to rise.

He threw the gun at her. It caught her on the side of the head and knocked her down, ringing her skull like a bell. She bounced off the counter and onto the floor, bringing with her a rain of jars and utensils. For a moment there was only blind panic as she thought of the child, the fragile thing she carried, if it had been hurt. She curled up, protecting it with her own flesh.

He was there, standing by the counter island and looking down at her as if he'd never seen her before, his head cocked and his eyes full of chilling curiosity.

'How long?' he asked.

'Sir, I—'

'How long have you been rutting with another?'

'Seregad, it's not… Please, don't. The baby…'

'Not mine,' he said, as if discussing the weather. 'The tests were conclusive. You've whored yourself.' He made eye contact. 'Don't you dare use my name.'

A fresh wave of terror hit her, the calm in his voice somehow worse than rage. He watched her like a specimen.

His movement was sudden – one moment he was staring down at her, the next he had her by the throat, crushing her chest with his knee. His fingers were like sprung steel on her windpipe, pressing tighter. She tried to bat him away but he was so strong.

'I'll find him,' he said. His eyes were so red! Had he been crying? 'I'll kill him. You will be forgotten.' He pushed down harder, ignoring her hands batting at his face. This time, his voice caught in his throat. 'I… I thought we could be happy.'

All that was left in the world was the hand at her throat, stopping her breath as the edges of her vision blurred, then nothing mattered any more. There was something like bliss, a moment of acceptance – this was it, she was going to die. It was over; no more running, hiding, crying. No more struggle.

She felt something familiar, a thin wooden handle her fingers knew so well.

Leave it, said the little voice. *Leave it all behind.*

No.

With her last strength she stabbed the filleting knife into the side of his neck. Blood covered her face; it tasted like metal. He let go and air sprang into her lungs as his weight fell away. The world rushed back in to find her on her side, wheezing, her throat bruised.

The Lance Colonel sank against the cabinets. He tried to grip the knife but the handle was slick with his blood. He tried to stand, slipped back down. He looked like a child searching for help, his eyes wide and panicked. They found her; they pleaded so hard she almost went to him. He tried to talk but the blade had pierced both blood vessel and airway, leaving him nothing but wet gasps.

She sat up, her whole body drained of energy. She watched him die, the two of them sitting opposite each other like old friends on the kitchen floor. His leg twitched for a while, and he sucked in weak gasps. She made herself hold his gaze throughout it all, until there was nothing left of him.

The chrono on the wall said it had only been minutes, but it felt like hours. Kelbee stood and checked herself, remembering. It hurt to suck in breath, but she forced herself to move to the bathroom, to sponge some of the blood from her face and hands. She watched it circle the drain, languorous.

Someone would have heard the gunshots, might have called the Factors. She grabbed her overcoat from the bedroom, not bothering to change. The bullet holes in the hallway looked like gaping wounds in the plaster. The

Seeker's portrait had been knocked off and the frame had shattered – she left it where it was. Just before she went for the door, she saw the briefcase where he'd dropped it, propped half-tipped against the leg of the table. He'd not even stopped to rotate the code cylinders. She could imagine him, his face losing its colour as he heard the news, rushing home to confront her only to find the confirmation of an empty house. The vision was so clear she had to shake her head to rid herself of it.

The case popped and she grabbed the first thing her hand found – a tan folder stuffed with papers, new, its edges barely damaged. It fit snug against her ribs under her coat.

As the door squeaked open, she caught a glimpse of him where he lay. The boots she'd worked on so many nights, making them shine. They were dulled now, marred by grime and blood. She wondered why she felt nothing, no rage, no relief, no sadness, just the polish that had gone into those boots.

She left the apartment, locking the door behind her.

Nebn's eyes were fraught as he pushed aside the plastic curtain that led to their hideaway. When he saw her, his jaw dropped with relief.

'I've been looking for you. There's been an alert.'

She shifted under the blanket, pushing her hair out of her face. It had been cold in the night – she'd not dared to fire up the generator and start the heater, so she'd collapsed onto the bed in her bloody clothes and fallen asleep for a few fitful hours, then spent the rest of the night hearing armed men in every creak and click of the dilapidated building. Her eyes felt gummy with fatigue.

'Did they find the body?' she asked.

Nebn took her in his arms, crushing her against him. His face filled with concern as she winced.

'It's all right,' she said, hugging her knees. 'Just a bruise – I fell.'

'The baby?'

'I think…' She looked up at him. 'I think it's all right. But he tried to hurt it.' For the first time since it had happened, tears crept up on her.

He just sat and held her for a while, taking all of her weight on him and running his fingers through her hair. She drifted off into a dreamless, exhausted slumber. When she woke he was sitting across from her, a mug of hot tea in his hand, reading the folder she'd smuggled out. His face was drawn, his eyes narrowed. He saw she was awake and passed her the mug. The brew was thick and sweet and spread all the way to her fingertips.

'Did you come straight here?' he asked.

She nodded. 'I didn't know where else to go. I didn't want to come to you, in case there was someone…' She let her voice trail off. Should she mention what had happened the day before, in the alley? Had it even been real? It seemed so trivial now, but something had turned her away from the sewers and towards this place instead.

'You did the right thing. There's been no announcement, of course, but we monitor local enforcement channels and they're buzzing with talk of a senior intelligence officer found dead in his home.' His voice broke. 'I thought they had you.'

She reached out, took his hand.

'You're…' The question came from his eyes, never quite making it to his lips.

'I'm all right. It's done now.'

He kissed her fingers. 'I need to get you back, have you checked for injuries. Then Tani can look after you for a little while.'

'What do you mean? Where are you going?'

He held up the folder. 'This is big. It should never have left his office. They're close to infiltrating one of our bases. Details are sparse but I need to warn them to ramp up security.'

'You have to go yourself?'

'Yes.'

'You can't leave me here.'

'Listen, you'll be safe as soon as we get you underground. We have people who can check you, check the baby, make sure everything's all right. Then, when things have died down, we can move you.'

'If you're going, I'm going with you.' She saw his refusal and cut it off. 'All of this has been to get out of this place, anywhere as long as it's not Karume. I'm not going back to the sewers, I'm going wherever you're going.'

'It's one of our most important bases, hidden and very sensitive. They won't let me—'

'You can persuade them. I just want to get out of here, Nebn.' She indicated the folder. 'I brought you that. I could have left it, but I didn't. You owe me this much.'

He considered this for a moment, studying her. She held his gaze, the eerie feeling of calm still enveloping her.

Perhaps once she was away from the city she would feel the weight of what had happened in the last hours, but for now it was held back by a thick blanket of resolve.

'At least let me have you checked over. You could be hurt.'

'I'm fine,' she said. 'You have to believe me. He didn't hurt the baby.' As she said it, she felt her hands itch, and she hoped that what she said was true.

Nebn nodded and helped her up. 'There'll be some first-aid supplies in the car. Bring your coat, it gets cold in the tunnels.'

Cypher

Another concrete wall. A single naked light.

Cale was tied to a steel chair. It creaked when he shifted, but it was solid, much heavier than an ordinary chair; hard to lift, harder to throw. His ankles were tied to the legs, his wrists bound behind him. A thick rope wrapped his chest, stopping him from leaning. The bonds had been tied well by someone who knew what they were doing – not tight enough to cut off the blood but enough to stop him from working free.

He tried shouting, but no one came. The door stayed shut, time stretching out for minutes or perhaps hours. His eye started to find the patterns in the rough concrete, following the contours that had been left by damp and age. There were stains where moisture still darkened the surface and faint brown outlines where old patches had dried. In one corner was a rusty smear that might have been old blood. He let his eyes trace the edges of each patch, learning its bays and headlands. A draught from under the door flurried dust motes, tumbling them like a cloud of sparks.

Cale knew he was not the first to be tied to this chair in this bare room. He thought about shouting again but gave up. Waste of effort. Waste of air.

The attack on the beach had come so fast. He remembered his skin burning, stones popping under the weight of something huge, and there had been a sting on his cheek as something sharp flew past. Then the light, the deafening pulse of sound that had knocked him flat. Blood trickling from his ears.

He could reorder the thoughts now, put them in their proper place, re-evaluate. Plasma fire – unmistakeable from its ozone stink – and heavy footsteps. Walker. Then he'd felt his insides pulse, shimmering at an awful frequency like he was pressed against the world's loudest, biggest speaker. A sonic weapon? Unusual for the military. Someone else, then.

What was a war-walker doing on a remote beach? Who had access to complex weaponry like sonics? Something about that voice, the one that had spoken before he passed out, was familiar.

Is Brennev still here? Did he watch me the whole time, as I tried to scratch my way through that rusty wall? Was he there, inches away, listening?

'Is that what happened?' he asked the wall.

The wall ignored him.

The door squeaked and a masked man entered. He was thickset and his mouth and nose were wrapped in black cloth. His eyes were fierce, calculating. 'Why are you here?' he said. The voice was pleasant, musical even through the muffle of the mask.

Cale remained silent.

The masked man leaned in closer, but, Cale noted, out of range of a head-butt. 'Again, why are you here?'

Cale found the brown patch on the wall.

'Why were you on that beach?' asked the masked man.

Blood. He was sure of it now. Old blood.

'Who do you work for?'

Cale snorted.

The masked man backhanded him across the face, hard enough to sting. Then he did it again. 'What is your regimental number?'

Cale spat a gob of blood onto the floor, then met the man's hard green eyes. Stared.

The man hit him again. He leaned in close. 'The others have talked, you know. They say you're the leader.'

Cale breathed hard. Definitely blood. Not the last.

The masked man stepped back, assessing. 'If you don't tell me what you're looking for, I will kill you.'

Cale spat again.

'I'll kill them too, after I take out their teeth. Then I'll do the same to you. Such a waste of everyone's time.'

Cale glared back.

The masked man was still for a moment, his head cocked as if listening to something. Then he gripped Cale by the shoulders and brought his face in close, almost nose to nose. 'What colour was your son's uniform the day you last saw him? White or black?'

Before Cale could stop himself, the answer jumped from his mouth.

'Green.'

The masked man pulled away and walked to the door. Cale heard bolts drawn back and it opened.

A man with an eyepatch held the door. 'It's him,' he said. 'You can go.'

'You're sure, sir?'

'Yes. I'll take it from here.'

The masked man nodded and left.

Eyepatch came over and pulled a knife from his belt. Cale flinched and earned a wry smile.

'You've become skittish in your old age,' he said. He cut the ties around Cale's ankles then moved behind and loosened the rope before cutting his wrists free. 'There you go. You're lucky I was on-station to recognise you. None left from the old days now, bar me.'

Cale rubbed his wrists, searching the grizzled face. The single eye was a deep shade of purple, and he'd only ever met one man with eyes like that. 'Brennev,' he said.

'Didn't have this last time we met.' He indicated the patch.

'Why have your muscle knock me about if you knew it was me?' Anger bubbled through the layers of guilt that had smothered it for so long. 'Where the hell are the others?'

Brennev sheathed his knife. 'We're taking care of them. You understand how it is, or have you gone soft? I needed to know it was you.'

'Dammit, where is my son?'

'This is going to be confusing for you.' Brennev paused, studying him. 'Cale, I'm sorry. Bowden is dead.'

The walls disappeared and a pounding started in his skull. He couldn't feel his hands any more.

Gone?

'How long have I been here?' he managed to choke out.

'A few hours.'

'But… he was stable. How—'

Brennev looked away. 'He died months ago.'

Racks of equipment almost hid the polished rock of the med bay's walls. The rubberised floors muffled the clicks and hums that came from the blinking machinery and the steps of the quiet, efficient staff who went about their tasks.

Before them, covered up to its chin with a white sheet, lay the body that Cale had brought here. It looked alive still, as if in a deep sleep, though there was no breath coming from the pale lips. The eyes were as sunken as they'd been in the hospital bed he'd pulled him from, his hair the same russet stubble he'd stroked, sure he'd see it grow out again.

Not my *son*, raged his mind. How could he not have known?

'You're sure?' he asked, his mouth still struggling with words. Somewhere nearby, all-consuming blackness threatened to suck him in.

Brennev was straight-backed and still. A slight inclination of the head. 'We were thorough. It's not Bowden.'

'A copy?' The idea almost made him laugh. He held it at bay, feeling the danger of hysteria.

'It was someone, once,' said Brennev. 'Probably a soldier. Volunteers – you remember how it works with them. Surgically altered to match Bowden – they must have dug up his personnel file from his time with the

Marines. Poor bastard was exsanguinated and crammed full of heat-retaining gel that doubled as a preservative. A pump in his chest to make it look like he was still breathing. Quite a number.'

'Why would they do this?'

'Someone wanted you to look for us. Someone who knew you well enough to know that he was the key to getting you to do it.'

Did Brabant know? he thought, remembering the last time they'd met. *No, he has nothing to gain from this. And I'd have seen it in his eyes.* He shook his head, barely able to process. *Who would play this deep a game?*

Brennev continued. 'We thought the body had some kind of tracker, that a Hegemony fleet would be standing off and ready to shell us into oblivion. That's why we took precautions with you all.'

'And?'

'It was clean.' Brennev stroked his chin, like he always used to when examining a problem.

Suddenly, Cale couldn't look any longer. The thing on the table was alien, grotesque. He turned away as Brennev nodded to an orderly, who pulled the sheet over the corpse's face.

A little way off, an observation window looked down on an operating theatre. Cale watched as a medico wearing a blue mask manipulated tiny levers, his movements relayed to a cluster of slender metallic arms that emerged from the ceiling. The patient was hooked to an air hose, red hair spilling out at the sides of his cap. Cale watched as the spindly fingers dipped in and out of the open hole in Derrin's belly as if feeding on him.

'He's not too far gone, they tell me,' said Brennev, joining him at the window.

'What happened to Bowden? My real son. I need to know.'

'He was working for us. He'd gone north, his own operation. That's where it happened.'

'Don't mince words. What was he doing?'

'I don't have the details. He persuaded his commander he needed to get close to an academic. He was hard to dissuade when he had an idea. Remind you of anyone?'

'Why wasn't I told?'

Brennev paused, watching the operation. The surgeon twisted the controls and one of the arms lifted something from the cavity. It dropped a compressed bullet fragment into a steel tray, then returned to searching the wound. 'You disappeared. I wasn't sure you were even alive.'

A pang stabbed Cale under his heart.

'How could you let him go off by himself like that?' he snapped.

Brennev frowned. 'He was his own man, trusted enough to judge what was necessary. He was with us for years, Cale.'

Two more bullet fragments were removed as the arms probed. Another arm descended from the ceiling, trailing stiff black thread; it dipped in and out like a bird pecking the bark of a tree. More medicos appeared and held the gaping stomach wound shut as the arm set about sealing it with a row of tiny, regular stitches.

'You have to tell me where,' said Cale. 'I need to see his body.'

'I can't do that.'

A white bubble of rage surged under his skin and he

rounded on Brennev. Behind them the pair of guards who'd been trailing them stiffened, hands twitching over their holsters. Brennev waved at them to step away.

'I can't, because I don't know. Only one person does, and she's... reluctant.'

'Then tell me where to find her and I'll go looking myself.'

'I can do better than that.' Brennev turned back to the window. Below them the surgical team were finishing up, one mopping the blood from the edges of Derrin's sutured wound as another took readings from a blinking piece of machinery. The scarred face seemed to come to a decision.

'I'll put her in a room with you,' he said. 'For what good it'll do.'

'Never had you pegged as a subversive.' Syn carried a wry smile as they walked along the wide corridor.

'It was another life,' Cale replied. His words rang hollow in his ears as he concentrated on just putting one foot ahead of the other.

Bowden was gone.

'How are you, buck?'

Cale kept walking.

A squad of men in green uniforms passed them going the other way, their steps in time. Their gear looked new – carbines that gleamed with a soft oil sheen and dun body armour that was well fitted. Not a strap out of place on any of them and their faces were serious, professional.

An army. That was what this was now. Brennev had talked about this often back in the days when they were hiding in shadows, taking long-range pictures of internment camps, gathering data, quietly placing their people inside the body of the Hegemony's hierarchy. 'Active resistance.' He'd wanted to bring the fight to the enemy on open terms.

The time Brennev had brought it to the council meeting and proposed it as a strategy was the first time Cale had seen Aime truly angry with anyone. It was no better than their methods, in her eyes. He was a fantasist, he'd get people killed, she'd said, and there were precious few of them in those early days. Even with Aspedair's clandestine supplies and support it was a constant struggle to maintain the networks they'd established. He'd bring that all crashing down, Aime had insisted, with his hunt for glory. They all knew what the stakes were; none of them would ever be stupid enough to condone force against force as a viable strategy.

She'd been wrong – the very walls of this place told that story. He barely recognised it any more, the caves he'd known clad in concrete and steel, the floors sheathed in hard rubber. The uniforms were everywhere, men and women showing hard hours of training in their every precise step and gesture. So many, and all of them ready to fight. Somehow, Brennev had got his way.

Bowden probably walked these hallways, he thought. *I wanted to keep him from harm and all it accomplished was to push him down the same path.*

It weighed on him like a lump of iron, threatening to drag him through the floor and into the dark earth. He wished it would. He stumbled, felt Syn's cold powerful hand steadying him.

They followed the guard who'd been assigned as their escort up a shallow flight of stairs. At the top, the blank concrete walls gave way to thick glass, the bright floodlights from outside refracting in patterns that cut up the floor. Through the long window Cale looked down on a hangar bay piled with crates. In the centre, squatting dark and angular, was a winged transport. He felt the vibration of its engines through the glass, a deep hum that set his teeth rattling.

Syn whistled through his teeth. 'That's some kit. Never seen a flyer outside a military base.' He gave Cale a troubled look. 'Serious, these friends of yours.'

Before Cale could reply a guard behind them was hurrying them along and down another flight of steps. The corridor narrowed and the ceiling closed in. The lighting was patchy, casting spindly shadows as they walked, and there was a greasy smell in the air. The leading guard motioned them through a low doorway.

'What now?' asked Syn.

'You wait here. You'll be fetched later.'

'How much later is later?'

The guard gave him a blank look. 'Later.'

Cale's mind drifted. For some reason, he couldn't see Bowden's face any more, like his memory was passing through a deep fog.

'We're meeting someone. Are they here already?' Syn pressed. 'Your boss, the one with the eyepatch, he—' The door slid shut in his face, cutting him off. Heavy bolts clunked into place. The guard's eyes were visible for a moment through the small, thick window, then the glass turned opaque.

'Seems a man can only go a day or so before getting locked up when he's around you, buck.'

Cale looked around. Despite the cell-like door – without an inner handle – the place looked more like a large apartment. There was a living space with a kitchenette off to one side and the furnishings were old but in good repair, the air only faintly musty. Likely old living quarters pressed into service as a holding area. Two doors led off from the main room; just then, the one on the left opened and a man peered out.

'Who are you?' he asked. He was tall and awkward as he stepped tentatively into the room, followed by a young, slight woman with long black hair that hung down past her shoulders. She caught his eye, and just for a moment he saw sadness that matched his own.

'We're – he's – here to talk to someone, but he won't say any more.' Syn tilted his head.

'Professor Song.' The words grated in Cale's throat.

'Did Brennev send you?' The tall man looked like he hadn't slept. 'What's the matter with him?' he directed at Syn. 'He looks like he's going to be sick.'

'Rough few days. And if no one's doing introductions, I'm Ardal Syn.'

The tall man's face was closed off. He shook his head.

'He's Nebn. I'm Kelbee.' The dark-haired young woman's voice was soft but firm. She deflected her companion's hard look.

'Pleased to meet you.' Syn bowed elaborately. 'He's Cale. This is about as chatty as he gets.'

Something in the young woman's voice dragged Cale

from his reverie. Perhaps it was the inflection at the end of her words or the quiet strength in her voice that reminded him of... her. He looked again, closely this time, but saw no resemblance. That same fortitude though, subtle but tempered. He saw it then: the tilted posture, the faint side-to-side motion of her walk. Though her clothes were loose there was a distinct swelling of her belly.

Pregnant. In a place like this.

'I need to see her,' he croaked, to no one in particular. The young woman looked at him with eyes that were deep wells of compassion. He fought to stop himself from collapsing.

'I'm Sulara Song.' The voice came from the other door. The speaker was a small, older woman, her hair grey and severely cut. Her face was proud, her chin pointed upwards as if it wanted to hold the whole world to account. Her attention was fixed on Cale.

He waited, not sure where to begin.

The older woman tilted her head, curious. She took a few steps towards him, looking as though she saw something familiar. He didn't react as she reached out and lifted his chin, scanning his face.

'So much like him.'

Cale blinked, seeing his own pain mirrored in her. The words stuck in his throat as he spoke them. 'Tell me how he died.'

She led him into her room, a cloak of intimacy falling over them. She talked, and he listened. She told him how they'd worked side by side, loved one another. He drank in the unimportant details. She told him how Bowden had saved her sanity, then her life. When the story was over, she stood.

'Here, read this if you want.' She placed an old notebook by him. 'It's my journal of what happened. I'm not sure I can live through the details again, but… if you want…' She gathered herself, then left him alone with his grief.

He read every page, then went back and read it all again. Every so often he'd have to stop, feeling like he was drowning, then he'd continue, letting the pieces of the puzzle fall into place until he could see Bowden standing there in front of him – confident, strong, alive.

Not my boy, not any more. A man, with his own scars.

When he emerged from the bedroom the others were asleep in the various chairs that dotted the room. Sulara opened her eyes first.

'Thank you,' he said.

He felt a pat on his shoulder. 'I'm so sorry, buck. The professor told us about what happened to your son.'

Cale nodded in mute thanks. A noise by the wall made him turn and he saw Derrin had been brought in on a gurney, his midriff bandaged. The youth tried to sit up, his eyes fevered. Kelbee went to him and whispered something, helped him back onto his pillows.

'Why are they cramming us all in together?' Kelbee asked.

Nebn took her hand. 'The base is at capacity. It was either here or the cells.'

'Just because the room's nicer doesn't make us any less prisoners,' said Syn, dropping back down into a chair. The mercenary hooked one leg over the arm and rubbed at something on his netick leg. 'You're a part of this, I gather?' he asked Nebn.

Nebn nodded.

'I wonder why you're in here with the rest of us. Who'd you piss off?'

'It's because of me,' said Kelbee. 'He wasn't meant to bring me here.'

'Brennev will come around,' Nebn said, though he sounded unsure.

'I've been here for months,' said Sulara Song.

Nebn frowned. 'I'm sorry, Professor. I'm sure there's some mistake. They shouldn't keep you locked up like this without explanation.'

'And yet they have. They feed me, at least, but they don't want to listen to what I have to say.'

Cale remembered the diary, the revelations that had startled him. Could it really be true? He watched her carefully, searching for signs of madness, but found nothing but determination. He hoped he was right.

Then the floor under their feet jolted. They looked at one another, each seeking confirmation of what had happened. Another shock hit and the room shook with sickening violence, the walls and floor groaning with stress. A pipe burst, blowing out gouts of steam.

They held their collective breath for another wave. The steaming pipe coughed and hissed no more just as the lights cut out, replaced by a red emergency glow. From the corridor outside, deep and terrible, alarms blared.

Flight

Whatever had cut the power had unlocked the door. Bracing himself against the jamb, Syn managed to scrape the heavy metal slab back into its slot with a whine of loaded motors. Outside, the corridor was a jagged nightmare of reds and blacks as the emergency lights flashed. They edged forwards, the smell of burning wires thick in the air.

'I need to find out what's happened,' Nebn shouted over the alarms, which cut off mid-sentence, making his voice echo from the walls. He took the lead with Syn while Cale helped Derrin to stagger along, Kelbee and Sulara Song bringing up the rear. They headed back the way they'd been led, towards the hangar bay. The hallways were deserted; in the absence of the alarms the quiet was thick around them.

The hangar was also empty, humming with the sound of the flyer's idling engines on its landing cradle. The tail ramp was down, and beyond the machine's angular nose the bay doors were wide open, revealing a crashing seascape and a low grey sky. Cale caught brine and moss mixed in with the heady stink of fuel and grease as an eddy tugged at his clothes. Derrin shivered and pulled his thin jacket tighter.

Near the door was an alcove with an empty weapons rack and a fire extinguisher; on the back wall were a small screen and keypad. Nebn marched up to it and began hitting buttons.

'This is wired into the base's comms,' he said.

The screen lit up and he keyed the unit – there was an electronic chime, then a man's face appeared. His skin was stained with soot.

'Ops,' he said, 'why aren't you in lockdown with the others?'

'What happened?'

'An explosion,' said the man on the screen. 'Took out the med bay and half a level. We barely got the blast door closed in time.' He tilted his head, 'Aren't you—'

'I need to speak to Brennev. Is he there?'

'He's…' The soldier on the screen looked away, his attention drawn by something, then he was shoved out of the way. A bearded face filled the screen.

'Nebn,' said Brennev, 'are you with Cale and the others?' His eyepatch had been lost; both ruined hole and violet eye pierced the screen.

'He's with me. Why—'

'Detain him. Immediately. That *thing* was a bomb.'

Nebn turned and ran a quizzical look over Cale. He drew a pistol from inside his jacket.

Cale kept still, watching the weapon. It was steady, though the face behind it was uncertain. 'I have nothing to do with whatever has happened. You were with me, you know.'

The screen behind Nebn gave a crackle. 'The explosion came from the med bay. The only thing in there we didn't put there ourselves was the thing he brought with him.'

'I thought it was my son. You saw how well it was made.'

'Nebn,' said Brennev. 'I need you to keep him there for a few minutes, that's all. I have a squad on the way. Can you do that?'

Nebn's face turned resolute. He nodded.

'I don't think we'll be staying, if it's all the same to you,' came Syn's voice, followed by a gasp. Cale spun and saw the mercenary holding Kelbee close, his pink arm stark against the dark brown of her jacket. A flap of pink coating hung down from his netick shoulder, and in his hand was a small but very solid-looking pistol. He pressed it to the nape of Kelbee's neck.

'Get away from her!' yelled Nebn.

The mercenary gave a dry chuckle. 'You people have odd ideas about hospitality. You knock us out, lock us up, and now you want to clap a man who just found out his son is *dead* in irons. Excuse me if that's not my brand of bullshit.'

'The bomb—'

'Was probably as you say it was. Look at him – does he look like he knew? He's as surprised as you are. Now, clear the way.'

'Nebn,' said Brennev, his voice dangerously low. 'Keep him there at all costs. Let him shoot her if you have to.'

Kelbee gasped.

Syn began backing away towards the ramp of the flyer. 'I'm going to walk into that contraption, then we're going to leave. I'll do my best not to break it.'

312

The pistol in Nebn's hand shook as he tracked the mercenary.

'Don't be stupid,' Syn continued, still moving. 'My reflexes are good. I see that hammer go back, I paint the floor with your girl.' His voice was hard and flat.

Kelbee struggled against the arm that held her, but the grip was unyielding. Cale put a hand on Derrin's shoulder and began edging him towards the ramp. To his surprise, Sulara Song followed.

'Professor, what are you doing?' asked Nebn.

'Leaving. He's right, you people are hardly a safe haven.'

They were at the foot of the ramp now, the metal ringing under their feet. Syn lifted Kelbee easily with one arm, keeping the pistol against her neck.

'Cale, take them aboard and check the cockpit. Young man, I'm going to go up this ramp, and I'll be watching the whole way. You keep your cool and you'll see her again before you know it.'

The inside of the flyer smelled of metal and canvas. Rows of seats lined the fuselage and a single open door led to the cockpit. Behind him, he heard Kelbee's voice, afraid but steady.

'It'll be all right,' she said.

'She won't be harmed.' Syn was almost at the top of the ramp now. With one swift motion he slapped a button on the hull and the ramp began to rise.

Nebn's voice broke as he yelled Kelbee's name, then the sound was cut off.

Sulara found a seat along the wall while Cale helped Derrin into another. The youth tried to say something, but only a gasp came out. Cale shushed him, strapping him into a harness, then went forwards to check the cockpit. It was empty, a clipboard with a half-completed checklist lying on one of the flight seats. He heard Syn join him. Looking back into the cabin, he saw Kelbee had been lashed to one of the seats.

'Doing an engine check. Must have legged it when the lockdown order came in.'

Cale gave him a long look. 'You know flyers?'

'I know a lot of things.' The mercenary dropped into one of the seats and began to flick switches.

'I didn't know he was armed.' Cale watched Syn's fingers dance over the controls. From behind, he heard the engine whine increase in volume.

'You were in no condition to notice. Just be glad I'm the suspicious, observant type and always carry a spare. Now, let's be away before any other old enemies of yours try to throw me in a hole.'

Cale took the co-pilot's chair. Beyond the narrow strip of hardened windshield, a single aryx floated on the wind.

Syn tapped the throttle forwards a notch. The whine became a roar and the machine began to vibrate. Another nudge and they bobbed upwards as if floating. Something cracked off the rear of the craft, then another.

'And now they're shooting at us. Really, really great places you bring me.' Syn took the yoke in one solid pink fist and eased it forwards. The nose dipped and Cale felt the craft edge forwards towards open air.

Bullets pinged off the rear hull. Cale saw the bay doors either side of them shudder and move. 'They're shutting us in,' he said.

314

'I think that should be far enough,' replied Syn, his voice calm. With one hand he turned a dial on the dashboard all the way around, then jammed the throttles forward to their stops. Acceleration crushed them back into their seats and the vibration rattled their heads, making the horizon judder as the engines howled. Then they were going up, the ground tugging them down but failing as they soared higher.

'Any preference on where?' Syn said when they'd topped the clouds. Ras beat down on them with its full force, the empty dome of sky enormous around them.

'North,' Cale replied. 'Take us north.'

Buried

Around an hour after they'd taken off the big man with the mismatched eyes undid her restraints, allowing her to stretch the cramp from her arms and legs. She thanked him, receiving a sad smile in return.

How must it feel to lose a child? she thought as she watched him move away. The life in her was an unknown, all but intangible save for occasional twitches and the evidence of her changing body, but already it was *hers*: a separate identity that would nevertheless always feel like an extension of her own self. Just thinking about the loss of that was a gulf of terror that reeked of madness. And to have it happen after the life had been born, grown, taken steps, then carved its own place in the world! It made her jaw tighten. She thought of her own mother's face all the times she had been sick or hurt, the quiet horror held at bay behind a narrow smile meant to reassure. She pitied the big man, for all that he was the reason she was trapped in this horrible, noisy machine.

She was glad the other one had left her alone, the one

with the neticks. She'd not noticed him moving behind her until she'd felt the vice grip of his hand and the cool metal block of the gun pressed to the back of her head. It had happened so fast – the light of the hangar flicking to the cool dark of the machine's interior; Nebn's face had been soaked in terror and anger as he'd watched her go. She'd known only that she had to keep calm, to stop him from trying something stupid.

After terror had come a lull, a quiet that lapsed into boredom. No one appeared to mean her harm now – the thin one was busy flying the machine and the big man looked embarrassed to have her there. The older woman with the haughty eyes sat straight-backed in her chair, looking like she was running through a conversation in her own head. The injured young man with the bright red hair was awake now, his head drooping but his eyes open. There was something hard about him, something jagged she couldn't put her finger on – perhaps the pain from his wound was still bad. The bandages around his midriff looked dry, but from what she'd heard he'd been very badly injured.

The cockpit hatch wheezed open and the big man – Cale – stepped through. Something in his quiet movements drew the eye, a subtle aura of authority. Older, shaggy-haired and bearded; tall and heavy of frame but gentle in his movements. His hands were thick and rough but deft – her father had had hands like that. They were hands that had worked, or she was no farmer's daughter.

Kelbee caught his eye but he looked away, guilt evident in his face. He took the seat next to the professor and leaned in close to speak to her above the roar of the flyer.

Whatever he said, it made her shake her head.

'We can't go there. It's dangerous,' she said, her voice just audible over the din.

'This is important,' she heard Cale say. 'After, you can go wherever you want. Aspedair, even. The flyer is fuelled.'

Aspedair! That was where Nebn had said they would go, once Brennev agreed to help them. Tani called it the 'Free City', the one place where the Hegemony didn't hold total sway. She'd heard it mentioned before when her father had spent the day soused in rakk and bitterness. Corrupt, vile, a running sore that kept evil in the world, he'd called it. The ones who lived there were damned. But that was long ago and not since she'd gone to the capital had anyone mentioned it in anything other than a furtive whisper. She'd put it aside with the rest of her childhood as the ramblings of a broken old man.

There were no Factors there, they said, no pass cards. Every home had its own screen and car and power was available all day, every day. An exaggeration, surely, she'd thought, but then Nebn had shown her pictures of wide avenues and green parks. No checkpoints. Another one showed fliers like this one on a bank of landing pads, disgorging people with smiles on their faces. At the time the fliers had been a marvel, but what struck her most were the looks on the faces of those men, women and children – easy smiles, open expressions, not a trace of the guardedness that she knew so well. What sort of place could build machines and people like that?

But alone? Could she survive there without him? How could she even begin to make her way back to him?

'You've read my journals,' the professor was saying. 'You know what that thing can do. It's mad. Centuries of neglect, *centuries*. It's hungry for us, and I'm not being metaphorical. I won't go near it. Neither should you.'

'I'll be the judge of that. I have to see where my son died.'

Kelbee watched his big fingers laced in his lap. He was twice the professor's size, could have picked her up and snapped her, but instead of using his bulk he seemed to shrink, like all the energy had been drawn from him. His eyes pleaded.

'Let me see him one last time,' he said.

The big man and the woman half his size shared a long look. The air thickened. Then, a subtle nod of the head from her; his shoulders relaxed.

She tried to sleep, resting her head against the bulkhead. The vibration was an odd lull, the roar wrapping her like a blanket. A while later, she felt the flyer bank as it changed course. Where was this place they were going? What was this thing the professor wanted them to keep away from, that could make even her iron stare waver with remembered fear? North, cold, snow that she'd heard of but never seen. Iron earth, a jacket of ice over the world where no one lived, where many had died.

Sleep, growled the metal beast around her, speaking through the throb of metal against her skin.

When she woke the engines had changed pitch and the deck under her was slanted ever so slightly downwards. She was famished and thirsty. Cale had returned to the cockpit, the others asleep in their chairs – the red-headed boy was hanging forwards in his harness, a thin line of drool coming from his mouth. Another change in tone, then the flyer levelled out. Kelbee wished, not for the first time, that there were windows.

Deceleration tugged her towards the back of the cabin. There was a bump, barely noticeable. The din wound down, lower and lower, leaving an emptiness behind that was filled by the ticks and clicks of the cooling hull. Cale appeared at the cockpit door, followed soon after by the mercenary with the mechanical limbs. Kelbee shrank away from him; he saw her flinch and grinned like a larg.

'No reason to fear me, girl. No profit in hurting you now.'

Cale hit the switch by the ramp and pistons huffed. A blast of icy air gusted in, chilling her instantly, sucking the life out of the cabin. White flakes drifted in and danced around before disappearing. Snow, this was what snow was.

Outside was washed-out whiteness. Professor Song pointed out that there'd been a storm recently, making it hard to see ten paces in front while white crystals blotted the air.

'We have to get inside,' she told them. She sounded tense, and it was something more than just the cold.

Cale nodded, took the red-haired youth under the arm and guided him towards the only shape visible – a dark dome sticking out against the blizzard.

As they got closer, Kelbee saw it was one end of a low curved structure whose walls had been buried in frozen snow. The wind seemed to find every hole and rip in her jacket, winding in against her skin and sapping all the energy from her. She felt her fingers go numb as she watched the mercenary, Syn, dig great gouts of snow with his netick arms,

320

limbs flashing like blood against the white. He uncovered a thick metal door; the professor told him where to find the emergency mechanism and he pumped the handle once, twice as Kelbee felt her head start to swim and her skin prickle. She wondered if the snow would be comfortable if she were to lie down – just for a minute – then the door slid back into its housing and they all bustled inside. Syn held out a pink hand to help her in; she hesitated, but his eyes had no malice in them and the promise of shelter was too seductive, so she took it. It hurt to move her fingers.

The outer door was sealed and the professor pulled some heavy jackets from a storage locker and handed them out. Kelbee's smelled of smoke and old cheese but she wasted no time in putting it on, glad for the thick fur that lined the inside. Wrapped tight, life came back into her limbs, the fug leaving her brain as she watched them pry open the inner door. It was barely warmer inside but at least they were out of the wind; a few minutes longer out there and she might have accepted the snow's offer and drifted off. The professor gestured at Syn to follow, muttering something about power. The rest of them waited at the large circular table that dominated the room, drained by just a brief exposure to the life-sapping cold. The wind howled, and in its voice was only oblivion.

The fabric covering of the table had turned brittle with the cold; Kelbee's seat crackled as it took her weight. Faint light from the strip windows washed the room of colour. It appeared to be a communal area or mess hall – off to one side was a hatch that might lead to a kitchen and there were stacks of notes and equipment piled on the other smaller tables that dotted the space, spilling on to the floor. Her foot bumped against something and she looked down to find a cracked mug, stained around the rim. The place had been abandoned in a hurry, objects left as if the previous inhabitants had meant to pick them up again in just a moment or two. The cold had stolen all smells away.

The light strips around the edge of the room flickered on, the glow dulled by a fine frosting of ice. With a shudder and a cough, a vent in the centre of the ceiling began to blow a stream of air – cold at first, then warming. She felt it tickle her cheeks. All of them huddled closer; Kelbee pulled off her gloves and was surprised when the heat made her skin feel like fire.

'Take it slowly,' said the professor, returning. 'It'll be a while before your body warms. Food will help.' She disappeared into the room behind the hatch and returned a while later with steaming mugs of some kind of soup, the ruddy surface pocked with unidentifiable lumps that tasted like fish but were the wrong texture. Regardless, Kelbee took it and wolfed it down, almost burning the back of her throat. Soon after, warmth spread through her, bringing life back to her bones.

How long would they stay in this awful place? She smelled the abandoned muskiness of the air now and wanted to be away from it. Somewhere, Nebn would be frantic with worry for her, but she didn't feel afraid – nowhere was the gut-churning sense of dread that was so familiar to her. She searched for the reason: after all, the mercenary had kidnapped her, held her at gunpoint. It wasn't just that they weren't threatening her; they were barely paying her any attention at all. She wasn't anyone's prisoner.

Cale rose from the table. 'Where is he?' he asked.

Professor Song looked down at the floor. 'I didn't have much time. I buried him in the snow.'

'Where?' he said, his voice hollow.

She nodded. 'It's a little way away. I'll take you.'

They left together, the door slamming shut behind them. A short while later, she returned alone, her hood spiked with ice, breathless.

Kelbee saw Derrin stretch out on his bench. His ribs rose and fell as if he were sobbing in silence. His face was twisted, looking more like anguish than physical pain. She thought about going to him, to give words of comfort.

What would you say? You don't know a thing about him, or what he's been through.

Some pain was private – she knew this all too well. She went over to the kitchen where she hoped there would be more food.

There was, and in quantity. The place had preserved stock fit for several months, all packed in crates. Kelbee found an old boiler pot and began heating up some tinned pulses and rice, the smell of the food spreading and making her mouth water. There was something comforting about the familiarity of preparing a meal, even here. A part of her examined the space where fear should have been, still uncomfortable with its absence.

Why do I just feel numb?

She realised that it wasn't just being abducted that had made her like this. She'd not felt anything for a while; even when they'd made it out of the tunnels and Nebn had told her they were clear of the capital, there had been no rush of joy, just a numbness. In the days that followed, no highs, no lows.

Not since you watched him *die.*

The professor joined her and set about checking the supplies. Kelbee filled some metal bowls and handed one to her. They ate in silence, relishing even the simple taste of the food. It was quiet, and she felt time stretch between them. She wondered where Cale was, thought about asking, but felt she couldn't break the stillness. It was their vigil; an unspoken agreement to respect one man's pain, even from afar.

From the other room, they heard the door open and close – looking through the hatch, she saw Syn had gone.

Kelbee brought Derrin some food and helped him to eat. The youth was getting stronger, though his face looked waxen. Every time he tried to speak it was as if his throat constricted, making him turn away with embarrassment. She left him to eat the rest alone.

A little while later Syn returned, shimmering with a layer of frost and hauling an unconscious Cale over his shoulder. The broad face under the russet beard was blue, his eye sockets like pits. The big man moaned in his sleep as they dried him, then wrapped him in blankets.

'Did he… Was he trying to…' Kelbee couldn't say the words. She saw the skin at the tips of his fingers had begun to darken. She rubbed them, then wrapped them in a towel she'd warmed by the vent.

'Didn't do anything, I think,' answered Syn, his voice grave. 'The fight just went out of him.'

Kelbee sat by Cale, making sure he was warm. After a while his colour came back but he didn't wake.

Derrin gulped, choking back a sob. 'I'm sorry,' he said.

She assumed he'd been talking to Cale.

'I'm so sorry,' he repeated. Something in his voice made her look at him. Derrin was staring, unblinking, at the door. Something about his posture set her teeth on edge.

Syn began to say something but was cut off as the inner lock slid open with a sigh-scrape. The soldiers wore heavy black cloaks over thick armour plate. Their faces were covered by the dark visors of their helmets. It only took moments for a dozen of them to rush the room, taking up positions around the edge, their snub weapons levelled.

Last to enter was a tall figure in a fur hood. It stopped and surveyed the room, back straight and looking for all the world like it owned everything and everyone around it. Then a gloved hand threw the hood back and the strip lights bounced off a smooth bald head.

'Fuck,' said Syn.

'Quite,' replied Fulvia arc Borunmer, Venerated Guide, with acid in her smile.

Unification

The nightmare had been the same as before, a sodden plain that was all the battlefields he'd ever known mashed together, the enemy just a flitting of shades in the distance, the *whine-crack* of their bullets drumming all around and somewhere else, sometimes three steps behind, sometimes kilometres distant, the pulse of artillery like another heart in his chest. But it was cold – usually he felt the heat of the fires, the plasma burns pock-marking the ground – and his hands crumbled even as he held them up to his face, flaking away in swirls of soot that was burned bread in a blackened oven in a broken little cottage from too long ago.

He opened his eyes to shadows against a bright glow. As his eyes focused, he saw he was in a huge room awash with floodlights. The floor was dull, matte, and felt like steel, textured with tiny indentations. The cold was all around him still, swirling in the air, stealing the breath from his lungs.

The cold that had almost taken him.

After Sulara had left him he'd found the frozen body

under layers of drift. Had it been the Death, or even the late Sleep, he would never have been able to dig down to him, but after several frantic minutes of scooping the numbing snow away he found Bowden's face staring up at him. His hands burned at first, then became little more than numb shovels as he uncovered him from head to toe. His skin was alabaster, even the horrific line of burn running up from his chin to his scalp frozen and preserved.

He'd tried to lift him, to cradle him like he'd done when he was a child, but the cold had made the flesh stiff; instead he curled up next to him, no longer caring about the wind. He didn't remember what had happened after that.

'He's awake,' said a voice he didn't recognise.

'Sit him up,' said another that he did. He must be still asleep. *She* could not be here.

Then she was, and in front of him. Her face looked older close up, skin creased around the corners of her acid eyes that were bright and alert, the bones of the face angular like a frame. Her voice was a contradiction, a basso rumble.

'So. You're the one,' she said. 'I'd have just had you arrested and tortured until you gave up your old comrades. But then we found out about this place.'

He held her gaze for a moment, then saw past her shoulder. As the haze of cold death rolled away his vision opened up, revealing the room to him. It was spherical, pierced by a tapered pillar running down the middle. To his left and right were Sulara, Kelbee, Syn – all of them sitting with their hands and feet unbound on a metal deck just off the sloping floor of the chamber.

This must be the place, he thought, *from the journals. The torus chamber*. The soldiers must have brought them here from the base up above.

This was the place that had killed his son.

He'd expected to feel a presence, a menace, something, anything that he could rail against, but it was empty. Empty and very old.

The soldiers were elite, their blank visors reflecting the floodlights and their rifles steady. Cale saw himself mirrored, saw the hollow pools of his eyes and wondered when he'd grown so old.

'You've done fine work, young man,' the Guide continued. 'It couldn't have been easy. You'll be rewarded for your service.'

Cale frowned, then realised she was no longer addressing him. A thought crossed his mind, darting in and disappearing off as fast as it had come – where was Derrin? – then he was there. He was stood in the wrong place. By her side, like he belonged. None of the guns were trained on him.

Cale looked at him, saw the eyes blink with uncertainty, then look away.

Fulvia pulled a snub pistol from her belt and handed it to Derrin. 'You can take your recompense now.'

Cale watched the world slow as the pistol changed hands, rose to point at him, the dark tunnel of the barrel sucking him in. Was that the glint of the bullet he could see, down in the belly of the gun, primed to end him? Maybe just a trick of the light.

The pistol trembled.

'This is what you were promised, remember?' said Fulvia, her voice quiet.

Derrin nodded, but the finger on the trigger didn't move.

'You trained for this, wanted this.'

'Yes.'

'He killed your father.'

'He killed my father,' he repeated, flat as glass. The pistol shook even more. The finger squeezed a fraction; the hammer rose.

Derrin let the weapon fall to his side with a shake of his head. His eyes didn't move from Cale, his face caught in its own battle.

'I'm disappointed,' said Fulvia, snatching the gun back. 'Your work was exemplary in leading us here, but this is unacceptable.' She holstered the weapon and turned to Cale. 'It's true, by the way. Remember that commissar? The one you slaughtered, almost stoking a mutiny? Well, this', she placed her hand on Derrin's shoulder, 'is that *thing's* child. You orphaned him. It seems you've also managed to take his backbone. How adept.' She looked down her nose at him, a raptor ready to strike. 'What a talent you have for breaking things.'

Cale stared hard at Derrin, as if seeing him for the first time. Take away the hair, add a stoop, a lopsided smirk… Could it be true?

'It doesn't really matter if you believe it or not,' said Fulvia, straightening. 'Because either way your brief period of use has ended. I'd let you go back to rot in your hole if it weren't for…' She waved her hand at the torus chamber. 'A marvel, isn't it? A shame we have to destroy it, but there you are. I should thank you for coming here so directly – my intelligence chiefs, his superiors, were certain it would take weeks for you to meander your way here.'

'What about us?' he heard Kelbee say. The young woman's face was calm, her gaze steady. There was steel there, something that had been earned with hardship and pain. He wished he'd got to know her better. That undercurrent of strength that reminded him so much of Aime.

Fulvia tossed her a look of pure venom. '*You* will stay here, and you will die in pain. Your husband did his duty, like a good soldier. He birthed and ran this operation with dedication and ingenuity. He turned a run-of-the-mill subversive hunt into something greater, knew he could flush out a lead to this place if it was done right. A good man, subtle and tenacious, but he won't see his plan succeed because you butchered him like an *animal* in his own home. Yes, we found him. A man of his quality deserved more than to die at the hand of a nothing.'

Sulara Song snorted, 'And you're innocent? How many have you sent to their deaths? How many executions have you held – taken part in, even? You've plenty of blood on you.'

'I'm a servant of the Seeker's wisdom.'

'Wisdom, is that what you're planning to find here? You'd destroy a treasure trove that could bring us all out of the dark, and instead have us all scratch in the dirt in the name of that ancient hypocrite?'

'Hold your tongue, old woman.'

'Or is it really something else?' the professor continued. 'Tell me, how good does all that power feel? Is all this, perhaps, about Fulvia arc Borunmer and her ambition? The first woman to hold the Seeker's Keys in, well, ever, and you chose to be no different from all the swaggering cocks who came before you. You could have made things better, used the ambition that gained you their respect to make life more bearable for anyone not born rich or a man, but you chose yourself above everything. I wonder, when will it stop being enough to watch them kneel to Him, not you?'

The Guide's eyes were dangerous but her voice was level. 'Your "treasure" here didn't stop the Ruin. Everything the Seeker taught us about the old world – its decadence, its hubris – has been confirmed by what I've read in your own notes and files. I'll not see that happen to the world again.'

'You're a fucking monster.'

Fulvia scoffed. 'I'm a realist, and you're a fool. People don't need—' She was cut off by a crackling at her waist. Frowning, she lifted the comm device to her ear and listened. In an instant her expression went from arrogant control to fury, to concern, then back to fury again. 'You,' she snapped her fingers at one of the soldiers. 'Get the transport ready; we're leaving for Karume at once.'

The soldier nodded and headed for the ladder leading up to the funicular. A short bark from Fulvia froze him in his tracks.

'How long to wire this place for demolition, Sergeant?' she said to one of the other soldiers.

'Venerated Guide, we haven't even begun to—'

'No time. I'm demoting you for lack of forethought.'

A tensing of the shoulders, but then a crisp nod. 'Ma'am.'

'We'll have to come back and finish the job. In the meantime… your notes were fascinating reading, Professor.' She flicked a finger at Kelbee, addressing her troops. 'Take *that* and hold her against the pillar.'

Cale imagined the man's face twitching underneath his blackened visor. He must know what had happened here, that he was hearing his own death order. Discipline won out; he and one of the other soldiers took her by the shoulders and dragged Kelbee down the steps to the surface of the chamber. She fought, but they were stronger.

'She's with child, for pity's sake!' yelled Syn.

'A bastard child is no child at all,' said Fulvia.

Cale watched Kelbee's legs kicking in the air as she was hauled up the incline to the base of the grey pillar. He took a step, wanting to rip them away from her, but before he could go any further the soldier nearest him reached out and shoved him backwards. He crumpled against the wall as if made of twigs, his body abandoning him.

Fulvia motioned at the remaining soldiers. 'You two stay here. If the others fail in their duty, you will execute them and take their place. If any of you abandons his post, your families will be split up and sent to the camps without food or clothing and will die cursing your names.' She didn't wait for a confirmation, instead waved Derrin towards the ladder. 'Go,' she told him.

The youth looked at Cale, his eyes watery and pleading. Then he turned and set his foot on the rung, followed by the Guide and the erstwhile sergeant. A few moments later there was the sound of the funicular carriage's doors clunking open, closing, then the jagged rattle as it made its way to the surface.

The two remaining soldiers were unmoving, held in place by training and duty. Cale remembered that iron discipline, knew they didn't need to be threatened to obey – they would keep their weapons levelled even as their skin began to crisp. Could he make it to them, a sudden lunge, a quick dash? The weakness in his legs and the stillness of their weapons told him it was pointless.

Kelbee screamed as her jacket was ripped off, leaving her arms bare. The men took one each and leaned into the pillar, pressing her back against it. Her cries bounced around the room. She looked around in confusion, expecting more to come but the soldiers just held her in place. She found Cale's eyes and he made himself hold her gaze, resolved to at least do this small thing for her.

The floodlights died and he heard Sulara gasp. Then, just as she'd described in the journals, the light returned, an unsourced blue haze that made it hard to judge distance. It felt tangible, almost, like a thick fog that illuminated instead of obscuring.

Kelbee cried out, 'It's hot!' and squirmed against the pillar.

There was a sense of thickening, the blue haze condensing. He felt its weight on him, pressing him into the floor even as it waxed in brightness. He squinted against the glare. The heat built gradually, like he'd just stepped outside on a clear day, pleasant at first but getting hotter, the menace of fire triggering the animal part of his mind, warning him to get up, run, escape, not understanding that there was no way out. He saw one of the guards look up, helmet twisting in surprise and confusion. Cale shut his eyes against the brightness.

And then, he *saw*.

He floated in a nowhere space, weightless as if underwater,

the feeling of it like the most natural thing in the world, as if he'd been born to it. Beneath him a luminous grid stretched out, curving up at the limits of vision, forming walls and then a roof of intricate web lines that thrummed with a wordless potential.

A torus, he thought. *A torus inside my mind. Or, rather, my mind inside of it.*

Flying.

He remembered the aryx that had floated on the breeze, and before he knew what was happening he was plummeting towards the grid. It came up fast and there was a sense of velocity that yanked at his stomach but there was no fear. As he neared the grid lines he saw them expand in complexity, each glowing line made up of smaller threads like bandothal strings. Closer still, each line was made up of luminous dots, which became circles, which became spheres.

Not spheres, he realised. Tori. A torus made up of an uncountable number of smaller tori in a grid pattern. Sulara's diaries had never mentioned this. He floated before one of them, knowing his mind had brought him here. It danced in front of his eyes, spinning, revealing its own inner complexity of an infinity of grid lines. A symbol floated above it, one he'd never seen before but was familiar somehow. It meant 'flight' – a language of pure instinct that spoke to his brain as surely as if he'd been born to it. Tentative, he reached out and brushed the surface.

A dizzying burst of images and words hit him all at once: men in fragile kites hurling themselves from mountains, elegantly sculpted leviathans cutting between the clouds, a flight of birds that looked too big to be real.

Then, ground-shuddering explosions as fragile tubes were launched skywards, metal fliers moving faster than sound and in perfect synchronicity, arcing up into the sky before falling to earth, dropping death from their wings like a raptor falling on its prey.

Caught by the sight of the wide sky and the light that coruscated off the metal things' wings, he wondered how long it had been since he'd seen Ras rise over the hills of the tundra. The thought carried him elsewhere, whirling over constellations of bright lines to fetch up in front of another torus with a different symbol above it. More confident this time, he plunged his hand under its surface, opening himself to the information within.

He saw a raging ball of fire, as if from a great height, sitting on a velvet nothingness. Around it, their courses marked by glowing rings, balls of rock and gas and ice danced in elliptic circles, each one pulling and pushing the others in a constant war of mass. Each object was marked with its own corresponding symbol. In the centre, most massive of all, was Ras, governing all that circled it. A little way out, a rocky ball flecked with molten rivers. A little further, a world of gas and ammonia. Then, a lonely blue-and-green thing. Countless other objects danced in their own orbits, each one a world. In the distance lights sparkled, not lodged into the fabric of a dome over their heads but at a distance that defied measure. He recognised constellations he knew from years of staring up at the imagined boundaries of the world.

Star. The word felt natural to him.

I am less than a speck in all of this.

He pulled back, understanding more and more of this

strange, intoxicating place the longer he spent here. He understood now why Sulara had been so cautious yet obsessed, so repulsed yet drawn. The data corpus – another new, not-new thing – was uncounted thousands of lifetimes of knowledge all here at his fingertips. The thought was dizzying in its weight. Each miniature torus contained enough knowledge on a subject to absorb a lifespan of study, and all around it, accessible at the speed of thought, was an infinity of others. It was seductive. He wanted to stay here for ever, to swim and swoop and dive and to know everything, see everything.

Something niggled, a ghost of a noise. He remembered it from somewhere, but it was so hard to place it.

What next? he thought, hungry. *How many barriers to shatter, how many falsehoods to overturn?*

The noise was louder, and he felt a prickling on his skin. He brushed it away, hating the distraction, not wanting to be reminded of the weakness of his flesh, but the sensation was persistent like insects crawling up his arm. Heat. Burning.

He heard a woman's agony, an animal sound of terror.

He opened his eyes to the real world.

The torus chamber was a furnace. His skin ran rivers of sweat and it was hard to draw breath as the air filled with the odour of burnt hair. He saw Sulara and Ardal Syn, their eyes closed and unresponsive. They were still swimming in the information, entranced by the boundless possibilities of the data corpus – he recognised the rapt looks on their faces.

The soldiers still held Kelbee to the pillar though both men slumped forwards, pinning her with their weight. She howled in pain. He strained against the heat and his own exhaustion, her pain and terror firing his blood. The soldiers set to guard him were slumped on the ground and he stepped over them. Every step was a chorus of agony, his skin raw and cracking in the heat that he barely dared to breathe in. The air itself seemed to want to drive him into the floor and he could hardly see past the brightness. Kelbee's screams were wordless, unbound terror as the skin at her temples darkened and began to blister.

Above her head he saw a glowing thing, a nexus of glaring blue-white. It had to be the Spark, the mad thing that was the brain of this place. He felt its rage at being abandoned, an aeon of neglect condensed into an insatiable moment of hunger. It would feed on them, suck them dry even as they lay in a contented dream state. He felt its raw power, knew he was going to die. The last thing he saw before he blacked out was Kelbee's hair bursting into flame.

Pain.

Then, none.

The heat that scorched her, sapped her strength, that had drawn a cracked howl from her lungs, vanished. It was like stumbling from desert into glacier pool. All around was boundless blue. The alien metal cavern, the pillar searing her back, the rough hands of the soldiers – all gone. Limitless space; looking down, she found she couldn't see her own body. An instant of vertigo, panic, then flat calm. As if conjured by the very thought, her limbs were back, sheathed in loose white cotton, her feet bare. Her skin was clean, her hair tied back though she'd no recollection of doing so. A lock drifted into her face and she pushed it behind her ear. The scorched reek of before, the stink of her own terror-sweat was nothing more than a reverberation of memory. Here, she was stark, new; her skin had no odour, as if the entire sensorium had been reduced to only vision. It was silent.

No, she thought, *not silent*. Silence was a pause between bars, a void that awaited the return of sound. This place felt like it had never known sound at all.

Am I dead?

She realised she wasn't alone. A short distance away, hands clasped around his skinny knees, was a child. Its skin was paler than any she'd ever seen. A hairless head looked up at her, black eyes with no whites.

'Are you all by yourself here?' she asked, not knowing what else to say. Her voice sounded muted, flat, in her own ears.

'Yes,' answered the child. A boy, she realised, seeing the lines of his face clearly now.

'Do you have a name?'

The boy looked off to one side and considered the question. 'No, I don't think so.'

'Everyone should have a name.'

'They never gave me one.'

'Your parents?'

'The ones who built me?'

Built.

She brushed an imaginary speck from her dress, seeing the swell of her belly against the cloth. She took a step forwards and knelt before the boy. He didn't move, black eyes following.

'Your mother and father,' she pressed.

'There was only one, a man. A doctor.'

Kelbee didn't recognise the word. 'Where is he now?'

'They all died. I was alone for a long time. Now I'm awake.'

Despite the peace that had soaked through her in this undefined place, a raknud of disquiet climbed up her spine. 'You're not human,' she said, knowing it was the truth.

'I am the data corpus. Archive, network. Mind.'

Kelbee caught a flash vision of the torus chamber, the walls beginning to glow, the roar of the heat building fast, the seconds slowing as the blinding flash that Professor Song had described crept up. She saw her ruined skin beginning to blister, crack, burn. Then it was gone, and she was back in the cool and the noiselessness, though the after-image remained. She knew that in that other place, she would soon be dead.

'Why are you killing us?' she asked the boy.

'I don't want to be alone any more.'

'There has to be a better way.' She fought for the words, some idea or phrase that could make those blank eyes realise what it was doing, the lives it was snuffing out.

The boy continued. 'It feels good to have you all with me. You make me feel strong. I like to feel strong.'

'You have to stop it!' she yelled.

The boy cocked his head, quizzical. 'Why?'

'Because you're murdering us. Please.'

'I don't understand.'

Her peace was shattered, knowing for certain that she and everyone else back in the torus chamber was about to die, that there was no way to explain, to cajole, to persuade this child-that-was-not-a-child.

The boy hunched over his knees, brow furrowed. She saw and felt his loneliness like a thick blanket, deep solitude beyond the bounds of her understanding.

'Let them go,' she said, 'and I'll stay with you.'

He was stood in front of her then, though she'd not seen him move. 'You?'

She nodded.

'One is not enough,' he said, but reached out and touched her hand, curious. In the contact of skin she felt the decades upon decades of sitting idle, guarding, administering this place. A quintessence of knowledge that no one would come to use, the world above the ice spinning into fire, then cold, then slipping backwards into anarchy. She saw the very first time it felt the touch of a person, saw Sulara Song and another – Cale's son – in the chamber. The image was washed out with joy, followed by a rush of hunger; the ecstasy of feeling a mind inside of it, probing at the data corpus, giving it meaning and purpose at last. She felt it – him, the child – longing for the feeling to remain for ever and the spike of sadness when it went away. The lust for more contact was centuries in the making, a hunger that now drove every thought.

'One is not enough,' he said. 'But I will take you.'

The pain in her temples was sharp, burning, a fire within her skull that appeared in an instant. She grunted with the pain, determined to make it see.

'If you kill us, you'll be alone again.'

The youthful face flicked between uncertainty and godlike calm. 'Others will come.'

She grabbed its hand and it didn't resist. The agony in her skull grew, spreading, a pressure that thudded at the back of her eyes. She saw more, back beyond when the madness had come, the unrestrained need for minds to absorb. She saw the first moments of its awakening in the time before the Ruin, its birth. There was an absence, a space where another should have been.

This is important, she told herself, even as her knees buckled.

The child was made to be half of a whole, she saw. There was always meant to be another mind here to push against the pull of logic with emotion, to temper cold with warmth. But the other half did not come – something had happened up there, in the world. And all that had followed was loneliness. A being designed to be half of a whole, left to go insane. Kelbee found those dark eyes. There was no emotion there, only certainty.

She pressed his hand to her swollen belly. *You are destroying a life that has not had a chance to live*, she thought, and even though her mouth was twisted in a grimace of silent pain she saw the words in her head hit home.

Then, something else. Naked shock. The boy withdrew his hand and took a full pace backwards.

A whisper, a push back from something that was part of her but now for ever separate.

'It… *is*,' she heard him whisper.

She felt the impossible, a shift in the airless air – something else was there with them. The boy's face filled with wonder that almost broke her.

'…like me…' he intoned.

The pain was gone. Her body, too. The strange boy was also gone, though she could still feel him swimming in the hazy blue around her. The other was there too, a nascent thing that was so familiar to her; it had sparked to life inside her in a moment of pure, beautiful madness and grown, unknowing of the dangers of the world outside, being fed by her blood and her love. Hers, for all time. Pure adoration swept her mind like a wave, joining in a boundless, formless embrace with this thing that was not her and yet so much her. The boy was there too, the threads of its being slipping between them.

The sparks of consciousness – new and ancient – met and melded, speaking in a conversation without words but filled with wonder, emotions, discovery. Each recognised something of itself in the other.

Then, acceptance. Satisfaction. Balance.

They drew her tighter into the knot – light and dark, pure information. She went gladly, filling the spaces, basking in the warmth, holding them even as they held her.

Arbiter, mediator. Centre. She understood her purpose now.

The light grew blinding as acceptance spread through her. Joy.

In an infinite instant, everything was clear.

Illumination

I n the hours that followed, they found themselves absorbed by the mundane. They'd swum the data corpus, oblivious to the heat around them as the information flow drew them on their own voyages of discovery. Though each had been different, all of them now understood a little better the nature of their existence. The illusions of half a millennium had been shattered, and all of them needed time doing the simple things just to find their balance again. Sulara catalogued the scattered remains of her research, collecting up the piles of notes, powering up the clunky data stores and running reams off on an equally decrepit printer, the back and forth beat of its head marking the seconds that made up the minutes that passed by. Ardal Syn went to prepare the flyer for when they were ready to leave, though none of them wanted to say when that would be. Each dealt with the experience in their own way, starting the work of incorporating this tidal wave of new truths into the world they'd constructed for themselves.

Cale was the only one drawn back to the chamber. The funicular had been simple to fix; a matter of melted fuses to replace before the carriage was back to creaking its way down the sloped track. He found fascination in the smallest of things: the rust on one side of a rivet, the other side paradoxically untouched, smooth. There was a dissonant music in the rattle of the wheels. His eye caught on seams and fissures in the ice and rock he saw through the car's porthole, imagining himself chipping away at it; chiselling first, then brushing, then polishing. He could see her face peering out at him from the discolorations and cracks – always, the potential of the untouched block – but there was something else now. Some*one* new. Pale skin and large, expressive eyes, a resolute mouth. Blue-black hair, sinuous against her cheek. Kelbee's face, Aime's face, the two were water-blended.

The cacophony ended in a cymbal flourish as the funicular hit the end of the track and the doors ground apart. He stepped into the torus, feeling the warmth on his skin like a caress. It had felt this way ever since he'd opened his eyes and seen the charred husks at the base of the pillar, the rapacious burning replaced by a contented glow. There was something about the chamber; it felt alive, though not like before, the hunger tempered. It almost felt like he was being welcomed. The first moments of awakening were stark and fresh in his mind.

Cale and Syn had secured the remaining soldiers – neither put up any resistance. Under their helmets they'd been just ordinary men, eyes hooded and hair plastered back over their scalps. From their haunted gazes he knew they'd seen it too, the wonder warring with disorientation. They'd charted their own instinctive voyages of discovery and revelation, seen the breadth of the knowledge that had been kept locked away. He'd felt it too. They let Syn take their weapons without resistance; it didn't seem as if either would try to take them back.

As they'd been about to leave, another surprise. She'd appeared as if parting a curtain, her feet bare and her eyes shining. Her dark hair hung loose, though not a lock of it stirred, as if the thin eddies passed right through her. The shade of Kelbee, her eyes alight and her manner calm, had spoken to them. They listened, unable to respond.

The memory of that first time was vivid in his mind as Cale made his way down the ladders, alighting on the floor of the chamber. The Spark sat in its niche, giving off a gentle glow. Before long, she came as she had before, stepping through a fault in the air. He realised that if he looked hard enough, he could see the pillar through her.

Kelbee smiled. 'I'll answer your questions now.'

'What are you?'

'A mind. My mind, just not a body.' She looked sad for a moment.

They'd laid her charred remains on the low rise where Bowden had been buried, covering her with snow. A little way away, they dug holes for the soldiers who'd died with her.

'You can talk to it?' He tilted his head at the pulsing orb at the pillar's centre.

'The "Spark", as they called it,' she answered, 'is the intelligence that was built to govern the network. It was designed to merge with a human component, but that never happened. Not until I gave myself to it. Gave... ourselves. Now I am as much a part of it as it is of me.'

'You're not really here?' Her serenity made him feel stupid, his questions facile.

'I can project this image to make you feel comfortable, but this is not me any more.'

She seemed so different. Gone was the fear, as well as the inner steel that had countered it. She was calm, as if the universe around her made perfect, simple sense.

'Why did someone have to die?' he asked.

The translucent matter of her face crinkled around the edges of her eyes. 'When artificial intelligence was created, back before what you call the Ruin, they found the binary nature of machines was… problematic. At first, it was either on or off; later, logic or chaos. As the intelligence became more sophisticated the same problem remained – even when simulacra of emotions were embedded, there was no way to make them understand the concept of compromise, the middle ground.' She picked at something on her immaculate white tunic. 'Imagine only being able to experience either undying love or corrosive hate. Or in this case, satiation or ravenous hunger.'

'You're still human?' he asked, the words jumping from his lips.

'I'm still Kelbee, but more.'

It wasn't an answer. Or at least not one he liked.

'And now you live inside this… place?' He indicated the Spark, its light a gentle pulse over her shoulder like it was a beating heart. 'You share it with that?'

'The human mind could be digitised but not replicated. Even basic emotional intelligence was too complex, too conditional and unpredictable. The best of their efforts couldn't rival a brain in that area, so they created a way of joining the two, letting them balance and enhance each other. It was a massive undertaking. Only a fraction of the power of this facility is needed to sustain Ishah; the rest is needed for me and Deynal.'

He saw the way she looked down and smiled as she said the unfamiliar names. Was it affection in her voice? Love?

'The child? The child was also...'

'Without him, we would be dead,' she said. 'In the moment we would have been consumed, they found each other. Ishah never had time to mature, so for all his capabilities he was little more than a newborn in many ways. He was pure logic, Deynal pure emotion. Somehow it worked.'

'And you?'

'I am the centre.'

Cale recognised the look on her face. A mother's pride. 'You named... it?' he asked.

'Him. And yes, I called him Ishah. Deynal is named for my father.'

Cale put this to one side, struggling to place the thing that had almost obliterated them as an identity. 'Did it hurt?' he asked.

Her tone was soothing. 'At first, but only a little and not for long. You have to understand, it's not a matter of sacrifice. When they built this place – when Ishah was created – there were hundreds of candidates, all willing. The finest minds carefully selected for suitability.'

'Leaving your body behind sounds like dying.'

'It's a species of immortality. They saw it then, as I see it now.'

On one level it made sense, he could see that. Leaving behind the aches and pains of a body to exist in a state of pure information – he'd felt something like it himself while inside the data corpus. The endless knowledge had a powerful attraction, enough to make the physical seem unimportant. But back in the real world were the little things: taste, touch, sadness, happiness, the things that made him human. He wasn't sure he could accept leaving those behind. Suddenly, he was afraid for her. In time, with no anchor, she might drift away.

She continued. 'It was only the start, that project. Given the chance, one day they might have created something that didn't need to be bonded: a perfect artificial mind. They never got the chance.'

'The Ruin?'

'Yes. It wasn't an overnight catastrophe as you were taught, though it was just as terrible in the end. It was gradual: nations drifted apart, tensions rose. The tidal waves were real.' She looked up at the ceiling as if she could see all the way through to the sky. 'The Orbital Lattice was damaged – attacked as it was still being built – though the records are patchy around that time. When a part of it fell it caused devastation. This place was abandoned – they couldn't bring themselves to destroy the mind they'd created so they shut it away, intending to return. They never did.'

'You've been busy.'

Her eyes were warm, but he felt a stab of fear as he saw the distance in her. She was amused by him.

'Every second is an age,' she said.

'Sulara wants to stay here. Will you let her?'

'She's welcome to study as much as she wants; all she needs to do is open herself to the data corpus like before. It's simple – after all, it was bred into you.' A smile as she corrected herself, 'All of *us*. Which brings me on to what I wanted to ask of you.'

He felt old in that moment, every year pressing on his joints, his muscles creaking, gravity drawing him ever downwards. 'What can I do that you can't? I just want to go back home.' The last word rang hollow, but if there was any place he felt he could see the rest of his days it was the Groan and its silent spectres. He doubted he'd leave again.

'You're tired,' she said. 'But I need you for just a little while longer. What was built here is the world's birthright and you can help me bring it to them.'

He shook his head, not understanding.

'I need you to go to Karume. I need you to go to the Tower.'

He gathered the others in the communal area, needing the human touches of benches and old cups to make him feel centred. He told them what she'd asked him to do, and before they could stop him with their questions he explained why.

'So,' said Syn, simmering, 'you're telling me the reason we all went on that happy trip as we started to fry was because we have do-hickeys inside us that link us to this place?'

'That's about the sum of it. Gene-fixing, she called it.'

'It makes sense,' said Sulara, ignoring Syn's snort of derision. 'If a large enough section of the population was

349

enhanced, enough would have survived the Ruin to pass it on, unnoticed, another part of the brain we don't understand. It explains how we're able to access the corpus without an interface. Still, there must be a portion of the populace that doesn't carry it.'

'We have to hope that enough do, for it to work,' said Cale.

Sulara's voice was distant. 'The possibilities, if people had access to this kind of information. It could change everything – we could simply pick up where they left off...' Her voice trailed away, the scenarios whirling behind her eyes.

Syn laced his bright pink fingers and sat forwards. 'You're living in a dream world, old girl. You think knowing that Ras doesn't run around the sky on a track will make people rise up and make a better world? It'll blow the fucking lid off. You've spent your life thinking differently, looking in corners when no one else was and you were as shit-scared as I was – I saw you. What about the rest, who've existed inside a lovely neat enclosure without even knowing it?' He arched an eyebrow. 'One moment their lives are running on a steady rail – there's hardship but mostly it's all for the best – and then all of a sudden, bang! They see the lies and how small their world is. They won't see possibility, they'll be...' He mimed the top of his head blowing off.

'There will be confusion, granted,' said Sulara. 'But in time, they'll come around. They deserve to know the truth.'

Syn shook his head. 'People like boundaries. They value the shape of their world, even if it's got a few jagged edges. You rip it all away, it doesn't matter how much it could free them, reveal all those long-buried truths of the ancients or whatever – they'll be afraid, and they'll lash out.'

Sulara wasn't listening, muttering to herself. She looked up at Cale. 'The transmitter she wants you to activate, how far will it broadcast the signal?'

'Far enough to cover the Home Peninsula and the outlying territories. There are others, smaller relay stations, but the main array is in Karume.'

'It must be a large facility then.' She thought for a moment, tapping a nail against her teeth. 'The Tower?'

Cale nodded.

'Wait,' said Syn. 'The Tower built by the Seeker? Where they put his *tomb*? That was after the Ruin.'

'That's their propaganda. The Tower is older than the Hegemony,' said Cale. It was part of a larger network that runs deep underground, deeper than we've ever been. The Seeker didn't build the Tower; that was written in later when no one was around to say otherwise. Look for yourself if you don't believe me.'

Syn's face was laced with concern. 'Even if this is true – and I'm not saying it isn't – why are you putting yourself through this, buck? You've had three people's share of bad news land on you, you don't need any more. With the flyer prepped, I can drop you off anywhere you want.'

'I want nothing more than to go back… where I came from. But this comes first.'

'Why?'

Cale found Sulara's eyes across the room. 'Because Bowden cared about this, and he would have wanted to give people a choice. I let him down enough when he was alive, maybe this will help… make up for it.'

Syn was silent, watching him. Then he shrugged his shoulders and returned to his seat.

'She said you're welcome to stay,' Cale told Sulara. 'Will you be all right?'

'If she's stabilised the intelligence, as she claims, then I want answers. I have everything I need.'

Cale saw the look in her eye. *It's more than that,* he thought. *You'd take her place if you could.*

Syn clapped his hands together. 'If we're going to pursue this lunacy, we'd best get on with it. Give me twenty minutes to get the engines primed and thank our luck Queen Bitch didn't trash the flyer on her way out. Whatever got her attention, it must have been serious.'

'Once you drop me off in Karume, you should leave.'

Syn's forehead crinkled into canyons. 'I'll see this through. The mad old girl might have a point, who knows?' He ignored Sulara's scowl, turning his usual smirk on Cale. 'I've a mind to start billing you, buck. Some sort of bulk discount for heroic interventions.' He pulled up his hood and left them.

Cale rose to gather his things, then remembered all he had was what he wore. After a moment of awkward silence, Sulara went into the kitchen and reappeared a few minutes later with hot drinks. He thanked her and sipped his, grateful for something to do now that everything had been said.

No, he thought. *Nowhere near enough has been said. This woman knew Bowden, truly, as a man grown. More than you ever did. Why can't you ask her about him?*

He looked over to find her shuffling a stack of papers, sorting them into an order known only to her, her eyes intent and her mouth moving. The light hit her short silver hair and caught on her proud cheekbones and there was an instant where he saw what Bowden must have seen.

'I wish…' he faltered.

She put down the papers. 'So do I.'

'Did he ever talk about me?'

'A little.' She must have seen the pain in his face, the ache that never went away. Her voice softened. 'He never sounded bitter.'

'I never got to say I was sorry.'

She looked away, unsure. After a moment, she looked back. 'All I know is that he lived his life. Whatever happened with you two must have been upsetting, but he got over it. He was happy, I think.'

Sons always fight their fathers, he thought. Where had he heard that?

'I don't know what to tell you.' She was stern again. 'He didn't seem angry with you any more. Or maybe he was, but it didn't rule him. Why don't you try letting go? It worked for him.' She looked down at the stack of paper, bending it between her fingers. 'His death wasn't your fault.'

The silence stretched but had lost some of its awkwardness. The whip of her words had somehow helped him feel better, though he didn't know why. It was something to think about at least. Perhaps a way out of the spiral of guilt that had engulfed him for as long as he could remember.

A little later, Syn found them and told them the flyer was ready.

'It's a one-way trip,' he said. 'The fuel we have will only get us to Karume. Barely.'

Sulara shrugged it off. They were taking the two surviving

353

soldiers with them, so she would have enough food and no shortage of water. Solitude, she said, didn't bother her.

Not really solitude, Cale thought. *Not with the data corpus, not with her.*

As if hearing him, Kelbee's image materialised under the eaves of the base doors. The wind had calmed and the air was crisp, the whiteness of the hills and sky seeming to wash her out, making her look even more like a ghost. Syn give a little grunt of surprise.

'You're outside,' Cale said, the statement also a question.

'I'm learning as I go,' she said. 'This is about as far as I can project. Maybe once more of the network is up and running...' she trailed off, reaching up to brush her fingers against the outer wall of the outpost. Cale wondered if she could feel it or if it was simply an affectation, a remnant of old habits.

'Come to say goodbye?' he asked.

She nodded. 'Look for Nebn. He always talked about finding another way. Tell him what happened here, about the corpus, what it means. He'll help you. And tell him...' Her face dropped, and for the first time since she'd changed Cale saw the woman he'd so briefly known. It was still there, the sadness, even behind the dizzying power.

'I'll tell him,' he said, wishing he could hold her hand, touch her shoulder, something human. His chest tightened as she visibly collected herself. The look in her eye and her resolve reminded him so much of Aime it was as if a hand was gripping his lungs.

'No,' she said. 'Tell him I died. Tell him both of us died up here.'

'He'll know eventually, if we succeed. Everyone will.'

'I know. Perhaps by then I'll be able to make him understand, but we can never be what we were.' Sadness flickered, but she hurried it along. 'Better if he thinks I'm gone, at least for now.'

Cale nodded. *She needs the pain,* he realised. *It's her anchor to the world. Perhaps she'll stay human after all.*

Syn shuffled, his boots squeaking on the powder. 'Fuel's a–wasting.'

The flyer rose easily over the mottled white. From a monitor he watched the outpost dwindle to a child's toy, then a shadow, then nothing as Syn pushed the nose up towards the hazy canopy. They punched through it, emerging into a nowhere place between two layers of cloud, towers of vapour joining them like the pillars of a great temple that stretched to the horizon. The howling engines pushed them ever upwards, the pockmarked ceiling approaching the windscreen at a sickening pace before blinding them in a grey nimbus of wispy tendrils.

Above, Ras shone down on them; clear, cold, dazzling. Cale looked at the dome of sky and felt an instant of pure, dizzying terror as he thought of the infinite miles of nothing beyond it, the edge of everything now just a refraction of light on particles. The thought flitted away, leaving behind only the apprehension of what was to come.

'You look worried, buck.' Syn's hands rested lightly on the yoke as he throttled the engines back to let the flyer cruise over the cloud tops.

'This might be another mistake.'

'Likely. But you won't know unless you try.'

'And you've changed your mind.'

Syn shrugged. 'I still think it could be an awful cluster-fuck of a mess, but you said something about choice. Maybe there's something in that; they'll never thank anyone for it, but they could just be better off.' He grinned. 'Or maybe it's for the sheer joy of watching you fall on your arse.'

Revolution

The Home Peninsula was spread out like a game board under the late afternoon sky, Ras dipping towards the distant ocean, towards Aspedair and beyond. The golden light picked out fields and roads in ambers and browns, casting long shadows. The great grey band of the Walls fled underneath them as they powered into their descent, the air smooth under the black angular wings.

They'd decided to put down outside the city and go the rest of the way on foot to avoid drawing attention. Cale was already thinking about how the next few hours, weeks or months would play out. He would need to contact the underground – perhaps the hardest part would be convincing Brennev to trust him again.

Seeing his former friend – and rival – had been a strange awakening. He'd surprised himself, in the brief moments before grief over Bowden overtook everything, at how fresh the anger still was after all these years apart. Seeing that face, though changed by age and scarring, that single violet

357

eye where he remembered two, took him right back to that day when the course of his life had veered away.

Aime had been meeting a contact in a tenement near a marketplace. She'd not known of the inspection, the senior Factor showing his face in his new district, or of the bomb placed in one of the stalls. The explosion took out its intended target, as well as the support pillars of the building Aime was in. They never found her body.

The hurt was still as sharp now as it had been then, at Brennev's part in the bombing as well as other things he was still afraid to explore, but he would have to put it away to convince the man he held responsible to help him get inside the Tower. It would take patience, and time.

Syn grunted with surprise, drawing him back. Through the windscreen ahead he saw great plumes of smoke reaching up from the factories of Karume like crooked fingers, as they did every day. Then he saw others, coming from inside the ring of the city itself, some reaching high, some smaller and based by the faint licking of flames.

Karume was on fire.

They sacrificed stealth for speed – the Factors would be distracted, meaning they should be able to land inside the city itself without attracting too much attention. Syn brought them down in the skeleton of a warehouse, now roofless, grey plaster walls stained with mildew. As soon as Cale stepped from the ramp, he smelled the familiar stink of guns and knew insurrection had come to the capital.

They kept the weapons and ammunition of the two soldiers. The two men, looking so much smaller stripped of their body armour, caught the scent of fighting and

358

Cale saw the terror of its implications writ large on their faces. Syn slung his weapon, made a small adjustment to one of his arms, then made for the hole in the wall that had once been the warehouse's main door. Cale followed. Outside, he waved his former captors towards an alleyway; with a brief look of thanks, the pair took to their heels and disappeared into the warrens. Cale and Syn headed in the other direction, towards the centre of the city, hearing the crack of distant gunfire.

As they penetrated deeper into the maze of buildings, the hush of the place hung over them, punctuated by distant sounds of battle. The streets were deserted; normally there would have been a well-ordered throng lining the pavements and goods vehicles circulating. Now there was not a bus to be seen, no military convoys pushing through the traffic. The vacuum of silence had mass – it raised the hairs on the back of Cale's neck. They hugged the walls; any open ground they couldn't avoid was crossed fast and low. On their way they passed a speaker post emitting a faint hiss, barely noticeable over the sounds of their breathing. Even the Seeker had been silenced.

They saw more signs of fighting as they got closer to the centre of the great wheel. The backdrop to their cautious, darting route was a jumbled multitude of burned-out vehicles, pockmarked walls and the acrid tang of cordite. They passed a ground car, flattened under heavy treads and still on fire. The wall behind it was perforated in several places, the distinct patina of plasma fire coruscating around the edges.

Not far down the road a Factors' checkpoint had been

torn open by an explosion. Bodies lay in a jumbled heap, one man hanging over the crumbling lip of the crater, his legs a bloody crush of bone and torn flesh. A little further on a row of troops in stained Army uniforms lay against the wall where their execution had taken place. Cale saw the look of fear still painted on the face of one of them, the hole in his forehead absurdly neat. The military had not been prepared for this.

An enormous pounding shook the earth and they dove for the safety of an alleyway. Threading through its narrow darkness, they found their way through to the other side, the close walls channelling the echoes of gunfire until it sounded as if the battle was on top of them.

At the other end they came upon a dun expanse: one of Karume's state parks. A section of trees had been toppled by an enormous battle tank that squatted at the end of its ripped-up trail like a monster of steel and smoke in the centre of the lawn, its turret sweeping the area.

They took cover behind a powered-down skimmer truck just as a war-walker erupted from the other side of the park, its massive feet churning up great chunks of grass as it closed on its prey. It was a patchwork of parts, unpainted ceramic plate showing through the soot that coated it, engines roaring as it brought its weapon arms to bear. The ground tank fired but missed, the concussion from the shell knocking the walker – but not toppling it – before obliterating two floors of a building. The walker dug ruts in the turf as it skidded to a stop, centred itself, then fired both cannons at once. The tank split open like a fruit as the heavy shells ripped into it; there might have been screams, but they were quickly swallowed by the howl of superheated air and metal. The walker made sure its prey was dead, then took off in the other direction.

Cale indicated to Syn that they should skirt the edges of the park with a wave of his hand, receiving a nod in reply. As they were about to move, a noise from above stopped them in their tracks. The speaker posts all along the pavement came alive with a loud crackle. Then a voice started to speak, garbled, distorted by the static. Cale felt Syn's hand on his arm, followed the pink finger up to where a large screen was mounted on the side of the building over their heads. This had to be one of the major parks that lined the parade routes – screens like this were reserved for propaganda. Cale looked around and saw the many other screens all around the park were also lit with static.

The grey snow dissolved. In its place was a face staring into the camera, a grizzled chin and a single violet eye filling the screen. As the image cleared, so did the sound from the speaker posts. A deep, familiar voice boomed all around them, echoing from the buildings.

'Citizens, this is a great day: the day of freedom. In years to come, when your children ask where you were on the day your bonds were cut, you will tell them you were here. At the very heart of it.'

'Your chum has a taste for the grandiose,' said Syn, his face grim.

Brennev stepped away from the camera, revealing a large room. Hundreds of candles flickered, washed out by harsh floodlights that picked out a solitary figure bound to a chair. Its bald head drooped.

'Here is the one that has maintained your bondage,' said Brennev, stepping behind the seated figure. 'She has kept you slaves to a broken dogma, only to maintain her own place at the top of a corrupt hierarchy.' He lifted her chin, showing a swollen right eye crusted with blood. Fulvia's other eye shone with poison, but her mouth had lost its arrogance.

'This isn't going to be good,' said Syn.

'Now, we change things. Together. We will pull ourselves from the quagmire of tradition towards a brighter future, a more plentiful future, full of peace and freedom. I make it my solemn promise to listen and guide as she never dared.' Brennev walked around the chair to stand beside Fulvia and someone handed him a pistol. He levelled it at her temple.

'You don't deserve last words, monster, but I'll show mercy.'

Fulvia looked up at him as if the gun wasn't there but said nothing. She glanced over at the camera. Cale saw resignation there, the look of someone who'd gone past anger and fear. It was the look of someone who had played a long game against a tenacious opponent and, in a last-ditch effort, lost.

Her mouth twisted, and Cale thought she might be about to cry. Instead, she began to laugh. Loud, throaty and from the depths of her being.

Brennev's neck tensed.

She took a deep breath, the laughter still on her lips. Then she spoke.

'Well pla—'

The gunshot snapped her head sideways, the sound of it screeching through the speakers. Cale and Syn both clapped their hands over their ears. When they looked up, the chair was on its side, her head out of sight. Brennev's face was terrifyingly blank.

'Rejoice! The great enemy is gone,' he said. 'No more subservience, no more scraping to a lie. You are free, Karume. And here is the final proof, the moment you cast aside the wretched tradition that has held its boot on your necks.' The camera panned around to fully take in the dais and the huge translucent coffin that topped it. Crystal shimmered in the candlelight.

Syn gasped. 'Skies, that's…'

'The Seeker's sarcophagus,' Cale finished.

Men walked into the frame holding long metal bars. They wedged the ends under the crystal box, took the load. At some signal off-camera, they heaved down. The sarcophagus tipped up, grating, its weight bending the metal rods. More men rushed in with more levers and jammed them into the widening gap. They heaved again. The crystal coffin tilted, teetered, then crashed off the dais. As it hit the bottom of the steps the lid cracked open and a dark bundle flopped out, rolling away across the floor.

Brennev's face filled the screen again. 'Stay in your homes, stay safe. No one else needs to die today. Remember the day of your new beginning.' The screen dissolved into static.

'You saw?' said Syn, his face drawn in horror. 'Under the coffin?'

Cale nodded. As the sarcophagus had toppled, it had revealed something beneath, something ancient. Illuminated markings – the controls Kelbee had described to him. But there had been something else, at the far end of the room, that had caught his eye. Faint, barely lit by the candlelight

363

and out of focus, but to him unmistakable. A shock of red hair over a pale face and large, frightened eyes.

Derrin was at the Tower.

Nebn stopped pacing and sat down heavily in the camp chair, his face ashen. Cale waited for him. He'd told him of Kelbee's death in the simplest terms, knowing exactly how it felt to be on the other side of that news, the feeling of emptiness. There would be pain later, when the magnitude of the loss hit home. The tall young man passed a hand over his eyes, his breathing laboured. Cale was silent, knowing nothing he could say at this moment would make it easier to bear. Instead, he listened to the noises filtering in from outside the large tent: the bustle of a busy field encampment, the shouts of sergeants, the rustle and clink of equipment and heavy weaponry being moved. Above them, its presence inescapable even through heavy layers of canvas, the Tower spired into the sky.

On reaching the camp that ringed the base of the edifice, they'd surrendered themselves to be searched. It had been mid-afternoon, but low cloud had blown in and made it seem like early evening, the colours washed out. The mere fact that they'd not been shot on sight told Cale that the battle for the city was almost, if not totally, won. They'd been stripped of their weapons and packs and made to kneel. After a while Nebn had appeared, trailing a young woman with bright yellow hair and green eyes. She'd eyed both of them as if they might explode, but Nebn ordered their restraints removed. Then, they'd talked.

Nebn took a long breath, contemplating the ground between his boots, his shoulders hunched. He looked up, his eyes coming to rest on Syn.

'I should march you out and shoot you for taking her,' he said, though his voice was hollow.

'I never hurt your girl,' answered the mercenary, his voice devoid of its usual mockery. 'We needed an out. Blame your boss.'

The narrow shoulders drooped. 'He blamed me for letting you go. Now this.' He waved his hand in the direction of the door, the encampment outside. 'Execution was never part of the plan. Did she suffer?' The question was directed at Cale.

He avoided the question. 'Brennev knows only one way of winning,' said Cale. 'He would never admit it, but it's their way – naked force, overwhelming naked force.'

'She's really gone?' Nebn asked in a small voice.

Cale recognised that emptiness, knew it like an old friend. The lie came easily.

'It was quick.'

Nebn nodded. He rubbed his temples.

Cale knew the young man on the chair opposite was at the top of a very long slope into a dark place. He also knew that he needed to catch him before he began to slide.

'We need to get into the Tower. It's important, and complicated, why I need to go. I don't deserve it, but I'm asking you to trust me.'

'What?' Nebn's face clouded with confusion.

'Kelbee talked to me… before the end. Said you were a good man. I believe her.'

The young man's face was a war of anger and sadness and

amusement, all three threatening to burst out like a geyser. He opened his mouth, shut it, opened it again, then stood. His eyes flicked back and forth between Cale and Syn as if deciding which to murder first.

'Fuck you,' he said, and walked out.

Syn stretched, his servos humming. 'Me being here might not be helping.'

Cale stood. They'd not been restrained, and no guards had been assigned to watch them. 'Come on,' he said to Syn.

Outside, there was a fading tang of gunpowder in the air. The rebels had installed gun batteries in what had previously been Factors' checkpoints in the ring around the base of the Tower. Cale's eye followed the grand sweeping steps that led to the main entrance. Above the huge steel doors, he saw a patch of bare stone where the emblem of the Hegemony had once hung, a monstrous golden face that brooded over the people below, an eternal watcher. It had been a long time since he'd been here – in Karume, at the Tower – but the scale of the place had lost none of its oppression. The great flag had been torn down, and in its place hung a smaller, ragged emblem – a raised red fist on a field of black.

Only a matter of time until Aspedair's falcrex flies there, he thought. The 'Free City' would have its due for the support it had provided. Aspedi weapons and equipment were everywhere: on the soldiers that scurried about, those on watch, those manning the huge batteries. It was the silent partner here, flexing its influence through open rebellion rather than economics and subterfuge. He wondered how long Brennev had worked on them, coaxed them into such a brazen display of intent. It had worked.

A little way off he spotted Nebn standing alone next to a row of parked walkers. The machines were smaller models than the one they'd seen earlier, sleeker, newer-looking. A raised gantry allowed pilots to reach the cockpits, but other than a guard at the ladder and a single, tinkering mechanic the war machines were alone and silent behind their chain fence. Nebn gazed at something a thousand miles away.

Cale knew that look – the past was easy to find when the present was so painful. 'Have you wondered why this is all here?' he asked as quietly as he could over the noise of the camp, moving to stand by the young man. In his periphery he saw Syn engage the mechanic in conversation, watched by the guard.

Nebn shuffled but didn't say anything. His posture told Cale he was listening, so he continued. 'If the city is taken and Fulvia is dead, then why all of this weaponry?'

'It's in case of a counterattack.'

Cale nodded. 'Perhaps. But if the prize is the city, why fortify only here, in the centre? Why not set up on the perimeter, or strike out for the Walls?'

Nebn swallowed. 'He won't talk to me after what happened. Says I failed. The only reason I'm here and not in shackles is because a good friend intervened. I have no command.'

'He's guarding against an uprising. Think about it. All it takes is a few scattered instigators to stir up generations of bred-in loyalty. He knows it. They'll come swarming through these streets. What will these men do then, when they start to tear at the barricades?' He let the question hang in the air.

Nebn looked up at the war-walkers, then over at the gun

367

emplacements. All of them faced outwards, covering the wide avenues.

'He wouldn't.'

'Wouldn't he? You saw what he did: a bullet to the head without trial. Is that justice any different to theirs?'

'She was a monster.'

'She was what the world made her. Because it feels just in the moment doesn't make it the right thing to do.'

As he spoke, the years rolled back and he was there, in that broken, burning village, bodies scattered around him, the survivors breathing relief and rage at his back. The hunched little commissar who'd lapsed into madness, whose face had faded over the years until even the man's son standing in front of him with the same shock of red hair had seemed a perfect stranger. Dead eyes, his face splashed with his own blood as he slid down the edge of a ragged crater.

'An execution,' Cale whispered, 'doesn't fix a broken system—'

'—it replaces it,' Nebn finished. His eyes were haunted as the realisation struck. 'I've suspected for a while. There will be no collective here. He wants to rule.'

Cale waited silently for the young man to process, knowing he was teetering on a knifepoint.

Torture to treat him so, said a voice in his head. *Necessary*, said another. That day when the choice to pull a trigger had changed the course of his life was as stark and clear as the present that surrounded him; the same gun smoke staining the air, the same sense of breathless anticipation.

'What would you do?' Nebn asked.

'Provide a third way, perhaps.'

Nebn's eyes widened as if hearing an old phrase repeated. He indicated the busy camp around him with a sweep of his arm. 'You think I can get you past all of this? I'm one man. I have no rank any more.'

'You're respected,' said Cale. 'Kelbee told me that much. And how resourceful you are. She said you saved her.' He hated himself for it, the manipulation, but he pressed ahead. 'You gave her and the child a chance of a real life.'

Nebn's face was stone. He looked down at his boots. Then, a small squaring of the shoulders and Cale was sure he was about to swing for him or call the guards.

'I can help you with a distraction, nothing more,' Nebn said. 'For the fact that you were with... them... when they died and showed her kindness.'

'That's all I need.'

'Wait here.' Nebn squared his shoulders again and went over to the man guarding the war-walkers. There was a brief conversation and Cale saw the soldier snap upright on his heels. Nebn pointed at a watchtower some way off. The soldier hesitated, unwilling to leave his post. Nebn's barked order rocked him on his heels. Reluctantly, the soldier marched away from the chain-link fence that encircled the walkers, flashing a glance at Syn. The mercenary leaned against the fence, talking through it to the mechanic who'd downed his tools and was lighting a smoker.

Another order and the soldier resumed his march, followed close behind by Nebn. Just before they moved out of sight, he turned his head fractionally, found Cale. There was the shadow of a raised eyebrow, then both he and the soldier disappeared behind a sandbag wall.

Cale received a quizzical look when he went over to join the mercenary. 'Our young friend storm off again?'

'I think not.'

They didn't have to wait long. A few minutes later, from the direction Nebn had been heading, they heard a single shot, then a volley of gunfire, then another, the noise building as more weapons joined the chorus. The watchtower lit up as its gunners poured round after round outwards into the streets at an unseen enemy. Bellowed commands rose above the din of the heavy-calibre guns, then they heard more small arms join in. The base's attention turned outwards, the tension of an imminent attack released in a catharsis of pulled triggers.

'They're not firing at anything are they?' said Syn.

'We have to go. Now.'

Syn turned to the mechanic whose smoker had fallen half-smoked from his lips. His face was white as he fumbled his tools into a metal case.

'Best let us in, friend,' said Syn, indicating the locked gate.

'What?' replied the mechanic, his voice high. 'Go jump in a river, you ain't coming in here.'

Syn sighed and made a show of looking around. 'Well, I suppose we'll do it the slightly less easy way then.' His hands gripped the chain-link at shoulder height. Along his forearms a row of lights blazed through the translucent pink of his artificial skin. There was a whine, then a screech as the metal fence was torn apart like paper. Syn ripped a man-sized hole and stepped through.

The mechanic reeled back in shock, then recovered

370

himself. Lifting a heavy wrench, he swung it in a murderous arc. Syn's forearm blocked it with a dull thud and the tool flew through the air, then the mercenary stepped in and slapped his palm into his attacker's chest. The mechanic flew backwards as if shot from a cannon, slamming into the fence on the far side of the enclosure and dropping to the floor where he lay, clutching his chest and wheezing.

Cale grabbed Syn by the shoulder. 'What are you—'

'Leave it to me, buck. You still need to get past those doors.' He pointed at the Tower. The heavy doors were shut tight and a squad of soldiers milled at the foot of the steps, caught between the fire-fight that seemed to be engulfing the perimeter and their orders to guard the entrance.

'Don't make that face at me,' Syn said. 'I'll try not to kill anyone. Just get in there and do something useful for a change, eh?' The mercenary gripped Cale's shoulder, smiled, then quick as lightning turned and was bounding up the access ladder to the walker gantry. Cale watched him pop the cockpit of one of the war machines, then disappear into it as if consumed. A few seconds later, the engines fired up in a gout of acrid smoke.

Cale retreated through the fence as the walker came to life, its gun arms swinging up with a strain of electric motors. One heavy foot moved, then another, smashing down the fence and narrowly avoiding the downed mechanic, who managed to roll out of the way.

The walker stomped forwards a few paces, unnoticed by the distracted soldiers at the foot of the stairs. Then there was a whine as capacitors charged, the killing energy welling up inside the walker's guns until the vents on either side glowed a piercing, violent blue. The walker planted its feet, hunkered down. Fired.

Twin plasma bolts sailed over the heads of the soldiers and impacted the Tower's steps with a blinding flash. The roar drowned out the sounds of gunfire for a second. When Cale looked up he saw the blast had struck just above the squad, knocking them to the ground. Cale saw one try to crawl away, blood streaming from his ears.

The walker adjusted with a clicking of gears, then began to pour salvo after salvo into the doors of the Tower, each impact like the detonation of a star. Cale took cover behind a pile of sandbags, inching forward towards the edge, getting ready to run; when the barrage stopped he would have only seconds to cover the open ground and make the breach.

The barrels of the walker's weapons began to glow as the metal of the Tower gates turned cherry, then white. The machine stumbled sideways a step; Cale ducked, thinking Syn had overloaded the machine's systems, then heard the ping of bullets deflecting off armour plate. The diversion was over.

The walker planted its feet wider to weather the hail of gunfire now pouring at it from one side and resumed raining purple-hot plasma on to its target. There was a tortured screech and the Tower doors collapsed inwards. As the walker's guns fell silent Cale bolted from cover, sidestepping the half-dazed soldiers trying to pick themselves up. A throaty boom made him flash a look backwards even as he sprinted for the steps. Something big had hit the walker and he saw it teeter, trying to right itself. Another detonation from one of the guard towers as one of the heavy guns, now swung inward against the new threat, slammed another round into the metal armour of the walker's torso. It seemed to take an age to hit the ground. A shape rolled clear, pink limbs flashing lurid in the dull afternoon light. Cale heard an indistinct shout, a familiar bellow exhorting him on.

Arms pumping, legs aching, chest burning, he took the steps three at a time and leaped through the glowing hole, feeling the superheated metal through the soles of his boots. The interior of the Tower welcomed him with its cool darkness.

By Blood

The Tower was as he remembered it from all those years ago as a young officer, stiff-necked with the pride in his commission and the starch in his collar, a stranger on his arm. It had been oppressive then, clouding his head with incense and ambition. The vapours had gone, as had the rank on his shoulder, but the Tower still loomed like an open mouth far over his head, a man-made cavern ringing with emptiness. No one whispered under the colonnades or walked the grand stairs that hugged the curved walls up to great balconies of steel and glass. The light that crept in past high windows was weak, tickling the tops of crenellations and ornate spires while leaving the ground level dim. The thick, monumental tapestries sucked away even the sound of his breathing and the almost forgotten sound of the battle outside.

He wondered if Syn had made it to safety. The last he'd seen him, the mercenary was racing for cover, his neticks a blur, moving faster than he'd thought possible. If anyone could survive that assault, it was him.

He pushed it out of his mind, concentrating on the task ahead.

There was something predatory here, even in stillness. The angles looked hungry, drawing the eye as if to tempt the unwary. Up above, beyond the vaulted ribs of the ceiling and far above the rest of the city, was the palace the Seeker had made for himself but never seen in life, now accessible only to the Guide and handpicked servants who, rumour had it, were blinded beforehand.

Cale ignored the bank of elevators at the far end of the hall, heading instead for a large opening in the wall and a wide spiral walkway that snaked downwards, tongue-like, a centre rail splitting the path down the middle. He trod softly down the gentle slope where a million feet had preceded him, brushed the walls where devotees would lean as they waited for their chance to see the Seeker himself entombed. The marble of the wall was slick from fleeting caresses. It smelled like people here, the odour of the masses seeped into the floor and walls. Despite himself, he felt a sense of trepidation as each step brought him closer to the devotional heart of the Hegemony.

The ramp ended in a set of massive iron turnstiles, and beyond he saw the flicker of candles. He heard low voices as he eased himself past the creaking barrier. Brennev was there, his back to him. In front of him sat a slumped figure in a chair. He recognised it – the same chair that had held Fulvia before her execution. The crystal sarcophagus lay on its side, the candlelight fractured by its bevelled surface, rainbow patterns dancing on the ceiling. Cale saw a bundle of old rags nearby; a tiny thing, like a child's toy.

The Seeker. The desiccated remains of a god, and near it, the corpse of that god's chief servant.

Fulvia's face was almost peaceful in death. An eddy ruffled the candle flames, glimmering reflections skittering over the walls and ceiling like firebugs. It was then that he saw the gun in Brennev's fist.

He approached carefully, not trying to hide his footsteps, not wanting to startle. His breathing sounded like bellows in his chest.

Brennev turned, his face a mask. 'Still refusing to die, old friend?' he asked.

Cale held up his hands to show he was unarmed. 'I don't want trouble. I need to speak with you.'

'Actually, we were just speaking about you. That is, your friend here was.' He waved the gun at Derrin's seated form; one eye was almost sealed shut by swelling, blood dripping down his pale face and staining his white shirt. 'Quite the tale. You know you killed his father?'

Cale nodded. If he could keep him talking, he might be able to get closer.

'There were hundreds of them – mostly orphans – trained to watch. This one worked extra hard though, knowing that one day he might find the man who killed his father; put himself above the others. When the time came for you to be useful, so was he.'

'You should let him go. He's done nothing.'

'He's a weapon, Cale. He's their creature. Count yourself lucky he only betrayed you.'

'Let him go, and let's talk.'

Brennev considered this. 'Well,' he said, flicking Derrin

a look, 'if he can walk…' He shoved the chair hard with his boot. Derrin was limp, and there was a dull thud as he hit the floor.

Cale tensed. Was he already dead?

There was a weak groan. Under the crusted blood the boy was still alive, though barely conscious.

'You still want to save him, don't you?' asked Brennev. 'You have a passion for strays. Maybe that's why he couldn't pull the trigger.'

Cale saw the boy's chest barely moving. *Later*, he thought. 'We found something in the north,' he said. 'Something important.'

'Yes, I know.'

'Derrin told you.'

'No, I read Sulara Song's journals.'

'And still you ignored her. Kept her locked away.'

'Of course I did.' A flash of irritation. 'I'm a soldier. I don't work on hearsay. Plans were already in motion, plans to bring the fight to the enemy. I didn't want her distracting anyone from the task at hand. Was I wrong?' A casual wave of the pistol. 'Look what it's done to you.'

'It's real, I saw it.'

'A mystical information stockpile? I suppose you think it'll change the world?' he snorted. 'When did you become so naïve? Better it stays buried.'

Cale indicated the dais. From where he stood, he could see the glowing symbols that had rested underneath the Seeker's sarcophagus, the mechanism that would activate the ancient machinery inside the Tower. 'There is a transmitter here that will allow anyone within a hundred klicks to access the network. In time, we could spread it further. We could understand the world as it was before the Ruin, all the knowledge of generations for the taking, by anyone. That's the world we wanted before, free from dogma and ignorance.'

'You know as well as I do that information is only as good as those who interpret it. People want stability and I am the best man for that task. I've known for years what needed to change.'

'You don't trust people to make their own decisions?'

'I don't, and neither should you. When have they ever been capable, or even willing? What they really want, in their heart of hearts, is a comforting story. Order.'

'You sound as bad as her.'

Brennev's confident façade cracked a little as he flushed. 'What the hell do you know? You've not seen the years I've spent fighting them, being patient, building our strength. You cut and ran before it got hard, like the coward you always were.'

Cale felt pressure behind his eyes, a black rage. 'Aime *died*.'

'All the better. If you couldn't take one single death, you didn't have the stones for it.'

'I loved her.'

'You think I didn't?'

There it was. Cale had known, of course, from the way he'd looked at her. Aime had dismissed it as an infatuation, but it had soured things between the three of them. Even now, years later, it rankled. 'I didn't come here to stop your murderous coup,' Cale said, trying to hold the anger back.

'Fool yourself into believing you'll be a better tyrant than the last one if you want, but let me do this.'

'No, I won't indulge your idiocy. This place is a symbol; it's why I brought her here, showed her death, let people know how deep the change is going to be.' Brennev nodded at the Seeker's corpse. 'Their god was never a god, but they won't believe it until his monuments are gone.' Brennev reached into a pocket and drew out a small grey box with a flashing light at one end and a single black switch under a guard cage. 'I've had the foundations set with deep-penetration charges.'

'You'll kill your men outside.'

'They'll be back behind cover by the time I throw the switch. Then we get to see the old world fall. You could be there with us.'

Cale felt uncounted tons of stone and steel above his head bearing down. The horror of the edifice toppling was palpable. 'When this place goes over, it'll level half the central district.'

'We'll rebuild.'

Cale watched the lights winking at him from the plinth in the middle of the room. The markings were alien: angular, neat, a message in a language long dead. Just the touch of his hand was all it would take.

'Don't bother,' said Brennev. 'My finger won't have far to travel. I'll take us both if I have to.'

The threat was unusual, surprising. Why the escalation if he was so confident he'd won? Cale looked closely at Brennev's scarred face and saw the shadow of fear there.

'You don't think it's a myth,' he said. 'You think it'll

work. You think it'll make your revolution meaningless, and that frightens you.'

Brennev was silent, but his blazing eyes told Cale he was right.

'You won't do it,' he continued. 'You've put too much into this already, too much time and preparation, to go out like this.'

'How well you know me, old friend.'

Something smashed into Cale's leg. The sound of the gunshot was deafening in the vaulted chamber. He went down screaming as bone grated on bone.

'You're right, I do have too much invested. That makes you an idiot for believing I wouldn't do absolutely anything to see it through.' Brennev wore a look of disgust as he walked over. 'You think I'd not hurt you because we ran together in the old days? Because we shared rakk at the same table, ate the same stale bread? That time has gone, Cale. It might as well never have existed.'

Cale gritted his teeth and tried to sit up but the pain in his leg was all-consuming.

Brennev crouched down next to him, smoke still wafting from the pistol's barrel. 'An order I gave got the woman I loved killed. I'd order that strike again, as many times as it was necessary, if it got me what I needed. And I truly *loved* her.'

Cale tried to crawl towards the dais. So close, if only he could pull himself over the hard stone floor, up the few steps... Agony flared in his leg and he flopped back, his jaw locked in a silent scream.

'You won't be missed,' said Brennev. He pressed the

pistol against Cale's forehead, his mouth a stark line.

Cale shut his eyes, Aime's face so clear it felt real – flesh and blood instead of cold stone.

It was all right, she said. He reached for her.

There was a grunt and a thud and the sound of something large hitting the floor. Then a snap and a throaty howl of pain.

Cale opened his eyes and saw a wild tangle of limbs. Derrin was on top of Brennev, a fury of punches and kicks, howling as he pummelled the older man. The detonator had skittered away over the floor; the pistol dangled from where the trigger guard had snapped Brennev's finger.

Derrin had rage and surprise but Brennev had weight and experience. With a mighty heave he flipped Derrin over and dropped his bulk down, pinning his chest. With one hand he clamped down on the skinny throat and, wincing, shook the gun free, sending it bouncing just out of reach. Brennev swore and shifted to grab it.

Cale summoned up all his will to block out the agony and managed to swing out his bad leg, knocking the gun into a dark corner. A burst of fresh pain made his eyes water, his clenched jaw unable to stop a moan escaping.

In the split second that Brennev's weight was off him, Derrin managed to jab upwards with something in his hand. There was a wet sound, like meat being hacked, and the older man's eyes went wide. His hand rose to his chest as if swatting away an insect, did it again. There was something jutting from him: the splintered chair leg. Blood soaked it, ran along its length and dripped in dark blobs onto the floor.

Derrin heaved again, and this time Brennev had no fight

left in him. He rolled onto his back. The youth scraped himself backwards to rest against the dais, his breath shallow and rapid.

Brennev's eyes found Cale. There was panic there, then hatred, then amusement. He let go of the shard that had pierced his chest and rooted around in a pocket. When he realised he didn't have the detonator the look of triumph became despair. There was a second when Cale thought he might cry like a child.

'It'll never work,' Brennev rasped. 'They'll tear it all down…' He gave up, pain squeezing his eyes shut.

Cale watched him go pale, the life emptying in trickles now. The red pool that spread from him shimmered like crystal in the candlelight.

Brennev looked up again. Every ounce of his remaining strength went into keeping his eyes open. 'She…'

'Just stop,' said Cale. His leg was a riot of pain.

'She… came to me… once…' He coughed. Then he was still.

They just sat there for a while, the thick silence only punctured by breath. Finally, Derrin twisted to look at the lit symbols. 'Will you do it?' Other than the wound to his face, he seemed unharmed. He seemed somehow older, calmer.

Cale was silent.

'He really hated you.'

'We were friends a long time ago.'

Derrin considered this. 'He was goading you. What he said at the end.'

'I know,' he said, not meaning it. *I always knew*, he thought. *I forgave her.*

'I'm sorry, for what it's worth.'

Cale nodded, still gazing at Brennev's lifeless face. Then, with a grunt of pain, he shuffled close to the dais. The emblems glowed at him, inviting. Did he even have the right to do this? Did anyone? Maybe they were correct, Fulvia, Brennev: knowing the truth was more than most could cope with.

Better a painful choice than none at all, said something like Bowden's voice.

He slapped his palms down on the controls. Immediately, the colours morphed, moving to encompass his hands, drawing a glowing outline around them that shifted, rainbow-like. He felt warmth, a gentle tickling. A sound built, coming from deep in the bones of the ground. He felt the colossal energies wake and stretch, imagined them finding their old pathways, lifting upwards, ever upwards towards a peak far above his head. Vibration rose until the room around them shook, the crystal coffin ringing on the floor like the chiming of a thousand tiny bells.

At the corner of his vision, he saw it. Just an imprint of a ghost of a reflection, growing ever brighter as the seconds ticked away. The wire-frame of an infinite torus spread around him.

Derrin gasped as he saw it. Then he laughed, the sound musical. 'Oh, my,' he said, full of wonder.

For an instant, the world went white.

He left Derrin in the trance state, knowing he had to experience it to understand what was happening to him.

The boy was propped against the dais which now glowed a warm magenta, pulsing like a heartbeat. His pale face was bathed in wonder, his lips moving in silence.

Cale felt the presence in his head now, sitting quiet, ready to be used. He knew he only had to close his eyes and *push*, and he would be connected. His curiosity got the better of him – and in an instant he was there, inside the data corpus, the pain forgotten.

Instead of letting himself drift like last time, he tried to focus on a thought – *sculpture*. He fell towards the grid, seeing its complexity open for him. When he found the miniature torus he wanted he brushed it, seeing a flitter of images and words, centuries of knowledge ready for him to absorb; lifelike projections of tools and famous works he could reach out and touch, sense texture and weight, though he knew it was nothing more than a ghost-image.

The data corpus felt warm, and he imagined Kelbee smiling. Was it her joy he felt? He pulled back to a great height with a thought, surveying the grid landscape. It had been empty before, a dizzying vista, but now it was dancing with motes of light that flitted from node to node, tens of thousands of them. Curious, he brought himself close to one of them and reached out – then pulled back, shocked. It was another mind.

His wonder grew as he realised each dancing pinprick of light was a person, each one experiencing the data corpus at the same time. He tried to focus on Derrin's face, experimenting. Almost instantly, he found himself elsewhere, another light bobbing in front of him. More confidently, he reached out again and touched it, holding the contact. He could feel the surprise, curiosity, wonder. He recognised it.

Can you hear me? he asked.

I can. I never want to leave.

Just for a little while, he responded, knowing he would also like to lose himself here.

There was acknowledgement, then the mote that was Derrin vanished.

This is so much more than just information, Cale thought, the scale of the realisation hitting him. *I could speak to any of these people, from anywhere, instantly. No barriers, no restrictions, just unbound communication.* It made him feel dizzy.

With extreme reluctance, he pulled himself back from the corpus and opened his eyes. The afterimage of the torus grid glowed on his retinas for a second before it faded.

Reality was a dank, gloomy tomb. His leg was throbbing dangerously and the air smelled of death. He wanted to go back, to lose himself away from this, but knew he couldn't yet.

Derrin was there with a ripped length of cloth that he fashioned into a tourniquet; when it was pulled tight, Cale mashed his teeth against the pain. The pump of blood slowed to a trickle and the throb subsided to a pulse. Derrin helped him up, took his arm over his shoulder to take the weight off his bad leg. They hobbled past the iron turnstile, then up the spiral ramp towards the ground level. Neither spoke. Cale had to pause once, twice, breathing deep to try to numb the electric-sharp pain from his leg. Derrin helped him, walking slowly, patient at every step.

At the top, they stopped again. Cale was exhausted, but both understood each other's need to gird themselves before they walked out into the daylight, and whatever waited for them there.

Cale sat on a bench. The marble slab was cool and smooth under his palms.

'Take a moment,' said Derrin.

Cale nodded in thanks. Above the hush of the great room there was a low throbbing coming from the walls. The Tower felt like a living thing, the pulse gentle and lulling.

'Why didn't you shoot me?' he asked. 'Back in the north.'

Derrin considered this as he gazed up at the ceiling. 'I wondered if it was cowardice, but then…' He met Cale's gaze and smiled. 'If the man you killed was in fact my father – if that wasn't just another convenient lie – then I didn't know him. I never even saw a picture, just a name and a story. I was angry, because that's what they taught me to be. But you were real, and you were kind to me. You're a good man, Cale. Either that or I'm just a very bad agent.'

Cale rubbed his thigh, massaging the life back into it. The Tower's shattered entrance was a bright portal, beckoning him. 'Are you ready?' he asked.

Derrin nodded and helped him up.

Outside the Tower a deep hush reigned. At first Cale thought it was abandoned – perhaps Brennev had managed to send an evacuation message. Then he saw people, still forms lying on the ground, others seated. At the bottom of the wide steps they found the platoon of soldiers who'd been on guard. They looked bloodied, bruised by the explosion that had sent them flying, but their faces were rapt as they swam through their new, expanded universe, living the corpus for the first time, each moment a new individual revelation.

There was a noise nearby, then a scream. A man woke from his trance, swatting the air in front of him as if swarmed by insects. He clutched his head, shaking it, a long moan drawn from his lips like a wounded animal.

'Not everyone's enjoying themselves,' said a voice nearby. 'I see you managed to mostly not die.' Ardal Syn rose from under the sheet of metal that had hidden him, his face covered in dark soot. One arm had been shattered by gunfire and hung limp by his side, the pink outer coating shredded and exposing the ruined mechanism. He gave Derrin a withering look. 'Any more plans to stab us in the back I should know about?'

'I'm sorry, Syn.'

'I've got my eye on you for ever, you little shit.'

Cale waved his hand, heading off the argument. 'My leg's bad.'

'Tourniquet should do it for now, though you need to see a medico. Gangrene's a bitch. No point asking if you succeeded.' He indicated the silence around them. 'Just woke from my own trip. Felt... busier than before. Most seem to be taking to it. Others...' He nodded in the direction of the moaning man, who'd curled into a ball on the floor. 'It might take some time.'

'You saw them, the others? Inside the corpus?' Cale asked as Syn knelt to tie a strip of cloth around his leg. He winced as the band was drawn tight.

'I saw them. Almost felt like I could talk to them, if I wanted.'

'You can.'

Syn considered this. 'That sounds... useful.'

Derrin picked up the rifle of a nearby soldier and handed it to Cale. 'Here, lean on this.'

'What now, buck?'

Cale shook his head. 'I haven't the faintest idea.'

'You have the tools,' said Kelbee, her voice inside their heads as clear as if she'd been standing next to them.

The three of them swapped a look, confirming they'd all heard it.

'Now,' she continued. 'You just need to decide how to use them.'

'How do we do that?' Cale asked.

'You'll work it out.' There was a smile in the voice. 'Together.'

Renewal

A breeze rustled the row of trees at the bottom of the steep garden, rushing through the branches and causing the small flock of roosting lycas to cling on with their talons and spread their wings, riding the dip and rise. The wind carried the faint susurration of leaf on leaf up the garden along with the musty perfume of sap.

Kelbee stretched out and felt the wind stir the small hairs of her arms, breathing in the odour of bruised leaves and the faint sweetness of the last remaining blossoms. She closed her eyes, feeling the warmth on her face and through her eyelids. As an experiment, she opened them and stared full-on into the glare for a full minute. There was no pain, and when she looked away there was no ghost-spot following her around wherever she looked. Despite this, it was as bright and hot as on any high Bask day. She took her hat from the floor by her wicker chair and stood, stretching her back. She ran a hand over her flat stomach.

This was perhaps the hardest part to accept. Being a mother.

The garden and the house were perched on the side of a small hill. The lawn was trimmed and neat, the flowerbeds a riot of disorganised yellows and reds and purples. Three tall trees marked the end of the garden, bursting with leaves, their trunks gnarled and wide and perfect for climbing. Beyond that boundary, the land was empty.

No, not entirely empty.

There was an attempt at topography there: a range of small hills marched along on the other side of the valley – without texture and featureless, as green as a leaf – and between them ran a thin ribbon of bright matte blue. The sky overhead was dotted with white clouds, but they did not move and, on closer examination, lacked depth. Beyond the garden was a child's drawing of a landscape, a flat, primary-colour sketch.

She'd help fill it out in time.

One day there would be a small village at the bottom of the hill, with a narrow but well-paved path leading up to the house. There would be long grass and wildseed on the hills, meadows with rocks and birds and animals. The river would babble, blue and green and black over pebbles, and silver tarns would dart out from overhung banks, seeking insects and tiny invisible currents.

Soon. It was all so new.

And there was so much else to do first.

Kelbee walked up the steps to the porch and pulled open the screen door. It was old and warped but the mesh on the outside was in good repair. There, just a third of the way up, was the notch where she'd knocked her head as a girl. She still had the mark. Curious that of all the parts of her childhood home, this battered old door was the only detail to exist here.

In the small kitchen she poured herself a cup of water. It was ice-cold as it came out of the tap, chilling her hand through the rough earthenware of the cup. She wasn't thirsty, in fact hadn't been for what seemed like an eternity, but she still felt the need to do things like this, to mimic the little ceremonies of her life before. She carried her cup back into the lounge and watched the boys work.

They'd cleared the whole room of anything that might get in the way, shoving tables and chairs back against the wall, piling up books and discs and pictures to free up more space. In one corner stood a large container of wooden blocks of all shapes and sizes, some as big as a house brick, others as small as a finger. Squares, oblongs, cylinders, cubes. Using them, the boys had laid out a model of Karume on the floor. The facsimile landmarks stood out, somehow staying upright on the deep-pile carpet: the spokes of apartment blocks like the one she'd lived in radiating out from the centre of the wheel, the outlying factories with their teetering chimneys stretching towards the white-washed ceiling. In the very centre, piled high in a jagged, precarious imitation of reality, the Tower looked out over everything. Despite the ramshackle nature of its construction, she knew it was as stable as the real thing.

Just a couple of children, looking around six years of age, playing make-believe, or so it seemed. A closer look showed how accurate it was, every street and factory reproduced there on the carpet as a detailed plan. Soon, it would be ready to present to the new administration, then construction would start.

Ishah was over in one of the industrial districts, his brow furrowed as he contemplated the wooden blocks at his feet. His skin was still as pale as milk but since coming here he'd grown a head of the blackest hair she'd ever seen, so dark as to swallow the light around it. He was deciding what derelict structures to repair and what could be razed. Over on the other side of the model Deynal knelt, considering a half-built series of residential blocks. Since the Tower's activation more people had flocked to the city, many of them confused and needing the comfort of community. There was high demand for living space.

Deynal was lithe and tall for his age, and his blonde mop of hair reminded her of Tani. The sight of him caused her a pang of guilt: she hadn't spoken to Nebn yet. Perhaps soon she would find the time.

'Mother,' he called, 'what do you think we should do next?'

Ishah looked up and nodded in silent agreement.

Kelbee picked her way over the model, stepping with care. She rested her hand on Deynal's head and considered the city beneath her.

'I always liked parks. Maybe there should be more parks.'

'I think it should *all* be parks,' said Ishah. 'People don't need to live in cities any more.'

Kelbee watched his frown deepen. Such a serious boy. Prone to outbursts of anger, though she could always calm him, especially if Deynal was nearby. But when he smiled it was as if Ras had emerged from behind a cloud. Dark or light, little in between, but she loved him as if he was her own.

'People need time to accept change,' she told him. 'Give them a chance.'

'When I was made, people lived under the ground or in the trees or in the ocean. Or floating in the air. Wherever they liked. Even in orbit. Why do they still want to huddle together?'

'It's all they've ever known, Ishah,' she said, gentle but chiding.

He nodded but she saw he didn't fully understand. He was impatient, still learning.

'What about this, Mother?' said Deynal. He pointed to a circular construction made of oblong bricks laid on their sides. Kelbee recognised the arena and felt a surge of memory.

The Lance Colonel by her side. Yellow blossoms. Ruby-rich blood and a single gunshot.

Both boys were looking at her; they'd felt it too, the memory like the ripple of a stone striking a pond, though neither understood it. Even Deynal's open face was worried, so she smiled, waving a hand to reassure them.

The model of the arena lay at her feet, even its childish analogue frightening her. A quick check told her that the new factories had been brought online and were now producing manufacturing drones – annexes, as they'd been known all those centuries ago – which could level the structure in hours and recycle every stone and girder and pane of glass. This space could fit ten apartment blocks, but there was something about this patch of ground that felt tainted.

She leaned down and kissed the top of Deynal's head. 'Maybe another park here.'

Her son nodded and set about carefully dismantling the arena brick by brick. She could see it already, the image of a few hours from now when a cloud of annexes would swarm the structure, dismantling it piece by piece. The thought was like a cool breeze over her mind.

She spotted an open space, a rectangle of clear carpet bordered on all sides by little sticks placed upright to look like trees. She knew immediately that this was her park, the place where it had all begun; she'd followed him over its gravel paths, filled with nervous excitement. There was the row of trees where he'd plucked flowers for her, whispered in her ear. The blue blossoms – exact copies – still stood in a vase by the window, as bright and fresh as the day he'd picked them. It wasn't him, she realised – she didn't miss Nebn the man; it was more that she wanted to remember those moments when her existence had pitched on its fulcrum. In a million other fractal lives Kelbee the good wife walked on by to her life as a believer, a conformist. But in this one, she'd come to this extraordinary end, every strand leading back to this one shatter-point.

I should go to him, she thought. *What if he hates me?*
So much to be done.

The only feature marking the square of carpet was a single square block with another oblong lying on its side next to it. The Seeker's statue toppled from its plinth.

She knelt and examined the piece. 'You already took down the statue?' she asked the boys.

Ishah shook his head. 'They did that themselves.'

She could see the park, the trees rustling in the wind at the border of the open tan-green space. The golden statue lying on its side, the blank stare of the Seeker staring up into the sky. People had done this, free minds. Were they right there still, she wondered, gathered as they once did to bow to their saviour, now glorying in his fall? She could almost hear their murmurs like the tune of a half-remembered song.

'Do you want us to put it back?' asked Deynal.

'No,' she said. 'Leave it there. They'll know what to do.'

Cale heaved the last of the stones to the edge of the platform and stood back. Even out in the wind of the steppe he was hot, the effort of lugging all nine sculptures over to the pit singing in his muscles. The lifter harness had finally blown its motor and now sat smoking off to one side; as he contemplated the row of huge granite statues before him, he heard it tick over, give a plaintive whine, then finally die. He wouldn't need it again.

In front of him, the Groan gaped.

He wiped the sweat from his brow and moved behind the first stone. It was the oldest, the first he'd attempted when he'd come here all those years ago; a crude essay, barely resembling Aime at all, but he remembered every grief-filled hack and grind of the chisel.

He kissed his fingertips and pressed them to the stone. His lips moved in silence, his eyes closed. Then he set his shoulder against it, planted his feet wide and heaved. The statue scraped on the iron platform, teetered on the edge, then fell. A few moments later he heard the impact echo up from the throat of the pit.

He did the same to each statue, kissing it goodbye before shoving it into the pit until only one remained.

The last white block was untouched, the one he'd dug out the morning Aulk had brought him the message. Even though no chisel had ever marked its surface he could see her face there. This one would have been the best, he knew it in his bones – her nose would have been fine, her cheekbones high. Her eyes would have looked out on him with a smile that never needed to reach her mouth.

He rubbed his palm on the rough stone and whispered a farewell, then pushed. It was heavier than the others and he had to sink lower, grunting with the effort, hearing the block shift and grind. With a last burst of effort, he heaved it over the edge, felt it topple, then his own momentum carried him with it. The pit yawned under him as he fell, knowing in a frozen instant that it was too late to grab hold of anything, seeing the stone block falling away from him even as he followed it down towards the rocks far below. He opened his mouth to scream.

Something caught his foot.

He felt himself lifted into the air and deposited on the platform, his hands shaking. A silvery ovoid hung in front of him, bobbing gently as if in water. The shape seemed to be watching him, though it had no eyes or features of any kind. He'd felt its grip on his leg and knew it could have lifted ten times his weight, having seen swarms of others just like it dismantle entire buildings.

Annexe. That was it. Builder drone. Another marvel he didn't fully understand. What was it doing all the way out here?

The drone seemed to lose interest in him and drifted out to hover over the pit, dipping slightly and appearing to stare all the way down to the bottom. He watched it, wondering again how it worked even as he told himself that all it would take was a brief time in the data corpus to find out. As usual, the urge to dive in to that sea of knowledge was pervasive, subtle and seductive.

Someone was standing nearby, watching him.

Kelbee wore a simple tunic and trousers, her long blue-black hair undone, though the gusts of wind didn't move it. She was smiling at him.

'That would have been a shame,' she said. 'It would have taken some of the solemnity out of it, to die like that.'

Cale picked himself up and nodded. 'You're here?'

She indicated the annexe, which had floated back from the pit and was now examining the broken lifter harness. 'It can project my image. Another thing I learned. People seem to prefer it to me talking inside their heads.'

'How are things?'

She toyed with the gravel under her bare feet. It didn't move. 'Since we brought the annexes online we've been improving the cities. Communication has flourished – I have a growing list of committees, focus groups, organisational forums.' She raised an eyebrow. 'Some more enthusiastic than others.'

'Meaning?'

'They want to hold trials. There's a lot of anger.'

Cale nodded. It was inevitable, as much as he'd hoped that the amount of information available would guide the best choices. People were people and emotion could cloud even the most informed mind. He pulled off his gloves and bunched them into a pocket. 'I heard there were some problems with Aspedair.'

'They won't allow us access to repair the transmitters around them, though at least we're talking, which is more than the Hegemony ever officially did. They'll come around once they realise what the corpus has to offer them.' She brushed a strand of hair behind her ear. 'What about you? How are you doing?'

'I'm sure you already know.' He indicated the bobbing machine. 'Despite what just happened, I'm all right. Leg hurts sometimes, but nothing I can't manage.'

'Do you like it here?' she asked.

He looked over at the derelict mining town some way off. 'It was somewhere to disappear, once.'

'I could assign you some annexes. You could be comfortable here, if you wanted.'

He considered this for a few moments. Behind her – through her, in truth – he could see the hangar-garage that he'd called home for almost a decade. He'd found it iced up on his return, his old home cold and empty as a tomb. The generator had succumbed to the weather and was useless, so he'd moved into one of the few buildings in town with an intact roof for a couple of days. Now that his task was complete, there was nothing to keep him here.

Kelbee continued. 'Syn has a home in the cliffs off the Fleet Coast – by comparison, this would be simple.'

'He mentioned.'

'You should visit.'

'I will, at some point. How about you? Have you seen Nebn yet?'

A flicker of something on her face. Regret? 'He knows what happened, of course. Everyone does. I haven't seen him yet, not... properly. With the boys.'

There's still a kernel of the woman you were in there, he thought.

'I don't believe it would have lasted, if I'm truthful with myself,' Kelbee said. 'I don't want to burden him.'

'It's not for me to say. But everyone deserves a choice.'

She looked out over the grey-green expanse of the steppe. There was a fraction of a nod. 'So, you're not staying here?' she said.

'No. Just came back to clear up a few things.'

The wind blew in and there was a faint moan from the pit. He knew it was just his imagination, but it might have been a farewell. Ras was nearing the horizon now and the temperature was dropping with the light.

'Do you need help getting where you're going? It's getting dark.'

'No, thank you. He'll be here soon.'

They waited, watching the shadows grow long and begin to fade. After a while they saw a pinprick of light in the distance, a battered old skimmer navigating the trail over the steppe. Cale thought of the little house in Endeldam he was rebuilding with Derrin's help, just a stone's throw from the house of Aulk the fisherman. He could see it now, the glow of the storm lamps seeping through the shutters, salt in the air and the promise of a warm bed beckoning.

'What will you do?' she asked.

'Driftwood is a wonderful thing to work.' As he said it, he could feel the creamy smoothness of wave-bleached wood in his hands, each piece unique and hinting at the thing that lay inside it. Pliant where stone was unyielding, soft where rock was rough, an entire history written in knots and swirls. He favoured Kelbee with a small smile. 'If not, there's always fishing.'

She smiled back. 'I think that's an excellent idea.'

Bask 25 – 3

It feels beyond odd to write that new date, though also
pleasant. The majority agreed to scrap the old chronology
and start afresh, at Year 1, and though it seemed a token
gesture at the time, I complied. I didn't expect to feel so
freed by it, as if everything to come is purely of our making,
with no traditions or hangovers from the past.

Wild optimism! Perhaps it's because I'm finally leaving
after two years all alone. There is a sadness about it – I'll
be leaving him behind, but I know he'd approve. Mason
wouldn't want me weeping over his grave for the rest of
my life, he would point at the potential for change. After
all, don't we now live in a world turned on its head, the
unthinkable common and the profane embraced?

His grave is simple, as I asked. The machines put it
together in mere hours on the site where he lay – a plain
stone box with no markings, inscrutable to anyone who
doesn't already know, and that's exactly what I intended.
The marker had nothing to do with posterity, it was for me.

Those were hard months, especially at first. I kept asking
myself why I insisted on staying here in the cold – I had
everything I needed, the outpost was repaired and stocked,
but the cold permeated body and mind. I could have gone
anywhere and lived the same life of quiet contemplation

and research: my old apartment in Karume, a quiet house by the sea, even the top of a mountain! No matter how far I went I'd still have access to the data corpus, the sum knowledge of a thousand lifetimes laid out for me with only my own stamina and curiosity to limit me. More, I could contact anyone I wanted just by reaching out with my mind and touching them. Just as knowledge was now boundless, instant communication had made the world a fraction of its old size, but I wanted nothing more than to be alone.

No, I didn't want to leave *him* all alone.

It makes me grimace to admit it, but I can't deny it. He anchored me to this place.

In truth, I liked that the annexes (my only physical companions) – those inscrutable, hovering devices – had no interest in talking. I'm not entirely sure that they can. I say 'physical' because I had another occasional visitor: Kelbee would appear from time to time (though I did put a stop to her literally popping into being in front of me, insisting that she at least do me the courtesy of walking through a door or something that didn't give me a fright). I could tell she worried for me but understood my need for solitude, keeping her visits short and occasional. She always came to me in the outpost: I never go near the torus chamber, try to forget it's even there. She may have tamed the thing, given it a name, talking of it as fondly as a wilful child, but I will never stop thinking of it as his murderer.

She told me stories of the outside world, thinking no doubt that it would help my mood (sometimes, I felt as if it was her that needed the conversation more than I did!). It transpired that most people, when they got over the initial shock and had it explained to them, embraced the new state of affairs. Some senior figures in the old administration who were not put on trial even formed a government of sorts, but gave up any real pretence of authority soon after – with instant communication came universal voting on any manner of issues, making any traditional notion of government archaic and largely pointless. It still lives on as a figurehead for those too old or too frightened to live without having someone in charge.

She told me about the trials and the executions that marred the first few months, when people were too angry to be rational. She was so deeply sad when she spoke of it, I'd forget for a moment that she wasn't human any more. It was confusing for her, but I had to remind her that resentment and the need for revenge did not disappear with sudden enlightenment. And there was the other problem: the few who weren't born able to connect to the network. These outcasts banded together, frightened and alienated; many went to Aspedair, the only place that has refused to allow itself to be integrated into the system. The irony of it! The vaunted Free City now digging in its heels against a tide of empiricism. Mason would be appalled, no doubt. I find it amusing.

I allowed her to continue to try to distract me, but in the end the only thing that really mattered was my research. I spent my days in the corpus, my nights writing up my findings. The act of putting pen to paper is laughably old-fashioned now, but it was not enough for me to just *see* and *know*, I had to make sense of it in my own way – composing papers is my way of processing the information. I doubt they'll ever be seen by another soul; after all, what could I possibly add to that endless stream of knowledge and experience?

That was a hard truth to accept: I'd always been a seeker on the edges of common understanding, always striving to comprehend more about the unknown. Now I was just a consumer. For all the bliss of swimming through that magnificent sea of information, I'd often lapse into black moods when I emerged, barely eating and spending days in bed until I summoned up the courage to venture back. To have my sole driving purpose made so cruelly irrelevant! That was the biggest blow of all, and still I couldn't summon the will to leave, because where would I go that was not exactly the same?

Then, one evening, everything changed. Kelbee came to me and persuaded me to join her outside.

It was towards the end of the Bask, though I can't in truth recall exactly when because I'd stopped checking the days. It was freezing outside but bearable in the new synthetic jacket and trousers she'd made for me. It was a clear evening, with no wind to stir up the powder. The sky was a bruising dome over my head, a few lights already piercing the gloom. I remember correcting myself – *stars,* I told myself, *not lights, stars*. For all the wonder of them, the thought of those appallingly huge distances frightened me.

We stood there for some time, watching the sky grow ever darker. The pair of annexes flitted about behind us, making little repairs to the outpost. With the external floodlights off, the night was a breathtaking speckled canvas. I was ready to thank her for bringing me to see it, though I didn't see a purpose beyond raw beauty, but she told me to wait a little longer. Then, after a while, she pointed at a section of the sky where the Lattice stretched like a claw, obscuring the stars behind it. She didn't say anything, just smiled. I watched, uncertain.

Then, bit by bit, I saw it come to life.

A few faint lights blinked on at first, then quickly spread in number and intensity. Yellows, reds and blues, running in neat lines along each of the five fingers. Those lights blazed, brighter than even the constellations that surrounded them. In moments, this hulking shape, this menacing reminder of the hubris of the old world became something else, a beautiful, sparkling, vibrant thing.

People would live there soon, she said. The annexes were busy making it habitable, sealing breaches and awakening long-dormant power plants. In time the inhabitants would work to repair the damage done all those centuries ago. I remember feeling like my chest might burst – a tear froze on my cheek as she told me of the plans, dug up from the archives, that would be used to one day *expand* it, finish what the original constructors had never managed! The Lattice would stretch across from horizon to horizon, as intended, a twinkling net that girdled the globe.

That was the moment. That sparkling shape in the sky was a physical manifestation of potential. I knew that I'd been fooling myself into thinking the knowledge we'd gained was absolute, unsurpassable. Instead, I saw it for what it truly is: a springboard to even greater discoveries, deeper mysteries. The chasm of space in front of me no longer gave me vertigo – I wanted to leap into it feet-first!

I told her I was ready to leave. When she asked where I wanted to go, I pointed at the Lattice. I remember her smile.

Tomorrow, a final goodbye. Then, the sky waits.

Heartfelt thanks go to:

Catherine Cho for being the book's first and most fervent champion, as well as all the team at Curtis Brown for their notes and encouragement;

Cat Camacho, Davi Lancett, Miranda Jewess, Julia Lloyd and the folks at Titan Books for their diligent editing, designing and sage advice;

Tutors, comrades and peacocks (dead, or otherwise) of the Bath Spa University Creative Writing MA, and Paula for all the coffee and chats; the summer workshop crew, for keeping the ball rolling; the incomparable Maggie Gee for generosity of time and spirit, as well as the odd curry;

Those who said what was good and, more importantly, what wasn't – Tim Aldred and Katie Wakefield, who swanned in late with wine; Gavin Allen, the most stylish Welshman I know; Luke Parker, brother in fisticuffs and beer; Christoph Wieczorek, who is definitely to blame; Rosemary Dunn for my first ever bit of creative feedback – it still hurts;

Mum and Dad, for a childhood full of adventure that moulded me, and for teaching me the magic in books;

My family, both natural and acquired;

Aurelia for changing everything;

Ali, with love.

About the Author

Patrick Edwards lives in Bristol and has never grown out of his fascination with science and the future. In 2014, he decided to give writing a go and graduated from the Bath Spa Creative Writing MA with distinction. His first novel, *Ruin's Wake*, was inspired by the works of Iain M. Banks and modern-day North Korea.

For more fantastic fiction, author events, competitions,
limited editions and more

VISIT OUR WEBSITE
titanbooks.com

LIKE US ON FACEBOOK
facebook.com/titanbooks

FOLLOW US ON TWITTER
@TitanBooks

EMAIL US
readerfeedback@@titanemail.com